Car... ...for her ... ...er, she put writer. Then it asked what Carol did for relaxation and she put down the truth – writing. The third question asked for her hobbies. Well, not wanting to look obsessed she crossed the fingers on her hand and answered swimming but, given that the chlorine in the pool does terrible things to her highlights – I'm sure you can guess the real answer.

USA TODAY bestselling author **Kat Cantrell** read her first Mills & Boon novel in third grade and has been scribbling in notebooks since she learned to spell. She's a former Harlequin So You Think You Can Write winner and former RWA Golden Heart finalist. Kat, her husband and their two boys live in north Texas.

USA TODAY bestselling author **Catherine Mann** has books in print in more than twenty countries with Mills & Boon Desire, Mills & Boon Romantic Suspense, HQN and other imprints. A six-time *RITA*® finalist, she has won both a *RITA*® and Romantic Times Reviewer's Choice Award. Mother of four, Catherine lives in South Carolina where she enjoys kayaking, hiking with her dog and volunteering in animal rescue. FMI, visit: catherinemann.com

Secrets and Seduction

Secrets and Seduction:
Playing Games

CAROL MARINELLI

KAT CANTRELL

CATHERINE MANN

MIX
Paper from
responsible sources
FSC
FSC C007454

This book is produced from independently certified FSC™ paper
to ensure responsible forest management.

For more information visit www.harpercollins.co.uk/green

Printed and Bound in Spain using 100% Renewable electricity at
CPI Black Print, Barcelona

MILLS & BOON

SICILIAN'S SHOCK PROPOSAL

CAROL MARINELLI

PROLOGUE

'A WOMAN WHO says she's your fiancée is in Reception, asking to see you.'

Luka Cavaliere looked up from his computer and saw the wry smile on his PA's face.

'I thought I'd heard it all until now,' said Tara.

Women would try anything to get an audience with Luka, but to have someone pretending to be his fiancée was a first. Tara knew from bitter experience that the woman in Reception was lying—the only thing that Luka ever fully committed to was work.

She certainly wasn't expecting his response.

'Tell Reception that she can come up,' he said in his rich Italian voice.

'Sorry?'

Luka didn't respond to Tara's question. Instead, he got back to the work he was doing on his computer. Certainly he did not need to repeat himself to his PA, nor explain things to her.

'Luka?' Still Tara hovered at the door, unable to believe that he knew who this woman was—he hadn't even asked for her name.

'Do you want a second warning?' Luka checked. 'I have already told you that I should not have to give out my instructions twice.'

'No, you want to *give* me a second warning so that soon you can fire me.' Tara's voice was thick with tears. 'You want me gone…?'

Of course he did.

'It's because we made love, isn't it?' she simpered.

He could correct her but he chose not to. Luka didn't make love—he had sex.

Often.

His wealth attracted shallow women, but his dark good looks and skills in the bedroom did not lead to the fleeting encounters that he preferred. Always they wanted more than he was prepared to give. He knew that he should never have got involved with his latest PA, especially when he'd just trained her up to be useful.

'I'm not going to get into a discussion,' Luka said. 'Send her up.'

'But you never said that you were engaged. You never even gave a hint that there was anyone else—'

Bored now, Luka thought. 'Take as long as you like for lunch,' he interrupted. Yes, he wanted her gone. 'Actually, you can take the rest of the day off.'

Tara let out a hopeless sob and then turned and rather loudly left the office.

The slam of the door made Luka's eyes shut for a brief moment.

It had nothing to do with his PA's brief outburst, or the noise from the door—it was what would happen in the coming moments that he was bracing himself for.

There had *always* been someone else.

And now she was here.

He stood up from his desk and moved to the window and looked down below to the London street. It was the middle of summer—not that he usually noticed. His life was spent in air-conditioned comfort and he dressed in the same dark suits whatever the month.

It was ironic, Luka thought, that he and Sophie, after all these years, should meet in London—the place of their far younger dreams.

Until recently he had always assumed that if they did come face to face again it would be in Roma, perhaps on one of his regular visits there. Or even back in Bordo Del Cielo—the coastal town on Sicily's west coast where they had grown up. He had only returned once, for his father's funeral last year, but he had been wondering whether he might go back one final time if Sophie's father decided he wanted to be buried there.

Luka still hadn't made up his mind if, when that day came, he would attend the funeral.

He knew that that day was coming soon.

And that, he also knew, was the reason that Sophie was here.

His hand reached into his jacket and he took out not a photo, not a memory; instead, it was a brutal reminder as to why they could never be.

He stared at the thin gold chain that wrapped around his long fingers and then he looked at the simple gold cross that lay in his palm. Yes, he would go to her father's funeral, for this necklace belonged in that grave.

It took only a few moments for Sophie to make her way from the foyer to his suite yet it felt like for ever as he awaited her arrival, but then came the knock at the door that he recognised from yesteryear.

How much easier might his life have been had he not answered the door that long-ago day? Perhaps, Luka thought, he should not respond to it now.

He pocketed the necklace and cleared his throat.

'Come in.' He managed a deep summons but, as the door opened, he did not turn around.

'Your assistant asked me to pass on the message that she's just resigned. Apparently I'm the final straw.'

The sound of her voice, though a touch stilted and measured, still held, for Luka, the same caress.

For a man who feared little, he was nervous to turn around.

Luka rather hoped that the years that had passed since they'd last met had not treated her kindly—he fleetingly hoped that a nice little drug habit might have aged her terribly, or that she was pregnant with triplets perhaps…anything that might douse the eternal flame.

He turned and found out that time had indeed been cruel, to him at least, for perfection greeted his navy eyes.

Sophie Durante stood before him again.

She was wearing a simple dress in the palest ivory that showed her curvaceous figure. Her glossy, long black hair was worn neatly up in a French roll when he remembered it spilling over naked shoulders.

Her neutral-coloured high-heeled shoes enhanced her toned olive legs.

He forced his gaze up but only made it as far as her mouth. Her full lips were pressed tightly together when he remembered them once laughing and smiling. Then he remembered them somewhere else, which was a rather inconvenient image to have sprung to mind, so he forced himself to meet those dark brown eyes again.

She was just as beautiful as he remembered and, just as they had at their parting, her eyes showed she abhorred him.

Luka stared back with mutual loathing.

'Sophie.' He gave her a curt nod.

He did not know how he should greet her—shake her hand, or kiss both cheeks perhaps?

Instead, he gestured for her to take a seat.

She did so; placing her designer bag by the seat, she neatly crossed her legs at the ankles.

'You look well,' Luka said, and hoped she might miss that he then cleared his throat—for those first delicate traces of her scent had now reached him and his mind was firing taunting glimpses of memory.

'I am well,' she responded, and gave him a tight smile. 'I am very busy, of course.'

'Are you working?' Luka asked. 'Did you ever get to work on the ships?'

'No.' Sophie shook her head. 'I am an events planner.'

'Really?' He didn't even attempt to hide his surprise. 'You were always running late for everything.'

He glanced at the ring on her finger—a ruby stone set in Italian gold. It was very old-fashioned and far from what he would have chosen for her. 'I have terrible taste in rings, it would seem,' Luka said.

'Don't!' she warned abruptly. 'You will never insult me again.'

He looked up and into the eyes of the only woman he had ever made love to as she asked him a question.

'Aren't you going to ask why I am here?'

'I presume you're about to tell me.' Luka shrugged. He knew damn well why she was here but he'd make her say it just for the pleasure of watching her squirm.

'My father may be released from prison this Friday on compassionate grounds.'

'I know that.'

'How?'

'I do occasionally glance at the news.' Luka's sarcasm didn't garner a response, though his voice was kinder when he asked her a question. 'How is he doing?'

'Don't pretend that you care.'

'And don't *dare* assume that I don't!' he snapped, and he watched her rapid blink as he continued speaking.

Seeing her, he had been momentarily sideswiped but now he took back control and made a vow never to lose his control with her again.

'But, then, that's you all over, Sophie. Your mind was always made up even before the jury had been chosen. I'll ask you again. How is your father?'

'He is fading, he is a little confused at times.'

'I'm sorry to hear that.'

'Isn't that what prison does to an innocent man?'

Luka stared back and for now said nothing.

Paulo was not as innocent as Sophie made out.

'Not that a Cavaliere would know about prison,' she added.

'I spent six months in prison awaiting trial, two of them in solitary,' Luka pointed out. 'Or were you referring to my father being found not guilty?'

'I have no wish to discuss that man.' She couldn't, Luka noted, even bring herself to say his father's name. How much worse would this conversation be if she knew the truth? he wondered. He could almost feel the heat from the necklace in his pocket. He was actually tempted to toss it across the desk to her, to end them once and for all.

'Just what are you doing here, Sophie? I thought we ended our engagement a long time ago.'

'Firstly, I don't want you to think, for even a moment, that I am here for any romantic reasons.'

'Good, because it would be an extremely wasted journey if that were the case.'

'However,' she continued, 'my father believes that you upheld your promise. He thinks we got engaged and that we now live together in Rome.'

'Why would Paulo think that?'

'It was kinder to lie and let him think that you upheld your commitment to me. I never thought he would be let out and now that he might be I need to keep up the pretence. I told him that the terrible things you said in court about me were in an attempt to protect him.'

'They were,' Luka responded. 'I said what I did in the hope of protecting him, or rather protecting you. You simply refused to see it from my side.' He looked at her for a very long moment and found he could not stand even having her in the same room so he shook his head. 'It wouldn't work.'

'It *has* to work,' Sophie said. 'You owe me.'

'I do.' Luka did not concede with those words. He knew she spoke the truth. 'But apart from the fact that neither of us can abide being in the same room together, I do have a life. I might be seeing someone…'

'I don't care if this upends your life for a while. This is going to happen, Luka. You might sit a rich man in your posh London office and live a jet-set lifestyle but you are *from* Bordo Del Cielo, you cannot escape from that. You might go through women like tissues but the fact remains we were promised to each other from childhood and where we come from that means something.' Luka let out a tense breath as she asked again. 'Will you help my father die in peace?'

'You want me to move in with you and pretend that we live together?'

'No, I read that you have an apartment in Rome… we will use that.'

'Why not yours?'

'I share with my friend Bella. You might remember her...'

Luka bit back a sarcastic response. From what he had heard, a *lot* of men might remember Bella!

'She runs a business from our home.'

As she spoke, he noted that Sophie ignored his slight sardonic smile, even though she must know what it insinuated.

'It would not be fair to disrupt Bella and it would look odd for us, as a couple, to be sharing a home with her.'

'And would this loving couple be sharing a bed?' He voiced the obvious question but she did not answer directly.

'It would look strange for us to sleep apart.'

'Would there be sex?' he asked, wishing a blush would rise on her cheeks, for Sophie to give some indication that this hurt like hell for her also, but she stared back coolly as she delivered her response.

'I would think not,' she said. 'Since that evening, given what happened, I have a phobia...'

Luka's eyes widened. Was Sophie saying that there had been no one since him? There was a small rush of giddy relief that he quickly doused but she hadn't finished speaking. 'But if that is what it will take for you to agree, then, yes, there can be sex.'

'I thought Bella was the whore.'

'We can all be whores,' Sophie responded with spite, and Luka looked at the beautiful yet hostile stranger whose innocence he had taken, never to return. 'So, yes, if sex is to be part of the deal—'

'No, thanks,' Luka interrupted. 'I don't need charity sex and, anyway, martyrs don't turn me on—it's extremely willing participants that do.' He watched the slight swallow in her neck and he knew, he just knew she was remembering how good they had been so he cruelly walked her down memory lane and, as he did so, he reinforced a truth. 'Surely you know how much I like a woman who instigates things.'

He'd thought she'd blush as he pointed out how she had been the one who had practically begged him to make love to her yet, rather than blush, Sophie surprised him with a shrug and a smile.

'Well, there will be no sex for us, then, because I won't be instigating anything. Are you going to do this, Luka?'

'I'd like some time to think about it.'

'My father doesn't have time.'

'Leave me your business card, Sophie, I'll call you when I've made up my mind.'

He watched as she went into her bag and for the first time appeared flustered. 'I don't have any with me.'

'Give me your number.'

'I will contact you.' Sophie stood and went to leave but at the last moment changed her mind. 'You owe me this, Luka, we were promised to each other. You took my virginity.'

He could only admire her for, unlike most women, she spoke of their time together without misty recall. In fact, she reduced it to cold fact.

Almost.

'Took?' he checked. 'What an odd choice of word. You see, from my recollection…' Now a blush spread from her neck and rose to her cheeks. He came around the desk and stood in front of her, and she backed up to the desk. 'Are you going to jump up, Sophie…or do your prefer a kitchen bench to an office desk?'

Now she was struggling to keep her cool.

'Why didn't I marry you?' He played devil's advocate. 'You being such a good Sicilian girl…'

'I told my father that it was my dream for him to walk me down the aisle. I told him—'

'Stop there,' Luka interrupted. 'I need to think about what I'm prepared to agree to but before we go any further there is something that you need to know.' They were face to face as he said it. 'I will *never* marry you.'

'You'll do whatever it takes.' The spitfire he had known was returning and she jabbed a finger into his chest to make her point. 'Whatever. It. Takes.'

'No,' he calmly interrupted. Despite the cool facade she had attempted, he knew that she was as Sicilian as the volcanic soil they were from, and as he watched her struggle to hold in her temper, he didn't suppress his slight triumphant smile. She was just as volatile and passionate as he remembered. Those traits in Sophie were everything he both loved and loathed.

'After what you did, after what you said about me in court…'

'Lose the drama, Sophie,' His voice was completely calm. 'I accept that I have a moral debt to you, given all that happened, but, even with several years' interest added, I do not owe you that much. I will agree to be your fake fiancé, but never your fake husband. Know that now, or get the hell out.'

He hoped for the latter. Get the hell out of my life, my head, my heart.

Just get out!

Instead, Sophie must have accepted his terms for she sat back down.

It was time to talk business.

Finally, together, they would face the mistakes of their past.

CHAPTER ONE

'HAPPY BIRTHDAY FOR TOMORROW!'

Sophie smiled as Bella went into her bag and bought out a neatly wrapped package.

'Can I open it now?' Sophie asked. She already knew what it was—a dress for her engagement party next week. Even though they worked as chambermaids, Bella was a talented dressmaker and Sophie had spent the last few weeks having sheets of paper pinned to her. She couldn't wait to see the real thing. Bella had kept it a complete surprise and Sophie didn't even know what colour the dress was.

'Don't open it here.' Bella shook her head. 'Wait till you get home. You don't want to get sand on it.'

Though tired from the shifts as chambermaids at the Brezza Oceana hotel, just as they always did they had come to their secret cove. It wasn't really a secret cove but it was tucked behind jagged cliffs and could not be seen from the hotel. The tourists didn't really know about it as the small beach was accessible by a path that the locals of Bordo Del Cielo kept to themselves. When the hotel had first been built, much to the locals' disgust, it was here that Sophie and Bella would come after school. Now, even though they worked together most days, still the tradition remained.

Here, where no one might overhear them, they came and sat, their legs dangling in the azure water, chatting about their hopes and dreams and voicing some of their fears…

Not all of their fears, though.

Bordo Del Cielo was a town of secrets and some things were too dangerous for even the closest of friends to discuss.

'Now I can get on with making my own dress,' Bella said.

'What is yours like?'

'Grey,' Bella replied. 'Very simple, very sophisticated. Maybe then Matteo might notice me…'

Sophie laughed. Matteo was Luka's best friend and had been Bella's crush for years, but he had never given her so much as a glance.

'You must be getting excited,' Bella said, and Sophie was about to smile and nod.

In fact, she did so.

'Of course I am,' she said, but her smile, the one she had worn so determinedly whenever her upcoming engagement was discussed, suddenly wavered and rare tears started to fill her expressive brown eyes.

'Sophie?' Bella checked when she saw that her friend was struggling. 'Tell me.'

'I can't.'

'Are you worried about…?' Bella hesitated. 'Sleeping with him? I know he might expect you to once you are engaged but you could tell Luka that you are a good girl and want to wait for your wedding night.'

Sophie actually managed a small laugh. 'That's the only part I'm not worried about.'

It was the truth.

Oh, she hadn't seen Luka in years but she had grown

up nursing a crush on him. Luka's widowed father was rich; Malvolio owned the hotel and most of the businesses and homes in town. Those Malvolio didn't own he took payments from for their protection. When Luka's mother had died, instead of struggling to raise his child, in the way Sophie's father had, Malvolio had sent Luka away. He had attended boarding school on the mainland but, every summer when he'd returned, to Sophie he'd looked more beautiful. She had no doubt that the years he had spent in London wouldn't have dimmed that.

'I'm actually looking forward to seeing Luka again.'

'Remember how you cried when he left?'

'I was fourteen then,' Sophie said. 'Tomorrow I'll be nineteen...'

'Do you remember when you tried to kiss him?' Bella laughed and Sophie cringed in recall.

'He told me I was too young. I guess he would have been twenty then.' She smiled at the embarrassing memory of Luka dropping her from his lap. 'He told me to wait.'

'And you have.'

'He hasn't, though,' Sophie said, her voice bitter. Luka's reputation was as undeniable as the waves that pulled at their calves. 'He didn't back then, he was already screwing around.'

'Does it make you angry?'

'Yes, but more...' She felt a familiar burn rise in her chest—little bubbles of jealousy at the thought of Luka with other women that did not ease when they popped, for it felt like shards of glass were being released in her throat. 'I want what he has had.'

'You want to date other men?'

'No, I want my freedom,' Sophie said. 'I want to have

experiences and chase my own dreams. I've spent my life taking care of my father's home, cooking his meals, doing his washing. I don't know if I want to be someone's wife yet. I want to work on the cruise liners…' She looked out to the sparkling ocean. Travelling, sailing on the seas had always been her dream. 'I wouldn't mind making beds for a living if I could do it on a ship. It's like you with your dressmaking…'

'That's just a dream, though,' Bella said.

'Perhaps not. Your application might be accepted. You might be off to Milan soon.'

'I got rejected,' Bella said. 'My drawings weren't enough for them and I'll never be able to afford models and photographers for a decent portfolio.' Bella shrugged her shoulders as she both tried and failed to convince Sophie that not getting in to study fashion design in Milan didn't hurt like hell. 'I could never have gone anyway. I need my wage to pay the rent. Malvolio would give my mother hell if…' Bella's voice trailed off and she shook her head.

Yes, there were things that should never be discussed, but with her engagement now less than a week away Sophie could no longer keep her fears in. 'I don't want to be pulled even closer into Malvolio's life. I don't think Luka is anything like his father but—'

'Shh,' Bella said, and even though they had the cove to themselves she looked over both shoulders just to make sure. 'Don't speak like that.'

'Why not?' Sophie pushed. 'We're just friends talking.'

Bella said nothing.

'I don't want to get married.'

There—Sophie had said it.

'I'll be barely nineteen. There are so many things

I want to do before I settle down. I don't know if I want to...'

'You don't know if you want to live with Luka in a beautiful home and be taken care of?' Bella's response was one of anger. 'You don't know if you want to be rich and pampered?' Bella was starting to shout. 'Well, I'd take it if I were you and count yourself lucky—after your engagement party Malvolio has told me to stay back. I'll be working the bar. This time next week I won't be making beds at the hotel, I'll be...' Bella broke down then and Sophie held her own tears in check. 'Like mother, like daughter,' Bella sobbed. 'I am not ashamed of my mother, she did what she had to to survive, but I don't want that for me.'

'Then don't do it!' Sophie shook her head furiously. 'You are to tell him no!'

'Do you think for a moment that he'd listen?'

'You don't have to jump to his rules. He can't make you do anything that you don't want to.' Sophie was insistent. She loathed the way everyone jumped at Malvolio's command, her own father included. 'If you can't say no to Malvolio then I shall for you.'

'Just leave it,' Bella pleaded.

'No, I will not leave it. When Luka gets here on Wednesday I'll try speaking with him...'

'It won't do anything.' Bella shook her head and stood. 'I need to get back...'

They walked down the little pathway together and Bella apologised for her outburst. 'I didn't mean to be cross with you. I understand that it should be your choice if you marry.'

'We should both have choices,' Sophie said.

They didn't, though.

Everyone considered Sophie lucky—that, because

of her father's connections to Malvolio, she would marry Luka.

There had been no discussion with the future bride.

They came out of the trees and onto the hilly street and walked past the hotel Brezza Oceana, where Sophie and Luka's engagement party would be held.

'Are you taking your Pill?' Bella asked, because they had taken the bus two weeks ago to a neighboring town so that Sophie could get contraception without the local doctor knowing.

'Every day.'

'I'd better get some,' Bella said, and Sophie's heart twisted at the resignation in her friend's voice.

'Bella—'

'I have to go.'

'Will I see you tonight at church?'

'Of course.' Bella attempted a smile. 'I want to know if you like your dress.'

They parted ways and Sophie was almost home when she remembered she was supposed to have stopped for bread, so she turned and raced back to the deli.

As she walked in, the conversation stopped abruptly, just as it often did these days.

Sophie did her best to ignore the strange tension and when it was her turn she smiled at Teresa, the owner, and ordered the olives and cheese she had chosen, as well as a large pane Siciliano, which was surely the nicest bread in the world, and then took out her purse to pay.

'*Gratuitamente.*' Teresa told Sophie there would be no charge.

'*Scusi?*' Sophie frowned and then blushed. She was being let off paying because she was marrying Malvoio's son, Sophie decided. Well, she wanted no part in that sort of thing and angrily she took out some money, placed it on the counter and then walked out.

'You're late,' Paulo said, when Sophie let herself into their home and walked through to the kitchen, where her father was sitting reading his paper at the table. 'You would be late for your own funeral.'

'Bella and I got talking,' Sophie said.

'What do you have there?'

'Just some bread and olives…' Sophie answered, and then realised that he was referring to the parcel she was carrying, but before she explained what it was she asked her father a question. 'Father, when I went to pay, Teresa said there was no charge. Why would she say that?'

'I don't know.' Paulo shrugged. 'Perhaps she was being nice. After all, you are there every day.'

'No.' Sophie refused to be fobbed off. 'It was uncomfortable when I walked in—everyone stopped talking. I think it might have something to do with my getting engaged to Luka.'

'What is in the parcel?' Her father changed the subject and Sophie let out a tense breath as she set down the food and pulled out some plates.

'Bella gave me my birthday present a day early. It's my dress for my engagement. I'm going to try it on when I have had my shower. Father…' As she cut up the loaf Sophie did her best to sound casual. 'You remember you said I could have my mother's jewellery when I got engaged?'

'I said that you could have it when you got married.'

'No!' Sophie corrected. 'You told me years ago that I could have it when Luka and I got engaged. Can I have them now, please? I want to see how my dress looks with everything.'

'Sophie I've just sat down…'

'Then I will fetch them if you tell me where they are.'

Her father let out a sigh of relief as the phone rang and, though not prepared to get her mother's jewellery, he happily headed out to answer the phone.

He was always making excuses. For years Sophie had been asking for her mother's necklace and earrings and always he came up with different reason why she couldn't have them yet.

'Father…' she started as he came back into the kitchen.

'Not now, Sophie. Malvolio has called a meeting.'

'But it's Sunday,' Sophie said.

'He said that there is something important that needs to be discussed.'

'Well, surely it can wait till Monday?'

'Enough, Sophie,' her father snapped. 'It is not for me to question him.'

'Why not?' Sophie challenged. She was sick and tired of her father being Malvolio's puppet. 'What is this *meeting* about? Or is it just an excuse to sit in the bar for the evening?'

Surprisingly, her father laughed. 'You sound just like your mother.'

Everyone said the same. Rosa had had fire apparently, not that Sophie could remember her as she had died when Sophie was two.

'Here,' Paulo said, and handed her a small pouch. 'These are her jewels.'

Sophie let out a small gasp and then looked at her father and saw that he was sweating and a little grey.

'This means so much.'

'I know,' Paulo said, his voice shaken. 'There are only her earrings.'

'I thought there was a necklace…' In all the photos

Rosa wore a simple gold cross but she could hear the emotion in her father's voice when he told her that he didn't have it.

'It was a very fine chain. I believe that it came off in the accident. Even after all these years I still look for it in the bushes when I take my walk in the morning. I wanted you to have it. I'm so sorry that I cannot give that to you.'

'Is that why you haven't let me have them?' Sophie asked. 'Father, I just wanted something…anything of hers…' She looked at the fine gold hoops, that had a small diamond in each, with tears in her eyes. 'And now I have her earrings. Thank you so much.'

'I have to go to my meeting,' Paulo said, and Sophie pressed her lips together. She didn't want to fight, especially not when he had just given her something so precious, but her father looked terrible and she really did want him to rest. 'I'll try and get back for dinner.'

Sophie simply could not hold her tongue. 'If Malvolio lets you.'

She saw her father's eyes shut for a brief moment before he turned and headed for the door.

Sophie knew it might be kinder to apologise and that she was maybe making things harder for her father by admitting her truth but she didn't like his involvement with Malvolio.

'Father, I don't know if I am ready to get engaged…' She held her breath as her father's shoulders stiffened.

'It is normal to be nervous,' her father said, but did not turn around. 'Sophie, I have to go.'

'Father, please, can we talk…?'

But the door had already closed.

Sophie walked around the small home and picked up a picture of her mother. She could see the similarities there—they had the same long black hair, the same dark brown eyes and full lips. Oh, Sophie wished she was here, just for a moment. She missed having a mother to give her advice so badly.

'I am so confused,' Sophie admitted to the photo of Rosa. A part of her dreaded being married, yet there was another part of her that longed to see Luka again, the man who had always filled her dreams. She had always looked up to him, had always nursed a crush on him, and she wanted her first kiss to belong to them and to be made love to by Luka.

What would Luka want, though?

She blushed in embarrassment at the thought of him returning and being forced to marry her.

No doubt he was dreading next weekend and returning to uphold his father's commitment for him to marry poor little Sophie Durante.

Was that the hold Malvolio had over her father? Sophie wondered.

Well, she didn't need charity and she would tell her father that.

She put down the photo, took her parcel upstairs and finally opened it.

The dress was exquisite. It was in the softest chiffon and the colour was a very pale coral. Sophie badly wanted to try it on but she had a very quick shower and washed her hair and then combed it before picking up the dress.

She slipped it over her head and looked in the mirror.

Sophie found she was holding her breath. All those hours standing as Bella had pinned sheets of paper had been worth it for this moment.

The dress was amazing. It was scooped low at the front and showed Sophie's cleavage. Of course, it would need a bra but even without it was somehow both elegant and sexy. It came in at the waist and then fell in layers, emphasising her curves when usually Sophie did what she could to downplay them.

Yes, she knew she should take it off but instead she put on her mother's earrings and found the lip glaze she had bought.

Working at the hotel, Sophie was used to seeing beautiful women but this afternoon, for the first time in her life, she felt like one.

Now she blushed for different reasons when she imagined facing Luka.

She wanted him to see her grown up.

Briefly she imagined his mouth on hers but a loud knocking on the door snapped her out of her daydream.

It sounded urgent and Sophie ran through the house but she smiled when she opened the door and saw that it was just Pino on his bike.

He was twelve years old and everyone used him as a messenger.

'Malvolio wants you to go to his home,' Pino said in a self-important voice.

'Malvolio.' Sophie frowned. She had never been to Malvolio's home. 'Why? What does he want?'

'I was just told to give you the message,' Pino said, balancing on his bike. 'He said that it is important and that you're to go there now.'

Sophie went and got Pino some money and thanked him but her heart was racing.

Why would Malvolio ask her to go to his home?

She had assumed that he and her father were meeting at the hotel bar.

Sophie thought of her father's grey complexion and

the sweat on his face and was suddenly worried that he might have been taken ill.

She slipped on some sandals and ran up the hill towards Malvolio's spectacular home, which overlooked not just the ocean but the entire town. Once there she took a breath and then knocked on the door. She didn't want to be there but he had summoned her after all.

No one ever said no to Malvolio.

CHAPTER TWO

'WHY DON'T YOU ask Sophie to come over?'

Luka let out a tense breath at his father's suggestion. Against his father's wishes he had been in London for the last six years, at first studying but now he was now starting to make a name for himself.

He had offered some financial advice to a boutique hotel, but when unable to pay him to implement the changes Luka had offered to work for them for a stake in the hotel.

It had been a gamble. For a year he had worked for nothing by day and earned money by working in a bar at night.

Now, though, the hotel was starting to flourish and Luka owned ten percent of a thriving business.

Luka had his start.

He could have it all here, he knew that.

His father was one of the wealthiest men in Sicily, and he should be stepping in now. His father thought he was back to settle down and start taking over his empire, but instead Luka was choosing to step out for good.

His time away had opened his eyes. With an increasing awareness of his father's corrupt ways he had chosen to stay away and had made only the occasional trip home to Sicily.

Deliberately he hadn't seen or spoken to Sophie in that time.

And in that time an awful lot had changed.

'It might be nice to spend some time with her before the engagement party,' Malvolio pushed. 'Angela will be at church all day and I know that there is a bible meeting this evening she wants to attend,' he said, referring to their maid. 'I'll go out and give you two some time—'

'There isn't going to be an engagement party,' Luka said, and met the eyes of his father—a man who he did not even recognise, for Luka had come to understand that he had never really known his father at all. 'Because there isn't going to be an engagement. I'm not marrying Sophie Durante.'

'But the two of you have been promised to each other since childhood.'

'That was your promise, not mine,' Luka said. 'You chose my future wife, the same way you have chosen for me to follow in the family business. I'm here to tell you that I am going to be returning to London. I'm not going to live and work here.'

'You can't do that to Paulo, to Sophie.'

'Don't pretend you care about them,' Luka said, and watched his father start to breathe harder as he realised the challenge he was facing.

'I won't let you do it to me,' Malvolio said. 'You will not shame the Cavaliere name.'

Luka jaw gritted. His father had no shame. His father took from the poor, from the sick, his father ruled the people of Bordo Del Cielo with an iron fist—*there* was the real shame.

'I will speak with Sophie's father and explain that I will not have a bride chosen for me. The same way that

I will not have my career, nor the place on this planet where I live, dictated to me.'

'You will destroy Sophie's reputation.'

'I am not discussing this,' Luka said. 'I am telling you that I shall speak with Paulo about my decision and then, if he will allow me to, I will talk to Sophie myself.'

'You are not returning to London, you will work with me. After all I have done for you—'

'Don't!' Luka said. 'Don't say that you did all this for me when I never asked for any of it.'

'But you took,' Malvolio said. 'You have lived in the best home and I gave you the very best education. I have a business waiting for you to take over. I will not let you walk out on that.'

'Let me?' Luka checked. 'It's not for you to choose how I live. I don't need your permission for anything.' He went to walk off but his father stopped him in the way he knew best.

Luka, at twenty-four, could have halted the punch that was coming to him but he did not. His father sent him crashing back into the wall and there was a gush of warm blood down his face. Not that it would stop Malvolio.

His only son, his only child was now turning his back on everything Malvolio had worked for and Luka had known that it would come to this.

Too often, growing up, it had.

As his head hit the wall his father thumped him in the stomach and as Luka doubled over Malvolio's fist came into his ribs, but all it did was reaffirm to Luka that his decision to leave for good was the right one.

While he did not hit his father, Luka pulled himself back to his feet and faced him. 'Clever men fight with their minds,' Luka said, as Malvolio raised his fist again. 'Whereas you instil fear…' He shrugged his father off. 'But not in me. The next punch you deliver will be returned,' he warned—and he meant it.

'You will marry her.'

Luka might not have fought back but anger raged through his veins. He loathed his father's assumptions and the way he dictated his life, and he told him so.

'I live in London,' he shouted. 'I date models now, glamorous, sophisticated women, not some peasant that you have chosen for me.'

'I have to go to a meeting,' Malvolio hissed. 'We will speak of this when I return.'

Luka said nothing, standing bruised and bleeding and a bit breathless as his father picked up his car keys and stormed out.

He headed up to his old bedroom and stripped off his shirt then went into his bathroom and examined the damage.

There was bruising to his ribcage and on his shoulder where it had met the wall. An old gash above his eyes had opened up and probably needed stitching.

Not now, though.

For now he would patch himself up and then head to the airport. He might call Matteo and ask if he wanted to meet for a drink but they would meet at the airport.

He was done with Bordo Del Cielo.

Sophie.

As he splashed cold water on his face he thought of her.

Yes, this would be hell for her, Luka knew that and it didn't sit right with him. Perhaps before he left for good he should go and speak with Paulo and maybe Sophie too.

He pressed his bloodied shirt over his eye and went

into his suitcase to find a fresh one. He hadn't unpacked. Luka hadn't even been back home for an hour before the argument had started.

He heard a knock at the door but ignored it.

Angela could get it, but then he remembered that she was at church.

There was another knock but more loudly this time, and Luka headed down the stairs and opened the door.

The breath that had just returned after his father had knocked it out of him stilled inside Luka now.

His voice, when it finally came, was low and curious, and even though he said but one word there was a slight huskiness.

'Sophie?'

He was struggling to meet her eyes. In the argument that had just taken place, as he had attempted to wrestle back his life from his father's control, things had been said about Sophie.

Things she did not deserve.

It had been said in the heat of the moment. Vile words in a vile row and Luka could taste bitterness along with blood in his mouth.

Now, though, as finally he looked at her, there was a pleasant silence. No other thoughts other than this moment.

Her eyes were the same, yet more knowing. Her mouth was full and she was wearing a little make-up.

Her hair was thicker and longer.

And her body—he could not help but briefly look down. The skinny teenager he remembered had left and in her place stood a very beautiful woman.

One whose heart he was about to break.

CHAPTER THREE

'LUKA?' SOPHIE FROWNED. 'I didn't think you were getting here till Wednesday.'

'There was a change of plan.'

'What happened?' Sophie asked.

'I decided to fly home earlier—'

'I meant to your face.'

'It's just a cut,' Luka said. 'An old cut that opened up.'

'The bruises are new,' Sophie pointed out, and he gave a pale smile.

'My father,' he admitted.

Sophie didn't really know what to say to that so she cleared her throat and got back to the reason she was standing at the door.

'I just had a message from Pino. Your father said I was to come here. That it was important.'

'I can guess why,' Luka said. No doubt his father had thought that one look at Sophie and he would change his mind. Well, he wasn't that shallow. He saw her frown as he explained things a little better. 'I think my father wanted us to be alone.'

'Oh.'

'You know how manipulative he can be,' Luka said.

She didn't answer. Everyone might think that of Malvolio but no one would ever dare to say it.

'Come in, Sophie.' He held open the door and after a moment's hesitation she stepped inside. 'We need to talk.' She followed him through to the kitchen, her eyes taking in his back and wide shoulders, and she felt very small and not in a nice way.

He was so glossy, so sophisticated, he was everything that she wasn't.

Of course he wouldn't want her.

And now, from the little he had said, and the way he couldn't quite meet her eyes, Sophie guessed she was about to be told that.

Yes, she had her doubts about the engagement—yes, she wasn't sure if she wanted to get married—but it felt very different from being told to your face that you weren't wanted.

'I just need to sort out this cut,' Luka said. 'Take a seat.'

She didn't.

'I don't know where Angela keeps the first-aid kit,' Luka continued as he went through the cupboards. 'Here it is.' Sophie watched as he pulled out a small first-aid kit and even smiled as his long fingers tried to open a sticking plaster while holding the shirt over his eye.

'It needs more than a plaster,' Sophie said. 'You need a doctor to stitch it.'

'I'll get it sutured tomorrow if it needs it,' Luka said. 'In London.'

He looked up and caught her eye but she didn't respond to his opening.

She'd damn well make him say it, Sophie decided.

'I'll do it,' Sophie said, because it really was a nasty cut. She took out the scissors then cut the sticking plaster into thin strips onto the kitchen bench, and as she did so Luka spoke.

'You look well.'

Sophie gave a wry smile. At least he had got to see her in her beautiful dress, she thought with slight relish. She knew she looked her very best and it was a rather nice thing to know when you were about to be dumped.

Let him think she ran around on a Sunday in coral chiffon with lip gloss and jewellery...

And no underwear, Sophie remembered, as she jumped up onto the kitchen bench and quickly put her dress between her thighs.

'Come here,' Sophie said, now that she had set up for the small procedure.

'I don't want to get blood on your dress.'

It didn't matter now if her dress was ruined, Sophie knew. This was the only time that he'd be seeing her in it. 'Oh, this old thing.' She shrugged. 'Don't worry about it.'

Luka went over to where she sat and stood as Sophie concentrated on closing the cut.

'Why were you two fighting?'

'We weren't fighting,' Luka said. 'He was taking out his temper on me. I chose not to hit him back. This one last time.'

'I hate how he treats you,' Sophie said, and her hand paused over the cut as she deliberated with herself whether or not to continue. 'How he treats everyone.'

She thought of Bella and if there was any good that could come out of this then she'd damn well find it.

'Bella's mother is sick,' Sophie said. 'She can't work and now he wants Bella to start doing shifts at the hotel bar.' She assumed, given that his eyes refused to meet

hers, that he knew what that meant. 'Can you speak
with him for me?'

'Sophie, before we discuss Bella I need to speak
first with you.'

'I get that you do,' she said, 'but I would like to speak
about this first'. Sophie persisted because she knew she
might lose her temper about five minutes from now.
Yes, she didn't want to be forced into a marriage but,
no, she didn't want to be left here either.

It wasn't just her pride that was going to hurt when
he ended things—now that he was back her heart remembered him.

Standing before her was the man she had cried herself to sleep over when he had left last time.

It had been a childish crush, a schoolgirl's dream, a
teenage fantasy, Sophie's head knew that but, having
him back, feeling him close, her heart was racing again
and her body wanted to taste first-hand her forbidden
dreams. Yes, soon that Sicilian temper might get the
best of her, so she would speak with him now, about
the things that possibly could be sorted, while there
was relative calm.

Relative, for her legs ached to wrap around him and
the tongue that went over her lips now was inadver-
tently preparing herself for him. 'Bella doesn't want to
work in the bar.'

She could sense his discomfort and guessed that it
had little to do with the pain from the cut, more the
subject matter.

'I'll speak to him,' Luka offered, 'but first I need
to speak with you. I was going to go and see Paulo—'

'Luka…' Her hand was on his cheek and she wanted
to halt him, wanted to kiss him, to make love and then
deal with the rest.

Please, don't say it, she wanted to beg.

Not yet, not until I have finally tasted you.

'Luka, I know this is difficult but…'

She was right. Luka was not looking forward to this conversation one bit. He wondered how best he could tell her his reasoning without destroying her belief in her father.

It was also difficult for other reasons.

Yes, Malvolio was a manipulative bastard and Luka knew that he wasn't shallow enough to change his mind just because Sophie looked sensational. Still, it was rather hard to stand there at eye level with the ripe swell of her breasts, with the warm, musky scent of her reaching into him and then to look into eyes that, Luka realised, knew him.

Perhaps their fathers had chosen more wisely than he had given them credit for, because the ache in his groin and the surprising pleasure of talking to her had momentarily upended his plans.

He had to go through with it, Luka knew.

He had to deny the attraction, the want that was there between them.

Her pupils were large with lust, and he was sure that so too were his as they stared back to her. How the hell did you tell someone it was over when you were hard for them? When you knew, just knew, that with one slip of your hand those gorgeous thighs would part?

He needed to tell her they were over now, right now, before he gave in to the kiss they both wanted, and so he spoke on. 'My father was angry because I told him I wouldn't be coming back to Bordo Del Cielo and instead I would be living permanently in London. I told him I wanted no part of his life. I said that I won't have him choose where I live, how I work—'

'Don't I get a say in where we live?' Sophie said, refusing to make this easy for him.

She wanted to slap him.

Now that he was here, she wanted not just her dreams of freedom and working on the ships, she wanted him too.

Luka, who had swum in the river with her, Luka, who had told her the night he'd left her aching to be kissed by him that she must wait. He had been twenty years old when he had prised her off his lap and she had clung to him like glue.

She wanted the kiss that he had promised her then.

Instead, she finished closing his wound and then put a large plaster over the top as she spoke. 'My father will be upset. He always thought that I would live close to him and that our children would grow up in Bordo Del Cielo.'

Don't do this, she wanted to warn, though she knew that he was right to.

'In my time away, I've come to understand things.' Luka ran a tongue over tense lips as he reminded himself that he was going to do this without criticising her father. 'The way my father conducts business, the way my mother used to turn a blind eye to terrible deeds...' She looked at that beautiful mouth in his unshaven jaw and he confirmed her darkest thoughts. Malvolio was pure evil. 'I don't want any part of it,' Luka said.

'I don't like the hold he has on my father,' Sophie admitted. 'I don't think my father...' She couldn't bring herself to say it but she tried. 'I think some of my father's dealings are also wrong.'

'That's his choice,' Luka said. 'And I am making my own. I don't think that a promise our fathers made on our behalf should be something we feel we have to adhere to. I think we should be able to date and fall in love with whoever we choose.'

'And have you been dating?' Sophie asked, and Luka said nothing. 'Because if you have then it doesn't seem very fair when I have kept myself for you. I haven't so much as kissed another man, even though I have wanted to.' That was a lie, she'd never want another man. She had only ever wanted him. 'I have been to dances and parties and nothing, *nothing* has ever happened.'

Luka remained silent and Sophie assumed then that he was serious about someone.

'Is *she* insisting we break up?' The jealousy in her voice was not faked. Sophie's skin prickled at the thought of him with another woman.

'There is no *one* she,' Luka said. 'I have not been serious about any one person in particular, but...'

'You have been dating?'

'Yes.'

'You've kissed, made love...' all the things she had guessed he would be doing, all the things she had wanted Luka to do with her '...while all the time you were promised to me.'

Her hand came up then and he would have accepted a slap to the cheek but, hell, he'd just got the wound closed so he caught her wrist.

'You still have good reflexes,' Sophie said, because she had watched him play sport, catch a fork, grab her arm before she fell...

Luka frowned at the light tone to her voice and turned his attention from the wrist he was still holding and then saw that she was smiling.

'Sophie?'

'Perhaps I am not best pleased that you have been

having fun while I keep myself pure for you, but maybe I am a little relieved too…'

He had never expected this reaction but, then, Luka remembered, she had always surprised him. Sophie had always made him either smile or want to tear his hair out in frustration. He'd never known what to expect from her.

'I thought—'

'You thought that I would cry and plead and say that you have shamed me. Well, I guess that in the eyes of everyone here you will have shamed me, but I don't care what they all think. I am nineteen tomorrow, Luka, and I want a life. I want more fun than I could have as your wife.'

'Were you ever going to tell me this?'

'I was.' Sophie smiled. 'But after we had made love. I went and got the Pill…'

'What, did you think I'd be more open to suggestion then?'

'That had crossed my mind.' She smiled again.

'You're really okay with it?' Luka frowned because this reaction had been far from the one he had been expecting.

'Of course,' she said, and then her voice dropped. 'Apart from one thing.'

Yes, she always surprised him.

'You still owe me that kiss.'

'Sophie, you don't end a relationship with a kiss.'

'Why not?' she said. 'I want you to be my first kiss.'

'Sophie—'

'It has to be you,' Sophie said, because quite simply it had to be. She sat on the kitchen bench and her hands went up and linked loosely behind his neck.

'Remember the party, the night you left for London?'

'Of course I remember.'

'Did you want to kiss me then?'

'No,' Luka said. Then she had been a girl, a teary teenager, now there was no doubt that a woman sat before him—and one who knew what she wanted.

'Do you want to kiss me now?' Sophie asked.

He answered with his lips. She felt the soft weight of his mouth and though she did not want to marry Luka, it did not mean she did not find him beautiful. Every kiss that Sophie had ever missed out on was made up for by this.

He held her face and his mouth was gentle. The last seconds of her lip glaze ensured their soft passage and his kiss was exactly as it should be, better even than anticipated. A soft tasting that had her hands move to his chest as they had ached to do on sight.

In her dreams he had crushed her mouth and his tongue had fiercely parted her lips, but in reality he had no need to for her mouth readily opened to his and mutually their kiss deepened.

Her palms pressed to his naked chest and as his tongue slipped in she slid her hands, loving the feeling of strength beneath the skin. His breathing was harsher as her hands moved over his flat, mahogany nipples and then it was Sophie who took his face in her hands.

She felt he was going to halt their kiss so her tongue pleaded for him not to. She wanted this just as he did.

She wanted his hand that was now stroking at her breast through the fabric of her dress and as her nipple thickened to the touch of his thumb he let out a small moan that sent a vibration to her core. He stepped in closer and her legs parted to enable him to. One hand still toyed with her breast while the other slid up the outside of her smooth thigh, but when he encountered

her naked bottom he stilled and pulled his mouth back
a little.

'Do you always run around with no underwear on?'

'You'll never know.' Sophie smiled and Luka returned it but when she went to kiss him he moved
his mouth back and she ached because he had halted.
'Please, Luka…'

'You said a kiss.'

'*We* want more than a kiss.'

She was so certain in that moment that she could
speak for them both.

'I'm not ending things *and* taking your virginity,'
Luka said. 'You've already got enough reasons to call
me a bastard.'

'Then don't give me another one,' Sophie warned. 'I
cried every night for a month when you left but I'm not
going to cry this time. You've had all my tears, Luka. I
just want a part of what was promised to me.'

'Which part?'

'This part.'

His eyes closed as her hand found him and she ran
her fingers over his length. Lightly at first but then she
pressed her fingers in a little.

She had never been shy around Luka.

She had never been shy.

She watched as he closed her eyes and felt the bliss
as he grew to her touch. The ache in her groin grew too
and so Sophie wriggled provocatively closer to the only
man she had ever wanted.

She met his ear and kissed it as he pulled her in firmly.

'I want you to be my first.' She stated her wishes. 'It
has to be you, Luka… It was *always* going to be you.'

CHAPTER FOUR

GONE WAS THE girl he had tipped from his knee all those years ago. Gone was the teary teenager. Instead of pleading, instead of crying, now she seduced.

Now she removed her hand from where it was teasing him and stopped the dance with her tongue on his ear so that she could watch his eyes open.

With a smile, in one lithe easy motion, she pulled off her dress and naked she sat before him, watching his eyes roam the lushness of her breasts.

'This part,' Sophie said again, and with her legs balanced on his hips she unzipped and freed him.

He was beautiful. His skin was soft and dark and together they watched her explore him till Luka could take it no more. He was there at her entrance and Sophie was guiding him in, her jaw tensing as he stretched her but the rest of her was loose and willing.

'Not here,' Luka said, even though it was contrary to his action, for he was inching just a little more inside her tight space.

'Yes, here,' Sophie urged.

They wanted each other's mouths yet the top of their heads were locked, watching as if from the edge of paradise as he inched in a little further. Bordo Del Cielo meant the edge of heaven and that was exactly where both of them were as he stretched her.

'Not here,' Luka warned again, despite her frantic pleas for him to continue. 'I'm taking you to my bed.'

He tried to zip up but with the protest of her kisses and the scent and oil of her on his fingers further turning him on it was like trying to reset a jack-in-the-box. He gave in and just kicked off his pants and got back to kissing her as he lifted her from the kitchen bench. With her legs coiled around him they kissed all the way up the stairs.

'Here,' Sophie said, when they were halfway up and he halted just to taste her deeper. He almost relented but then reminded himself of a part of the need for getting to his bedroom.

'I've got condoms in my case.'

'I told you we don't need them.'

They just made it to the bedroom and he dropped her onto the bed but, unlike the last time when he'd had had to peel her from him, now, loose-limbed, she let herself fall—because this time Sophie knew that in a moment he'd join her.

'I told you I've already gone on the Pill,' she said, watching the delicious sight of him kneeling and trying to open up his case.

'It's for protection.'

'I've never needed protection from you.'

Innocent, Luka thought, but only to a point. Her words were more seductive than any he had ever heard. Nothing would usually halt him—sheathing was, to Luka, second nature. Not with Sophie, though, because he wanted the naked bliss of them together. Later he would scold her, and warn her not to trust another with such a choice. She was right, though; she needed no protection from him.

'I know what I want, Luka.'

He came over to the bed where she lay and like a panther he crawled with stealth that had her writhing until he was with her, and she would never forget his smile.

'I'm going to talk to you later.'

'You're going to make love to me now, though.' Sophie smiled back.

'Are you nervous?'

'I've never been nervous with you.'

It was true. Around him she was not nervous. How could she be scared? Sophie briefly pondered when the mouth that made her shiver returned to hers.

They kissed naked and long and then he left her mouth and blazed a hot, wet trail down her neck and then to her breasts, where he licked the warm skin, avoiding her aching nipples till her hands guided his head. It was Sophie who moaned as his mouth captured her and sucked deeply, not once, not twice, but over and over till she twitched and writhed. How could she be nervous when her body just came alive to him?

She loved how he gave the same attention to the other breast and yet she was almost pleading for him to stop because he had lifted just a fraction of the lid and she was greedy for the treasure he would bring.

Luka knew it.

He knelt up for a moment and looked down at her.

Her mouth was swollen from his kisses, her breasts were wet and her nipples erect, and there was a small purple bruise on her perfect skin that his mouth had made.

'Luka…' Sophie liked the warmth of his eyes and

the affection of his gaze yet she was on fire. He was intimately stroking himself against her as he had downstairs, but there was no holding back as there had been then—this was just a moment of pure decadent indulgence.

She felt like his instrument, tuned purely for him to play to perfection, and he did. She looked down and this time watched him disappear further in.

'It might hurt,' Luka said.

'It had better.'

He laughed and toppled onto her. His weight was half on her and yet not enough; she liked the feeling of being lost beneath him—how the sight of the ocean from his window no longer existed, how the bark of a dog in the distance receded, how it was late in the afternoon and she welcomed the light just to see his closed eyes as he kissed her. Sophie's friends had needed wine, or long dances, some had demanded the promises of a love that would never die before this.

All Sophie needed was Luka, for this was just how it was supposed to be.

Luka was torn. He wanted to taste her breasts again, he wanted to kiss and make moist every inch of her skin, he wanted the musk of her sex on his tongue, not just his fingers. Badly he wanted her to come to his mouth, but he was as impatient to be inside as Sophie was to be taken.

Later, he told himself.

There would be time for that later.

Like a chip to his skull, somewhere he refuted that, because they ended today, this was it.

Yet there, in that second, Luka knew he would take her again, that this was not the end.

And, yes, he could feel her impatience. Her hips kept

lifting, her mouth was more demanding and then there was almost anger as he removed his kiss.

'Luka.' She was breathless.

'Now!' Luka said, that one word taking such effort to deliver.

'Yes, now,' she said, but then she saw his slow, teasing smile.

'I mean *now* is when you can get anything you want from a man.' He was referring to her earlier innocent thinking. 'Not after…'

'I'll remember that for the future.'

She did not understand the flare of possession in his eyes as she spoke of others, but she didn't have time to dwell on it for he took her then. Luka seared into her and swallowed her sob with his mouth.

It hurt, far more than she had expected it to, far better than she had ever dared dream. He filled her and stretched her and, when she thought she knew what it was to be his lover, still further he went tearing at virgin flesh and then stilling as her body fought to acclimatise to him.

She forgot how to breathe until he gathered her right into him and hooked his arm beneath the small of her back.

'Luka…' Sophie didn't even know what she wanted or what it was she was trying to say, but as he started to move any pain was forgotten because with each thrust he made her more his. His mouth was by her ear now, and he spoke as he did in her dreams. 'I won't hurt you…' he said, when she now knew that he would.

The pain of being taken by him was receding. It was the pain of being left by him that was now starting to make itself known.

She wished that her body didn't love him so completely. She wished that he would take her deeper, harder, faster, rather than deliver, as he was now, the slow torture of his love, because that was exactly what this felt like.

As her legs coiled around him, even as she urged him on, Sophie was frantically trying to hold back.

How do I let you leave? she wanted to sob as her orgasm gathered.

'Luka…' She said it again as she started to come and the intensity scared her.

'Let it happen…' Luka said, and his rapid thrust gave her no choice but to do as his body commanded.

Inwardly he beat her to match his rhythm but it wasn't that that had her toppling over the edge, it was Luka, and the feel of his shoulders tense beneath her hands. It was the last look at the world without fully having the other, this strange brink they both found themselves on. Luka was in that beat before coming, past the point of no return when he felt her pulse to him and he just unleashed. Nothing could ever top this, he knew. Her intimate pulses beckoned and he gave in to the tight, soft warmth of her endless caress.

For Sophie it was the sensation of falling but not a gentle one.

Every bump, every sob, every fear seemed enacted in slow motion. She wanted to curl up in protection but his hands held down her arms. She hoped for a moment of clarity but he was pounding her senses again. Kissing her hard as his climax receded and then thrusting again, giving up the very last of himself as she lay there, knowing she had nothing left to give.

She had been taken.

CHAPTER FIVE

'SO THAT'S WHAT it feels like,' Sophie said.

'Not usually.'

They were lying in his bed and watching the evening sun over the ocean.

Sophie's head was resting on his chest and she watched a cruise liner glint in the distance.

'Not *usually*?' she checked.

'Truth?' he asked, and she nodded. 'There is usually a knot of disquiet.' He took her hand and he placed it just beneath where his ribs joined, and he pushed her fingers in. 'Just there.'

'Why?'

'I don't know,' he admitted.

He moved his hand to the same place on her. 'Do you have it?'

'No,' Sophie admitted. 'No knots, no disquiet.'

She knew what he meant, though, as she tried to imagine a moment where the man lying there wasn't Luka.

It felt written in her DNA that this time belonged to him.

'You really want to work on them?' Luka asked, and they must have both been looking at the same thing because he voiced her thoughts.

'No, I really want to be a guest on one of them.' Sophie smiled. 'But for now working on one would be wonderful.'

'What would your father say?' Luka asked.

'What *will* my father say?' Sophie corrected, because it was going to happen, she was determined, but she answered his question. 'I don't know how he's going to react,' she said, listening to the thud of Luka's heart as he stroked her hair. So much had changed now. 'I guess people will understand that I might want to get away after the shame of you dumping me.' She laughed and dug him in the ribs but then she was serious. 'I don't know how my father will be about it but I don't think I can factor that in when I make my choice… I don't know if I want to stay here in Bordo Del Cielo, Luka. There is too much past…'

They were the same, Luka realised.

'I think my father is up to no good,' Sophie admitted. 'I love him yet I want to get away from him. I want no part in that type of life.'

During his last years at school Luka had started to question the way things worked here and he had fought hard to go to university in England. There, his eyes had been fully opened as to his father's ways and from that distance he had decided to stay away.

Sophie had worked it out from here, Luka thought.

Or was starting to.

'My father doesn't work, he sits in a bar most of the day and into the night. What are these meetings he says that he has to go to?' She looked up from his chest and instead of giving her an answer or avoiding the subject he offered the unexpected.

'Come to London with me,' Luka said.

'With you?'

'You could apply to the cruise liners from there. I

could help you to get on your feet. I am a part owner of a hotel, you could work there till you get your dream job...'

Sophie lay there, thinking about it. She wasn't surprised that he part owned a hotel—Malvolio would have seen to it that his son was looked after.

'I have a flat,' Luka said. 'You could stay with me for a while.'

'Stay with you?' Sophie blinked. 'I don't know if that would work out...'

'Why not?'

'Luka, while I accept this is a one-off, I really don't want to be there if you bring another woman home...'

It angered her that he laughed and Sophie climbed from the bed. 'I'm going to have a shower and then I have to go to church...' She stopped talking when she saw the sheets that bore the evidence of what had just taken place. 'Oh.'

'I'll sort it all out,' Luka said. 'I'm not going to leave them for Angela. Go and have your shower...'

As Sophie did so she thought about what Luka had suggested and she thought too about her cross response.

It was true.

She somehow had to hold in her jealousy at the thought of him with someone else. She'd agreed to break things off, a part of her had even been happy about it and certainly she had been relieved...

That had been before they'd made love, though.

How could once with Luka ever be enough?

He had taken her, left her exhausted and sated.

Now, though, even the recent memory was bringing her back to sensual life. She soaped her tender breasts and saw the bruise that his mouth had made. Her sex was hot and swollen and as Sophie soaped the last traces of him away she wanted him again.

She walked out with a towel around her to the sight of a naked Luka changing the sheets. Now from a relative distance she could admire his naked beauty. He was tall and lean and she could see the muscles on his thighs as he bent to rather haphazardly tuck in the sheet. His shaft, though soft against his leg, lifted a little from the movement and she wanted to take the sheet from his hand and get back to bed.

'Is that the first bed you have ever made?' Sophie teased, trying to keep things light.

'It is the first bed I have ever made in Bordo Del Cielo,' Luka answered. He looked to where she stood and wondered if what he had to offer would be enough. She thought him rich and, in London, he wasn't.

Yet.

'Sophie, I have a small flat in London…' Luka would explain it all to her later, he decided. He would go into detail about how he had removed himself completely from his father, that his ways were honest. But he wasn't going to do that here, and anyway there was something else that needed to be addressed before they got to family stuff. Today was about them, about the possibility of a future away from Bordo Del Cielo. 'What you said before about me bringing another woman home if we lived in London, I would not do that to you. In the same way I wouldn't like it if you were staying with me and saw anyone else…'

'I don't understand what you are saying.'

'I'm saying that I don't want it to be over between us. Maybe I don't want to commit to marriage, or getting engaged just yet, it is far too soon for that, but we can date,' Luka said. 'Once we get to London we can go out and get to know each other away from our families. We can do things our way, without all the pressure and expectations.'

Sophie could feel the goose-bumps on her bare arms as she realised that Luka wasn't just offering her a way out of Bordo Del Cielio but a way out *with* him.

'Can I still apply to work on the cruise liners if we are going out with each other?'

'Sophie,' Luka said. 'Tomorrow you are nineteen, of course you must follow your dreams and do the work you want to.' He threw a sheet at her. 'For now, though, you can help me do this...'

Sophie took the sheet and started making her side of the bed. 'Does anything smell better than a sheet dried in the sun?' Sophie asked, because at the hotel it was all starch and bleach.

'One thing does,' Luka said, and he beckoned her to cross the bed. Unabashed, wanting the same as him, she climbed over to him, kneeling up as he stood. 'You do.'

'And you,' Sophie said.

They kissed a slow, long kiss that she wanted to go on for ever but it was Luka who halted things—the sky was turning orange, he could hear the bell in the distance, summoning everyone to church. He had no intention of going himself but he knew that Sophie would be expected to be there so he pulled back. 'I'll go and get your dress. You said you needed to be at church.'

'Soon,' Sophie said.

'You'll be late,' Luka said.

'I'm always late.'

'When we're in London, we can spend the whole day...' He didn't finish. Her towel was slipping and Sophie let it fall. His lovely erection was nudging her stomach as they kissed some more.

'I want to kiss you there,' Sophie said, and now, when she lowered her head, Luka didn't remind her that there was somewhere else she needed to be.

She kissed down his stomach until his erection was too tempting at her cheek to ignore. He held the base as she tasted him first with her tongue then kissed him along his thick shaft and then Luka removed his hands.

Sophie felt giddy as she ran her lips over the salty tip.

Together they would go to London; they would get to know each other's bodies.

The world was theirs.

'Like this?' Sophie asked, and then parted her lips and took him a little way in.

'Like that,' Luka agreed. This, for Luka, was more intimate than sex. More private. He would prefer to give rather than take but he went with it now. His hands were in her hair and she felt the building pressure. 'Deeper,' Luka said, and she obliged, taking him in as far as she could as her tongue swirled on his shaft.

His powerful thighs started to buck a little, his hand coiled her hair into a long ponytail and Sophie loved the traction—the tightness to her scalp gave her delicious direction but then cruelly she stopped.

'Now?' Sophie said, hovering over him, and then she looked up and smiled as he swore. 'Is now a good time to get my own way?'

'Why the hell did I tell you that?' Luka both laughed and groaned. 'What is it that you want?'

'Can Bella come too?' Sophie asked. 'Just till we get on our feet?'

'Sophie…' Luka tried to come up with a reason why she couldn't but, what he hell, he knew Bella and Sophie had been friends for ever and it might make it easier for

Sophie to settle in. 'Sure,' Luka said. 'Bella can come too. Now, get back to work.'

Laughing, happy, she did so. Her hands moved and held his taut buttocks. He let her hair fall and what went on behind the black curtain was a private tasting. Sophie rested on her heels, her sex on fire as Luka didn't try for gentle. She loved his passion, how he told her exactly what he wanted—which was simply more of the same. It was hot work and then he swore again, and it was right to swear because things could never be the same as he swelled in her throat, she pulled her head back and caught him first on her tongue, tasting and swallowing him down, more turned on than she thought possible. But then she realised he hadn't finished, and the sound of him gently swearing as he came over her lips and into her hair had her close to climax.

'Tonight...' Luka scooped her up to him, told her he would wash himself out of her hair, right now in the shower, and then, 'I shall go and speak to your father tonight.'

Not yet, though. He saw her so flushed and aroused and ready that he pushed her back on the bed. Too giddy to stand, he knelt on the floor. She would take a minute. Luka knew. She was almost there. He could see her wet, sore and swollen, her clitoris erect, and God help him but he never wanted them to get out of bed.

Sophie watched, shocked and laughing, as he pulled her to his mouth, and she lay there longing for the building pressure in her to release to his lips. She would later wish she could somehow hold that moment, for it was a time that belonged only to them. A time of pure happiness. A moment without shame, where the future was bright, where dreams were coming true, but then a crashing noise doused her in panic.

There was the sound of footsteps running up the stairs.

A lot of them.

Her first thought was that Malvolio had come home, though there was too much noise for it to be only him, but then the police shouted out that they were being raided.

Luka threw a sheet over her. The bedroom door splintered and as it was kicked open he lay over her as gruff voices told them not to move.

'Non muovetevi!'

Sophie closed her eyes in terror as Luka was hauled from the bed to the floor where he was cuffed.

'Stay still,' Luka warned her. 'Just stay calm.' Then he shouted to them to fetch her clothes but all they gave her was one of Luka's shirts.

'Not in church this evening?' The lewd comment only added to her embarrassment and terror as Sophie attempted to cover herself.

'Say nothing,' Luka warned her. His voice was the only calm in the room but then it changed as they pulled Sophie's hands behind her back and put on cuffs. 'Why are you cuffing her?'

'I don't know what's happening...' Sophie said, and then she looked at Luka, met his eyes and in that moment she did know.

This was about their fathers.

'Say nothing,' Luka said. 'I'll get you a lawyer.'

It had all been perfect and now she had been plunged into a hell that burned ever hotter. Sophie was unceremoniously marched to a car. The entire congregation of the church, it seemed, had come out and were watching from the other side of the road. It was mortifying. The only saving grace was Bella, shouting to her friend,

'I'll get some clothes and bring them.' She was already running down the hill towards Sophie's home.

There was no time to thank Bella. Instead, Sophie's head was pushed down as she got into a police car, but it didn't come close to the loving way Luka's hand had, only moments ago, guided her head.

'Poutana...' She heard the whispers—some even said it loudly. The people she had grown up with had all turned on her in one night and very soon she would start to understand why.

'I suggest you *don't* take your boyfriend's advice and that you do speak,' Sophie was told as the car started to drive off

Sophie said nothing. She trusted Luka to sort this out and she knew that she'd done nothing wrong. She rested her head against the window and lifted her hands to her tousled hair, feeling her mother's earring, then moved her fingers to her other ear.

It was gone.

'My earring,' she started, and then stopped. She would speak with Luka later. It had to be in his bedroom, or maybe on the path as she had been led out.

She looked down at the car floor, wondering if she had lost it when she'd been pushed in.

'So where's your father tonight?' she was asked, but Sophie refused to answer. She had given up looking for her earring and was now back to staring unseeingly out of the window,

'There's Luka's father,' the officer said, and Sophie started to breathe faster as she saw Malvolio being led by the police from the hotel. 'I wonder where Paulo is,' the policeman said. 'Let's take the scenic route.' But instead of the beach road they were heading now towards the hotel and into a small side street, the same street that

Sophie had walked down just a few hours ago. Now, though, it was filled with firefighters and the deli was alight with flames.

'You were in there this afternoon, weren't you?' the officer checked, and there was no point denying it so Sophie nodded.

'Your father went and visited them this morning,' the officer said. 'For the third time.'

It was then, Sophie knew, time for her to start talking.

CHAPTER SIX

'SOPHIE DURANTE.'

Sophie stood as her name was called.

It had taken six long months to get to the trial.

After the arrests she had been released without charge the next morning but her father, Luka and Malvolio had all been charged with various offences.

The last six months she had spent living with Bella and her mother because, even from prison, Malvolio still ruled Bordo Del Cielo. Her father's house had been signed over to him to pay for Paulo's lawyer.

Sophie had been allowed a few short, monitored visits with her father.

She would have preferred to have seen Luka.

It was a terrible thing to admit perhaps, but at every visit she had ached for just a glimpse of him and she could no longer look her father in the eye.

'You will hear many things in the trial,' Paulo had said. 'Some of the things will be true, but most are lies…'

Sophie simply didn't know what to believe.

Trinkets and jewellery had been found in their home. Souvenirs, the police called them, for they had all belonged to victims.

Sophie knew they had not been in her home, she'd cleaned it after all. But she also knew that her father,

though perhaps not a killer, had not been entirely innocent either and it hurt like hell to know that.

'Malvolio would send me to warn people—it doesn't
mean that I hurt them…' Paulo attempted to explain.

'You went, though,' Sophie shot back. 'You terrified
them just by passing on the warnings. Why would you
say yes to him?'

'Sophie, please—'

'No!' She would not simply ignore the facts. 'You
chose to say yes to him and, please, never say that you
did it for me. He kept us poor.'

'You have Luka.'

Sophie let out an incredulous laugh. 'Don't tell me
you said yes to him just for that. I'd have had Luka with
or without your help.'

She was confident of that.

Almost.

She couldn't wait for the trial to be over, to go with
him to London…to take up those tentative dreams and
to run with them.

Sophie looked at her father. He looked so grey and
gaunt and she knew she had to win the battle to forgive him and stand by him, for she was the only family that he had.

'After the trial you can get away from Bordo Del
Cielo and start over again,' Sophie said.

'I'm not leaving your mother.'

'She's been dead for seventeen years! Father, I am
going to be leaving. I'm going to move to London with
Luka. I just want to get away from here and all the
people who have judged me.' She ran a nervous tongue
over her lips for there was one thing she felt her father
ought to hear first from her. 'You will hear things in
court about me too, father. Things that you won't like.

That afternoon, when the raids happened, Luka and I… we were together.'

'Sophie, you and Luka were practically engaged. You have nothing to be ashamed about. Walk into that court and give your evidence with your head held high.'

How, though?

As her father was led back to the cells Sophie asked, as she always did, if she could visit Luka.

He had no one. His mother had died years ago and his father was locked away.

'Non ci sono visitatori ammessi.'

Again she was told that no visitors were allowed and then she found out that Luka had been placed in solitary.

'Malvolio too?' Sophie challenged. 'Of course not.' She answered her own question.

Luka wasn't a security risk, Luka wouldn't contaminate the trial, that would be Malvolio.

'He rules even in here,' Sophie called out as she left on the eve of the trial.

She took the bus back to Bordo Del Cielo and walked down the street.

Teresa's café was all boarded up and the locals shunned her. If it weren't for Bella and her mother. she would have had nowhere to go.

If it weren't for Luka, she wouldn't even be here, a still small voice told her.

She was so cross with her father that there was a temptation to simply take the next flight and leave him to his fate, given all he had done.

But Luka…

He was the reason she was here.

Sophie halted at Giovanni's the jewellers when she

saw him at the window, adding a new stand to the wares. 'Anything?' she asked when he caught her eye, because she was still hoping against hope that her earring might have been found and handed in.

Giovanni shook his head and disappeared back into the shop, leaving Sophie standing there.

No one wanted to be seen talking with her.

She peered in and looked at the new offerings in the window. There was a huge emerald-cut diamond set on the prettiest rose gold band and she couldn't help but let her imagination take flight.

She wanted that ring on her finger.

Or rather she wanted the engagement that had never taken place.

Walking back to Bella's, she tasted the salty sea air and thought of Luka alone and locked away.

He had no one.

Well, he did, he had her, but there was no way to let him know, apart from to do as her father said and to walk into the trial with her head held high. She would not be ashamed about what had taken place between her and Luka that afternoon.

She was here only for him.

Sophie tried.

Throughout the trial, as a witness she had not been admitted to the courtroom, but today she was being called to give evidence and, though dreading it, though embarrassed at the thought of some of the salacious details of that day being examined, though scared for her father, what had sustained her was that today she would see Luka.

And she did.

Walking into the courtroom to take the stand, finally

she saw him. Those navy eyes met hers and he gave her a small encouraging smile. He looked thinner, leaner and sharper. The scar above his eye had had little medical attention for it had healed badly and even from the witness stand she could see it purple and raised. His hair was cut far too short and Sophie could see the anger that simmered beneath the surface, though not towards her, for his eyes were kind when they met hers.

She awaited the barrage of questions and let out a breath of relief when the rather embarrassing moments of the police raid were skimmed over.

'You knew that Teresa was upset with you that day when you went into the deli?'

'I did?'

'And you asked your father why she might be upset?'

'I just mentioned it in passing when I got home.' Sophie swallowed, her cheeks going a little bit pink as they made it sound as if she had been questioning her father. 'I thought it was to do with my upcoming engagement, that because Malvolio would be my father-in-law...'

'Just answer the question.'

Sophie frowned, as she did on many occasions over a very long day of questioning. Malvolio and Luka had the same lawyer, her father had a different one, yet even he wasn't asking the pertinent questions.

'The souvenirs that the police say they found in my home...' Sophie attempted, for when she had been arrested, over and over the police had spoken about trinkets that had belonged to the deceased or come from buildings that had been destroyed. She wanted to explain they had never been in her home. That she had kept the house and would have known if such things were there.

'We'll get to that later,' her father's lawyer said, yet he did not.

Sophie left the witness stand and now that she had given her evidence she was allowed to watch as the accused were cross-examined.

Malvolio went to the witness stand a sinner but the questions were so gentle and so geared for him that he left the stand looking like a saint and walked away with an arrogant smile.

She sat bewildered as her father took the stand. He seemed weak and confused. Sophie once stood and shouted as his own lawyer misled him but Bella pulled her down.

'Quiet, or you will be asked to leave.'

'It's not fair, though,' Sophie said.

None of it was fair.

Yes, her father admitted, a second visit from him meant there would be trouble if bills were not paid.

A third visit was the final warning.

'I had no choice but to do as Malvolio said.'

It was, Sophie knew, a poor defence.

And then it was Luka.

In a dark suit and tie, his skin was pale from months of being locked inside. He wrenched his arm from a guard who led him, still as defiant, still as silent as he had been on the day of his arrest.

He would not lie to save his father.

Luka refused to lie.

It was not in him to lie and he wanted no part of his father's life so he had decided that he would speak the truth.

The truth could not hurt him.

Or so he thought.

He looked out and nodded to his close friend Matteo, who had been there every day to support him, and then he looked at Sophie. He tried to let her know with his eyes that he had this under control.

But ten minutes into his testimony he started to glimpse his father's game.

'Did your concerns about Paulo's dealings play any part in your decision to not go ahead with your engagement to his daughter Sophie Durante?'

There was a gasp around the courtroom and Sophie stared ahead as Bella took her hand.

'Sophie and I had decided to make our own arrangements for the future,' Luka answered in a clear voice.

'We'll get back to that but first can you answer the question? Did you have concerns about Paulo's dealings?'

'I had never really given Paulo much thought,' Luka answered, though his voice was not quite so clear as he delivered his response.

'Did Sophie tell you that she had concerns about her father's activities?'

His already pale face bleached and he looked into Sophie's eyes briefly. He had sworn to tell the truth but he could not have Sophie's own words be the reason for Paulo being put away.

'No, she did not.' For her, Luka lied under oath.

'So what you did discuss that day?'

'I really can't remember,' Luka answered.

'Because you were busy in the bedroom?' His lawyer was working more for Malvolio, Luka knew it now. Luka didn't have anything to hide so the lawyer would work to secure his father's freedom by throwing Paulo under the bus.

'I'm confused,' the lawyer continued. 'On the afternoon in question you said to your father that you were going to end things with Sophie, yes?'

'Yes,' Luka answered. 'However—'

'Malvolio was upset,' the lawyer broke in. 'In fact, you got into a fight when you spoke poorly about the woman he had chosen with care for you. You said that you did not want to marry a peasant of his choice. Correct?'

Sophie closed her eyes and then forced them open as Luka was forced to admit that, yes, that had been what he had said.

'I was trying to separate myself from my father—' He didn't get to finish.

'You told your father that you preferred the more glamorous, sophisticated women in London to Sophie. Now do you see the reason for my confusion? Sophie Durante came to your home…'

'My father sent for Sophie so that he could move the souvenirs to Paulo's,' Luka said. He could see what had happened now. Six months locked up, two of them spent in solitary, had given him a lot of time to think. His father hadn't been hoping to get Sophie and him together, Luka was sure of that now. Malvolio must have been tipped off about the raids and would have wanted the souvenirs out of his home and in Paulo's.

Only no one wanted to hear his truth.

'Sophie Durante heard that you were about to renege on your promise to marry her. She turned up at your home on a Sunday afternoon to dissuade you and you ended up in bed that same afternoon, or rather you had sex in the kitchen.'

'No.'

'You are saying nothing happened in the kitchen?' the lawyer checked.

'As I have said, I had had a fight with my father, Sophie was sorting out the cut above my eye…'

'Oh, I see—you were bleeding so profusely that she was left with no choice but to take off her dress to stem the bleed…?' the lawyer asked, and Sophie sat burning with shame, completely humiliated as the courtroom laughed.

'My father had suggested that Sophie come over before I told him that I did not want to get engaged. He wanted her out of Paulo's house so that he could move—'

'Did Sophie Durante want to be out of that house too?' the lawyer interrupted. 'Was Sophie concerned that her father was engaged in criminal activity? Did she tell you she wanted to get away from him?'

Luka broke into a cold sweat, he could feel it trickle down his back. He was doing everything he could to stay calm, to somehow give his version of events, but there was no right answer.

His father had a brilliant lawyer, so too did he, and he was, Luka could now see, being used to discredit Paulo.

If he answered yes to the question then he put Paulo away for life.

'No.'

'You are under oath,' the lawyer reminded him.

'No, she did not say that.' Luka's voice was clear as he decided that bedroom talk had no place in the courtroom.

'You did tell your father, though, that you were not going to go ahead with the engagement?'

'Yes.'

'And you told Sophie the same. Yes or no?'

'Yes.'

'Luka.' The lawyer really was the smiling assassin

as he looked at his youngest client, whose father was paying the hefty bill. 'How can you expect the court to believe that there was no conversation—?'

'We were *otherwise* engaged.'

'*After* you had ended things?'

'Yes.'

'Nothing was said about her father?'

Luka did what he had to.

'There really was little conversation.'

'It makes no sense.'

The lawyer was about to pounce again but Luka got there first and turned to the judge and shrugged his shoulders. 'I think that Sophie might have been trying to get me to change my mind about ending things by trying to seduce me so I took what was on offer.' He looked out towards the jury and then back to the judge as he shamed her. 'Am I on trial for my libido?'

The laughter that went around the courtroom ended the testimony.

But as Luka left the stand she did not look at him.

Luka knew that he might have saved her father from conviction by his own daughter's words.

But it might just have killed the two of them.

CHAPTER SEVEN

SOPHIE, EVEN DAYS LATER, could not bring herself to look at Luka as the defendants stood to hear their fate.

'He didn't mean it.' Over and over Bella said this to Sophie, who had held in her formidable temper since Luka had said those words. 'The lawyer gave him no choice.'

The villagers sniggered as she passed, there were whispers everywhere she went, but now, as the verdict was about to be delivered, there were no smiles or laughter in court.

All knew that the six-month break they'd had from Malvolio's clutches might end today.

'Luka Romano Cavaliere—*non colpevole.*'

Despite her anger, Sophie let out a breath of relief and she did lift her eyes to look at him. She didn't expect his eyes to be waiting for hers, yet they were. For a small slice of time they stared at the other and the courtroom faded.

He gave her a nod that apologised, that said he would explain things, that soon he would be with her.

'Here comes the verdict for Malvolio,' Bella whispered.

'Malvolio Cavaliere—*non colpevole.*'

'No!' Bella gasped, and Sophie clutched her friend's hand as the fat brute smiled over in their direction.

Malvolio had wanted Bella for a long time.

Pandemonium broke out as, terrified now and determined to appear loyal to Malvolio, the spectators in the courtroom applauded. Sophie simply lowered her head and tried not to weep.

She knew what was coming.

Her father was so frail he could hardly stand.

Paulo Durante—*colpevole*.

Her father would be taken to the mainland for sentencing, the court was informed, and would serve out his time there.

He would die in prison, Sophie knew that.

She watched him being led away and though she was still angry at him she knew she was the only person that he had so she called out to him, 'I'll be there for you...'

She would be.

There were cheers in the streets as Malvolio left the court a free man, though Sophie didn't hear them and neither did she wait to speak with Luka; instead, she went to Bella's to start packing.

'I'm going to Rome to be near him and you need to leave too,' Sophie urged Bella. 'Malvolio is back, all his yes-men are still here.'

'I cannot leave my mother,' Bella said .

'She will understand...'

'I can't, Sophie, she is so sick.'

There was a knock on the door and Bella went to answer it as Sophie continued to pack.

'No,' Sophie said as Bella returned. 'I don't want to see him.'

'It wasn't Luka,' Bella said, and Sophie looked up when she heard the strain in her friend's voice. 'It was Pino with a message for me. There is to be a big celebration tonight at the hotel, everyone is to be there. I am to work in the bar.'

'No!' Sophie was adamant. 'You are to come with me to Roma.'

'I can't leave her now,' Bella said. 'I know that you have to leave and not just to take care of Paulo—you are the scapegoat now. Everyone knows it is Malvolio but that is not what that will say to his face.' Bella started to cry. 'I don't want my first to be Malvolio. I know you think I should just say no to him.'

'I know that it is not that simple.' Sophie put her arm around her friend, who took a cleansing breath.

'When my mother has gone, and it won't be long, I will come to Rome and be with you. But not now. I need to be here for her in the same way you need to be there for your father.'

There was a knock at the door and Bella went to answer it and after a moment came back and this time, Bella told Sophie, it was Luka here to see her.

'I have nothing to say to him.'

'He says he's not leaving till he has spoken with you.'

He wouldn't leave, Sophie knew it.

Her shame and hurt from the words he had said in court the other day was still there inside her. Her fear, her panic about her father seemed to be swirling into a concentrated storm as finally, for the first time in six months, they would speak.

She stepped out of the small bedroom and there Luka stood in the hall. 'Congratulations,' she hurled at him. 'You and your father walk free, while mine is to be imprisoned on the mainland. Where is the justice?'

'There is no justice,' Luka said. 'Can we go for a walk?'

'Just say what you have to.'

'Not here,' Luka said, and looked over to the bedroom that Bella was in.

'I trust Bella,' Sophie said, 'And, given all that was said, I trust her far more than I trust you.'

'You know why I had to say what I did.'

Somewhere deep down Sophie did. Right there, in the midst of her turmoil, she did know that so she nodded and called to Bella that she was heading out for a short while.

They walked from Bella's home down the street and past the hotel Brezza Oceana, not talking at first. Cars were starting to arrive, there were flowers being brought in through the foyer. Clearly the hotel was preparing for a large celebration.

And, Sophie knew, Bella would be working there tonight and every other night that Malvolio dictated.

Yes, her heart hurt right now.

'Will you be going to the celebration tonight?' Sophie broke the strained silence.

'No,' Luka answered. 'I am having nothing more to do with my father.' They walked further on and they came to the small path that only the locals knew about and they walked down to the cove.

It felt strange being here with Luka when usually she came with Bella, and she told him that. 'We always called it our secret cove. I guess everyone does that, though.' She tried to make small talk but found it impossible, the hurt was too great.

Luka didn't even try.

'Sophie, tomorrow I am leaving for London. I want you to come with me and Bella too. Matteo is also leaving, though no one knows that yet. He will go along with things tonight and make out that he is pleased to see my father released but tomorrow he's getting out.'

'Bella can't leave her mother,'

'Bella has to,' Luka said.

'She won't. I just spoke to her and she says that she can't leave and I understand why. Her mother needs Bella to be working to pay the rent. She used to own her own home till *your* father took it from them to *help* cover the medical bills.'

Luka knew that, he knew it all now, but hearing the slight acid in Sophie's words that inferred his father's dealing were somehow anything to do with him had anger building within him, yet he fought to stay calm.

'I have to support her choice,' Sophie said.

They kept on walking and it was strange that a place could be so picture perfect and yet so sordid.

'Sophie, will you come with me to London?'

'No,' Sophie said. 'I need to be close to my father. I'm going to go Rome and live there.'

'If you come to London with me then I can pay for you to visit him frequently.'

'I don't want you paying for me,' Sophie said. 'God, you're as arrogant as your father. Well, let me tell you—I would rather work as a *poutana* in the bar with Bella than go to London with you. Have you any idea of the shame, to stand the court and hear that?'

'Sophie.' He grabbed her arm and swung her around to face him. 'You know why I said what I did. I did all I could so that what you said to me would have no bearing on your father's verdict.'

But she didn't want to hear it.

'Go and live in London, Luka, and party with your models, who only want you for looks and money. You'll suit each other. Take the head start your father's filthy dealings gave you.'

'He gave me nothing.'

'Please,' Sophie scoffed. 'I'll do better on my own that I ever could with you.'

'Are you sure about that?' Luka checked.

'More than sure.'

'Some welcome,' Luka sneered, and then shook his head. 'I've been in prison for six months, two of them spent in solitary, where the thought of seeing you was the only thing that kept me sane.'

Luka had had a lot of time to think and in that time the only thing that had kept him going had been her and the memory of that afternoon—sheets that had smelt like the sun and the future they had dared to glimpse. He had walked out of court and straight to the jeweller's. It had been closed, of course, but he had gone around to Giovanni's home and asked him to open up, and his first purchase had been the thing he craved most.

A future with the person he loved by his side.

'What exactly did you say to your father?' Sophie demanded. 'I want to hear it.'

Now, instead of looking to the future, Sophie wanted to examine the past.

'I've just been found not guilty, Sophie. I've just had my past and my all my dealings examined. I never thought I'd have to come out to be to be retried by you. I lied under oath for you.'

'I don't care about your lies under oath,' Sophie said, her eyes blazing with anger. 'I care about the parts that were true. You go to London, Luka, you go with your glamorous women, you don't need to take the *peasant* along...'

It was that part that had killed her, that part that made her want to curl up right now and hide for ever, but instead Sophie came out fighting. She had never felt good enough for Luka, and hearing what he had said about her to his father had been more shameful than being paraded half-naked in front of the village. 'You weren't lying under oath then, Luka.'

'It was a row that I had with my father. What I said was wrong, I know that. Sophie, I thought it the moment I opened the door to you and saw you standing there, so beautiful…'

Unwittingly he had hurt her again. The Sophie he had seen that day had been dressed in her finest, but he couldn't know that. All his words did were reinforce her silent fear that if he knew the real Sophie, she wouldn't be good enough.

From the ruins she had to dig deep to find her pride.

'I'll never forgive you for that,' Sophie spat. 'I'll never forget the shame of my first lover calling me a peasant.'

'Well, it was it clearly true.' He hit completely below the belt but, hell, he was hurting. 'Do you really think I want to be standing arguing, with you acting like a fishwife, on the night I get set free? I want champagne, Sophie. I want laughter and a beautiful woman.'

'And?' she demanded.

'That about does it for me,' Luka said, and shrugged her off.

CHAPTER EIGHT

HE DIDN'T FEEL ANYTHING.

Or rather, Luka thought as the car took him from the airport to Bordo Del Cielo , the feelings that he had were perhaps not at they should be on the day of his father's funeral.

Yes, he was grieving.

Just not for Malvolio.

It had been five years since Luka had been back.

At least physically.

More than Luka cared to admit, his dreams regularly brought him back to this place.

The car turned and he looked out at the glittering Mediterranean and then another turn and there spread out before him were his childhood and teenage years.

The church, the houses, the rivers and roads that were all etched in his heart were on view now. Memories of summers and Christmases long gone when he had lived a life with the promise of Sophie in his future.

It had been a promise that he had backed out on, Luka reminded himself.

Today, on the day that his father was buried, when surely there should be a layer of grief for his father, instead it was all for Sophie and for that small slice of time they had been together.

She still resided in his heart.

With the benefit of hindsight he had often rearranged that day in his mind so that they had left for London as soon as she had come out of the shower, before the raid, before everything had fallen apart.

He arrived at the church and as he stepped inside Luka could only give a wry smile for it was practically empty.

Defiant only on Malvolio's death, no one attended.

There was just Angela the maid, sitting midway down the aisle, and Luka gave her a nod and then headed to the front.

There was the sound of the door opening and he turned around because, yes, hope remained.

False hope, Luka thought as Pino, once a young boy on his bike, now a young man, came in and took a seat.

Luka nodded to him also but as he sat through the short service still his mind turned to Sophie.

She should have been here.

Had she cared for him, she would have been beside him today.

The burial was a sad joke.

Malvolio had paid for his own funeral and the huge oak casket with its glitzy trimmings went almost unnoticed, for everyone had chosen to stay at home.

Pino headed off and after Luka had thanked the priest he walked out of the cemetery with Angela.

'I have put on some refreshments,' Angela said, 'back at the house. I wasn't sure how many would be attending. I don't think I'll be hungry for a long time.'

Luka gave a wry smile. 'You know, for all his power and wealth he had nothing,' he said. 'Nothing that matters anyway.'

'I thought Matteo might come with you today. I hear that the two of you are doing very well.'

'He is in the Middle East on business. He offered to come but I really just wanted to do this on my own.'

Or not on his own. Still his eyes scanned the street, hoping against hope that she might yet arrive.

He should leave now.

Luka knew that.

His lawyers were taking care of the estate. Luka could barely stand to hear the details—his father owned Paulo's home and Bella's mother's too.

That was the mere start.

Most of the town had been handed over to his father in times of weakness or ill health, with the promise that Malvolio would take care of everything.

No wonder the church had been practically empty. No doubt the moment Luka left they would celebrate the end of his father's dictatorship.

They would, Luka knew, have reason to celebrate properly soon for he had instructed his lawyers carefully.

He needed nothing from his father's estate. It would take some work and a lot of unravelling but, in time, all the homes that his father had procured through less than honourable means would be returned to their rightful owners or their descendants. The locals would only find that out long after he had left Bordo Del Cielo, though.

They arrived at his car and Luka looked at Angela's tired, strained face.

'How long until I have to leave the house?' Angela asked.

'You don't ever have to leave,' Luka said. Yes, he was handing it over to his lawyers, but he did not want

Angela spending another night in fear. 'I will be transferring the house into your name.'

'Luka!' Angela shook her head. 'Bordo Del Cielo is a popular holiday resort now, the properties are expensive.'

'It is your home,' Luka said. 'Hopefully, now it can be a happier one.' He gave her a small smile. 'Can I ask you to keep it to yourself for a little while?'

Angela nodded tearfully.

'Come back to the house,' she said, but Luka shook his head.

'There are few good memories there…'

'Come back for a little while at least.'

There was one good memory, though, and after a moment of quiet thought Luka nodded.

He hadn't been home since the night of the police raid.

On his release, after pleading with Sophie to join him in London, instead of going to the bar to celebrate his and his father's freedom he had sat on the sand, going over and over Sophie's words.

He went over them again now as he stepped into the kitchen and remembered her sitting on the bench and tending to his eye.

'I might take a look around,' Luka said, and took the stairs, trying and failing not to remember their frantic kisses there, and then went into his old bedroom.

It was like entering a time warp.

Angela must have dusted it but it was just as he had left it.

Luka closed his eyes as he remembered that afternoon before it had all gone so wrong.

He thought of the plans they had made and their hopes for the future. Now, with the wisdom the years had afforded and after so many fleeting relationships that never came close to what he had found with Sophie, he knew that what had been born that day had been a fledgling love. It had to have been for there had been nothing close to the same since. Not just the sex, but the conversation, the sharing, peering into the future with one another and picturing themselves there—not clearly, they'd had but a few hours together, of course, but there had been the chance of a future and it had been stolen from them that same day.

He opened up his bedside drawer, expecting nothing, an old notebook perhaps or a school report. He used to hide them from his father—they had never been good enough. What he found, though, made him sit on the bed with his head in his hands.

Her earring—just a thin gold loop with a small diamond where the clasp met, but it was the only tangible thing he had from that day and he examined it carefully as memories rushed in. He remembered her standing at the door and how that tiny stone and the sparkle it had made had brought attention not to the earring but to her eyes.

She should have been here today, standing beside him. If she cared at all she'd have made the effort, wouldn't she?

'Did you ever look her up?' Angela asked a little later as they drank coffee.

'Who?' Luka attempted.

'The woman you were promised to for half of your life,' Angela said. 'The woman who walked out of this house dressed only in your shirt as the whole town looked on. The woman you shamed in court. I'm sure you don't need me to tell you her name.'

'I had no choice to say what I did in court.'

'I know that.'

'Sophie didn't, though.'

'She was young,' Angela said, and Luka nodded.

'She was more upset about what I said to my father about her being a peasant…' Luka smiled as he rolled his eyes. 'And so, to make things worse, I went and said it again on the beach, the night of my release…'

'To Sophie!' Angela exclaimed, but then smiled. 'She is so like her mother. Rosa could skin you alive with her eyes… I remember the day she turned up here, shouting at Malvolio to leave her family alone…' Her voice trailed off. Even if he was dead, some things still weren't discussed, but Luka nodded.

He could remember that day just a little. Rosa had knocked on the door and had stood shouting down the hallway.

He'd forgotten that, Luka thought. He would have been eight or nine…

'You were younger then too when you said those things and you were also just out of prison.' Angela broke into his thoughts. 'Perhaps it wasn't the time for common sense.'

Again, he nodded.

'So, *did* you ever look her up?'

'I sat in a car outside Paulo's jail day in day out for a month a couple of years ago,' Luka admitted. 'Then I found out that he was in hospital and not even there.'

'You never visited him?'

'I couldn't face him,' Luka admitted. 'He took the fall for my father. When I found out that he had been sentenced to forty-three years…' Luka gave a tight shrug. 'The wrong man was put behind bars.'

'Paulo wasn't entirely innocent either.'

'I know that. I don't know what my father's hold

over him was but surely he could have said no at some point or just left.' Luka gave a tight shrug, weary from thinking about it. 'He didn't deserve forty-three years, though, and for my father to walk free.'

'You never saw Sophie after she left for Rome?'

'Never,' Luka said. 'It is like she disappeared...'

'I am sure she still visits her father.'

Luka nodded. 'Maybe I *should* go and visit him.'

He was older now—he could face Paulo...

Perhaps he could visit him and ask after his daughter.

Maybe he and Sophie deserved a second chance because, as sure as hell, the years hadn't dimmed the memory. Absence really did make the heart grow fonder because Luka was in the agony of recall again.

And still angry again at her words towards him.

He had never compared her to *her* father.

Paulo was no innocent—he knew full well what two visits from him meant.

Never would he have thrown that at Sophie.

She wasn't like her father, though, Luka thought. She was as volatile and explosive as Rosa.

'I'm going to look her up again,' he said to Angela. 'I will go and see Paulo and make my peace with him.'

'And ask where his daughter is?' Angela smiled.

'I have an earring that needs to be returned!' He smiled; he hadn't expected to smile today but he did. It hurt to be back here but it had cemented some things in his mind.

He and Sophie deserved another chance.

'She might be married,' Angela said. 'She might—'

'Then it's better to know,' he said.

It was the not knowing that killed him.

It hurt too much to be here, Luka thought. He wanted

the future, he wanted to explore if there was still a chance for him and Sophie, so he drained his coffee and stood.

'I'm going to head back.'

'Do you want to go through his things first?'

'Just take what you need,' Luka said. 'Get rid of the rest.'

'His jewellery?' Angela said. 'Don't you want that at least?'

'No.' Luka shook his head. He was about to tell Angela to sell it and keep what she made but then he hesitated—no doubt his father's jewellery hadn't all come by honest means and he did not want Angela in trouble for handling stolen goods.

'I will drop it in to Giovanni on the way to the airport,' Luka said, referring to the local jeweller 'He can melt it down or whatever.'

Angela led him up the stairs and into Malvolio's bedroom.

There was nothing he wanted from here.

He opened up a box and stared at his father's belongings with distaste and then Luka's heart stopped still in his chest and then started beating again, only faster than it had been before.

'Can I have a moment?' he said, and somehow managed a vaguely normal voice. He didn't even see Angela leave but she must have because a moment later he looked up from the jewellery box and she was gone, the door had been closed and he was alone.

Luka watched his hand shake a fraction as it went into the heavy wooden box and pulled out a simple gold cross and chain.

Yes, he remembered Rosa.

Luka had heard in court how things worked and

knew that her necklace must have been taken as a souvenir after her death.

Did Paulo know? Luka wondered.

He looked at the door.

Angela too?

He felt sick as he started counting dates in his head. Yes, he remembered Rosa shouting down the hallway, telling Malvolio that it would be over her dead body before she gave up her home.

The next memory?

Her funeral. Paulo, holding a smiling Sophie, who, at two years old, had had no real idea how sombre the day had been.

He remembered his father delivering the eulogy, telling the packed church how he would support his friend and little Sophie.

Even though he had surely been responsible for Rosa's death?

Was that why Paulo had always said yes to his father? Was that the hold that he'd had over him? Had Paulo done whatever had been asked of him just to keep Sophie safe from the same fate?

Poor man.

Luka had always considered Paulo weak.

Now he glimpsed Paulo's fear. He had done whatever it had taken to protect his child, and Luka knew that he had to help free him.

He would get his lawyers onto it this very day, Luka swore there and then. He would get an apartment in Rome and work for however long it took to secure his release.

There would be no contacting Sophie, though, Luka knew.

There could be no second chance for them now.

He knew Sophie well enough, and she would never forgive him if she knew that it had been his father who had killed her mother.

Never.

The glimmer of hope he had just started to kindle, the fleeting hope for some reconciliation with Sophie, died then as Luka pocketed the necklace.

All he could do for her now was fight to set her father free.

CHAPTER NINE

'I saw Luka.'

Sophie had always known that she might hear those words one day but when Bella actually voiced them, for a long moment Sophie did not know how to react.

So much so that she said nothing and just lifted her side of the mattress and carried on making the huge king-size bed.

Sophie had known that Bella wanted to speak with her. As well as sharing a very small flat in Rome, they worked as maids in Hotel Fiscella—a luxurious hotel in the very heart of Rome.

The manager, Marco, had, at first, refused to put them together, knowing that they came from the same Sicilian town. However, when a gap in the roster had given him no choice, Sophie and Bella had set out to prove him wrong. They worked very well together, although they chatted a lot!

Now, though, Sophie was silent.

'I just saw him in the elevator when I went to collect the guest list for our floor.'

'He's not on our list? Sophie checked in horror, but thankfully Bella shook her head.

'Looking at the way he was dressed and held himself, he would be on one of the top floors,' Bella said, and that told Sophie he was doing well.

The hotel was indeed luxurious but the top floors were reserved for the rich and famous.

It had been five years since Sophie had last seen him.

Five years since that walk on the beach.

She knew that Malvolio had died a few months ago. Her father had been diagnosed as terminally ill on the very same day that she had heard the news. After that she had read that Luka had bought an apartment in Rome and now lived between here and London.

Sometimes Sophie was nervous that she might see him in the street, that she would face him in her maid's uniform when she had sworn she could do better without him. That she might face him in the street was bad enough, but knowing that he was at the hotel was far too close for comfort.

'Why would he stay here when he has an apartment?'

'I don't know,' Bella said. 'But it was definitely him.'

When they had read that Luka Cavaliere had purchased a residence Sophie and Bella had even gone to the library to use the computers and had done a virtual tour of the apartment. It had been a foolish thing to do because Sophie found she could picture herself there and all too often did.

'Did he recognise you?' Sophie asked, but Bella just laughed.

'As if he would even glance at a maid! Though I stood behind the bellboy's trolley just in case he looked over.' she admitted. 'But he didn't.'

'I don't want him to see me like this,' Sophie said in sudden panic. 'I don't want him to see that I am still a chambermaid. What if I have to deliver a meal to his room?'

'Don't feel ashamed.'

'I'm not,' Sophie said. 'I just don't want to give him the satisfaction of seeing how little I have moved on.'

'You won't see him. I heard him say he was going back to London this afternoon.'

'Good.'

'What else do you want to know?' Bella asked.

'Nothing.' Sophie shook her head. 'I don't even want to think of that man.'

It was all that she did, though.

Every night when she fell, exhausted, into bed he was there, waiting for her in her dreams. Every morning she awoke cross with her subconscious and how readily it forgave Luka, for her dreams varied from sweet memories of a sun-drenched childhood to a torrid recall of their one passionate afternoon.

They finished making up the bed in silence and Bella went in to do the bathroom while Sophie dusted the flat surfaces of the hotel suite.

Sophie didn't want to ask questions; she wanted to shrug her shoulders and carry on with her day as if a bomb hadn't just dropped in her world, but, of course, that wasn't possible.

She walked into the bathroom and Bella smiled in the mirror that she was polishing when she saw her friend hovering in the doorway.

'Who was he saying it to?' Sophie asked. 'Who was he speaking with?'

'A woman.' Bella's voice was gentle yet the words hurt so much.

'Was she beautiful?' Sophie asked, and Bella screwed up her nose. 'I didn't really notice.'

'I want the truth, Bella,' she said.

Her friend nodded. 'Yes, she was beautiful.'

'Did she have a name?'

'He called her Claudia.'

'And how did he look?' Sophie asked.

'He looked well.'

'Very well?'

'Well, the last time I saw him he was just out of prison so, of course, he looked better than that.'

Sophie knew her friend was trying to downplay things for her.

'His hair is longer now but still very neat. He still has that scar over his eye.'

'Did he look happy?' Tears were in Sophie's eyes as she asked the question, though she never let them fall. It was ridiculous that the man she hated, the man that had caused her family so much pain could still move her so much. That jealousy could rise in her just knowing Luka was carrying on as he always had—dating and living his life—while she Bella worked as maids in a hotel and could barely make ends meet.

'Luka never really looked happy,' Bella said. 'That, at least, is the same.'

Sophie was quiet.

Bella was right—to others he never looked happy. He was sullen and dark but with her he had laughed and smiled.

She had been privy to such a different side of him.

Knowing that Luka had been here in the hotel had Sophie on edge all day, and it was a relief to get away from work.

All she wanted to do was go home and sleep but instead she changed out of her maid's uniform and into a skirt and a T-shirt and then took the bus. She had to stand nearly all the way to the prison infirmary her father had been moved to.

Once there she put on a ring that had belonged to Bella's mother and signed the visitors' book.

Her bag was searched and she was patted down and then she was allowed in.

'Sophie!' Paulo's face lit up when he saw her walk onto the ward. 'You don't have to come and see me every day.'

'I want to.'

Now that he was in the infirmary, visits could be daily, and Sophie knew full well that he had little time left.

'How is Luka?' Paulo asked.

Her father's mental health had deteriorated throughout the trial and by the time he'd got to Rome he'd been a shadow of himself. He had never been a strong man, and was an exhausted man now.

Sophie just wanted him to know a little peace so she had lied to her father over the years and pretended that she was with Luka.

'He's busy with work.' Sophie smiled, grateful that her father was easily confused and very forgetful. 'He says hello and that he will try to come in and visit you soon.'

'Bella?'

'She's still working at the hotel.'

It was the same questions most days and Sophie knew the routine well. She took out some fruit she had bought for him. A lot of her money went on bringing in Paulo treats, even though she couldn't afford to.

'This is too expensive,' her father said, when she gave him a large bowl of raspberries, which had always been his favourite fruit. When she'd been growing up, they had been a very rare treat.

'Luka can afford it,' she said, and the bitter edge

to her voice had her father frown, and Sophie did her best to rectify her small outburst. 'He's a good man,' she said.

'If he is such a good man, why hasn't he married you?' Paulo asked.

'I've told you that,' Sophie said. 'He knows how much I want you to walk me down the aisle. We are waiting for that day when you are released...'

It was never going to happen. Paulo did not have long left, maybe a few weeks of life, yet his jail sentence was forty-three years.

'I want to see you married in the same church your mother and I were,' Paulo said.

'I know that you do.' Sophie smiled. 'It will happen one day.'

'Maybe,' he said, and Sophie swallowed back tears at the sudden brightness in his voice. 'The director said this morning that things are looking hopeful.'

'Of course there is hope,' she said, and squeezed his frail hand.

'We will know next Wednesday if I am going to get out.'

Sophie looked up and smiled as a nurse came over.

'The director wants to speak with you, Sophie.'

'Thank you,' Sophie said, and stood. 'I'll be back soon,' she said to Paulo, and walked with the nurse, assuming that she was going to get a health update.

She was led through the prison infirmary and to a corridor of offices and there she met a tired-looking woman, who gave Sophie a warm smile and offered her a seat.

'He's more confused than ever,' Sophie said. 'Now he thinks he is getting out of here on Wednesday.'

'He might be getting released,' the director said, and

for a moment Sophie wondered if the chair had been moved for it felt as it the ground had just given way.

'Your father's hearing has been brought forward. We have signed all the forms and have done all we can for him at this end.'

'I don't understand—I didn't even know there was to be a hearing.'

'We are hoping that your father can be released on compassionate grounds. He is no threat to anyone, really he is too weak to go to anywhere other than a hospital or be nursed in your home.' She gave a small shrug. 'Now it is up to the judge to decide but the lawyer who is working on his case is a very good one.'

'I didn't even know there was a lawyer looking out for him.'

'When patients come into the infirmary and their condition is terminal, we try to have their cases reassessed.'

'Why wasn't I told this was happening?'

'It all came about very speedily. When Legal looked at his file they thought there might a possibility for a mistrial but your father does not have time for that. It was thought best to try to get him released on compassionate grounds.' She smiled at Sophie. 'I don't want to get your hopes up but I think in just a few days you might well be able to take your father home.'

Sophie smiled.

It was wonderful news, unexpected and amazing.

And yet it was terrifying too.

She had built a world in her father's mind. One where she lived with Luka in a beautiful flat in Rome, not a scruffy apartment that she and Bella shared.

She had told her father that Matteo and Luka were

still friends, which they were, according to the business press, but she hadn't seen him in years.

The only truth she had told was that Bella worked at Hotel Fiscella, only because once Bella had had to visit on her behalf and had worn a coat over her uniform, which her father had seen.

Paulo was confused enough not to question too many things and there was a lot that he didn't remember.

He simply believed that Luka had kept his word and had got engaged to his daughter.

How could she tell her dying father it had all been a lie?

How could she tell him that she had nothing and that, apart from her friend, she had no one?

'I called you in,' the director continued, but it was as if Sophie was hearing from a distance, 'so that you can start to make plans for his release.'

Sophie managed to thank the director and she even went in to kiss her father goodbye. Once outside again, though, she ran from the hospital and took the crowded bus. When she got off, she raced along the cobbled streets and up the small stairwell, where she wrenched open the iron security door and called out to her friend.

'What?' Bella asked, when she saw her stricken face.

'Pa may be being released...'

Bella let out a shocked gasp. 'That's fantastic news.'

'I know that but how can I bring him here when I have told him that I am engaged to Luka, that we live in a beautiful home?'

'You can't tell him the truth,' Bella said. 'Your father deserves to die knowing that his daughter will be looked after.' Bella's eyes filled with tears. 'My mother didn't know that peace. I think that night Malvolio got released and sent me to work had her go to her grave with a broken heart. It's not going to happen to your father.'

'Oh, so I just produce a luxury apartment? I could just get a photo of Luka, perhaps, and blow it up and sit him in a chair. I know my father is confused but he's not mad…'

'No,' Bella said. 'You are to go and see Luka and tell him that he owes you this much…after the way he shamed you, after all that he said in court, he can damn well go along with things for a while.'

'Do you think I could pull it off?' Sophie said, but then shook her head. 'I can't face him like this.'

'You won't have to,' Bella said. 'I can still sew, I can make you the most sophisticated, elegant woman he has ever seen. You can blow those London women out of the water. He will eat his own words.'

Sophie thought for a moment. 'Luka *could* do it,' Sophie agreed. 'He's a Cavaliere after all. They better than anyone know how to lie under oath.'

CHAPTER TEN

'COULD YOU DIRECT me to Luka Cavaliere's office?'

Sophie stood at a large reception desk and did everything she could to keep the slight tremble from her voice. She was determined to get this right, even if it meant practising her cool façade on the receptionist

'Is he expecting you, Ms…?'

'No, he's not expecting me.' Sophie shook her head. 'If you could just tell me what floor he is on…'

'I'm sorry, but Mr Cavaliere won't see anyone without an appointment.' There was just a slight *something* about the receptionist's voice when she said his name. Her words were tinged with affection and Sophie was quite sure she knew the reason for that.

'For me he would make an exception.' Sophie stared the woman down but it didn't work.

'There *are* no exceptions.' The receptionist smiled her pussycat smile and Sophie glanced at her name badge.

Amber.

'Excuse me,' Amber said as her telephone rang, 'but I need to take this call.'

Sophie stood there as she was summarily dismissed. The beautiful receptionist picked up the phone and started talking but when she had completed the call she blinked, as if surprised to see that Sophie was still there.

'Can I help you?' She frowned.

'You can, Amber,' Sophie responded. 'Please let Mr Cavaliere know that his fiancée is here and that she wishes to see him.'

'His fiancée?'

Sophie watched two spots of colour spread over the woman's cheeks and her cold blue eyes glance down at Sophie's ring finger. 'That's right!' Sophie was the one smiling a pussycat smile now. 'If you could let him know…'

'And your name is…?'

Sophie didn't respond to the question. Luka would know exactly who she was. She pictured his expression when he took the call that would tell him she was back in his life.

A little flustered, the receptionist picked up the phone and relayed the news that Mr Cavaliere's fiancée was there and then gave Sophie a guarded smile. 'I've told his PA and she's going to speak with Mr Cavaliere. If you'd like to take a seat…'

Sophie walked across the elegant foyer to the large leather sofas. She caught sight of herself in the mirror and was relieved for all the effort that she and Bella had made to get to this day.

Bella had, as it turned out, been raiding the bins that they emptied at the hotel for years. Anything that one of the rich guests had thrown out she had squirrelled away.

Beneath Bella's bed were two boxes packed with luxurious clothes.

'This one,' Bella had told her as she held up an ivory silk dress, 'had a little lipstick on the front. She couldn't even be bothered to send it to be dry-cleaned. And these...' She held up some stunning stilettoes. 'They needed to be reheeled, that is all.'

There were coats, jackets, skirts, even nightdresses.

Together they had selected her wardrobe for today and with Bella's skilled hands the rather large ivory dress now clung to Sophie's ripe figure.

The shoes had been reheeled and Sophie's toes had been painted to match her fingernails.

She had flown into London that morning on the red-eye and would be flying back tonight.

The little money they had been saving to fly her father's body, on his death, back to Bordo Del Cielo they had decided to spend on making his last days a dream come true.

Who would guess that Sophie's regular clothes and shoes were in a hired locker at the airport?

Luka must never know.

She had been to a hairdresser's to have her hair put up and then she had changed into the dress Bella had made for her and gone to the make-up counter at an exclusive department store.

She stood as the receptionist came over. 'Mr Cavaliere says you are to go straight up. I'll walk you to the elevator.'

Sophie wanted to turn and run, to ask for a couple of minutes to check her make-up, or for a glass of water for her very dry mouth, but instead she nodded and crossed the foyer.

His office was on the twenty-third floor and her stomach seemed to have been left on the ground as she sailed closer to him.

The elevator doors opened and Sophie was met by a tearful woman who told her that she was the final straw and then let her know that her fiancé was a cheating bastard…

'You can tell him when you go through that his assistant just resigned!'

Sophie merely smiled.

Ah, Luka, she thought, just a little glad for the chaos she had made for him.

Like a witch, she walked through the corridors of his life, delivering little hexes.

She looked around for a moment, taking his world in. There was a large walnut desk, which presumably had been his assistant's because a computer was on and there was half a cup of coffee by its side, as well as a mirror.

There was the quiet hum of the air-conditioning and fresh floral displays stood on the side tables. The carpet was thick beneath her feet—luxury at every turn.

And there, behind that closed door, Sophie knew, was Luka.

The last time she had knocked on his door he had opened it holding a shirt over his cut and naked from the hips up.

She doubted she'd be so lucky again.

She refused to let him glimpse her nervousness by hesitating and she knocked confidently on the door.

'Come in.'

Confidence faded as, after years of self-imposed abstinence her senses momentarily flared in false hope at the return of his voice.

Still, Sophie barely recognised her hand as it reached for the handle on the door, the nails glossy and painted, and it wasn't shaking, as she had thought it would be.

She was ready to face him.

For her father she would get through this.

Into his office she stepped and Sophie stood for a brief slice of time, accepting that again they shared the same part of the planet.

It must be difficult for him also, Sophie knew, and that was confirmed when he didn't turn around. She gave them both a moment to acclimatise to the other's presence—the air was a little thicker there and made no room for the rest of the world.

Still he did not turn and so she spoke to his straight back and broad shoulders.

'Your assistant asked me to pass on the message that she's just resigned. Apparently I'm the final straw.'

Don't turn around, she wanted to warn him.

Not just yet.

Don't let my heart see you until it's beating slowly again, but of course it was too late. Slowly he turned and she met navy eyes that, Sophie knew, were better served warm. Today, though, she was grateful they were cold, for it allowed her to maintain a necessary distance when instinct told her to run, though not from him.

It would actually, Sophie thought, be easier to run across the room and hurdle the desk in her tight dress. It would be far more natural to be in his arms than to simply stand in a room apart from him.

He offered her a seat and she took it.

She told him the reason that she was there—that her father might be being released and of the lies she had told about them.

He pushed every button and so, despite her very best efforts to stay cool, within a few moments she was standing, backed against the desk by him and jabbing her fingers in his chest, telling him that he would do whatever it took to make things right for her father. That he would be her fake fiancé, that he owed her that much.'

Surprisingly, he agreed, but then he told her he would *never* marry her. In fact, he spelt it out. 'I will agree to be your fake fiancé but never your fake husband. Know that now, or get the hell out.'

There was a brief stand-off but finally Sophie sat.

'Do you want a drink?' Luka offered, and reached for the phone. 'I can have some lunch sent up…' He frowned in slight annoyance when his call wasn't immediately answered.

'She resigned,' Sophie reminded him as he replaced the receiver.

'So she did.'

'You could perhaps ring down to Amber,' Sophie said. 'I'm sure she'd be only too happy to assist Mr Cavaliere…'

Perhaps because he heard the disdain in her voice Luka gave a soft, mirthless laugh.

'Have you slept with every woman in this building?' Sophie asked.

'All the good-looking ones,' Luka said, and then shrugged. 'I don't have to explain myself to you.' He stood. 'We'll go and get lunch.'

'I don't want to go out for lunch and sit and reminisce. I want to talk…'

'Sophie, I can assure you that I don't want a cosy lunch and a trip down memory lane. I have a meeting at two that I need to be back for and I'd like to have eaten by then.'

They took the elevator down and Sophie smiled a pussycat smile again at Amber as they walked through the foyer.

'You've got a nerve coming here and calling yourself my fiancée,' Luka said. He was furious that she could, within the space of half an hour, completely disrupt his life. Amber was sulking, Tara was gone and now, given he had just agreed to be her fiancé, the next few weeks would be a sexless hell, lying in bed beside her.

'I have nerves of steel,' Sophie said.

Almost.

Until she'd gone to Rome, she had hardly been out of Bordo Del Cielo and now she was in a foreign city with a man who was so familiar he felt encoded. It seemed wrong not to touch, not to hold hands, but instead to walk painfully apart down the busy street.

They entered a restaurant and were led through to the back—clearly he came here often because they greeted him by name. The waft of the aroma of herbs and garlic made her feel a little sick.

There was a flurry of menus but Luka shook his head. 'No wine.'

'Am I business?' Sophie checked, as the wine waiter walked off.

'If you were business,' Luka said, 'there would be the finest red breathing now.'

'If I were pleasure?'

'Champagne in bed,' Luka said. 'Just one glass for me, though. I'd have to get back to work.'

'So too would Amber?' Sophie flashed.

'I always give her the afternoon off afterwards,' Luka retorted. 'I'm nice like that.'

She was angry and more so when she saw that Luka was ordering for her—no doubt he didn't think her capable.

'I can order for myself,' she flared.

'I'm sure you can,' Luka said, 'but I have about thirty-two minutes before I need to get back, I'm hungry, angry and I'm guessing you still eat pasta… This isn't a nice lunch, Sophie, this is sustenance because I didn't have time for breakfast.'

'Why was that?' She couldn't resist raising her eyebrows and then she knew she had gone too far because he leant across the table and put her straight back in her place.

'Don't ask me about these last years Sophie. You could have been in them, you chose not to be.' The waiter came back with two bowls of pasta and Sophie sat bristling as he refilled her water.

She never cried.

Never.

She almost did now, she could feel this sting at the back of her nose. Oh, it wasn't quite bread and water. But almost. She got pasta and thirty-two minutes of his precious time—she got his attention, but the irritated version of it.

How might it have been?

'So you work as an events planner?' Luka checked. 'Full time?'

'No.' Sophie shook her head. 'I mean yes, but I have cleared my diary, given that he might be getting out of prison…'

'That must have cheered your clients.'

'I handed them over to a friend in the business.'

'Good,' Luka said.

They talked business, or rather they discussed cold facts.

He told her about his Rome apartment and while she was there he called the management and told them his fiancée would be moving in.

'Over the weekend,' Luka said, but as Sophie went to protest he hung up.

'The judgment isn't till Wednesday.'

'You'll need time to get your bearings and move some of your things over. Give your name at Reception and they will give you a key and help with your luggage. I'll be there Tuesday night...'

'Maybe we should wait to see what happens in court.'

'We'll just have dinner, sort out some final details...' Luka glanced at the time. 'I need to get back.'

Sophie went to stand but he gave her a look that had her halt. 'What are you doing?'

'I was going to walk back with you.'

'Why?' Luka asked. 'We have said all that we need to for now. I will see you on Tuesday night. I have a lot to sort out between now and then. Just give me your number in case I need to contact you.'

'I'll contact you.'

'Fine.'

He walked out of the restaurant and Sophie sat there, watching him disappear into the street, and not once did he look back.

'Could I have the bill?' Sophie asked, but the waiter shook his head.

'It's been taken care of.'

She looked at the businessmen ordering coffee, at the groups of laughing friends sharing desserts and the loving couples taking their time over a leisurely lunch with wine.

It was a long ride back to Heathrow.

Yet it felt like a very quick flight back to Rome.

She arrived at Fiumicino airport, where Bella was waiting for her.

'*Credeva voi*?' Bella asked.

'Yes, he believed me,' Sophie answered.

Luka believed she was rich.

Luka believed she was successful.

Even at her very best, he still did not want her.

CHAPTER ELEVEN

'THIS COULD HAVE all been yours,' Bella said, as they walked through Luka's apartment in Prati on the eve of judgment day for her father.

They had picked up the keys in Reception and had declined help with her luggage, but as they'd let themselves in both had been blown away.

Yes, they had seen it online, but walking through it was breath-taking. The tall arched windows were beautifully dressed in heavy fabric. The décor was a mixture of antiques yet there was every modern luxury.

'There's an internal elevator,' Bella said. 'Shall we go up to the rooftop?'

Sophie shook her head. 'I'll explore there later.'

It was agony to be here and to know it was his.

Bella had been busy and now in the wardrobe in the main bedroom hung elegant dresses, skirts and jackets and some shoes. Bella had lent Sophie her mother's heavy silver hairbrush and that was in the large bathroom, along with expensive toiletries they had bought. But even with everything they had managed to cobble together over the last few days, even with all their resources pooled and their savings almost spent, it was just a tiny drop in the ocean compared to Luka's obvious wealth.

'Doesn't it make you feel jealous?' Bella pushed.

'I chose not to go to London with him, remember. Anyway, who knows what would have happened if I had gone? We might not have got on,' Sophie pointed out 'One romantic afternoon doesn't mean that we would have lasted a lifetime. And, anyway, I want nothing that has Malvolio's name attached to it.'

'Luka works hard.'

'We work hard,' Sophie said. 'The only difference is we didn't get a step up on the ladder. Our parents didn't give us a share in a hotel to kick our careers off.'

It was easier to resent him, to sound jealous. It was far easier then admitting the truth—that she missed him so much, every single minute of every single day.

And as for the nights…

'What time is he getting here?' Bella asked.

'Any time now,' Sophie said. 'We're going out to dinner to make sure our stories match.'

'Well, just be as expensive as the women where we work. Don't say sorry to staff and don't…' Bella gave her a smile. 'You'll be fine. Oh, I got you a present. Actually, two…'

'Bella!' Sophie scolded when she saw the latest phone. 'We can't afford this.'

'Yes, we can. You can hardly pretend to be an event planner and not even have a phone. When you're done with Luka, I want it if you don't.'

'What's this?' She opened the second present, which was a heavy bottle filled with very expensive perfume. 'Bella…'

'What woman wouldn't have perfume in the bathroom.'

'We didn't have the money for that.'

'Oh, well…'

'You stole this?'

'Yes, I did,' Bella said. 'And I don't feel guilty and I don't feel ashamed. If that's the worst thing I do then I am glad to do it for you.'

Sophie opened the perfume and sprayed it on her wrist and then squirted Bella, who laughed but then it faded.

She had a question of her own.

'Did he say anything about Matteo?'

'Nothing.'

'I thought they were in business together...'

'We really didn't talk that much.'

'I'm scared I'm going to find out that Matteo is married. I know he must think I'm still a whore.'

'Matteo paid for you,' Sophie pointed out.

There was so much shame for them both.

'I still think about him all the time,' Bella admitted. 'Do you think he remembers me?'

'Of course he must,' Sophie said. 'But it was years ago, Bella. If seeing Luka again has taught me anything it is that people move on. Luka is busy with his life, his women. He has long since moved on from those days. So too must we. When all this over, you and I are going to chase our dreams. I don't care what it takes but you are going to go design school and I'm going to have a career.'

'On the ships.'

'Who knows?' Sophie said. 'But I'm not going to spend the rest of my life mourning Luka. I want this over and done with.'

'I'm going to go,' Bella said.

'Thank you.'

Bella forced a smile. 'I want all the details. Imagine you and Luka sharing a bed after all this time...'

Sophie smiled as her friend left but alone she walked nervously around the apartment. The bedroom mocked her, the bed mocked her. It was hard to believe that soon she would be lying in there at night with Luka. That wasn't all that upset her. It wasn't just the thought that he had lain in this bed with others that had bile rising like a volcano.

It was that Luka had had a life, a good one.

But without her.

Alone she walked around and then pulled back the antique gate and stepped into the elevator, it was small but luxurious, and she stepped out to a view that under any other circumstances would have taken her breath away.

Now, again, she was close to tears.

Rome glittered before her, the view better than any from the hotel because you were actually in it. She could hear the noise from the street below and see the Colosseum and the Vatican. The light was fading and soon the streets would pulse with nightlife yet it was not this view she craved.

She had never ached to be back in Bordo Del Cielo till now—there were too many dark memories there. Since seeing Luka, though, she craved to be there. She wanted to get back to her secret cove and to be near water that was so clear and cool that it took the sting out of summer.

Unable to bear it, Sophie headed back down but there was no relief to be had there, for having worked out a room for her father she walked down the main corridor and peered into the bedroom she would share with Luka.

The room was magnificent, better than the presidential suite at the hotel where she worked.

The furnishings were heavy and masculine and it would take more than a silver hairbrush and a few dresses in the wardrobe to detract from the male energy that stopped her from going in.

The bed was wide, dressed in muted jewelled tones, and she could not imagine herself lying there with him.

Worse, she tormented herself by imagining him lying there with another woman.

'Sophie?' His deep voice made her jump and then spin around on her new high heels.

'I didn't hear you come in.'

'Did you expect me to knock?'

'Of course not.' She could hardly bear to meet his gaze. She had seen him angry, she had seen him arrogant and aloof, but she had never seen him like this—there were lines fanning from his eyes and his mouth was grim, his complexion tinged grey, and his tension palpable.

He looked as if he was dreading this just as much as she was.

'Where do you want to go for dinner?' he asked.

'We could have something to eat here.'

'I would guess that we'll be eating here rather a lot,' Luka said. 'If your father gets off, I doubt we'll be going out very much.'

'I don't expect you to be here all the time,' Sophie said. 'We can say that you're busy with work.'

'He's dying, Sophie,' Luka said. 'And if I were engaged to you, if I did love you, your father knows that I would do more than put in a few cameo appearances.'

'Of course.'

'I'll give you a tour,' he offered, but Sophie shook her head.

'I already know my way around.'

'Have you organised a nurse for him?'

'I thought it better to wait and see what happens to-morrow,' Sophie said, although the truth was there was no way she could afford a private nurse for her father.

'I'm going to go to court in the morning,' Luka said. 'I'll text you with what's happening.'

'Why would you go to court?'

'To save you from having to go,' Luka said, and with that simple sentence her heart just about folded in on it-self because that was the type of man she had lost. This was what being loved by Luka would mean. 'Have you any idea how big it is going to be tomorrow with the press and everything?' he checked.

'I'm starting to,' Sophie said. 'I saw on the news that the press are already camping out by the court.'

'They think he's going to be there when the ruling is made,' Luka said. 'Hopefully he can slip out of the in-firmary before the press work it out. Is there anything else that I need to know?'

'I don't think so. We can talk over dinner.'

'I've changed my mind about dinner,' he said.

'Where are you going?' Sophie asked, as he went to walk out.

'What the hell does it have to with you?' he asked.

'If we're supposed to be engaged…'

'The games begin tomorrow, Sophie.' He came right up to her face. 'Tomorrow we lie in that bed, tomorrow we pretend that we care. I've just realised that tonight I don't have to even pretend that I like you, so I won't. I intend to enjoy my last night of freedom before *my* sentence begins.'

He walked off and Sophie knew she should hold her tongue but it had never been her forte. 'Oh, I'm sorry to have thrown such a spanner into your charmed life.'

'Charmed?' Luka turned. 'Tell me, Sophie, what part of my life exactly is charmed? I've worked eighteen-hour days for this. You talk as if it has been handed to me on a plate.'

'The share in a hotel from Daddy was a rather nice start.'

'He had nothing to do with it. I worked for that myself,' Luka said. 'What I didn't say in court was that I knew for years that my father was rotten to the core and that your father was his yes-man. So, tell me more about this charmed life, Sophie. When I came back to London I practically had to go on my knees to my partners at the hotel. Six months in prison takes some explaining. Do you really think my colleagues embraced me on my return? Do you not think that I had to prove over and over that I could be trusted?'

She stood with pale lips as he told her how things had been for him.

'Do you not think that when somebody looks me up and finds out that I was in prison, awaiting trial, for six months that it doesn't slur my name? I took nothing from my father. I have done everything I can to make right what he did. I handed back everything that man gave me. The only thing I couldn't return was the education. You can't unlearn things unfortunately but God knows there are things I've tried to forget...'

He was talking about them, Sophie knew it. He was back in his bed and taking her for the first time with his eyes. 'I washed my hands of Bordo Del Cielo. I only came back that time to rid myself of you once and for all. I should never have opened that door to you!' Even before she could move he grabbed her wrist. 'Slap me again...' Luka warned.

'And you'll slap me back?' Sophie challenged, and she didn't understand because he almost smiled.

Yes, he almost smiled because on so many levels she matched him and in so many ways he adored her. How he would love to end this row in a different way, to kiss her right now into submission, yet he refused that pleasure for himself.

'Slap me again,' he amended, 'and before the finger-marks have faded the engagement will be off and you can tell your father why if you must. I mean it, Sophie, and you should know that I don't give second warnings.'

She stood there and he had won but even as he passed the finish line he kept on sprinting.

'I'm going out now and I'm going to be with a woman who does not question, a woman who is sweet and warm…'

'Give Claudia my love,' Sophie spat, and hoped that the fact she knew his lover's name meant that she sailed past him on shock value alone, but Luka just grinned at the jealous snarl to her voice.

'Claudia?' Luka checked.

'You were with her at Hotel Fiscella.'

'Because Matteo and I are thinking of buying it,' Luka said, and Sophie was grateful that she had handed in her notice as she realised how close she had come to having Luka as her boss. 'Claudia is one of my lawyers.'

'She was there for the purchase of the hotel?'

'No,' Luka said. 'I hired her to get your father released.'

She stood there frozen to the spot, hating how he was always one step ahead, how this man continued to sideswipe her.

'Why?' Sophie asked. 'Why would you hire a lawyer to get my father out?'

No, he didn't tell her about the necklace burning a hole in his pocket and the hellish guilt that had made it his mission to see Paulo freed.

'For this moment, Sophie.' Luka lied. 'So that you would come to my office and ask me to be with you. For the pleasure of lying in bed with you and doing *nothing*...' Black was his smile.

'Why do you hate me so much?'

'You'll work it out,' Luka said. 'I'm going out now. I'll see you tomorrow when the real games begin.'

CHAPTER TWELVE

SHE DIDN'T WANT her father to be released.

Sophie decided she must surely be the most terrible daughter in history because at midday, when still nothing had been said on the news, when still the judge had not ruled, she had this brief fantasy that his application would be denied and she could walk out of the apartment and away from Luka without a single word.

Instead, late in the afternoon, she got a text.

Your father has left the infirmary and will be with you shortly. The judge made his ruling in private for security reasons. It will shortly be announced.

Aside from the hell of what lay ahead, Sophie still wondered what sort of a nightmare her father's release might have been without the well-oiled machine of Luka's life swinging into action.

She saw on the news the crush of reporters both at the court and another group that was now outside the prison infirmary and she shuddered at the thought of her and Bella dealing with this.

Even as the journalists jockeyed for position at the prison gates Paulo was sitting in Luka's home.

'I thought Luka would be here,' Paulo said.

'He was at court,' Sophie said. 'He has been keeping me up to date with all that is going on.'

'It is a beautiful home,' her father said, and then he looked at the view from a huge leather chair. 'Is there a balcony? I would like to breathe fresh air...'

'There's a balcony in your room and there is also a rooftop garden,' Sophie said.

'I would never make the stairs.'

'There's an elevator.' Luka deep voice caught her unawares and again, to the sound of him, she jumped, not that her father noticed.

'Luka!' She heard the sheer joy in her father's voice as he pushed himself to stand and then she watched Luka's eyes briefly shutter as he embraced the old man.

'Thank you,' Paulo said in a heartfelt voice as he took Luka into his arms. 'Thank you for all you did. I know it was you who got me out...'

'Nonsense.' Luka's voice was gruff. 'The judge was right, there were many mistakes made at the trial. You deserve to have your freedom.'

'You knew it was Luka who was behind this?' Sophie checked.

'Of course,' Paulo said. 'There are not many files that just happen to be picked up. I knew that it had to be you.'

'Father?' Sophie frowned because her father sounded far more together than he had in recent weeks. 'Were you pretending to be confused?'

'Sometimes.' He smiled.

'He's not really sick,' Luka said, and then he saw Sophie's horrified expression at the thought that they might be stuck in this lie for ever so he relented. 'That was a joke.'

'Ha-ha,' Sophie said, and then she looked at her father and she knew in her heart that he didn't have long and yet somehow he was here and they were together.

It was agony.

For Paulo the best wine sat breathing up on the rooftop. Sophie had spent the long day waiting for news, cooking her father's favourite pasta sauce, which he ate with relish.

'It tastes of home,' Paulo said. 'Almost.'

She glanced at Luka's plate.

It was untouched.

She watched as Luka poured three glasses and her father reached for his.

'Should you be drinking?' Sophie checked. 'You are on a lot of medication.'

'You are your mother's daughter.' Paulo laughed. 'I just got out of prison.'

'Even so...'

'You worry too much,' Paulo chided.

'Someone has to.'

Luka glanced over at Sophie's slightly bitter retort. She had dealt with so much, that Luka knew—moving so that she could be close to her father, giving up her dreams of working on the cruise liners.

Letting go of them?

Had that been what she had been doing on the beach that night? Luka briefly pondered.

What did it matter now?

The past was closed.

They just had the present to get through and despite Paulo's slight second wind from his release, Luka knew the charade would not play out for long.

'So.' Paulo looked over at Luka. 'What are your plans for my daughter?'

'I learnt a long time ago that it is foolish to make

plans on Sophie's behalf,' Luka responded. 'She is her own person.'

He looked at Sophie's tense expression. There was a curl of thought forming but he soon lost that thread because Paulo was making grand plans.

'I'd like to have a party,' Paulo said. 'We never toasted your engagement.'

'There's no need for a party,' Sophie said. 'We don't need a fuss to be made.'

'I would like to celebrate.' Paulo was insistent. 'Just a small gathering.'

He started to cough and Sophie took him inside, leaving Luka sitting out there.

'Please, Sophie,' her father said as she helped him to bed. 'I want some photos for you to keep. I want a night we can all remember…'

She didn't need photos to remember this, Sophie thought as she came out of her father's bedroom.

'He's asleep,' she said.

'Lucky him.' Luka's response was curt. 'I might take one of the spare rooms—' Luka started, but any hope of pulling that particular piece of wool over Paulo's eyes faded as his bedroom door opened.

'Could you bring me my wine from the table?'

'Father!'

'Stop fussing,' Paulo said. 'And can you show me how the radio works? I would like to fall to sleep to music.'

As Sophie headed up to the rooftop garden he smiled at Luka. 'Where do you two sleep?' Paulo checked. 'Just in case I need Sophie in the night. I won't come in, of course. I'll just knock.'

'Sophie sleeps in that room,' Luka attempted. 'I have the main one.'

'Please!' Paulo was laughing as Sophie reappeared

with his wine. 'Your fiancé is trying to tell me you have separate rooms! I am not that old-fashioned that you have to pretend.'

'Great!' Luka hissed, as they finally closed the door to his room.

'I told you that he'd never buy us sleeping apart.'

'I just never envisaged the hell it would be.'

Sophie went into the bathroom and undressed. She put on a small nightdress and took a few calming breaths before heading out.

Luka wasn't about to scuttle off to the bathroom to change and was still stripping off as she slipped into bed.

'He wants this party.'

'Then he can have one. I will call Matteo,' Luka said. 'I'll ask him to fly in.'

'He might let it slip that we haven't been together very long.'

'Why would he let it slip?' Luka frowned. 'Matteo knows what is going on, he's a good friend. He knows that this is all just a ruse.'

'You've told him?'

'Why wouldn't I tell him, Sophie? We work together, we are in business together, we grew up together. I don't keep secrets from people who matter to me any more.'

'I could ask Bella.'

'Whatever you want. I'll ring him now.'

'But it's nearly midnight.'

'Yes,' Luka snapped. 'I'm early to bed tonight.'

'Can you go one hour without reminding me about your active sex life?'

'Why does it bother you so much, Sophie?'

She didn't answer.

Luka laughed at her non-reaction and got into bed.

He called Matteo and lay chatting to his friend. Yes, it was hell being engaged, he told him, and then he was serious.

'We're going to have a small party for Paulo,' Luka said. 'Will you be able to fly in? Sophie might ask Bella...' There was a pause before Luka spoke again. 'Of course it's not a problem. Bring anyone you choose.'

He hung up.

'He can only make it tomorrow,' Luka said.

'Tomorrow?'

'He has an important meeting to prepare for in Dubai. Is tomorrow a problem?'

'Of course not.'

'Oh, and he's bringing his girlfriend.'

Sophie decided against asking Bella. She knew how crushed she be to see Matteo with another woman.

'I'll keep it simple,' Sophie said, thinking, as she always had to, about money. 'I might just make his favourite meals...'

'Get it catered,' Luka said. 'Today was an exception. I understand you wanted to give him a taste of home tonight but I'm telling you this much—if you were my fiancée you wouldn't have spent the day slaving and making sauce when there are the best restaurants across the street. Get someone to come and dress the garden and organise the music...' He stopped then. 'Sorry, I forget that you're an events organiser.'

Sophie was sure he knew she'd been lying.

'Is he driving you mad yet?' Luka asked, and Sophie gave a reluctant smile, because her father was driving her a little crazy. 'Are you starting to remember why you were only too willing to leave?'

'A bit,' Sophie admitted. 'I am sick of him saying I am just like my mother.'

'She had him under her thumb,' Luka said.

They lay in bed and it felt impossibly awkward, or at least it did for Sophie. Luka seemed completely fine with it. His hand was beneath the sheet and she blinked when she realised he was arranging himself in his underwear, then he saw her shocked look but merely shrugged.

'I've got an erection. I'm just moving it.' He grinned at her shocked expression. 'Don't worry, I'm not going to come near you.'

'You're in a very good mood.'

'I know,' Luka said. 'I thought it would be hell but I'm really enjoying myself. I like seeing your father free and I love watching you edgy and able to do nothing about it.'

Then he did the cruellest thing.

He kissed her on the tip of her nose and two minutes later he was asleep.

CHAPTER THIRTEEN

LUKA WOKE UP AND for the first morning in his life it was the right face on the pillow next to him.

He examined her beautiful face and he looked at where one breast had fallen out of her nightdress. Their legs were loosely entwined, hers over one of his and beneath the other.

She was loyal, she was fierce and she matched him.

He knew their dance, even if it had only been a short one.

He knew the steps, for their souls were familiar.

And she would never forgive him for what his father had done.

If she did, it wouldn't be for long. In the heat of the moment his father's sins would be raised and then hurled at him in her, oh, so Sicilian way.

And he would not live like that.

He wished it were different.

If he could change one thing about her, would he, though?

It would be like trimming the corner off a work of art, or like removing one letter from the alphabet and watching one's words fall apart.

'Why are you staring at me?' Sophie asked as her brown eyes opened to his.

'Because you're in my bed and there is not much else to look at.' Then his eyes drifted down to her exposed breast and he gave a lazy smile as she tucked herself in.

'See,' Luka said, 'it's rude when I rearrange myself, but not when you do.'

'Hard again, Luka?' Sophie smiled.

'That's for me to know,' Luka answered, and didn't even roll over as she climbed out of bed and went to her wardrobe.

She had no idea what to wear. Bella had made her plenty of stunning clothes but none were very practical for making coffee so instead she took out one of his shirts.

'How's the phobia?' Luka asked. 'Last time you put on one of my shirts there were ten policemen in the bedroom. You seem remarkably calm—no flashbacks?'

She didn't bother answering him. Instead, she went to make coffee and didn't look up when Luka came through. He was wearing a suit and looked ready for the office.

'I thought you'd take today off.'

'No.'

'I thought—'

'I have an office here in Rome and I have a lot of work that needs to be done. Anyway, I thought it might be nice for you to have a day with your father, without being on edge with me here.'

'I'm going to take him in some breakfast,' Sophie said.

'The doctor is coming at nine to check up on him,' Luka said, and he put a credit card on the bench.

'What's this for?'

'The caterers and things.'

'I can cover that,' Sophie lied. She really had been

intending to spend the day cooking and doing what she could to prepare for tonight.

'Please, don't say you will get this. You asked me to go along with things as if we were together. Well, that is how it would be. Book the caterers, get the garden looking beautiful. I have never heard of your business so I don't know how easy it will be for you to arrange things with no notice. Use my name, you won't have a problem'

She didn't have a single one.

It was strange to have the world at your fingers, courtesy of the Cavaliere name.

Except people didn't jump in fear when she rang and said that she was organising a last-minute gathering; instead, they seemed genuinely happy to help.

And so she enjoyed herself amidst the saddest of times.

The columns of foliage and scented trees were decorated with tiny lights that would come on at sunset. A string quartet had been arranged and the food had Sophie's mouth watering even as she made her selections.

Hearing her father cough and struggle to catch his breath, Sophie knew this would all be over, long before the credit-card bills came in.

'What's this?' Paulo asked.

'A new shirt and suit.' Sophie smiled. 'They just need you to try it on so they can take it in.'

Yes, to Sophie, Luka's life *was* charmed.

And so she had a beautician come to Luka's home and sat on a velvet chair in the bedroom as her thick black hair was spun into heavy ringlets and her eyelids were painted a smoky grey.

'Red lips…' the beautician said, but Sophie shook her head.

In her bag, still there, was her once-used lip glaze.

She wondered if it would all have dried up but, no, it went on easily.

'Just touch it up through the evening,' the beautician said. 'And try not to play with your hair or the curls will drop.'

Sophie chose her dress from the selection Bella had made. A simple black dress that went with the shoes she had worn on the day she had walked into his office was her choice. She tried it on and let out a small hiss of frustration. The front was far too low and as for the back there wasn't one.

Luka walked in as Sophie stood staring in the mirror, trying to fathom if she'd be safe without a bra.

He saw first her back, glossy and brown, with black ringlets snaking down it. He looked down and saw the muscles of her calves drawn lean in high heels and he walked over, anticipating her slight jump as he came into view in the mirror.

'I'm sorry about all this,' Sophie said.

'Don't be sorry.' Luka shrugged. 'I agreed to go along with this. Of course your father would want a special night.'

'Thank you.'

He looked at her lips and told himself he was imagining things because they were the very lips he had kissed that long-ago day. He looked down at the gape of unrestrained cleavage and thick nipples that jutted from the fabric.

'I forgot to pack my backless bra...'

'Those bras are the ugliest things I've ever seen.'

She could feel a shiver on her back, so light she thought it might be his finger, but she realised he was holding a drink with one hand and removing his tie with the other.

It was the nerves on her spine that were leaping in hope.

'I'll change,' Sophie said, turning to go to the wardrobe, except Luka didn't step aside and she walked slap bang into him.

His drink he held steady.

It was her heart that seemed to spill on the floor.

'You'll wear that,' Luka said. 'You'll wear what turns me on.'

'Why?' Sophie demanded. Why the hell would he do this to them?

'Mortification of the flesh,' Luka answered. 'It's my new game.'

He undid his shirt and she could feel the tense pinch of her nostrils as he took it off and she would hold her breath till he headed for the shower.

He didn't, though.

Instead, he went to the wardrobe and took out a clean shirt.

'Aren't you going to shower?'

'There's no time for that.'

'Luka, please...'

'Do I smell?' He came over and lifted his arm and she simply refused to breathe him in. 'No, I showered this morning. You get me in the raw...'

She wanted him clean and sterile—she didn't want his heady scent.

'See?' Luka smiled at her pale face. 'It's a good game. Well, it is for me. I keep forgetting you don't like all that business...' He did up his shirt and Sophie chose to get out.

'I'm going to help my father get ready.'

'No need.' His eyes did not leave her alone for a minute. 'I brought a nurse back with me. Another one will take her place at midnight. They come with the best references and I have done the necessary checks.'

'I take care of my father.'

'Of course you do,' Luka said. 'But as a daughter, not a nurse. I was thinking today that if I had a child, not that I ever will, but if I did I would not want them looking after me in that way. Enjoy him as your father now.'

'I can't afford a nurse.' Her words were shrill, her admission reluctantly dragged through strained lips, but Luka didn't even blink.

'You know,' he drawled, 'they're the first honest words to come out of your mouth. We need to head out there. Matteo and Shandy will be here soon, I believe they're getting engaged in a few weeks…'

'Shandy?' Sophie said, resentment prickling for Bella, for her heart would break when she found out that Matteo was about to get engaged. 'What sort of a name is that? Is he bringing a horse?'

'Oh…' Luka gave a low laugh. 'She's back.'

'Who?'

'The *real* Sophie,' Luka answered. 'I keep glimpsing her but then you tuck her away. Bring her out, Sophie. Don't worry, I can handle her.'

The *real* Sophie took the elevator with him up to the rooftop garden.

Her father was there, thanks to the nurse.

And so too were Matteo and Shandy.

'You've done well,' Luka said.

Sophie had. The garden twinkled with lights, the string quartet was softly playing and the waiters were waiting to pounce.

'It's been so long,' Sophie said, and kissed Matteo's cheek.

'Just not quite long enough,' Matteo said, and Sophie jerked her head back.

He hated her too, only she didn't understand why.

'This is Shandy.' Matteo introduced the glossy blonde and Sophie looked at her. With her long legs and slightly protruding teeth, she actually did slightly resemble a horse.

'Shandy.' Sophie kissed her on both cheeks too and met Luka's eyes.

She would behave, Sophie swore.

The food was delicious.

Porcini mushrooms with black truffle pappardelle, the sauce thick and creamy and mopped up with bread rich with herbs and olives, but, Paulo mused, 'It cannot beat Sicilian *panne*...'

'Nothing beats Sicilian,' Sophie said.

She meant it for Bella, for her friend, she meant it to remind Matteo of the woman who was not here tonight, yet it was Luka's eyes she met as she said it.

'No.' She put her hand over the wine glass as the waiter went to pour.

'Enjoy yourself.' Luka smiled. 'I am.'

He liked the real Sophie; he liked watching her attempt to rein herself in as he invited her to come out.

Both were, both knew, playing the most dangerous of games.

Dessert was pure heaven—thick cassata that was as rich and as liqueur-laced as it had been more than a decade ago when he had denied her that kiss.

And then tiny *cannellonis*, the ricotta tart with lemon, refreshing to the tongue.

'Limoncello.' Paulo smiled as he sipped the drink of home, and then he stood on frail legs as Sophie sat.

'Tonight makes up for many things,' Paulo said. 'Tonight I sit with old friends and new...' He raised a glass to Shandy, and Luka and Matteo did the same.

The glass felt like lead to Sophie but she raised hers too.

Then she had to listen to her father say how right she and Luka were. That they were simply meant for each other.

'Luka was twelve when his mother died. I remember Sophie crying that night for his pain.' She had forgotten that. Deliberately. To escape the pain, she had avoided their past and now her father walked them both through it.

For appearances' sake Luka's hand was over hers but it was hot and dry and there was no caress from him as her father exposed the love that was lost.

'When we had a party for Luka moving to London, I remember Sophie coming down the stairs. She had put tissues in her bra. She wanted Luka to notice her...

'"In time," I told her. But she was fourteen and impatient and did not want to listen to me,' He looked at Sophie. 'Listen to me now. You and Luka's time is now. Don't ever waste it.'

Then it was Luka's turn to speak.

He cleared his throat and thanked their few guests. Out of the corner of her eye Sophie could see that her father was fading. Smiling but fading, and she was so grateful to Luka to have given him this night.

'Paulo, we are so happy to celebrate this night with you. I am very blessed. Some might say that I have a *charmed* life...' He looked at Sophie and with a smile that did not reach his eyes he painted her heart black.

'That is because of you, Sophie...' He offered her his hand and Sophie stood. 'I know you have your ring, but I wanted something to mark this night.'

She opened a box and there was a fine bracelet and she read the inscription:

'*Per sempre insieme.*'

Together for ever.

She wanted to hurl it over the balcony and to the street or throw it across the floor, but instead she handed it to her father, who was putting on his glasses to read what had been written.

'We should go soon,' Matteo said to Shandy.

'Why?' Sophie challenged. 'When we're having so much fun?'

'You could stay here,' Luka offered, but Matteo shook his head. 'It is good to check the hotel out...'

'Where are you staying?' Paulo asked.

'Fiscella,' Matteo answered, and Sophie shivered and hoped that Bella wasn't working there tomorrow. 'Luka and I are thinking of buying it,' he explained to Paulo. 'It is a nice old hotel but it needs a lot of refurbishment. I want to see for myself a few things.'

'Doesn't Bella work there?' Paulo asked, and Sophie tensed, especially when she felt the scrutiny of Luka's gaze.

'She does.'

'Doing what?' Matteo asked.

'She's a chambermaid,' Paulo answered. 'Isn't she, Sophie?'

'Well, I guess it gives her access to a richer clientele.' Matteo's response was surly and, taking Shandy by the hand, he led her to the floor to dance.

'I thought you would wear your mother's earrings

tonight,' Paulo said. 'You wanted them for your engagement.'

'They didn't go with the dress.' Sophie's answer was brittle and Luka noted it.

'Come on,' Luka said. 'Dance.'

I don't want to dance with you, she wanted to say. *I don't want to be in your arms because there I might convince myself that this is real.*

He held her at her waist and she could feel his cheek by hers and it was their first dance and had to be their last because it nearly killed her to be back in his arms.

Yet she didn't want their one dance to end—ever.

'Why did you get me that bracelet? Why would you have engraved "Together for Ever"?'

'What did you want me to have inscribed? *"Né tu letu né iu cunsulatu"*?'

She looked right at him with narrowed eyes as he delivered a very apt Sicilian saying—'Neither you happy nor I consoled.'

'Do you need consoling, Luka?' Her smile was mean with seduction.

'Are you happy?' Luka asked, and saw that her smile struggled to stay on. 'Do you miss it?'

'Miss what?' Sophie hissed, yet she knew what was coming and she was right, for he practically echoed Bella's words.

'Everything we could have had.'

'You ended things with me,' Sophie said. 'You came back to Bordo Del Cielo just to say you didn't want to marry me.'

'Oh, you are so good at rewriting history, Sophie,' Luka refuted. 'I ended the old us, we were just starting anew. It was you that ultimately broke things off.

You who refused to come to London with me. So,' he asked, 'do you regret it?'

If she said that she did, then she admitted her love. And if she admitted her love, then it made the last years wasted, and that shamed her more than being led to a police car dressed in his shirt.

Instead, she clung to her pride as she fought not to rest her head on his shoulder. 'No.'

'Then you're more of a fool than I thought.'

'Oh, I'm a fool now, am I?' Sophie retorted. 'A peasant and a fool.'

'You'll never let it go, will you? Always you let your temper get the better of you,' Luka said into her ear, and she fumed silently in his arms as one by one he took out her faults and examined them as their bodies swayed to the music and turned the other on. 'Your quick tongue…'

'My slow tongue…' Sophie said, and he laughed a dark laugh at her attempt to change the subject.

Yes, the old Sophie was back.

'It won't work, Sophie.'

'Ah, but it already has,' she said, because she could feel him hard against her and certainly, for Luka's sake, one dance must now become two.

'You should be careful who you tease,' he said into her ear. 'I have no problem sleeping with you and then walking away.'

'You would do that, wouldn't you?'

'Oh, yes,' Luka said. 'So don't play with fire.'

It felt strange to be both angry and turned on, to want and to resist.

'Why do you loathe me?' Sophie asked. 'You have a wonderful life. And why does Matteo hate me?'

'Because I'm boring when I'm drunk,' Luka said. 'I guess I tend to complain about you.'

'And why do you hate me so?'

'Many reasons.'

'Such as?'

'You held what my father did against me. You compare me to him when I never did that to you.'

'My father is a good man.'

'Perhaps, but he is not completely innocent.' He dropped a kiss on her burning shoulder and there was nowhere to hide, no row that could be had in the public arena she had made for them, and resistance was agony.

'Don't make him out a saint,' Luka said.

'I don't.' Sophie closed her eyes as his face came back to her cheek.

'What else?' she asked.

'Your inability to back down, to admit you were wrong,' Luka said, and then he warned her what he was about to do. 'I'm going to kiss you now. I'm going to kiss you and there is nowhere you can go and nowhere you can hide, and I am going to remind you what you let go. You are going to taste what you must now miss every day.'

'A small kiss is hardly going to have me on my knees.'

'Who said small?'

'There are people present. My father...'

'Would he not expect us to kiss at our engagement party? Just pull away when it gets too much...'

'Luka, you seem to think I still want you. I told you, I don't want anyone.'

'Oh, that's right—your phobia...'

He pulled his head back so she could see his black smile.

'When you need me to stop, I shall.'

Sophie blinked. She already needed him to stop and he had barely started, but just the graze of his lips was too much, just the press of his mouth was too dangerous.

He was necessarily cruel.

Necessarily because their mouths needed each other, and it was a relief just to give in to mutual want.

The shiver along her spine this time came from his fingers, and it was Sophie's tongue that caressed his.

Just the tip.

That cool, muscular tip that stroked hers enough to remind their scalding bodies of the fire they'd once made.

'Enough for show,' Sophie said, and pulled back.

Just not enough for them.

'I'm going to see Matteo off.' Luka ran a slow tongue over his lips and tasted her again. 'Your father looks as if he needs to go to bed.'

He left her burning.

As Luka saw their guests off, Sophie took the elevator with her father and the nurse.

'It is good to see you so happy.'

'We are happy, Dad,' Sophie told him, as she saw him to his room. 'You can see how Luka takes care of me. You don't have to worry any more.'

'But I do,' Paulo said, then turned to the nurse. 'Can you excuse us, please?'

The nurse nodded and they walked into his room. 'You have no idea how good that feels,' Paulo said.

'What?'

'To ask for privacy and to be given it. You have made my final days happy, Sophie, but there is more that I want. I need to walk you down the aisle. I want to return to Bordo Del Cielo...'

'The journey will be too much for you.'

'Then I will die returning home to my Rosa.'

'Father...'

'Sophie, don't say no to me. Let me see you and Luka marry in the same church that your mother and I did, now, this weekend. I won't see another one, this much I know...'

How could she say no to him?

'I'll speak to Luka.'

CHAPTER FOURTEEN

SHE WALKED INTO the bedroom. Luka was lying on his side, his back to her and the sheet low on his hips.

She didn't know if he was awake or asleep but she knew that she had to tell him between now and the morning that she had told her father they would marry. She headed into the en suite and started to undress then realised she had left her nightdress in the bedroom. Rather than going back in there, she undressed and wrapped herself in a towel then took off her make-up and brushed her teeth.

Luka was going to be furious, Sophie knew.

But, hell, he must surely understand the impossible situation her father had put her in. He was days away from dying—of course he wanted to go home one last time, of course he would want to see his daughter married to the man she supposedly loved.

Loved?

She didn't love Luka, she abhorred him, Sophie told herself, but then she caught sight of her lying eyes in the mirror as she rinsed her mouth.

Her body loved him, she knew, because it hadn't just been hard work and few hours to spare that had kept her from other men, it had been the utter lack of wanting them when she looked at them. She'd had a few kisses that had tasted of plastic compared to being devoured by the man on the other side of the bathroom door.

She stepped into the bedroom.

'Luka…' Her voice was perhaps a little too quiet for someone who was truly trying to wake another, but when he didn't respond Sophie decided that she'd tell him in the morning, and she slipped out of her dress and panties.

'What?'

He didn't turn and Sophie reached for her nightdress as she spoke. 'It will keep till morning.'

'Tell me now.' He turned then and he wished he hadn't for despite the darkness he could see her naked body with arms raised as she pulled on her nightdress.

He should turn away quickly, yet he didn't. Instead, in that brief moment everything he'd imagined was verified. He had been trying to ignore her, willing sleep to come before she slipped into bed beside him and now he had to endure another night fighting instinct.

Sophie met his eyes and denied the sexual tension between them. 'My father…' She kept her voice calm. 'I couldn't get out of it.'

'Get out of what?'

'He wants to go back to Bordo Del Cielo as soon as possible. He wants to visit my mother's grave.'

'I'll arrange the flight, you can go with him. I'll make up some excuse about work as the reason I cannot be there. I never want to go back.'

'He wants us both to go with him, though,' Sophie said. His eyes were fixed on hers and her skin prickled with heat as she continued. 'I've said that we will marry this Sunday.'

He said nothing and she stood there awaiting his response.

'Luka?'

'Are you going to stand there all night or get into bed?'

Sophie took a tentative step forward, pulled back the sheet and slipped in.

Her heart was thumping. The tension in the room was almost unbearable—a mixture of fear at his response and a deep, thick arousal. She knew he was turned on, and so too was she; she could not catch her breath, though she tried to keep it even.

'Did you hear what I said about us?'

'I heard.'

'You didn't respond.'

'I have already told you where I stand on that—I will never marry you.'

'But I've told him that we shall.'

'Then you'd better hope that he dies before the service is due to commence.'

'Luka…' Fury bolted her upright but he pulled her down and pinned her.

'What?' he demanded. 'Say what you were going to.'

'You can't mean that.'

'Oh, I mean it,' he said. 'I'll go along with it, I'll go back home with you and get involved with the preparations. I'll say and do all the right things right up until the church but know this—I won't be standing at the altar when you get there, Sophie. You'll be jilted in front of the town.'

'You hate me so much that you'd do that to me.'

'I hate you as much as I want you.'

'That doesn't make sense,' Sophie said, yet even as the words left her lips she had worked out what he meant. He hated her fiercely, judging by the erection now pressing into her thigh.

'I'll make it clearer, then,' Luka said. 'I hate you as much as you want me.'

'But I don't want you. I don't want anyone,' Sophie said. With every cell in her body she lied and she knew he knew it. 'Will you marry me, Luka? I'm not asking for forever…'

'You miss the very point.'

'Luka, can we start again?' Sophie drew in a breath. 'Can we put the past behind us and start anew?'

'Without examining it?' Luka checked. 'Without accusing?'

'Yes.'

'How very convenient, Sophie, because then you don't have admit you were wrong. You get to wipe the slate clean for as long as it suits you.'

'What does that mean?'

He got up and headed to the safe where her mother's necklace was kept and opened it.

Just hand it to her, he told himself.

Simply give her the benefit of the doubt.

Hand it over to her and see what she says.

'You want a clean slate?' Luka checked.

'Yes,' Sophie said. 'I won't raise what was said in court.'

He stared at the cross and chain; he almost believed she could do it until Sophie spoke on.

'I won't bring up the other women.'

'But. You. Just. Did!' Luka shouted in exasperation, and took out the earring instead of the cross. She was nowhere ready for the truth. 'You're still the fourteen-year-old kid padding her bra.'

'Meaning?'

'You haven't grown up, or rather you haven't moved on.'

'Still the peasant.'

'One row,' Luka shouted, 'one cross word and you hurl the past back at me. So where's the clean slate, Sophie?'

'Keep it down,' she said. 'I don't want my father to hear us row.'

'He can't,' Luka said. 'These walls are soundproof So row away, Sophie, say what you have to. Here...' He tossed her a piece of gold.

Just not the right one.

'My mother's earring.'

'I found it in my bedroom,' Luka said. 'Come on, Sophie, say what you have to.'

'I don't want to row.'

'You want to make love?' Luka checked.

She ran an eye over his naked body and when most might avert their eyes from an angry erection, Sophie frowned.

'I don't think it has love on its mind.'

Uh-oh!

Luka walked over and she refused to flinch as he shredded her flimsy nightdress.

'You'll have sex with me yet you won't go through with the marriage?' Sophie checked.

'Yes,' Luka said. 'And if you knew my reputation you would know many of my girlfriends have complained about the same thing.'

'Ah, but you don't make love to them the way you do with me.'

'You don't know that.'

'I do know that,' Sophie said, and looked right into his eyes. 'Absolutely I do.'

'That's a very confident assumption for someone who's only had sex twice.'

'Once,' Sophie corrected. 'We only did it—'

She never got to finish. His mouth was hard on her hers and he kissed her then as he had wanted to on the dance floor.

He kissed her hard until she was kissing him back, her fingers knotting in his hair.

'Remember, I don't want charity,' Luka said, as his thighs parted her legs.

He made her back down.

With his refusal to go further, he tested their patience to the edge.

'It isn't charity,' Sophie said, as she guided him to her heat.

'Some phobia.'

He exposed her lie and she didn't care, as long as he took her now.

Yet he didn't.

And neither did he leave her hanging on; instead, he knelt up.

'What are you doing?'

'Picking up where we left off.'

He lowered his face to her and confirmed her desire for she was wet and swollen and a moment away from coming to him.

She tried to scramble away from him, but he held her hips down; she wanted them face to face, not this intimate, raw exploration where there was no place to lie.

And, Sophie thought as he pressed his long tongue in over and over again, she was wrong to berate him for past lovers.

She should handwrite them all thank-you notes because his mouth was sucking on her clitoris now and his fingers were probing her along with his tongue, and she was sobbing as she came to him.

'Luka…'

He was kneeling between her parted legs, pulling them apart when they ached to close in on the orgasm he had just delivered her.

'What?' Luka checked, as he nudged a little way in. 'Do you want to me stop?'

He would.

The bastard would.

'Or,' Luka said, 'I go deeper.'

She could hear the sound of them, feel the tease of him that had her beating below again.

'Just come,' Sophie said.

'I told you, I loathe martyrs.'

He rested on his heels and pulled her hips down and carried on his cruel tease, there but not, in but not enough.

'Or,' Luka offered, 'we could try something different…'

'Like?' Sophie asked, and he suppressed a smile.

He could feel her mounting tension, he was holding down her hips as they rose in his hands.

'Something dangerous,' Luka said, and she nodded her head, set now on a rigid neck.

And so he kissed her like the first time.

When they'd tasted sweet and new.

He toppled onto her as he fully entered her again, and he brushed her wet lips with his as she clawed at his back and then gave in.

They made love.

They might well regret it tomorrow, but that was for then.

Now he kissed her like he only ever would kiss her, and Sophie just drank it in.

She smiled and she pushed back his damp hair just

to see him, just to feel it. She stopped fighting and started caressing and they rolled, made love to each other, nipped, sucked and tasted, and came.

And came again.

Guns were down.

Walls were gone.

She accepted his temporary truce as they made up for lost time.

CHAPTER FIFTEEN

'I DON'T UNDERSTAND YOU.'

They were the words he awoke to the next morning. He stared at the face that belonged on his pillow.

'Where did the other earring come from?' Luka asked, because she was wearing both.

'I always carry it in my purse,' Sophie said.

She would carry her mother with her for ever, Luka knew. If the truth was ever revealed she would never forgive and he was right not to trust her with his heart.

Some things were too big to come back from.

'You don't understand me, Sophie, because I won't let you.'

He rose from the bed.

'Will you let me try?'

It was the calmest they had ever been, like sweeping up the debris after a wild party that neither regretted.

'No,' Luka said. 'Sophie…' He sat on the bed and took her hand. 'We had a love that most people never know. You know that saying…better to have loved and lost—'

'I *hate* that saying,' Sophie broke in. 'I hate that saying more than any other. Who wrote that?' Sophie demanded.

'Tennyson.'

'Well, he was wrong.'

'I agree,' Luka said. 'I wish I'd never loved you.'

'But you did.'

'I did.'

'And you don't now?'

Luka wasn't that good a liar so he gave her a kiss instead. A nice one, not a loaded one. A sweet one, if, between them there could be such a thing.

'In a few days this will be over,' Luka said. 'We're going to get back to our lives knowing that we did the right thing by your father. It will be easier on us both once we get to Bordo Del Cielo.'

'How?'

'I'll check into the hotel and, like a good groom, I'll stay well away from the blushing bride-to-be.'

'Not as blushing as I'll be when you jilt me.'

'I can't marry you, Sophie. I can't be your fake husband. I can't stand in a church and exchange vows that I know we can't keep.'

He got up and headed to the bathroom.

'Hey, Luka,' Sophie said. 'I wished I'd never loved you too.'

The calm did not just belong in the bedroom.

A new presence had arrived with the dawn, though no one fully acknowledged it.

The colour seemed to have drained from Paulo's irises, Luka noticed as he wished him good morning.

And as Sophie passed her father his coffee and his shaking hand reached for it, it was a natural transition for her to lift the cup to his lips and help him to drink it.

The nurse stood, about to help, but Sophie shook her head.

'I've got this.'

So too had Luka.

He was so kind to Paulo and so engaged in organising the quick wedding that there were times Sophie had to catch herself because it felt real.

'What about the evening?' Paulo wheezed.

'The hotel is already holding a function,' Sophie explained, and she looked at Luka, but he shook his head. There was nothing he could do. It had been the first thing he had sold. 'The hotel is under new ownership.'

'We don't need that hotel,' Paulo said. 'Before it was built we would party in the street. I remember my wedding to your mother—we came out of the church and straight into a feast. Perhaps you could ring Teresa at the deli and see if she can sort out the food and the drinks...'

'Pa...' Sophie looked over to where her father sat. 'Why would Teresa want to help us when you—?'

'Sophie.' Luka stopped her from continuing and then watched as Sophie walked out onto the balcony. He could see her hands gripping the railing as she fought not to confront her father. Despite Paulo insisting he wasn't confused, he seemed to live between the long-ago past—when Rosa had been alive—and then the present, as if he had simply erased the damage that had been caused in between.

'*Scusi*,' Luka said to Paulo, and walked out to join her.

'He gets confused,' Luka said patiently.

'He gets confused when it suits him.'

'No,' Luka said. 'I don't think he can reconcile what he has done. He needs to go home. I can see that now.'

'No one will be talking to him, though,' Sophie said. 'Have you asked Matteo to be your groomsman?'

'I have.'

'And what did he say?'

'That he'll move things around so that he can be there.'

'I want Bella there too.'

'I'm not sure if that's wise,' Luka said. 'Matteo will be with Shandy. You know a bit of what went down between him and Bella.'

'I believe that it was Bella who went down,' Sophie said. 'And your friend paid for the pleasure.'

'You don't let a single thing go.'

'You refused my offer of a clean slate,' Sophie pointed out. 'So tell your friend that, however uncomfortable Bella's presence might make him, she'll be there.' She rubbed her temples and dragged in air. 'I need to sort out some accommodation for us.'

'That's all sorted,' Luka said.

'How?'

'Come on.' Luka led her back inside then he addressed her father. 'Paulo,' he said in a very practical voice, 'you will be tired after the ceremony. Perhaps we could have a few people back to your home…'

He gave a pale smile as Sophie let herself back in but then Paulo spoke. 'I don't have a home there any more.'

'Yes, Paulo,' Luka said, 'you do. Since his death my lawyers have been sorting out the properties that my father acquired. You have your home to return to. It is all there, nothing has been changed. Angela has been taking care of it.'

For this gift to her father Sophie could almost forgive Luka for not loving her enough to remain in her life.

'I have a home,' Paulo sobbed. 'Your mother's dress will be there, Sophie. You can wear it for the wedding.'

'No!' It was Sophie who interrupted Paulo. 'I'm not wearing my mother's dress. I'm not my mother…'

'Sophie, please,' her father begged, but on this she stood firm.

'I don't want a replica of your marriage, Pa.' She was caught between the truth and a lie. 'I want our marriage to be different.'

She was torn, completely, as she walked out of the lounge and into the bedroom.

'What was all that about?' Luka asked, having followed her in. 'I thought you were trying to give him the wedding of his dreams before he dies.'

'Remember that you said if this was real, if we were in love…?' Sophie turned the tables on him. 'Then my father would know I would not be simply agreeing to everything. My father sees those times through rose-coloured glasses. If we really were marrying…'

'Go on.'

'What's the point in going on?' Sophie demanded. 'Why should I tell you the wife and woman I want to be when you're not even prepared to be there to find out? Why should I trust you with my dreams again when you won't let me into your heart? You can have sex with me. Luka, you can be kind to me, you can argue with me if you must, but don't ask for my private thoughts when we both know that you're planning to walk away from me.' She couldn't continue speaking. 'I'm going to Bella's.'

'We need to get organised for tomorrow.'

'I am organised,' Sophie said. 'We have the church booked, we have your plane to take us. I'll call Teresa and then I'm going out.'

It was amongst the hardest of calls she had ever made. Teresa was as cold and as hesitant as before, but, Sophie guessed, work was work for her and perhaps it was because of the mention of the Cavaliere name that Teresa agreed to cater back at the house for the wedding.

'*Grazie,*' Sophie said, and hung up.

She collected her bag from the bedroom and gave her father a kiss on the cheek.

'How long will you be?' Paulo asked.

'You'll be in bed by the time I'm back.' Sophie smiled. 'I'll see you in the morning. Just think, Pa, this time tomorrow you'll be back in Bordo Del Cielo. You can sleep well tonight, dreaming of that. I love you so much.'

It was getting harder and harder to say goodnight, never knowing if this would be the last time.

She went over and gave Luka the necessary kiss. 'Soon,' Sophie said, as she lowered her head and kissed his mouth then whispered into his ear, 'we'll be living apart…'

'What time will you be back?' Luka asked.

'You're not my husband yet.' Sophie smiled with her lips but not with her eyes and then she moved her mouth to his ear. 'Dawn,' she whispered, 'so, as said, you can sleep well.'

She could not stand another night spent next to a man she could never have so she headed to the door, but Luka followed her out.

'The plane leaves at seven.'

'I'll be back well before then.'

'Tonight might be our last chance to talk…'

'What's the point?' Sophie said. 'There's nothing left to say. We both know what you're going to do to me. You're wrong, Luka, I'm not fourteen, you don't have to prise me from you knee. I'll be at the church, and if you're not…' Sophie shrugged. 'I'll survive. I've had an awful lot of practice.'

She held it together until she made it to the apartment and only there, with Bella, did she finally let her guard down.

'He says he wishes he'd never loved me.'

'At least you have known love… Better to have—'

'Don't,' Sophie warned. 'If you start quoting Tennyson, I'll scream!

'Who's Tennyson?'

'I don't really know,' Sophie said, 'but I don't think he understood the heart…'

But maybe he did, because the thought of never having known Luka's love filled her with dread.

'He's going to jilt me.'

'More fool him,' Bella said.

'And I had a bit of an argument with my father. He wants me to wear my mother's wedding dress and I said no. I don't want a marriage like theirs.'

'I'm already making your dress,' Bella said. 'I guessed that this might happen when Luka agreed to get engaged so I've already started it. I kept some money back from our savings and I bought some chiffon from the market. I will work on it through the night.'

'I'm going to be there with you, Sophie.'

'No.' Sophie shook her head because despite her brave words to Luka she could not put her friend through that. 'You have to work, and anyway…'

'Anyway?'

'Matteo will be there and…' Sophie could hardly bear to tell her, but Bella already knew.

'I know that he has a woman,' Bella said. 'And I know that she's stunning. I'd love to come and be your bridesmaid, Sophie. And don't worry about work—as of this morning I am suspended.'

'Bella?'

'I got in a lot of trouble,' Bella said. 'I spilt an ice bucket on a guest's lap when I was delivering the breakfasts to the room.'

'An ice bucket.'

'It was mainly cold water. I tripped but his girlfriend kicked up a fuss and called for the manager. It was a simple accident. The room was dark. I didn't see him— or rather they didn't hear me come in with breakfast… They were otherwise engaged.'

Sophie looked up to the sound of venom and mischief in Bella's voice and her mouth actually gaped for a moment before speaking.

'You threw a bucket of iced water over Matteo?'

'I did.' Bella grinned. 'So, you see, now I am free to be at your wedding and I'm going to make your the wedding dress. Sophie, you're going to be the most beautiful bride.'

'Even if he doesn't get to see me?'

'Oh, he'll see you,' Bella said. 'I'll make sure Matteo takes a few pictures as you arrive.' She hugged her friend and recited a Siclian saying. *'"Di guerra, caccia e amuri, pri un gustu milli duluri."'*

In war, hunting and love you suffer a thousand pains for one pleasure.

'The pleasure will be yours,' Bella said.

'It won't be, though,' Sophie said.

She was tired of the old ways, tired of false pride and sayings that spoke of revenge.

She was tired, so tired of hollow victories.

Maybe she had grown up.

Sophie wanted the man she loved.

CHAPTER SIXTEEN

SOPHIE'S FLIGHT BACK to Bordo Del Cielo was very different from the one she had taken when she had left.

Then she had been nineteen—confused, hurting, angry and just so glad to be getting away.

Now she was confused but the hurt was different.

Paulo was asleep in the bedroom area; Bella was sitting in one of the luxurious chairs with a curtain around her because she didn't want anyone to see the dress she was making for her friend.

Sophie sat beside Luka, staring out of the window and watching the land she wanted to love but which had cost her so much come into view.

'I was wrong,' Luka said, and she turned.

'Oh, you are so wrong,' Sophie said. No doubt he was talking about something else but all she knew was that he was wrong not to give them this chance.

Luka gave a soft, wry laugh as if he knew what she was thinking. 'I thought you were lying when you said that you were an events planner but I know few women who could organise a wedding in a couple of days.'

'It's easy to when you know...' Sophie shrugged. 'Well, let's just say I'm not too worried about how the cake is going to look and whether Teresa has had enough notice.' She looked right into his eyes. 'How could you even consider doing this to him, Luka?'

'How could you have done this to us?'

His words didn't confuse her, they ate at her instead.

She remembered standing on the beach, confused and ashamed and shouting, when their mouths should have been kissing.

She remembered hurling the sins of his father at him when she should have loved him first.

The plane came in to land and they sat in silence, but as they hit the tarmac, as they hurtled down the runway, Sophie didn't care if the plane lifted now and took them away.

But it came to a halt and they were home.

'I'm not perfect...' Sophie turned to him '...but I'd fight for us.'

'Nice speech,' Luka said. 'Tell me, though, Sophie—when did you ever fight for us? Did you come to my father's funeral? You would have known I had no one, the hell it would be to come home...'

'I was going to,' Sophie said, 'but I had just found out that my father was terminally ill.'

'He still is,' Luka replied, unmoved. 'You've held up the death card and I'm here. That's not an excuse not to show up on the day you would have known I needed you the most.'

He accepted no excuses for her carelessness with their love.

Did she sit there now and tell him the truth?

That he was right?

It hadn't been her father's illness that had stopped her contacting him.

Did she tell him she couldn't have afforded it?

Would a man like Luka accept as an excuse that she'd had no money? That he'd have had to wire her the fare?

'Did you fight for us on the beach, when I pleaded with you to come with me?' Luka asked.

'No.'

Her single word moved him. She did not kick up with her usual defence as to how he had shamed her in court.

'So when did you fight for us, Sophie?'

'I'll fight now.'

Luka said nothing.

He just stood as the passengers disembarked.

'I'll see you to your home,' Luka said.

It was a strange ride.

Her father never stopped coughing. There was the angel of death in the car with them and turned backs on the streets as Sophie looked out.

Yet it was home.

And it was somehow beautiful.

'Do you remember…?' She stopped.

Eight years old to his fourteen, she had found Luka crying for the first and last time, washing blood from his face in the river.

'Did you fall?' she had asked.

'Yes, I fell.'

They had sat eating nectarines and she had looked at his bruised, bloodied nose and closed eye.

'One day,' Sophie had said, 'you will be taller than him.'

'Who?' Luka had asked, because then he had still been loyal to his father.

'Taller than any man in this town,' she had said.

'I remember,' Luka said, and she did not turn or jump to the sound of his voice.

Here it felt normal.

Here they were as entwined as the vines and the roots beneath them.

They passed the school where she had left at fifteen to work in the hotel.

'I cried the day I left,' Sophie admitted. 'I wanted to learn all the poems. I wanted to sort out the maths…'

'You have the cleverest head on the planet,' Luka said.

'Yet I can't work us out.'

'We're here,' Bella said, and Sophie looked as they turned from the hotel and into her street.

It was the same, except different.

The neighbour's house had changed and was *tastefully* renovated. 'It smells of London.' Sophie winked as she waved to her weekender neighbours.

'I'll leave you here,' Luka said, having helped Paulo up the path.

'You're not going to come in for coffee?'

'I'm going to go and check into the hotel,' Luka said, once he had ensured everything was okay. 'And then I am meeting with Matteo.'

He didn't want to go in.

He didn't want to see just how poor his father had kept them.

'I might go for a walk,' Bella said. 'I would like to look at my old home, even if there are other people living there…'

Sophie looked at Luka but he gave her a slight shake of his head and pulled her aside. 'I haven't told everyone what I am doing. I don't want anyone feeling beholden. My lawyer will contact people once I've gone. Bella will find out soon enough that she has a home.'

Thank God for the nurse, because she took an exhausted, overwrought Paulo to his room for some oxygen and medication.

'It is your last day as a single woman,' Paulo wheezed. 'You should go out with Bella.'

'I'm just happy to be home.'

Sophie was. Though it felt so strange to be back.

Happy her father was settled, she set to work. There was a lot to be done and also there was Teresa to pay.

She walked into town, trying not to look up. She didn't want to see Malvolio's home spreading out over the top of the hill.

She didn't want to glimpse the bedroom where she and Luka had first made love and she averted her eyes as she passed the church where tomorrow he would leave her standing.

Sophie walked into Teresa's deli and, just as they had the last time she'd done so, the people in the deli fell silent. Angela was there, chatting with Teresa and a couple of other locals, and Sophie felt her cheeks turn to fire as she stepped up to the counter.

'I've come to pay for the catering for the wedding tomorrow.'

'*Gratuitamente*,' Teresa said, and Sophie was about to slam the money down, as she had all those years ago, but she chose not to.

She was older and wiser now, even if she'd prefer not to be at times.

'Teresa, I know it must be difficult for you to know that my father is back. He just wants to see Luka and I marry...' Just as Sophie always did, she held back her tears. 'That is all we are here for, to give my father some peace in his final days. Soon we'll be gone and out of your lives for good.'

'Sophie?' Angela asked. 'How is Paulo?'

'He's weak. He just wants to be home and to see me married.' She put down the money. 'We don't want any trouble.'

She walked out of the deli. A part of Sophie wanted to go to the beach, to sit there a while and remember days when life had seemed so much simpler, but instead she made her way home.

Bella was back from her walk and busy finishing off the dress, and Sophie dealt with the flowers and cleaning the house, as she had done so many times before. But then Paulo awoke and declared that he wanted to visit his wife's grave.

It was a long slow walk to the hill.

And agony to walk back down.

Spare me from your grief, she wanted to plead to her father as the nurse took him, weeping, to bed.

'Another walk?' Sophie smiled as Bella again headed out with a full face of make-up.

'Who knows who I might bump into?' Bella smiled.

Almost the moment she left there was a knock at the door and, no, it wasn't Bella to recheck her make-up, it was the priest.

'Do you want to let your father know I am here?'

Sophie nodded.

He looked so tired when she went into his room and Sophie knew then that tomorrow might not be the embarrassment she was dreading. Luka had been right. The journey, no matter how luxurious, had depleted him and visiting Rosa seemed to have taken the last of his strength.

'The priest is here,' Sophie said. 'Do you want me to send him through?'

'Please.'

She went out to the garden and lay on a sun lounger

and tried not to think of what was happening. Her heart seemed to still as she felt a shadow fall over her and she looked up into the strained features of Luka.

'You're crying.'

'No,' Sophie corrected, 'because I never cry. I don't think I know how to. I'm just tired.' She looked up into navy eyes. 'The priest is in with my father. He is making his confession. I would expect him to be some considerable time.'

He sat down by her knees on the sun lounger but she shrank away.

'Please, don't be a hypocrite,' Sophie said. 'Don't offer me your arms and then remove them tomorrow. I'm drained, Luka. I'm tired of being a parent to my father. I'm exhausted from absorbing his tears so I'm going to sit and watch the sunset and then I'll get up and put on my green dress, as per tradition, for a Sicilian bride on the eve of her wedding.'

'About tomorrow—'

'I'm not even thinking about tomorrow, Luka,' she interrupted. 'The day will bring what it shall bring and I'll survive it.' She looked up as the priest came out and stood to see him out.

'He's made his confession.'

Luka heard the priest's reedy voice as Sophie saw him out.

It was, Luka knew, time for him to make his confession.

Just not to Sophie.

Paulo was sitting in bed, holding his rosary beads and a picture of Rosa, but he turned and smiled as Luka made his way over and joined him.

'Is it good to be home?' Luka asked.

'It is,' Paulo said. 'I have made my confessions. Most of them anyway.' He looked at Luka. 'How long will you two pretend to be together for? Till after my funeral?'

'What are you talking about, Paulo?'

'I'm not a fool. I've always known that Sophie was lying to me. I knew, with what you said about her in court, that you were over before you even started.'

'She doesn't forgive easily.'

'She is like Rosa.' Paulo smiled. 'Even if I believed at first you were together, we do see the news in prison. I've read about your affairs and your scandals. I've seen the many beautiful women that you've dated.'

'You went along with it?' Luka frowned as he sat on the edge of the bed.

'She thought it made me happy knowing she was being taken care of.'

'Yet here you are you are. pushing for us to get married, even though you know it is a ruse. Why?'

'Because for all the mistakes I have made in my life, that wasn't one of them. You two are right for each other. I hoped that maybe being forced to spend time together you both might see that. It didn't work though.'

'No,' Luka admitted.

'It's time to be honest,' Paulo said. 'Now, while we still have time to be.'

Luka gave a small nod.

'You paid people a lot of money to work on my case these past months. What happened to make you suddenly want my release?'

'I always thought you were weak,' Luka admitted. 'I saw you as my father's yes-man but then I found something and I realised then that you had been protecting the person you love most.' He went into his pocket and handed Paulo the cross and chain. 'I found this amongst my father's things.'

Paulo let out a small cry as he took his beloved wife's cross and chain and pressed it to his lips.

'You knew her death was my father's doing, didn't you?'

'Not at first but eventually I did,' Paulo said. 'Malvolio wanted to build the hotel on the foreshore but there were families, including Rosa and I, who did not want to sell our homes.' He took a moment to take some long breaths from his oxygen mask and then continued speaking. 'I said to Rosa that we should move away and just leave Boro Del Cielo but she would not be run out of town—she said that someone had to stand up to him.' It was the most difficult conversation. With every sentence Paulo paused to breathe. 'Rosa went to see him to give him a piece of her mind. A few days later there was a car accident. I didn't connect the two at first. I was grieving and Malvolio was the white knight, the friend...' He started to cough.

'Enough,' Luka said.

'No.' Paulo was insistent that he finish. 'He said to put differences aside—he organised the funeral when I could not. He spoke at the service when I had no words. When I told him that I could not stand to be in the home we had loved he moved me here...' Paulo looked around at what had been his and Sophie's home. 'It took a few months for me to come out of the fog and start to see what had happened. He had got us out of our home by any means. By then I knew what he was capable of. He never threatened that harm would come to Sophie—instead, he said how lucky she was that he would look out for her, that our children would one day marry.'

'But the implication was there?' Luka asked, and Paulo nodded.

'When did you know?' Paulo asked.

'About Rosa?' Luka checked. 'When I found her necklace amongst my father's things, although I knew that he was corrupt long before that. It's the reason I rarely came home.'

'You came home that day to end things with Sophie?'

'I did,' Luka said. 'I just wanted to break all ties with this place. It wasn't that easy, though.'

'Love never is,' Paulo said, and held out the chain to Luka.

'Why are you giving this to me?' Luka asked.

'I would have liked to be buried holding it,' Paulo admitted, but then he shook his head. 'If I was then Sophie would have to know what had happened.' Paulo spoke his absolute truth. 'She would never forgive you, Luka. I know my daughter and the fact that your family was involved in her mother's death is something that she would not be able to forgive. Take the necklace and throw it the ocean when I am gone,' Paulo said. 'I will take your secret to the grave.'

'It's not my secret,' Luka said.

'It can be,' Paulo said. 'Sophie loves you and you love her. You do not need this hanging over you. Please.' He gave the cross and chain one final kiss and handed it back to Luka. 'Never tell her the truth. There is no need.'

Luka pocketed the chain and walked out from the bedroom to the lounge. There was Sophie and she gave him a tired smile.

'How is he?'

'He's okay.'

'You?'

Luka didn't answer. There was lie in his pocket and he didn't know how to handle it. Her own father had told him that their love could not survive it, but as he went to walk off Sophie halted him.

'I was wrong, Luka. I should have come to London with you that night.'

'Why?'

'I just should have. I was angry and I blamed you.'

'When did you decide this?'

'Just now.'

'Five years after the event,' Luka sneered. His emotions were everywhere. 'You let it fester for five years.'

'Luka…'

'So what happens when the shoe drops, Sophie? What happens when the next bombshell hits? Am I to wait another five years for you to come around? Am I to wait again for you to swallow that Sicilian pride?'

'You refuse to give me that chance.'

'I do.'

CHAPTER SEVENTEEN

'REMEMBER HOW WE used to sit here?' Bella said, as they sat bathed in sunrise with their calves dangling in cool water.

'I do.' Sophie smiled. 'I also remember the terrible row I had here with Luka.'

'It is a glorious day for a wedding.'

'A wedding that isn't going to happen,' Sophie said.

'He loves you,' Bella said. 'I can see it in him. Luka would not leave you standing in the church. He would not have come to Sicily just to shame you.'

'He told me he would never go through with it. Is it wrong that I wish my father would die before three p.m., just to spare him the shame?'

'I think so.' Bella smiled.

'Luka is as stubborn as I am.' Sophie sighed. 'He accuses me of being Sicilian as he trips on his own pride. I'm going to be jilted.'

'You could always have a fall this morning.' Bella smiled again. 'Slip on one of those rocks up there…'

'I could,' Sophie said. 'Or I could get a cramp, swimming, and you have to save me but I swallowed so much sea water that I was too weak to make it to the church…'

They laughed, they sat at the water's edge and laughed, and it felt so good to do so.

'Let him jilt me,' Sophie said. 'Let's really give the people of Bordo Del Cielo some scandal again. The girls are back in town!'

'Sisters in shame,' Bella said.

Sophie looked at her dear friend, who was terrified about today too.

'Are you scared to face Matteo?'

'I'm ashamed to face him.'

'He paid for a night with you, remember. You wouldn't be a whore if it wasn't for his money.'

'I know,' Bella said. 'If he tries anything I will tell him he can't afford me now!'

They laughed again and then Bella stood. 'Come on, we have a lot to do today.'

'You go back,' Sophie said. 'I might just sit here a while.'

'I will give your pa breakfast.'

'Thank you.'

Alone she sat and stared out at the water and at the cargo ships and cruise liners so far out on the horizon.

Out of reach for ever.

She was going to cry.

It hit her as surely as the sensation that she might vomit.

It felt like thunder rising in her chest and, like a cat hiding, she moved to the shelter of the cliffs and curled into her knees and wept.

For the father she would soon lose.

For the future devoid of Luka.

But most of all for the love she *had* known.

A love that could never be replicated or surpassed. She was exhausted, not just from the past but already from a future without him. How she loathed the poets she did not understand, but even with a lifetime to study them she wanted one that matched her, that told her how to deal with a future without Luka in it.

'You're going to startle,' Luka said. 'As you do every time I approach.'

'Well, I've never had the chance to get used to the sound of your voice,' she said, and wiped her eyes and looked up. 'So, yes, every time we meet in the future, expect me to jump. How did you know I was here?'

'Bella told me. She is sitting in the morning sun with your father. Matteo and I met her walking back…'

'Walking back from what? Your stag night?'

'There are no bucks' nights in Sicily,' Luka said. 'We did our best, though. We drank at the hotel till it closed and then walked along the shore.'

'You should go,' Sophie said. 'It's bad luck to see me on the morning of the wedding.'

'We've had our share of bad luck,' he said. 'How is your father this morning?' he asked, and this time she didn't accuse him of not caring.

She knew that he did.

'He will live to see his daughter jilted.'

Luka sat down beside her.

Paulo would know why he could not go through with the wedding. It should not be her father who would have to explain things to Sophie. It was for that reason he sat down to tell her, and braced himself for the most difficult conversation of his life.

'Why do you hate me, Luka?'

'As I said before, there are many reasons.' It should be odd that he took her hand to break her heart, but to Sophie it wasn't. 'Remember the night we parted? How angry you were, how you refused to give me a chance to explain? How you compared me to my father?'

'I was nineteen years old then.'

'No, Sophie, that's my excuse when I go over that time,' Luka said. 'I was younger, I was just out of prison, I had no idea what was going on. I had said things in court that I regretted, things I know I would handle better if they happened today. I'd run rings around that barrister now.'

'I know that you would.'

'I've changed,' Luka said. 'You haven't.'

'You mean I'm not sophisticated enough for you?'

'I mean your fire remains.' He snapped his fingers in front of her eyes. '*That* is how long it takes for you to make up your mind, Sophie—you decide things in an instant and nothing will change your mind.'

It was true, Sophie knew, for almost the second he had opened the door to her she had fallen in love and nothing had dimmed that.

'Almost nothing changes my mind,' Sophie refuted. 'I regret the words I said. I was confused, I was hurting...'

'I know that,' Luka said. 'How long did it take for you to see things from my side? To calm down?'

'I don't know.'

'Nearly five years,' Luka said. 'It has taken you until we are on our knees, till we are all but over, for you to see things from my side.'

'No, I knew almost straight away.'

'What did you do about it?' Luka challenged. 'Did you try to look me up in London? Did you do anything to let me know that you were wrong?'

'No.'

'Only now will you admit that you can see things from my side, that you were wrong.'

'Are you saying that I have to be perfect?'

'No,' Luka said, 'I love your stubbornness. You would

argue the sky was purple. I love your fire and that you are pure Sicilian yet it is what will ultimately tear us apart.'

'I don't understand,' she said. 'Is it because I lied?'

'Tell me your lies,' Luka said. 'Let's do this once and for all. Tell me your lies and secrets and I'll tell you mine.'

'Why?'

'Because the truth can't hurt us any more than this does.'

'I'm poor,' Sophie said. 'Bella and I are as poor as church mice and we fooled you with my wardrobe and phone.'

Luka just smiled.

'You knew that?'

'Not really. Though I did wonder about you being an events manager,' Luka admitted.

'I'm a chambermaid.'

'You were when I met you.'

She loathed that she hadn't moved on but he melted that fear with four words. 'I loved you then.'

'You don't care?'

'I don't care about money and things. I admit that I like not having to worry about it and, yes, I like nice things but, at the end of day, if it all falls into the ocean I would survive without it. My father had more money that a team of accountants can trace and yet he was the poorest man I have ever known.'

'I'm sorry.'

'For what?'

'For not being there for his funeral.'

'It doesn't matter.'

'It does. My father has done a lot of things wrong but I still love him.'

'My father did worse.'

'The hurt is more, then,' Sophie said. 'I don't think you can ever remove love. Even when by others' standards it deserves to be removed, even by your own... Love is not a whiteboard, Luka, it doesn't come with an eraser.'

'I can't make a good man out of him,' Luka said, 'but there were times when my mother was still alive that I remember with some affection. After that...' He shook his head. 'So what are your other lies?

'I feel like I trapped you that day we first made love. That you didn't see the real me. I am the peasant you despise. When you opened the door I was dressed in my finest with my mother's earrings, some make-up that I was trying out for our engagement, the dress...'

'Sophie, I hate that I said that to my father about you. I can't take it back, just explain that it was a row between him and I. It should never have been replayed in court. As to trapping me, well, I spent six months in prison, and within that time I spent two very long months alone when I thought about that day a lot... Do you think, when I replayed that time, I recalled that you were wearing your mother's earrings?'

He moved his head and he kissed the lobe of her ear, kissed it with such tenderness that it was as if it was the most important layer of skin that had ever existed. 'Do you think,' he asked, 'when I touch you that I remember the make-up?' His mouth moved to her eyelids and again he was so gentle and Sophie started crying because she knew, she just knew that right here, right now, he was kissing her goodbye; she just didn't understand why. 'I promise you, Sophie,' he said, his mouth moving down her neck, 'when I recalled that time, not once did I think of the dress you were wearing. I thought of these...'

He slipped the knot from her top and her breasts were naked to the morning sun and to his mouth.

'When I go over that time,' Luka said, and his fingers moved up her dress and to the silk of her panties, which were damp as he slid them down. She moaned as his fingers slipped into her. 'I remember you naked... I remember taking you for the first time, and the noises you made.'

He pushed her slowly down and onto her back. It was Sophie who slipped off her panties as Luka unzipped. Half-dressed but naked to the very soul, she stared into his eyes.

'When I come, every time I remember this...'

He seared inside her, and his face was over hers, and Sophie didn't try to hold back the tears as together they revisited that day.

'I remember you coming. I remember how I tried so hard not to.'

He moved up on his elbows and looked down at her. 'I don't want to come because when I do...'

'You're going to leave me, aren't you?'

How could he be making love to her while nodding that, yes, they were over?

She had lived in the moment just once in her life. That afternoon when the dog had ceased barking, when the surroundings had faded, Sophie had glimpsed the present, and she found it again now.

The past slipped away and the future was unseen, and she kissed the man she loved. She kissed his mouth and his rough cheek, she kissed the scar she had closed and, try as she might not to just yet, she started to come to him.

'Don't,' Sophie begged, because once Luka came it was over, but his tide was coming in.

She knew from the only body she truly knew—his.

His moan was one of pain as he released because it signalled the end, but even in the last throes Sophie might have lost her heart but her head remained and she looked into his navy eyes as he offered her one last chance.

"Will you fight for us?" Luka asked.

He pulled out, he dressed and then he dressed her and he asked her again. 'Now, with what I have to tell you, will you fight for us as you promised?' He went on, 'Will your words still be kind and wise when we face a test?' He placed a gram of gold in her hand and it felt like a weighted ball, with no burden lifted, as he handed it over to her.

'I found it when my father died. I came back to Bordo for the funeral and I was going through my father's things.'

'Your father did this... You...' She halted, tripped over her words. She tried to remember she was fighting for them but she was breathless on the ropes in her mother's corner.

'You see, Sophie, with this you can win every row. You can take the shame of what my father did and give it to me over and over. But I can't live like that. The reason I will never marry you is this—I have lied under oath to protect your family. It didn't work. I have lied on the Bible, I have attempted over and over to edit the truth. No more. I will not stand in a church and lie and take you as a temporary wife when the truth is I will love you for ever.'

Anger, rage, fury, hissed at an unknown target.

'I don't care if you're poor. I don't care if you have

lied, cheated…whatever…' Luka continued. 'You do what you have to to survive but I know my limits, Sophie. I know I love you. I accept you but I cannot compromise with this. I cannot take more of his shame. I cannot say sorry any more for a person I am not. Know that.

'I love you,' Luka said. 'I love the life we could have, but I care about myself too. I have dreams and ambitions and I will never be brought to my knees again for that man.'

'Luka, how long have you known?'

'When he died.'

'And you never guessed before then?'

This was her mother who had died—*her mother*!

'I need to know. How long have you had your suspicions?'

'I can remember your mother coming to our house. She was angry at my father for trying to get them out of their home. Your father had warned her they should leave yet she refused…' Luka tried to look with adult eyes at a child's past and then he lost his cool.

'I won't let you do this to us, Sophie,' he shouted. 'You want facts? I found out for sure a year ago. I have known for a lifetime he was rotten to the core. If you want a dissection then get a dead frog—they don't bleed and anyway their blood is already cold. Mine's warm. My heart beats. I won't let you do it to me.'

She came out fighting then.

Sophie pushed herself off the ropes that bound her and entered the ring.

For them.

'You criticise me for comparing you to your father, yet over and over you compare me to my mother. Not just you,' Sophie said, 'but my father, the whole town

does. "She is like Rosa…"' The only sound was silence.
'I am like her, just as you are like your father. But you
are not him. You are arrogant, you are clever and you
are strong, but you are good. I am fierce, I have a temper, but I would listen when the man I love told me that
we had to leave. Did I march to your father and demand
Bella's freedom of choice?' Sophie shouted. 'No. I offered to and when she said no, when she said she must
stay, I respected her choice…as I have to respect that
you can't marry me.'

'I can never be your fake husband, Sophie.'

She looked at him.

'Can we get past this?'

'I don't know,' she admitted. Questions were swirling, dates and times and anger and blame, and Luka
smiled at her honest answer.

'You get to decide, Sophie. I'll be there today. Jilt
me if you think I deserve it for what he did. Score your
point for your fleeting victory but I win because I know
you will regret it for ever if you don't show up today. No
one ever shall, or ever could, love you as much as I do.'

'You love me so much that you invite me to end
us—?'

'I love you so much,' Luka interrupted, 'that I won't
relegate us to a poor future. I would rather have sex with
a stranger for the rest of my life than lie next to you cold
and blaming. I would rather have half a marriage, half
a life, half of me, if I cannot have all of you. For you
to deny me that part of you…for you to hold me hos-
tage…' He shook his proud head. 'Fight with me about
things if you want to, be every inch Sicilian. Call me
on what my father did once. I might get that, but if you
call me on it twice…'

And Luka dared accuse *her* of being Sicilian!

'I don't give second warnings,' Luka said. 'My father was responsible for the death of your mother. I will not let his sins, or your anger, bring me to my knees. If you walk into that church,' Luka warned, 'then you'd better know that it's for ever. You only walk towards me if you can love me more than the shadows of our past. If you can't, then it is better for both of us that you walk away.'

Luka did the nicest thing then.

Her breast was precariously close to falling out again so he redid the tie to her halter-neck and rearranged her dress. He looked after her in a way that no one ever could and he demanded that she match that care.

Always.

'Show up or don't,' Luka said. 'Hate me at your own peril.'

'What will you do if I don't turn up?'

'Nothing,' Luka said. And it was, for Sophie, the darkest response he could deliver. 'If you don't show for our wedding then nothing will happen, not ever. I will wish you luck for the future, I will accept that our love could not survive. I'll be proud of you for having the guts to admit it and,' he added, 'I will get on with my life.'

He left her on the rocks.

He left her spinning like a Catherine wheel.

There was a retort she could deliver.

A proud last word, perhaps.

There was comeuppance still to be had.

Or there was a shiny new future?

CHAPTER EIGHTEEN

'YOU LOOK WONDERFUL,' Bella said.

It was possibly the most beautiful dress in the world and might, Sophie knew, remain unseen.

He had left her with seven hours to grow up.

She was down to twelve minutes.

'Are you scared he won't show up?'

It was no longer a town of secrets but what had happened on the beach Sophie had kept to herself.

This was between her and Luka.

She was scared that *she* might not. Scared that her rapid tongue could not hold its fire.

Sophie pulled out the necklace.

I love you, she said in her head to her mother. *I come from you but I am not you.*

'It looks like the one in the photos that your mother wore,' Bella said, as she helped her to put it on.

'It is the one my mother wore,' Sophie said, and she felt Bella's hands pause on her naked shoulders.

Bella knew, Sophie realised.

Here there were secrets even amongst the very closest of friends.

Her mother would probably have known and would have told Bella the truth long ago. The whole town would have been able to see what a small child could not.

Rosa had gone and confronted Malvolio.

A few days later she had died.

'Why didn't my father insist that they run?' Sophie asked. She knew the answer—Rosa, with her stubbornness and pride, had been right to want to stay.

Dead right.

'Can you ever forgive him?'

'Malvolio?' Sophie scoffed. 'Never.'

'I mean can you ever fully forgive Luka for what Malvolio did?' Bella asked, but hushed as Paulo walked in.

'Their names don't belong in the same breath,' Paulo said, his eyes filling with tears when he saw that Sophie was wearing Rosa's chain.

'But they do belong in the same breath,' Sophie corrected. 'Just as I belong in the same breath as my mother. Just as I look like her and act like her at times. I'm not her, though.'

'I know that.'

'Even if she's not here, I've learnt from her…'

'The cars are here,' Bella said.

'Go,' Sophie said to Bella. 'I will see you at the church.' She gave her friend a hug. 'Good luck with Matteo.'

She stood alone with her father.

'You are your mother's daughter. That is not always a compliment. I wanted to leave here, to get away. She told me to stand up to him, to fight for what was right.' Sophie stood as her father shook his head. 'So I did. I had our tickets booked to leave. I wanted to get out of here…'

'You were right.'

'I would rather have been wrong.'

'Malvolio *is* Luka's father,' Sophie said. 'At times

they will belong in the same breath. I don't want a marriage where there are things that cannot be discussed or names that can never be mentioned. I nearly lost Luka, not once but twice. I am not going to do that again. I shan't make the same mistakes as...'

'Me?'

'As so many people did,' Sophie said, more aware than ever how words could hurt so very much. 'You did the best that you could for me. I know that.'

'Not really.'

'Yes, really.' Sophie smiled at her father. 'You got one thing very right—you chose the perfect husband for me.'

'You and Luka belong to each other.'

'We do.'

It wasn't just the bride who was nervous on a wedding day, Luka was finding out.

The groom stood at the altar when, for the longest time, he had thought that he never would.

Luka had long ago accepted that he and Sophie were over and, given that he had known he would never love like that again, he had decided he would remain single.

Until this morning.

This morning he had chosen for their sakes to take the biggest gamble of his life and to reveal the truth.

Her own father thought that Sophie could never forgive him and Matteo too was tense.

And so he stood on his wedding day not even knowing if Sophie would show up.

He didn't care about the public reaction if the bride didn't show.

He cared only about them.

'Whatever happens—' Matteo started, but Luka halted him.

'She'll be here.'

He had confidence in them, in the love they had found that long-ago afternoon.

And he was right to.

He turned around and there was Sophie, dressed in a simple white dress that reminded him of yesteryear. Today her black hair was worn down, as he preferred, and dotted with summer jasmine. In one hand she loosely held a bunch of wild Sicilian poppies and they were as sexy and as decadent and as heady as her.

The delighted, stunned look on her face when she saw the packed church was something he would remember for ever.

They loved her and understood too just how hard it had been for Paulo.

He was home, where he belonged, and ready now for his daughter to leave properly.

She walked towards him and Luka could see the glimmer of her mother's cross.

Guilt, fear, shame left him as her eyes met his.

Sophie walked and then, as her father let go of her arm, she ran—those last few steps she ran—to the shield of his arms and the freedom they afforded her.

To him.

Luka kissed the bride before the service had even started.

They needed that moment even if it made the priest cough.

'You're here,' he said.

'So are you.'

'Always.'

Paulo stood, even though he was offered a seat.

Luka turned just once and his eyes met Angela's and thanked her.

She, he was sure, was the one who had told the rest of the townsfolk to give these people the chance they deserved and to forgive Paulo now, while they still could.

Their vows were heartfelt.

'I love you,' Luka said. 'I always have and I always will.'

'I love you,' came Sophie's response. 'I always have and I always will.' Then she deviated from the priest's words for she made a small addition. 'And I shall *try* to remember that in all that I say and do.'

No one understood why the groom laughed.

Matteo was the perfect groomsman, even if cynicism was written all over his face, for just yesterday Luka had told him this wedding would never take place, that it was a sham.

But for now he went along with it and handed over the rings.

And tried not to glance at the bridesmaid!

Luka slid on the ring and then he too deviated from tradition, for he went into this pocket and took out another ring and placed it next on her finger.

It was rose gold and the diamond was emerald cut and stood high, and Bella stared at it for a moment, her eyes filling with tears.

She remembered staring in Giovanni's window and a diamond catching her eye.

The hope that when Luka got out, that one day...

There wasn't time to dwell on it for now.

They were man and wife.

The church bells were ringing loudly in Bordo Del Cielo today and as they stepped out, it was to a *true* Sicilian celebration.

The street was lined with tables and dressed in ribbons and flowers, the trees were lit with lights that would glow brighter as evening fell.

Angela and an old friend were helping Paulo out of the church.

'Dance with your father,' Luka said.

She did.

And to hear him laughing and proud was the best medicine for both of them…but then she was back to Luka's arms.

She glanced over his shoulder and smiled. Bella and Matteo were dancing a duty dance, not that it looked like duty for Bella—her eyes were closed and her head was resting on his chest. Only Matteo looked as if he was struggling.

'He's angry,' Luka said. 'He thinks that she is still…' He looked down at Sophie. 'I want to catch up on all the years we have missed, I want to know everything.'

'You shall.'

'Your father is so happy.'

'He wants us to have a baby now.' Sophie smiled.

'You could lie and say you are…'

'Knowing him, he would live for another nine months just to make sure that we were telling the truth.'

'We are,' Luka said. 'This is for ever.'

'That ring?' Sophie asked. 'Is it from Giovanni's?'

Luka nodded. 'As soon as I got out of court I went and bought it. I wanted to take you to London, not as a friend or a date. Those months in prison had taught me many things…'

Sophie could hardly stand to think of all she had dismissed that day, all the foolish pride she had held onto just to be right.

'I can afford something nicer now.' Luka offered.

'Nothing could be nicer,' Sophie said. 'It belongs with me.'

'So do you.'

EPILOGUE

SOPHIE LAY IN that delicious place between sleep and waking and for a moment she thought she was dreaming.

The lap of the sea, the slow motion of rising and falling with the waves, and Sophie knew she was awake.

She was on honeymoon with Luka.

They were taking their time to sail from Corsica to the Greek islands, stopping where they chose to and just enjoying the journey.

Life was better than she had ever dreamed it might be.

It had been an emotional time. Her father had held on long enough to know that Sophie was expecting a baby. He had seen a summer and a winter in his beloved town and finally he now lay with Rosa.

Sophie lay there thinking about the past months.

It had been Sophie who had thrown her mother's necklace in the grave. It was her mother's, not hers.

She didn't want to wear it day in, day out.

Instead, she wore her mother's earrings, for they spoke of the happiest days with Luka.

And there had been so many of them.

Yes, she was stubborn, but never about that.

'Morning,' Luka said.

'Where were you?'

'Thinking,' he said. 'About us. Are you happy?'

'So happy.' she said, and then looked into his navy eyes. 'And cross with myself for all the time we wasted.'

'We needed that time,' Luka interrupted. 'We were young, there was a lot of pain and little of it was of our making.'

'Even so.'

'We know that what we have is precious,' he said, and she nodded. 'Had I married you when you were nineteen you might have always resented that you never got to work on the cruise liners.'

'No.'

'Yes.'

He smiled and always it made her stomach fold over and in on itself. He was so stern and serious with others, but so open with her.

'And had we got together after the court case and then later found that chain…' Luka thought about it. 'I needed to find out about my father away from you.' It was Luka who brought the name up at times and he was so grateful that her eyes didn't flash in anger; instead, they could hold his gaze as they explored the pains of the past. 'This is our time.'

'So you don't think I was wrong?'

'Sophie…'

'I didn't make us waste all those years?'

'Sophie,' he warned, but he was smiling. 'Come on, let's go and see the sunrise.'

'No, come back to bed,' she grumbled, but Luka shook his head and she got out of bed, put on her sarong and tied it then headed up to the deck.

The sky was gorgeous and just dipping out of navy and the stars were fading.

'Where are we?' Sophie asked, and then she paused as for the first time she saw her home from the sea.

The sun was rising over Sicily and their yacht was close enough that she could make out the familiar landscape—the church where they had not only married but where both their parents rested. She could make out Luka's home, the beach where they had made love.

'I used to sit there every day with Bella,' Sophie said. 'Dreaming of the future, wondering what our lives would be like. I used to picture myself on a cruise liner out on the seas…'

'And now here you are.'

'I'm here with you,' Sophie said, and then she told him a deeper truth, one she hadn't told Bella. Not because she was scared to, she simply hadn't dared admit it to herself, for it had seemed pointless that long-ago day.

'Even though I didn't want to be married, I wanted you then. I wanted it all, I just didn't know how it could happen. How I could be out on the ocean and sailing the seas and somehow be with the man I loved. Yet here I am.'

'We can dock,' Luka said. 'Spend a couple of days there if you wish.'

Sophie thought about it. The people would make them more than welcome. They had their homes back and Bordo Del Cielo was thriving now.

Yet there was no need to go back, no need to visit.

Not now

One day maybe.

They were having a daughter, and they would take her back and, far more gently than they both had, she would learn about her past, about the pain and the beauty of the land that ran through her veins.

But not now.

Now, as Bordo Del Cielo awoke, it was Sophie and Luka that were the glint of a boat on the horizon.

They were out there, together, and living their dreams.

* * * * *

PLAYING MR RIGHT

KAT CANTRELL

One

The building housing LeBlanc Charities felt the same as every other time Xavier had set foot in it—like he'd been banished. Despite sharing a last name with the founder, this was the last place he'd choose to be, which was too bad considering he'd been forced to walk through the door nearly every day for the last three months.

And would continue to do so for the next three months until this hell of an inheritance test drew to its conclusion. Xavier's father had devised a diabolical way to ensure his sons danced to his tune long after he'd died: Xavier and his brother, Val, had been required to switch places in order to receive their inheritances.

So the ten years Xavier had spent learning the ins and outs of LeBlanc Jewelers, plus the five years since he'd taken over the CEO chair and broken his back to please his father…none of that mattered. In order to get the five hundred million dollars he'd have sworn he'd already earned, Xavier had to pass one final test. But instead of being required to do something that made *sense*, the will stipulated that Xavier would become a fundraiser in Val's place at LeBlanc Charities and his brother would assume the reins of LeBlanc Jewelers.

Even three months after the fact, Xavier still foamed at the mouth if he let himself dwell on how unfair and impossible the terms were. His father had betrayed him, bottom line. While Xavier had been putting enormous energy into connecting with his dad and basking in the glow of being the favored son in blissful ignorance, Edward had been plotting to posthumously show his sons how much he really hated both of them.

In that, Xavier and Val were alike. It had been a surprisingly effective bonding experience for the brothers who shared similar faces and not much else. Though twins, they'd never been close, even choosing completely different paths as adults. Val had followed their mother into LeBlanc Charities and thrived. Xavier had gladly shucked off anything remotely resembling charity work in favor of the powerful CEO's office at one of the world's largest and most profitable diamond companies.

All for nothing.

The terms of the will had sliced off a huge piece of Xavier's soul and he'd yet to recover it.

Bitter did not begin to describe his feelings toward his father. But he used that bitterness as fuel. He would not fail at this test. Success was the best revenge, after all.

Xavier had swept into his new role at LBC with gusto…and despite his fierce need to ace his task, he still hadn't gotten his feet under him. It was like his father had stacked the deck against him, somehow. The problem was that the will stipulated Xavier had to raise ten million dollars in donations while doing Val's job. No easy feat. But he hadn't given up yet, nor would he.

Even at 6:00 a.m., LeBlanc Charities teemed with life. The food pantry operated seven days a week, fifteen hours a day. It was ludicrous. A huge waste of capital. Oftentimes, the volunteers reported that no guests had darkened the door of LBC during the early morning hours, yet they always kept the light on.

Changing the operational hours of the food pantry had been one of the first of many executive orders Xavier had come to regret. He'd changed them back, but Marjorie Lewis, the tiny general of a woman who had been a surprisingly effective services manager, had still quit. Sure, she'd told Val—her *real* boss, as she'd informed Xavier—that her mother had fallen ill with a long-term condition. But Xavier knew the truth.

She hated him.

Nearly everyone at LBC did, so that was at least consistent. The staff who reported to him at LeBlanc Jewelers—his *real* job, as he'd informed Marjorie—respected him. Did they like him? Who knew? And Xavier didn't care as long as they increased profits month over month.

LBC was *not* the diamond industry. No one here *owned* any diamonds, except for him, and he'd stopped wearing his Yacht-Master watch after the first day. Marjorie had pointed out, rather unkindly, that the people LBC helped would either assume it was fake, try to steal it or paint him with the ugly brush of insensitivity. Or all three.

Therefore, a five-hundred-thousand-dollar watch now sat in his jewelry box, unworn. Talk about a waste. But he'd left it there in hopes of garnering some of that mythical respect. Instead, he'd met brick wall after brick wall in the form of Marjorie, who had rallied the troops to hate him as much as she did. And then she'd quit, leaving Xavier holding the bag. Literally.

Yesterday, he'd worked in the food pantry, stocking shopping bags the hungry people LBC served could grab and go. The families took prepacked boxes. Once a day, LBC served a meal, but Xavier stayed out of the kitchen. Jennifer Sanders, the meal services manager, had that well under control and also agreed with the popular opinion that Val walked on water, so anything Xavier did paled in comparison.

Like he did every morning, Xavier retreated to his office. Val's office, really, but Xavier had redecorated. He'd ordered the walls painted and new furniture installed because if this was going to be his domain, it shouldn't remind him every second that Val had been here first—and done it better.

Xavier pushed around the enormous amount of paperwork that a charity generated until his brother popped through the door. Thank God. Xavier had started to wonder if Val would actually show up for their planned meeting about the missing services manager. After Marjorie stormed out, the majority of the day-to-day operations management fell to Xavier and that left precious little time to plan fundraisers that he desperately needed to organize.

Val had offered to help with the interview process, which had been a lifeline Xavier had gladly snagged, without telling his brother how much he needed that help. If the terms of his father's will had taught him anything, it was not to trust a soul, not even family.

"Sorry I'm late." Val strolled into his former office and made a face at the walls, flipping his too-long hair out of his eyes. "If you were going to paint, at least you could have picked a color other than puke green."

"It's sage. Which is soothing."

It was nothing of the sort and did not resemble the color swatch the decorator had showed him in the slightest. But Xavier had to live with it, apparently, because LBC didn't have a lot of extra money for frivolous things like painting. When he'd tried to use his own money, Marjorie had flipped out and cited a hundred and forty-seven reasons that was a bad idea. Mostly what he'd gotten out of her diatribe was that LBC had a negative audit in their rearview and thus had multiple microscopes pointed at their books.

Meaning Xavier needed to watch his step.

"Who do we have on tap today?" Val asked pleasantly as he sprawled in one of the chairs ringing the director's desk that Xavier sat behind.

No one was fooled by the desk. Xavier didn't direct much of anything. He would have claimed to be a smart man prior to this inheritance test, but LBC had slowly stripped away his confidence. At his normal job, he ran a billion-dollar company that was one of the most highly respected jewelry operations in the world. LeBlanc was synonymous with diamonds. He could point to triumph after triumph in his old world. This new one? Still Val's baby even though Xavier's brother was currently helming LeBlanc Jewelers with flair.

Xavier stopped his internal whining and picked up the single résumé on his desk. "After you ruled out the others, this is the only one. The candidate has experience similar to Marjorie's but with a women's shelter. So probably she's a no-go. I want someone with food-pantry experience."

"Well, that's your call." Val's tone held a tinge of disapproval, as if wanting someone with experience was the height of craziness. "Do you mind if I look at it?"

He handed the résumé to Val, who glanced over it, his lips pursed.

"This Laurel Dixon is the only new résumé you've got?" Val asked.

"From people who are remotely qualified, yeah. So far. I posted the job to the usual sites but we've had very little response."

Val pinched the bridge of his nose. "That's not good. I wonder if our little inheritance experiment has made the rounds. I would have expected more applicants, but if you've scared off all the candidates, I'm going to be in a world of hurt when I step back into my position here."

That stung, but Xavier didn't let it show. He never did. He'd learned to school his emotions at Edward LeBlanc's knee from an early age. CEOs didn't wear their hearts on their sleeves or they lost the respect of their workers. That lesson had served him well—until his father had upended everything in one fell swoop.

"This is not my fault," Xavier responded evenly, though Val's point wasn't lost on him. *Marjorie.* Again. He wouldn't put it past her to have poisoned the well of potential applicants, but there was no way to fix that now. "If you're going to blame anyone, blame Dad."

Val's expression didn't change as he waved the résumé. "We should interview this candidate. What other choice do you have? No one says you have to keep her if she doesn't work out."

"Fine."

Xavier picked up the phone and left a message at the number listed on the résumé. He didn't have time to argue the point or let his feelings get in a twist because Val was throwing his weight around. This was all temporary, and as Val had so eloquently pointed out, he'd be back in the saddle again soon, anyway. Little that Xavier did would make a difference in the long run.

Since they didn't have much regarding Marjorie's replacement to meet about, after all, Val apparently thought that was a license to ask a few barbed questions about how things were going operationally at LBC. They were interrupted by a brisk knock on the door.

Adelaide, the admin who had been a disciple of Marjorie's, poked her head into the office with a sweet smile for Val. If he hadn't seen it himself, Xavier wouldn't have believed she knew *how* to smile.

"There's a Laurel Dixon here to see you," she said. "About the position."

Xavier had called her less than thirty minutes ago and he'd said nothing about coming by. Only that he'd like to schedule an interview.

"No notice," he said quietly to Val. "That's a little bold, don't you think?"

It tripped his sixth sense and not in a good way. Downtown Chicago was not known for having great traffic patterns, so either she lived really close by or had already been on her way here.

Val raised his brows in challenge. "I'm already impressed. That's the kind of go-getting I like."

Of course he'd say that and manage to make it sound like Xavier was in the wrong at the same time. "I'd rather send her away and schedule a real interview. After I've had time to go over her qualifications."

"She's here." Val shrugged. "What's there to go over? If you're unsure, I'll do the talking."

"I can talk," Xavier fairly growled. "I just don't like surprises."

Or anyone stepping on his toes, which was what he got for stupidly mentioning to his brother that Marjorie's exodus had caught him sideways. Val had taken full advantage of that show of weakness, too, storming in here like a victorious hero and earning adoring glances from his staff.

Val just grinned and flipped hair out of his face in true slacker fashion. "I'm aware. Don't sweat it. I came by to handle this problem. Let me handle it."

When hell froze over. "We'll both interview her. Adelaide, show her in."

Val didn't even bother to move to another chair like a normal person would. You positioned yourself behind the desk as a show of authority. Val probably didn't even know how to spell authority. That's why his staff loved him, because he treated them all like equals. Except everyone was not equal. Someone had to be in charge, make the hard decisions.

And that person was Xavier, for better or worse. Val could step aside. This was still Xavier's office for three more months.

Laurel Dixon walked into the room and Xavier forgot about Val, LBC…his own name. Everything else in the world went dim. Except for her.

The woman following Adelaide looked nothing like Marjorie, that was for sure. She looked nothing like any woman Xavier had ever met. Long, lush sable-colored hair hung down her back, but that only held his attention for a split second. Her face was arresting, with piercing silvery-gray eyes that locked onto his and wouldn't let go.

Something otherworldly passed between them and it was so fanciful a feeling that Xavier shook it off instantly. He didn't do *otherworldly*, whatever the hell that even meant. Never had he used such a term in his life to describe anything. But nothing else fit, and that made the whole encounter suspect. Besides, it was ridiculous to have any sort of reaction to a woman outside of desire, and even that was rarely strong enough for Xavier to note. Most, if not all, of his encounters with females could be described as mildly pleasurable, at best.

This woman had *trouble* written all over her if she could elicit such a response by merely walking into a room.

Coupled with the fact that she'd shown up without an appointment—Laurel Dixon raised his hackles about ten degrees past uncomfortable.

"Ms. Dixon." Val stood and offered his hand. "I'm Valentino LeBlanc, the director of LBC."

"Mr. LeBlanc. Very nice to meet you," she said, her clean voice vibrating across Xavier's skin with a force he couldn't shake.

He'd have said he preferred sultry voices. Sexy ones that purred when aroused. Laurel Dixon's voice could never be described as carnal, but that didn't seem to matter. He instantly wanted to hear it again. It was the kind of voice he could listen to for an hour and never get bored.

This was supposed to be an interview. Not a seduction. Actually, he'd never been seduced before, at least, not that he could recall. Usually he was the one making all the moves and he wasn't all that keen to be on the receiving end with a woman who wasn't even supposed to be here.

"Xavier LeBlanc," he announced and cleared his inexplicably ragged throat. "Current director of LBC. Val is just passing through."

She flicked her attention from Val to Xavier. This was the part where he had to stand and stick his hand out. Laurel Dixon clasped it, and when no lightning bolts forked between them, he relaxed an iota. That's when he made the mistake of letting his gaze rest on her lips. They curved up into a smile and *that* kicked him in the gut so hard, he felt it in his toes. Yanking his hand free, he sank back into his chair, wondering when, exactly, he'd lost his marbles.

"Two for the price of one," she said with a laugh that was just as arresting as her face. "I applaud the fact that you have such different hairstyles. Makes it easier to tell you apart."

Automatically he ran a hand over his closely cropped hair. He wore it that way because it looked professional. The style suited him and the fact that Val's too-long hair marked him as the rebel twin only worked in Xavier's favor. "Val gets lost on the way to the barber."

Despite the fact that he hadn't meant it as a joke, that made her laugh again, which pretty much solidified his resolve to stop talking. The less she laughed like that, the better.

"We weren't expecting you," Val said conversationally and indicated the seat next to him, then waited until Laurel slid into it before taking his own. "Though we're impressed with your enthusiasm. Right, Xavier?"

Figured that the second after he'd vowed to shut his mouth, Val dragged him right back into the conversation.

"That's one way to put it," he muttered. "I would have liked to schedule an interview."

"Oh, well, of course that would have been the appropriate thing to do," she admitted with an eye roll that shouldn't have been as appealing as it was. "But I'm so very interested in the job that I didn't want to leave anything to chance. So I thought, why wait?"

Why, indeed? "What about directing a food pantry excites you so much?"

"Oh, all of it," she answered quickly. "I love to help people in need and what better way than through one of the most basic fundamentals? Food is a necessity. I want to feed people."

"Well said," Val murmured.

Since his brother could have written that speech word for word, Xavier wasn't surprised he'd been moved by her passion. It sounded a little too memorized to Xavier's ear, and his gut had been screaming at him from the moment he'd first handed Val Laurel Dixon's résumé.

Something about her was off. He didn't like her. Nor did he like the way she unsettled him. If he had to constantly brace himself to be in her presence, how could they work together?

"Your experience is on the sparse side," Xavier said and tapped the résumé between them. "What did you do at the women's shelter that will segue into a services manager at a food pantry?"

Laurel launched into a well-rehearsed spiel about her role, highlighting her project management skills, and wrapped it up by getting into a spirited back-and-forth with Val about some of her ideas for new outreach.

His brother was sold on Laurel Dixon. Xavier could tell. Val had smiled through the entire exchange. Sure enough, after the candidate left, Val crossed his arms and said, "She's the one."

"She is so not the one."

"What? Why not?" Val dismissed that with a wave without waiting for an answer. "She's perfect."

"Then you hire her. In three months. I'm still in charge here and I say I want a different candidate."

"You're being stubborn for no reason," Val shot back, and some of the goodwill that had sprung up between them as they navigated the Great Inheritance Switch—

as Xavier had been calling it in his head—began to slide away.

His caution had nothing to do with stubbornness and he had plenty of reasons. "She's got no experience."

"Are you kidding? Everything she did at the women's shelter translates. Maybe not as elegantly as you might like, but you only have to deal with her for three months. After that, I'll be the one stuck with her if she's the wrong candidate. Humor me."

Xavier crossed his arms. "There's something not quite right about Laurel Dixon. I can't put my finger on it. You didn't sense that, too?"

"No. She's articulate and enthusiastic." The look Val shot him was part sarcasm and part pity. "Are you sure you're not picking up on the fact that she's not an emotionless robot like you?"

Ha. As if he hadn't heard that one before. But obviously Val had no clue about what really went on beneath Xavier's skin. Xavier just had a lot of practice at hiding what was going on inside. Edward LeBlanc had frowned on weakness, and in his mind, emotions and weakness went hand in hand.

"Yeah, that must be it."

Val rolled his eyes at Xavier's refusal to engage. "This is not the corporate world. We don't hire people based on how well they rip apart their prey here in nonprofit land. You need someone to replace Marjorie, like, yesterday. Unless you have a line of other options hidden away in the potato closet, you've got your new hire."

The damage was done. Now Xavier couldn't readily discount Laurel Dixon as a candidate, though the barb had hit its mark in a wholly different way than Val probably even realized. No, this wasn't the corporate world and his raging uncertainty might well be rearing its ugly head here.

His father had done a serious number on him with this switcheroo. Xavier was only just coming to realize how many chunks of his confidence were missing as a result. How much of his inability to take an applicant at face value had to do with that?

Everything was suspect as a result.

"I'll deal with Laurel Dixon if that pleases your majesty," he told Val. "But I'm telling you up front. I don't trust her. She's hiding something and if it comes back to bite you, I'm going to remind you of this conversation."

Odds were good it was going to come back to bite Xavier long before it affected Val, who would leave to go back to the world of sane, logical, corporate politics in a few minutes. Xavier, on the other hand, would be working side by side for the next three months with a new services manager who made his skin hum when he looked at her.

He had a feeling he'd be spending a lot of time avoiding Laurel Dixon in order to protect himself, because that was what he did. No one was allowed to get under his skin and no one got an automatic place on Xavier's list of people he trusted.

Hopefully she liked hard work and thrived on opportunities to prove herself. Xavier was going to give her both.

Two

When Laurel Dixon had decided to go undercover at the LeBlanc Charities food pantry to investigate claims of fraud, she maybe should have picked a different position than services manager. Who would have thought they'd actually hire her, though?

They were supposed to admire her enthusiasm and give her a lesser position. One that gave her plenty of access to the people she needed to interview on the down low and plenty of time to do it. Instead, she'd been handed the keys to the kingdom—which should have put her in a great place to dig into LBC's books. Donors needed to know that LBC wasn't on the up-and-up, that they were only pretending to help people in need while the thieves lined their own pockets.

Except thus far she'd had zero time to even think about how to expose the charity's fraudulent practices.

Of course, a lot of that had to do with one infuriating man named Xavier LeBlanc.

Just because he arrived at LBC at the ungodly hour of 6:00 a.m. and worked through lunch didn't mean the rest of the world had to do the same. But they'd all done it, Laurel included, though she didn't suffer from the same sense of anxiety the other staffers seemed to feel around their interim boss.

But what was she supposed to do, stroll in at nine and draw attention to herself? She'd taken this job under false pretenses. And she couldn't back out now.

Ugh. This was what she got for trying a whole different approach to investigative reporting. This was supposed to be her big breakthrough story. The one that would fix her reputation in the industry while appealing to her sense of fair play and her drive to help people at the same time. If she went undercover, surely she could get the facts for the exposé, and this time, there would be no embarrassing counter-story exposing the lack of foundation for her accusations.

Embarrassing and nearly career killing. Thanks to social media shares and the eternal stores of video, her blunder would never be forgotten. But she could give her audience something else to play with. As long as she didn't make a single mistake with this investigation. When she blew the whistle on LBC, it would be career *making*. A triumph that would erase the mistakes of her last investigation.

Or so she'd laid out in a foolproof mental plan that ended up having a remarkable number of holes.

Instead, she'd spent her first few hours on the job following Adelaide around as the admin explained how Xavier envisioned things working around LBC—and how fast he expected Laurel to get it that way. Apparently, the old manager, Marjorie, had left operations in a bit of disarray when she'd left, but Mr. LeBlanc couldn't be bothered to tell her his expectations himself.

At one o'clock, she'd had enough.

Feigning hunger and fatigue, she begged off from Adelaide's cheerful tour of the facility and bearded the lion in his den. She didn't mind hard work, but only if there was a distinct payoff, and so far, she hadn't seen one. It was time to shake things up.

Xavier LeBlanc glanced up at her sharp knock, his deep blue eyes registering not one iota of surprise or curiosity—nothing. It was a great trick, one she wished she knew how to replicate. It would come in handy as she pretended she knew what the hell she was doing at this new gig.

In lieu of that, she'd settle for a mentor who could give her the insight she needed.

"Got a minute?" she asked and didn't wait for the answer. He would see her whether he liked it or not. How was she supposed to figure out who was responsible for the fraud inside these walls if she didn't keep the man in charge very, very close?

His gaze tracked her as she waltzed right into his office with confidence. He seemed like the type who wouldn't appreciate a mousey approach.

"What can I do for you?" he asked, his sinfully sexy voice rumbling in his chest.

She missed a step. His sexiness quotient really shouldn't be something she noticed. At all. Xavier LeBlanc wasn't allowed to be sexy. He was her boss and she'd been hired based on a lie. One she'd told with good reason, and all of the experience on her résumé was real. But still.

None of that equaled free rein to be attracted to the man behind the desk. And none of that stopped her insides from quivering as his gaze slid down her face to her mouth. He'd done that in the interview more than once and she'd blown it off then. She thought she'd been mistaken. That they'd been stray looks that didn't mean anything. She'd imagined it.

Today? Punch in the girl parts.

She could no more pretend it hadn't happened than she could ignore it. Did Xavier have any clue how unsettling it was to have a man who looked like him slide his gaze to your mouth as if he couldn't decide how to kiss you? Not if. *How.* Because it was happening and he wanted you to anticipate it.

Okay, she had to ignore that. She had a job. Two jobs. Neither were going to go well if she didn't pull it together. Besides, he hadn't done or said anything inappropriate. Likely she was still imagining it.

"Adelaide is a sweet lady," Laurel began. "But I don't get the impression she's fully communicating your vision as well as I would hope. Would it be possible for you to be a little more hands-on?"

In a totally nonpervy way, of course, she added silently as the atmosphere in the room went dead still. Totally could have phrased that better. More professional. Less *I want you on this desk right now.*

Xavier's eyebrows lifted a fraction. "What, exactly, are you asking me to do?"

Oh, man. Surely he didn't mean for that to sound as leading as it did. But then, she'd started it. Was he expecting her to finish it?

Her mind immediately filled in those blanks with several things she could ask him to do. Curiosity was both her strength and her biggest weakness, and she almost never hesitated to investigate things she was dying to know, like whether Xavier's shoulders felt as strong and broad as they looked and how he planned to kiss her.

Of course, she'd never say that out loud. She couldn't. Well, okay, she totally *could* and she had a feeling Xavier would deliver. But she wouldn't. It was highly unethical, for more reasons than one.

But she couldn't get the sudden and sharp images out of her head of what might happen if she did take the hint in his voice and really laid out what she might like. Nothing wrong with a little harmless fantasizing about a sexy man, was there?

"I, um…" *Voice too husky. Not professional. Focus.* She cleared her throat. "It's my first day. I was hoping you and I might talk about your expectations."

Good. That didn't sound like the lead-in to a seduction scene at all.

"I expect you to manage the operations of this charity," he said succinctly. "Nothing more, nothing less."

"I got that part." Sexy, but either Xavier was obtuse or he had way more confidence in her than he had a right to. "But this is your vision I'm executing. I don't know anything about you or your ideas for how things should work. Tell me what my typical day should look like."

Xavier lifted his hands from the keyboard of his laptop and laced them together in a deliberately precise gesture that had the mark of a man demonstrating his patience. His hands were strong and capable, with long lean fingers that she had to stop envisioning on her body.

"That's what I asked Adelaide to do. If she's failing to—"

"No, no." *God*, no. The last thing she'd intended to do was put a spotlight on Adelaide. The poor woman probably had nightmares about Xavier as it was. "She's great. Very helpful. But I want to hear it straight from you. We're going to be working very closely together, after all."

"We're doing nothing of the kind. I hired you to be invisible and ensure that I never have to think about the operations of this place."

Oh. That was not going to work. Laurel leaned forward and laced her own hands together near the edge of the desk, mirroring his pose. "See, that's exactly that sort of thing that Adelaide could never convey. She showed me where departments are and introduced me to people. But I need the mind of Xavier LeBlanc to mesh with mine so we're in sync. Tell me what you'd do. That's the best way to ensure you don't have to think about things, because I will instantly know how you'd want something handled."

And that philosophy had the added bonus of filling in the gaps of her skill set, not to mention allowing her to grill him on how much he knew about the fraud. Her sources had been volunteers in the food pantry and they had given her several credible tips about substitutions that didn't make it into the books, among other things. What she already knew was likely the tip of the iceberg. In her line of work, there was always more to discover.

But she needed to know how high up it went, if Xavier knew about it or if this strange and unexplained switch between the brothers had removed the real culprit from LBC.

Maybe the mysterious switch had its roots in the fraud. She had to know.

At the same time, she couldn't make mistakes. If Xavier's brother had spearheaded or approved the fraud, she had to find proof. Of course, it could have started with Xavier's reign, which added to the complexity of the investigation. It was a wrinkle she hadn't seen coming but adhering to Xavier's directive to be "invisible" wasn't going to reveal even a tiny slice of what she needed to uncover.

Xavier's gaze skittered over hers again and she had the distinct impression he didn't quite know what to do with her. Good. An off-kilter man spilled secrets he meant to keep close to the vest. She relaxed a smidgen. This undercover business couldn't be too hard. Or, rather, she couldn't allow it to be. This story was too important to the people LBC should be serving instead of cheating. The story was too important to her career.

"Here's what I want, Ms. Dixon." His low voice snaked through her and she tried really hard not to react, but she didn't have his ability to be stone-faced. Neither did he miss her reaction, absorbing it with a long, slow pause laden with things unsaid. "I want you to ensure LBC operates smoothly enough that I can focus on fundraising. Outside of that, I don't care what you do."

She blinked. "Sure you do. You're in charge. Everything flows uphill, right?"

That was the core of an investigative reporter's philosophy, the one they taught in Digging for Facts 101. Follow the money. The guy in the corner office was always the place to start because he made all the decisions. If anything illegal was going on, it usually went all the way to the top.

Of course, this situation had the added layer of the guy at the top not being the normal guy. All at once, she hoped Xavier would be in the clear and she'd instead be taking down his brother. Which would be a shame, because she'd genuinely liked Val.

She couldn't let her personal feelings compromise the

investigation, as they had in her last story. She couldn't afford to *like* anyone in this situation.

"Indeed it does," Xavier finally said.

His gaze still hadn't left hers, and if she hadn't known better, she'd have thought he might be fighting some of the same attraction she was. Surely he had his pick of women. He wasn't trying to be sexy as a come-on; it was just a natural part of who he was and she didn't for a second think he'd turned it on specifically for her.

"Great, then we're on the same page. You're in charge and I'm here to execute your orders. What would you like me to do first?"

"Explain why it seems like you're flirting with me."

Laurel's lungs seized and she choked on a breath. Tears leaked from her eyes as she coughed, and if she was really lucky, mascara streaks were even now forming below her lashes.

"What?" she asked when she recovered. "I'm not flirting with you."

If anything, he was the one exuding all the come-hither vibes. At times, it was so strong, she was barely hanging on by the fingernails.

His implacable expression didn't change. "Good. It would be a bad idea to get involved."

Oh, well, *that* was a telling statement. Not "You're not my type." Not "You've mistaken me for a heterosexual." *Bad idea to get involved.* That meant he felt all the sizzle, too.

Interesting.

How much closer could she get to Xavier LeBlanc and would that benefit her story? Or simply benefit *her*? The man knew his way around an orgasm—she could tell. And while this exposé lay at the pinnacle of her personal goals, she couldn't help but want to investigate her reaction to Xavier as a man.

She had a core-deep desire to *know* things, and at this moment, Xavier topped the list.

"A bad, bad idea," she repeated and crossed her fingers behind her back. "I solemnly swear that I will refrain from all double entendres, loaded statements and anything that could be construed as flirting while you and I are working so closely together."

"I didn't say we'd be working closely together," he corrected, and all at once she wondered what it would take to get him well and truly rattled to the point of revealing something unintended.

If she hoped to dig up enough dirt for an exposé, she'd have to figure it out. Everyone had their tipping point and people had spilled secrets to her in the past, often before realizing it. Usually that happened after she'd gained a measure of their trust, though.

How ethical was it to seduce it out of someone? She'd never tried that particular method before and there was no way to deny the idea excited her. Which meant it really was a bad idea. But still viable. She needed more information before fully committing.

"Oh, come on. We just hashed that out. You're in charge, I'm here to do exactly what you say but not sexually and we're both going to ignore the chemistry. Where, exactly, did I lose you, Mr. LeBlanc?"

At that, he actually laughed, and the heavy, rich sound did flippy things to her insides. His deep blue eyes speared her and she got all caught up in him in a very nonprofessional way. Yeah, there might not be a whole lot of choice in the matter and she might not be the one doing the seducing. It was delicious to contemplate, either way.

"I'm not lost. Just...reassessing," he said.

"That sounds promising. Why don't you share your vision with me, at least, and we'll take it from there?"

"Vision for what?"

He'd leaned into the space between them and she was having a hard time concentrating. Xavier had a very potent presence that had latched onto her skin in a wholly disturbing way. "For, um, LBC. As a charity. What's the vision? Mission statement? That kind of thing."

"Feed people," he stated bluntly. "What more is there?"

"A lot. At the shelter, our goal was to give women back some control in their lives. Provide them with choices. The shelter part was just one of the mechanisms we employed."

That had been satisfying work, even as a means to an end as she put herself through college. Sure, she'd had to fudge the dates a little on her résumé and leave off the last few years of employment so no one knew she'd worked for a news channel—which had subsequently fired her. But her drive to help people through knowledge hadn't changed. She still believed in the value of nonprofit organizations, particularly those that served people at the poverty line.

That's why it was so important to expose the fraud here. The money funneling through this organization should go to the people who came through the doors in need, not toward lining someone's pocket because they saw an easy way to skim profits.

Xavier's face turned to granite, which was his default more often than not. "You seem to forget I'm just filling in. This is not my normal world."

All at once, the information she craved had nothing to do with LBC and everything to do with Xavier LeBlanc himself. He was such a fascinating puzzle who gave very little away. She wanted to unlock him in the worst way. "But your brother mentioned that your mother started this charity fifteen years ago. Surely you've been involved to some degree."

"What you see is the sole extent of my involvement." He waved at the desk. "This is where I'll sit for three more months, and in that time I need to hold the best fundraiser this place has ever had. Mission statements are not my concern."

She blinked, but his expression didn't change. He was serious. Okay, wow.

"You're going to have a very big problem, then. People don't give money to fundraisers. They give to a cause they believe in. Your job is to make them believe in it. Don't you think that in a city like Chicago there are a hundred—a *thousand*—places for people to donate? How do they decide? You help them decide by passionately pitching your mission statement to them."

"I'll take that under advisement." In the long pause, they stared at each other without blinking. "You've done fundraising before. Did you apply for the wrong position here?"

Yes. Yes, she had.

That was all the opening she needed to segue this potential disaster into something more her speed. "Perhaps, but only because you posted a job opening for the wrong position. Sounds like you need someone in your back pocket to tell you what to do, not the other way around. Were you not aware that you have serious deficiencies in your operating philosophy?"

Xavier leaned back in his chair as his gaze narrowed. "Can I be honest with you, Ms. Dixon?"

Oh, God, yes. Please spill all your secrets, Mr. LeBlanc.

"Only if you call me Laurel."

His lips lifted into a brief smile that she fully expected meant he was about to argue with her. But he didn't. "Laurel, then. You need to understand what's happening here and I'm choosing to trust you, which is not something I do lightly."

His tone or his smile or her own conscience tripped something inside. Guilt plowed through her stomach out of nowhere. It was one thing to dig deep enough to learn someone's secrets when they were scamming, but she had no evidence Xavier was even involved in the fraud. What if her investigation caused problems for him?

Ugh, she was getting way ahead of herself. Her sources were credible and if there was something to uncover, Xavier would likely be happy that she'd done so. It was a public service, really. Surely he'd respect that.

"I'll do my best to be worthy of that trust."

He nodded once. "Then I have a confession. I am not well versed in how to run a charity. I do need help."

She very nearly rolled her eyes. This was him being honest? "I already figured that out."

"I'm doing my best to keep that nugget of truth from the rest of the staff," he said wryly. "Which is why I try to stay out of their areas of expertise. That's where you come in."

"I hear you. You want to hide out here in the office while everyone else does the dirty work." She stared him down as his eyebrows came together. "Too bad. You signed up to run LBC. Now do it. I'll help. We'll be partners."

She stuck out her hand and waited. She needed him, whether she liked it or not. Whether *he* liked it or not. And the reverse was also clearly true. They would do this together or not at all. If she had a partner, the less chance she had of screwing up.

Xavier let her sweat it for about thirty seconds and then reluctantly reached out to clasp her hand for a very long beat that neither of them mistook for a simple handshake. There was too much electricity, too much unsaid for that.

The less she let him focus on that, the better.

Three

Partners.

That was a concept Xavier liked a whole lot, given his distinct impression that Laurel Dixon was hiding something. He liked it even better that she'd been the one to suggest working together. The closer he kept her, the easier it would be to keep an eye on her.

He trusted her about as much as he'd trust a convicted car thief with the keys to his Aston Martin.

But he also understood that his lack of trust wasn't specific to Laurel. If he really wanted to get honest about it, his inability to stop being both suspicious and cautious had probably been at least half of Marjorie's problem with him. That's why he'd thought a hands-off approach with the new services manager might work best. Not to mention the fact that he couldn't shake that weird, misty feeling that sprang up inside whenever he was in the same room with Laurel Dixon. He'd hoped to avoid examining that by staying away from her.

Ms. Dixon had blown that plan to smithereens.

Jury was still out on how much wreckage he'd have to step over. Especially given the instant and volatile chemistry between them, which he'd been wholly prepared to pretend didn't exist until she'd so eloquently refused to let him. So that was a thing. The next three months should be incredibly taxing and exceedingly painful, then.

"Partners. What happens next?" Xavier asked Laurel once he'd dropped her hand, though the severed contact didn't eliminate the buzzing awareness arcing between them at all.

Not that he'd expected it to. Regardless of what he called the vibe between them, it wasn't going away. The trick was managing it. Which meant it would be a bad idea to touch her again, and of course, that was all he could think about.

"Follow me."

She slid from the seat she'd perched in when she first came into his office and glanced over her shoulder, perhaps to ensure he was doing as she commanded. As if he'd miss a second of whatever she had up her sleeve. Not likely.

Xavier trailed her to the receptionist's desk. Adelaide's eyes widened behind her bifocals as they approached and taut lines appeared around the woman's mouth. He nearly growled at her just to see if she'd actually come out of her skin. What good was it to have people afraid of him if he couldn't have fun with it occasionally?

Before he could try it, Laurel flipped a lock of her long sable-colored hair behind her back. "Today is your lucky day, Addy. You're in charge from now on. Mr. LeBlanc has given you a promotion."

"I did not. *Oof.*" Laurel's elbow glanced off his ribs,

leaving a sharp, smarting circle of *shut up* below his heart. "I mean…yeah. What Laurel said."

Adelaide's wide-eyed gaze flitted back and forth between the two of them as if she couldn't quite get her bearings. He knew the feeling.

"That's very generous, Mr. LeBlanc," she squeaked. "But I don't understand. A promotion?"

"Exactly." Laurel beamed so brightly, Xavier could see the rays from his position behind her. "To Services Manager. You're going to take Marjorie's place."

Wait, what? That was going a little far. If Adelaide had been remotely qualified or interested in the position, she would have applied for it the second the job posting had gone up. What, exactly, was Laurel up to?

"Are you sure about this?" he muttered in Laurel's ear and caught her elbow a hairbreadth from his ribs, holding it tight just in case she was stronger than she looked.

Clearly she had a plan and intended for Xavier to follow it. The elbow to the ribs indicated that if he wanted to have a conversation about her tactics, she'd indulge him later.

"You know everything about this place, Adelaide. Tell Mr. LeBlanc," Laurel instructed with a nauseating amount of cheer. "You gave me such a thorough tour of the place that I thought it would never end. There's not a nook or cranny at LBC that you don't have some sort of insight into. Is there?"

Obediently, Adelaide shook her head. "No, ma'am. I've been here seven years and started in the kitchen as a volunteer. I love every last board and nail in this place."

"I could tell." Laurel jerked her head at Xavier. "Mr. LeBlanc was just bemoaning the fact that he didn't have anyone to help organize a fundraiser that LBC so desperately needs."

Oh, dear God. That was not what he'd said. *At all*. But before he could correct the grievous misrepresentation that gave everyone the impression he was being a big baby about the tasks laid out for him, Laurel rushed on.

"I figured, this is Addy's opportunity to really make a difference. Step up and show us all what she's made of. You just do what Marjorie did and that'll leave me free to help Mr. LeBlanc get some money flowing in. Are you good with that?"

When Adelaide smiled and clapped her hands like she'd just been given the biggest Christmas present, Xavier's mouth fell open. Hastily, he closed it before anyone figured out that Laurel Dixon had just shocked the hell out of him. He didn't shock easily, and it was even harder to remember the last time he'd been unable to control his expression.

The two women went back and forth on the logistics for a furious couple of minutes until Xavier couldn't take it any longer.

"So, that's it?" he interrupted. "Adelaide, you can do what Marjorie did and everyone's good with that?"

Both women swiveled to stare at him. Laurel raised a brow. "Sorry, did we lose you again? Yes. Adelaide is in charge. She'll do a fantastic job."

Xavier should have asked more questions back in his office, like whether *partner* meant something different where Laurel had come from. When she'd thrown out the idea that they'd be working closely together, he'd reassessed his idea of how their interaction might go. And he'd come to the conclusion that perhaps she *could* come to him for approval on the budget, or maybe to get his help vetting new volunteers. That sort of thing.

He had not once suggested that she sign herself up to take over his inheritance test. That was *his*. He needed to prove to his father—and himself—that he could and would handle anything the old man threw at him. Ten million dollars was a cheap price to pay in order to get back on even ground, regain his confidence and lose the edge of vulnerability he'd been carrying since the reading of the will.

No one was allowed to get in the way of that.

"Excuse us, please," he said to Adelaide through gritted teeth.

Pulling Laurel back into his office, he shut the door and leaned on it, half afraid she'd find a way to open it again despite the hundred and seventy-five pounds of man holding it shut.

Instantly, he realized his mistake.

Laurel's presence filled the room, blanketing him with that otherworldly, mystical nonsense that he couldn't think through.

"What the hell was all that about?" he demanded and couldn't find a shred of remorse at how rough it came out. "You shuffled off all your duties to Adelaide—without asking, by the way. What, exactly, are you going to be doing?"

"Helping you, of course." She patted his arm and the contact sang through his flesh clear to the bone. "We have a fundraiser to organize. Which I'm pretty sure is what I just said."

The trap had been laid so neatly that he still hadn't quite registered whether the teeth had closed around his ankle or not. "You don't have enough experience fundraising."

She shrugged. "I do have *some*. What's your hang-up about experience? Adelaide doesn't have any experience." She accompanied that statement with air quotes. "But she's been learning on the job for years by following Marjorie around. She'll do great."

"Running a charity takes an iron fist," he shot back instantly. "Not an owl face and a lot of head nodding."

Laurel just laughed. "Owl face? Better not let her hear that. Women who wear glasses don't take kindly to name-calling."

"I didn't mean—" The headache brewing behind his eyes spread to his temples. "I called her an owl because she just stands there and looks wise. Instead of telling people what to do. I— Never mind."

Laurel Dixon had officially driven him around the bend. And now Adelaide had just been given a promotion that she seemed super pleased with. He couldn't take it away, though likely he'd have to spend a lot of time following *her* around to make sure she didn't drive operations into the ground. Hiring Laurel had been one thing, because at least he could blame that on Val if it didn't work out, but this was a whole other mess.

One he had no graceful way of undoing without upsetting the admin. Or Laurel, who might do God knew what as her next trick.

"Okay. Fine," he ground out. "Adelaide is Marjorie. She's going to be great. You're going to help with fundraising. Are you going to be great, too?"

"Of course."

She flipped a lock of hair over her shoulder again, and he couldn't help but wonder why she wore it down when her hands were constantly fiddling with it. She should wear it up. Then he wouldn't be tempted to put his own hands through it just to see if it felt as satiny and lush as it looked.

He crossed his arms. No point in tempting fate. "Fantastic. What's the plan, General?"

"Nicknames already?" Her long eyelashes swept her cheeks as she treated him to a very long, pointed once-over that lingered in inappropriate places. "I thought that wouldn't happen until much later in our association. Under...different circumstances."

In bed, she meant. The implication was clear. And he definitely shouldn't be feeling the spark of her suggestion in those inappropriate places. "It fit. Can't help it."

"Don't worry. I like it." The atmosphere in the office got a whole lot heavier as she stared at him. "And I like that you've already clued in that I don't sit around and wait for things to happen to me."

"I knew that a half second after Adelaide told me you were here for an interview that I hadn't arranged," he told her bluntly. "You're an easy read."

Something flitted through her gaze. A shadow. He couldn't put his finger on what she had going on beneath the surface, but that gut-deep feeling told him again she had something to hide.

How many secrets might she spill if he did take her into his bed?

Once that thought formed, he couldn't stop thinking about it. He wasn't like that, not normally. But Laurel had barreled right through what he'd call his *normal* and redefined everything. Maybe he needed to return the favor.

"I'm pretty transparent," she agreed readily, but another layer dropped into place over her expression.

She was a terrible liar. Or perhaps he was just incredibly tuned in to her, which didn't seem to have a downside. Other than the one where he'd just been boxed into a corner and had no graceful way to avoid spending a lot of time in her company.

"I probably see more than you'd like," he told her, and she blinked. This was a fun game. "For example, I'm pretty sure that you just maneuvered yourself into a position as my fundraising assistant because you can't stay away from me."

He didn't believe that for a second, but he definitely wanted to hear what she'd say to counter it.

Her eyebrows inched up toward her hairline and she relaxed an iota. "Well, that's a provocative statement. What if I said it's true?"

Then she'd be lying again. She had a whole other agenda, one he hadn't figured out yet, but if she wanted to work it like the attraction between them got top billing, he could play along. "I'd say we have a problem, then. We can't get involved. It would be too...sticky."

Her lips curved at his choice of words, as intended. "That's a shame. I'm a fan of sticky."

"Stickiness is for candy." All at once, a very distinct image sprang into his head of her on his desk naked with a caramel melting on her tongue. His whole body went stiff. "I like it best when things are uncomplicated."

At that, she snorted, moving in to lay a hand on his arm in the exact opposite of what this back-off conversation had been intended to convey. He'd wanted to catch her off guard but so far she'd held her own.

Reluctant admiration for this woman warred with bone-deep desire and flat-out irritation.

"Please," she muttered with a sarcastic grin as she squeezed his forearm. "You're the least uncomplicated man I've ever met. At least do me the courtesy of being honest about the fact that you're not attracted to me, if that's what's going on."

Oh, nicely played. She'd put the ball firmly in his court. He could take the out and claim he didn't feel the heavy arousal that she could almost assuredly see for herself, giving her the opportunity to call him out as a liar.

Or he could admit that she made him hotter than asphalt in a heat wave and call a truce.

He went with option three: ensuring she fully understood he didn't dance to her tune.

"I don't think honesty is on the table here. Do you?"

The atmosphere splintered as she stiffened, but to her credit, she kept a smile on her face. "Touché. We'll go back to ignoring the chemistry, then."

"That's best." And not at all what he'd been talking about, but he also hadn't expected her to voluntarily blurt out her secrets. All in good time. "Now, about this fundraiser…"

"Oh, right." Her hand dropped away from his arm—finally—and she got a contemplative look as if she really had given away her job with the intent of diving into his hell with gusto. "We should attend someone else's fundraiser and take notes."

"That's—" he blinked "—a really good idea."

One he should have thought of. That's what he'd do in the diamond trenches. If another jewelry outlet had a strategy he liked, he'd study it. Why not apply the same to charity?

Laurel smiled, putting some sparkle in her silver-gray eyes. "I'll start researching some possibilities and then we'll take a field trip."

Fantastic. If he couldn't stay away from Laurel, then he'd settle for spending as much time in her company as he could until he figured out her agenda. If it was merely to indulge in their impossible-to-ignore chemistry, then he might find a way to be on board with that, as long as he could protect what was his at the same time.

Jury was still out on just how difficult she'd make it.

Four

By Friday, Adelaide had Xavier's vote of confidence. She really had been studying at Marjorie's side for quite some time, showing off a deep knowledge of all things LBC, and she made sound decisions without a lot of deliberation. The staff responded to her as if she'd always been in charge, and he liked her style.

Not that he'd tell her that. She managed to convey a fair amount of dislike for him with pretty much every word out of her mouth and sometimes without saying anything at all. It was impressive.

But it felt like LBC was running smoothly for the first time in forever. Since Marjorie had dropped her set of keys on his desk with a clank and turned on her heel. Maybe even before that. So he gave Adelaide a pass on the disdain. She didn't have to like him as long as she did her job so he could do his. Or, at least, pretend to do his until he figured out how to turn the tide in his favor.

Laurel poked her head through his partially opened office door, sable hair swinging. "Why am I not surprised to find you behind your desk?"

"Because this is where I work?" he offered blithely.

In the week since he and Laurel had become "partners," he'd learned that he had almost no shot at responding to a question like that to her satisfaction. He'd given up trying and went with the most obvious answer.

She made a noise with her tongue that could easily be mistaken for a ticking clock. "Because you're hiding now that Addy has it all under control, more likely."

He lifted a shoulder. "Must not be hiding well enough. You found me."

"I was looking for you." The rest of her body followed her head as she slid through the cracked door uninvited. "Probably I'm the only one who is, though."

"For a reason, one would hope," he shot back pointedly before she launched into yet another discussion about how he could do more to interact with the staff. Laurel's job had somehow morphed from Services Manager to Fundraising Assistant to Xavier's Keeper. He hadn't figured out yet how to veer her back into something a little less invasive. "I am actually doing paperwork."

If staring at paperwork counted, then it wasn't so much of a lie. Otherwise, he'd stopped doing paperwork an hour ago and instead had been stewing about the latest fundraising numbers.

He was short. A lot. He had less than three months to raise north of seven million dollars and the near impossibility of the task writhed in his stomach like a greasy eel. As a result, he'd spent a lot of time sorting through fundraising ideas on his own, which was something he'd outsource to Laurel over his dead body.

The trick was engaging her enough so that she *thought*

she'd snowed him into this partnership, when in reality, he only let her have enough rope to bind them very closely together—strictly so he didn't miss whatever she had up her sleeve. Sharing the actual work with Laurel wasn't happening.

Thus far, she hadn't seemed to clue in. She barged into his office at her leisure to discuss what had become her pet project. He'd bet a hundred K that she'd spotted a notice in the society pages about the Art for Autism Association fundraiser tonight and she'd come by to announce she was dragging him along to it, pretending it wasn't a date when, in reality, it was a great excuse to spend the evening together without admitting she wanted to.

He'd put up some empty protests and eventually let her think she'd talked him into it. Getting out from underneath the eyes at LBC sounded like an opportune way to dig a little deeper into Laurel Dixon and whatever it was about her that niggled at his suspicions.

She curled her lip at the printed pages under his fingers, eyeing the black type as if she could actually read it from that distance. "Good thing for you I have something much more exciting to put on your agenda. You're taking me on a hot date tonight."

Oh, God, yes. The scene spilled through his mind without an ounce of prompting. Laurel in a little black dress—backless, of course, designed to make a man's mouth water—and sky-high heels that did amazing things to her legs. Her voice would be lowered enough to keep their conversation private. Hair down and brushed to a high gleam. She'd take his breath away the moment he opened the door and he'd never quite get his equilibrium back until maybe the next day...

What was he *thinking*?

Xavier sat back in his chair and crossed his arms with

feigned nonchalance in case his initial—and so very inappropriate—response got too big to stay under his skin and started leaking out of his pores.

And this even though he'd *known* it was coming. It was just…she'd called it a date, after all, and in the process, uncovered his previously undiscovered craving to do it for real. What was he supposed to do with her?

Laurel was so much more dangerous than he'd credited.

"We're not dating." A token protest. It was only a matter of time before he figured out how to keep his wits about him as he seduced the truth out of her. Meanwhile, he had to play it like he still planned to keep her at arm's length. All the balls they had in the air should be exhausting. "We've covered this."

Instead, it was invigorating.

She waved it off. "Yeah, yeah. This isn't a real date. You're taking me on a field trip. I found a great foundation doing a unique fundraiser. Tonight."

Pretending it was not a real date he could do. In fact, it got a righteous *hallelujah*. Silently, of course, but still. His arms relaxed and dropped into his lap. "Fantastic. Where?"

"Art gallery." She glanced at her watch, her attention already galloping away from this conversation into whatever else was going on in her brain. "I called as your representative and they were more than happy to take your money. The lady even sent a courier over with the tickets. I have to leave now so I can pick up a dress and get my hair done. I have reservations at LaGrange at eight. Meet me there."

Like hell. He did things the right way when it came to taking a woman to dinner. Especially one he wanted to keep close for more reasons than one. "We'll need time to strategize. I'll be at your house at seven thirty to pick you up."

Her eyebrows lifted and he couldn't help the smug sense of satisfaction that crept through him. Laurel wasn't so easy to surprise. He'd have to repeat that a whole bunch more, simply because he liked the idea of knocking her off balance before she did it to him.

"Well, then, I have to say yes to *strategizing*."

Innuendo dripped from her voice and the suggestion pinged around inside him, doing interesting things down below. He let the charged moment drag out because it suited him and then smiled. "Wear black."

"Duh. You, too," she suggested with a once-over that clearly said she found his jeans and T-shirt lacking in some way.

"I've been to my share of society events. I think I'm good." Finally, he'd have a chance to slip back into his old self, the one that wore three-thousand-dollar suits to the office as a matter of course. He could even pull his Yacht-Master out of the box in his closet. "See you at seven thirty."

She lifted her chin in amused acknowledgment that he'd won that round and took off to do whatever female rituals she'd lined up to get herself ready for tonight.

Xavier was dressed in his favorite tux by seven, but forced himself to cool his heels. Laurel did not need any ammunition, and showing up early would clue her in as to how much he'd been anticipating this not-a-date—and not just because he had an agenda of his own for the evening. He wanted to see her.

Labels were simply a mechanism to drive them both toward what they wanted using acceptable parameters. They'd be spending the evening together in formal wear, eating dinner and attending an art show, all of which could lead to something very good. Sure, it was pitched as an opportunity to scout out how another charity did fundraising, but they were both adults who shared a sizzling attraction.

There was no reason he couldn't enjoy the results of seducing her, even if his motives weren't entirely pure. Women who hid things didn't get to be self-righteous about how their secrets came to light.

Besides, if she hadn't wanted to play with fire, she'd have picked a fundraising field trip with a lot fewer matches. Like the 5k run through Highland Park that the Chicago Children's Advocacy Center had on tap for tomorrow. No chance to get the slightest bit cozy in the middle of the day while sweating your butt off. Probably that's what they should have signed up for.

But he had to be honest and admit that he liked a good fire, himself. As long as he was the one controlling the flame.

The moment he rang Laurel's doorbell at 7:31, she swung it open as if she'd been standing there waiting. Clearly *she* had no qualms about letting him know she'd been eagerly anticipating his arrival. And then his brain registered the woman. Whatever illusion he'd cooked up that had given him the idea he might have the slightest iota of control vanished like smoke in a hurricane.

Holy hell. "Laurel…"

His brain couldn't form coherent sentences after that. She was so far past gorgeous that she bordered on ethereal. Angelic. Something a man with far more poetry in his soul than Xavier LeBlanc would have to immortalize because all he could think was *wow*.

Black was Laurel's color. There was something about it that paired with her skin and eyes to make both luminous. The dress was exactly the right length to be considered modest, but also to make a man wishful. And her stilettos—sexy enough to make his teeth ache along with the rest of his body.

"I got lucky," she said with a laugh, like everything was fine and his entire world hadn't just been knocked from its axis. "This was the first dress I tried on and the price tag wasn't the equivalent of my mortgage."

"It's…" *Perfect*. But his tongue went numb. He swallowed. What the hell was wrong with him? It was just a dress. With a woman inside it. He'd participated in hundreds of similar scenarios where he'd picked up a date at her door.

But none of them had ever intrigued him as much as this one. None of them had irritated him beyond the point of reason. None of them had caught him off guard as many times in a row as Laurel. None of them had stirred something inside that he couldn't explain or even fully acknowledge.

It was far past time to stop ignoring it and start figuring out how to deal with it.

Because he still didn't trust her. No matter what. He couldn't think of her as a hot date or he'd never regain an ounce of control—and he needed control to get through the evening. She was his companion for a fundraising research trip. Nothing more.

"You look great," he said and cleared his throat. That husky quality in his voice would not do. "If you're ready?"

He extended a hand toward the limousine at her curb and waited as she locked the door behind her, then he followed her down the sidewalk, trying to keep his eyes off her extremely nice rear. The dress wasn't backless but it did dip down into a V beneath her hair, which she had worn down. She didn't seem to ever put it up, which he appreciated. Hair like hers should never be hidden in a ponytail or bun.

And he'd veered right back into thinking of her as a woman instead of his partner in all things fundraising. The problem was that she wasn't really his partner and he didn't want her in that role. But he had to do *something* with her now that she'd shuffled off daily operations to Adelaide, if for no other reason than because Val liked her and had asked Xavier to keep her around. Dinner and an art show it was, then.

The atmosphere in the limo bordered on electric, and he cursed the fact that he'd specifically instructed his staff to skip the champagne because this wasn't a date. It would have been nice to have something to occupy his hands.

Come on. You're better than this.

"LaGrange is an interesting restaurant choice," he said more smoothly than his still-tingling tongue should have allowed. "A favorite?"

Laurel shrugged, drawing attention to her bare shoulders. They were creamy and flawless, like her long legs. This field trip was either the worst idea ever conceived or sheer brilliance. He couldn't decide which.

"I've never been able to score a table there, but oddly enough, when I throw your name around, people jump." She winked. "Don't judge, but I'm enjoying my ride on the Xavier LeBlanc train."

Hell on a horse. The train hadn't even left the station yet and she was already impressed? He bit back forty-seven provocative responses about what else might be in store for a woman on his arm and opted for what hopefully passed as a smile. "I know the owner of LaGrange. Not everyone jumps when I say jump."

"I don't believe that for a second," she murmured.

"You seem like the type who takes no prisoners. Tell me about running LeBlanc Jewelers. I bet you're magnificent in the boardroom."

As ego strokes went, that one could have done some damage, but he'd caught the slightly off-color tinge to her tone. She was fishing for something. That alone put an interesting spin on the conversation. He couldn't help but indulge her, mostly to see if he could trip her up enough to spill bits of her agenda.

"I'm magnificent in every room." He let that sink in, gratified by her instant half smile that said she caught the innuendo. "But in the boardroom, I do my job. Nothing more."

"So modest. I read up on LeBlanc Jewelers. It's almost a billion-dollar company, up nearly 20 percent since you took over five years ago. That's impressive."

The reminder tripped some not-so-pleasant internal stuff that he'd rather not dwell on tonight. "Again. That's my job. If I didn't do it well, the board wouldn't let me keep it. What about you? Once we organize a fundraiser for LBC and I go back to LeBlanc Jewelers, what do you envision yourself doing?"

Val wouldn't keep her in the role of fundraiser, or, at least, Xavier didn't think he would. Honestly, he didn't know what Val might do and that was at least half Xavier's problem. The inner workings of his brother's mind had interested him even less than LBC, and that had left him clueless when thrust into this new role. Xavier had helped Val through some sticky mining contracts, and Val had sat in on the interview with Laurel, but then they'd drifted back into their respective corners. Their relationship didn't feel any more cohesive. Maybe by design.

They'd never been close. But then Xavier had never been close to anyone except his father. That betrayal would likely always be fresh enough to serve as a reminder of what happened when you trusted people enough to let them in.

"I'm fine with seeing what happens," Laurel informed him without a lot of fanfare. "I'm not much of a five-year-plan kind of girl."

That piqued his interest. "So you'd describe yourself as spontaneous?"

What was he hoping to get out of a question like *that*? Nothing remotely professional or even anything in the realm of strategy could come out of something that sounded more like first-date small talk. She should shut him down.

But she nodded, treating him to a smile that had secrets laced through it. "I'm full of surprises. And I like them, too."

That made one of them. "I'll keep that in mind. Tell me about your fundraising experience. I never did hear what qualified you to be my strategy partner."

Good. That was exactly what they needed to be talking about. No more first-date type questions that made him to want to get to know her better, as if they had some kind of future.

"I worked in a women's shelter," she said. "The women who came in looking for help...you can't see them with their slumped shoulders and tired eyes without wanting to pour everything you've got into erasing all that defeat. I didn't have any of my own money to give, so that meant I had to be creative in how I ensured we never had to turn away a single one due to lack of funds."

He blinked away the miasma of Laurel that had fallen over him as she caught him up in her passion. It was easy to see her point about people donating to her cause simply because she believed in it enough to get them to open their checkbooks. And easy to see why he'd yet to turn a corner on his own donation task—because he had none of that passion. For anything. Let alone LBC.

"I had to succeed," she continued somewhat fiercely. "Failure meant there was a woman out there who couldn't leave a bad home where she and maybe her kids were being hurt. I couldn't have that on my conscience. So I didn't fail."

"Failure is never an option." *That* part he knew all about.

Her brief smile didn't reach her eyes. "Right. That's why I wanted to help you. We'll be a formidable team because we're exactly alike, you and I."

"We're…um, what?"

"Alike. Peas in a pod." She circled an index finger between them. "You need to succeed at this fundraiser so badly that you hired someone to take over operations so you could focus on it. Because you can't fail. I get that."

She wasn't supposed to be getting ideas about anything other than a fundraiser that would fill LBC's coffers. Her canny insight crawled through him in a way he didn't particularly like, mostly because he didn't enjoy being so transparent when his goal had been to uncover *her* vulnerabilities. "I hired you to replace someone who had resigned. Reading into the subtext is not in the job description."

Laughing, she shook her head. "Lucky for you, that skill came with the rest, so you got it for free. If I'm wrong, say so. Otherwise, let's be real with each other. That's the only way for a partnership to work."

She wasn't wrong. But that didn't mean he had to announce it. Her comment had been founded on the premise that he cared whether or not their partnership worked. Not so much. He liked depending on Xavier LeBlanc only.

"We're here."

Wisely, she didn't press him on it and chose to exit the limo. But the knowing look she shot him as he extended his arm to sweep her into the restaurant said she was still analyzing subtext and had likely concluded that he'd changed the subject on purpose.

And hell if he didn't admire a woman who could do all of that without breaking a sweat. He'd have to work extra hard to stop admiring her. Otherwise, he might end up liking Laurel Dixon, and that could not work out well when his sole goal for the evening was to seduce her into a false sense of security, then prove his suspicions about her.

Five

Laurel was in a lot of trouble.

The longer she stood at Xavier's side and covertly watched him contemplate the chocolate sculpture, the more she wanted to crawl all over him and have her wicked way. If he would unbend enough to let her. And if it wouldn't compromise everything she was trying to do with LBC.

But…

The things a tuxedo did to that man's body defied description. He wasn't just good-looking or handsome. Xavier was lip-licking, finger-smacking, eat-him-all-up *hot*. It took considerable effort to pretend she was focused on the edible art surrounding them at the gallery sponsoring the autism benefit.

Dinner had been hard enough, when she'd gotten a solid hour just to look at him. Now he was close enough to touch and holy hell did she want to indulge her piqued curiosity.

If he tried to kiss her, she feared she wouldn't be able to stop herself from a thorough investigation of how good that could get.

As a distraction, she let the video play in her head of her greatest nightmare—the rebuttal story proving that Laurel had falsely accused the mayor's office of collusion. A rival news channel produced evidence that Laurel's sources weren't credible. That story had been all over the place the morning after she'd broken hers. Honestly, she was lucky the mayor had agreed not to press slander charges even after she publicly apologized and posted a retraction.

The shame of having made a mistake of that magnitude would never fully go away.

But ensuring she had all the facts *this* time—that was happening. Xavier was the key.

Which meant she had to stop imagining what his bottom lip would feel like between her teeth.

"I think it's supposed to be the *Venus de Milo*," Xavier commented finally and glanced at Laurel. "Do you see it?"

Yes. Art. That was a much better distraction. They were at an art show, supposedly doing field research on fundraising. "Um…yeah, I can kind of see the resemblance. If you squint and pretend that blobby thing at the top is a head."

He let his mouth curve up into a half smile. "Actually, that's what I do when I look at the real *Venus de Milo*. I skipped art appreciation in college."

She had to laugh because art wasn't really her thing, either. "I skipped everything in college in favor of working my butt off to graduate with no debt."

"That's admirable," he said as they moved to the next

edible art contribution, a replica of Monet's *Water Lilies* made out of crushed hard candies.

So far, they'd seen the chocolate statue of questionable composition, a portrait of Homer Simpson formed from Rice Krispies cereal and a very good representation of a fish tank laid out in a cast iron skillet with whole sardines posed to look like they were swimming through sage seaweed.

"Life Savers," Xavier declared with certainty as he swirled his finger in the air around one of the lilies. "The candy, I mean."

"Jolly Ranchers," Laurel said just to be contrary, though what she'd hoped to get out of that, she had no idea. Xavier didn't get riled. Ever. That was one of his most maddening qualities. No matter what she did, he took it in stride, never raising his voice or really seeming to get emotional about much of anything.

She had a perverse need to find out what *would* get him riled. What he was passionate about. What might pull him out from behind his corporate facade. Or, at least, what might move him enough to throw caution to the wind and act on the sizzling chemistry between them.

Because, honestly, nothing could distract her from wanting to know what it would be like between them. She could guess. Fantasize—and had done that a lot. But nothing satisfied her itch for knowledge. If she'd been the one in the Garden of Eden, no snake would have been required to entice Laurel into eating that apple; she'd have been climbing a tree trunk the first day.

Which was a problem.

"You think?" Xavier responded mildly, true to form.

Laurel rolled her eyes with a laugh. "Of course. Jolly Ranchers shatter when they break, like ice or glass. Life

Savers crack into big chunks. See the long shards in the leaves? Definitely Jolly Ranchers."

He crossed his arms, the art completely forgotten as he contemplated her, intrigued. "Spoken like a woman with experience breaking things. Do you have a temper I should know about?"

"Maybe I get a little spirited on occasion, sure. But I only destroy candy for fun."

"I must know more about that."

She shrugged and opted for honesty. "I like to see what happens."

"To what?"

"To everything." She spread her hands wide. "Curiosity is the spice of life. What fun is it to just unwrap a Jolly Rancher and stick it in your mouth? I want to know what happens when you hit it with a hammer. When you light it on fire. When you drop it in an ant bed. How can you *not* want to know?"

"I absolutely do." His gaze dropping to her lips as if she'd been talking about an entirely different kind of knowledge, of the more carnal variety. "I want to know everything, too. Tell me."

She swallowed as the vibe between them picked up strength, humming through the heavy atmosphere. It was so electric it became increasingly apparent there would be only one way to discharge all that energy and it wasn't an art discussion.

The real question was—would they opt to act on it?

"Well, that's the thing," she said, leaning into the conversation almost automatically. Xavier had this powerful draw that made her want to be closer to him. "You can't *tell* someone what's going to happen. You have to want to jump into that void yourself. Go on a voyage of discovery because you can't stand being in the dark.

What's over the horizon? Best way to find out is to sail toward it yourself."

"Curiosity," he said with a lift of his chin. "Isn't that what killed the cat?"

"Because the cat used up all nine of his lives," she informed him loftily. "I'm only on, like, number five."

He laughed, and the rich sound pebbled her skin with goose bumps. When was the last time she'd noticed the way a man laughed? But Xavier didn't laugh very often—and wasn't that a shame? She liked what it did to her, liked being the one to entice him into it.

What more could she entice him to do?

"I'm a fan of your approach to life," he said.

The compliment spread through her like she'd just gulped the first sip of hot chocolate after playing in the snow. "More where that came from."

"Really? Like what?"

He'd uncrossed his arms at some point and somehow they'd drifted to a space between two exhibits where they weren't impeding the flow of traffic. Glitzy couples strolled past them in both directions but she had a hard time concentrating on anything other than him. She'd just noticed that his eyes turned this incredible shade of deep blue when he forgot to be impersonal and let his face reveal that she'd captured his interest.

"See? Now you're getting it. You have to ask questions, dive in. That's when you find out what happens."

Her voice had dropped in deference to their close proximity and she had to admit it was also partly because she didn't want to burst the bubble that had formed around them. Being inside this circle of two did fascinating things to her insides. She didn't want to stop discovering how deep this thing went.

"What if the thing that's going to happen turns out badly?"

The undercurrents sped up as he leaned against the wall, his gaze tuned in to hers with laser sharpness. They'd moved on from talking about approaches to life to something else entirely.

"Well, you don't actually know that's going to be the result. Right? Again, part of the discovery process. Maybe it'll be very, very good. There's really only one way to answer that question."

"I'm starting to see that point," he muttered and then cursed. "This attraction between us isn't going away, is it?"

Well, that was blunt. She might be a pretty big fan of his approach to life, as well. She couldn't help the smile that spread across her face. "God, I hope not. I like the way you make me feel."

"That makes one of us."

But he punctuated that potentially deflating statement by brushing a chunk of hair from her temple with the back of his hand, lingering along her cheekbone with absolutely no apology. His touch zinged through all her empty spaces inside, filling her instantly with heat and light.

"You don't like the crazy energy of being like this with someone?" she asked somewhat breathlessly, but there was no way to help it. The man gave her lungs amnesia and they totally forgot how to function.

He was going to kiss her. She could feel the anticipation climbing. It was in the weight of his hand as he turned it against her cheek and cupped the back of her head.

"Not especially. I'm not used to a lot of crazy going on inside," he admitted and seemed as surprised that he'd said it as she was. The comment was far too personal. But then he shrugged. "You have this unique ability to pull reactions from me that I don't know what to do with."

That sounded so promising that she leaned into his hand. "This is the part where you experiment until you figure out what to do with me."

Heat stole through his gaze as his fingers caressed her hairline. "I know exactly what to do with you. It's me I'm not so sure about."

"We're partners, remember? We'll figure it out together. Step this way, sir, and prepare to be amazed at what's just behind this curtain."

He smiled, as she'd intended, but didn't immediately pull her into the kiss she was aching for.

"Sure you want to pull that curtain back? Pandora's box is a real thing, you know. Once you open it, then it's too late. You can't stuff everything back inside."

Yeah. That was a thing. Her *worst* thing.

She'd jumped off a cliff plenty of times and only realized a half step too late that she'd lost her parachute. But she hadn't splatted on the ground nearly enough times to kill her curiosity. Besides, she'd scraped herself off the sidewalk every single time and managed to limp away from the scene on her own two legs, so…

She wrapped her fingers around his lapel and drew him into her body. Slowly. The anticipation was too good to rush. He let her extend the moment before their lips met and then he took over, claiming her mouth with such ferocious need that it robbed her of her balance.

Falling into Xavier LeBlanc was, bar none, the most exhilarating experience of her life.

He consumed her from the inside out, his mouth lighting every nerve on fire. Not a little flame like the kind that sprang up when you struck a match, but the blow-torch variety. Huge, encompassing and bright, spreading so fast that it got dangerous instantly.

She wanted his hands on her. His heat. His skin. She wanted to know what he looked like when she brought him pleasure, when he came. What color his eyes would be when he peeked up at her from between her thighs.

If she got him naked, would he finally break and show her something other than absolute control? That she'd like to see. Because, so far, he was missing the abandon she'd hoped for if they got up close and personal.

What would it take to make him lose control?

Seeming to sense she needed more, he deepened the kiss. His hot tongue slicked against hers, heightening her arousal to epic proportions. The kiss took her to another dimension where she could do nothing but feel and she never wanted to return to earth.

But then his mouth lifted from hers a fraction and he murmured, "Wanna get out of here?"

Laurel crashed into reality with a sickening thud. Of course she wanted to follow him into whatever bed, limo or hot tub he had in mind to continue this, especially if it meant figuring out his magic buttons.

But she couldn't.

How could she? She wasn't Laurel Dixon, charity director and future lover of Xavier LeBlanc. She was an investigative reporter who had a bad track record of screwing up when she let herself get distracted by a source.

And that was all this man could be to her right now—a source.

She couldn't afford to have her ethics compromised in her investigation, either. If—when—she found some-thing off in LBC's accounting, she did not want the fact that she was sleeping with the boss to shade what she did with the information.

Fine time for this realization to surface. *Before* she'd started kissing him would have been better.

Through some effort of will she'd never possessed before, she pulled free of his delicious embrace and stepped back, hoping like hell her face wasn't broadcasting how much she hated having to do so.

"Forgive me if I gave you the wrong impression," she said smoothly and tucked a lock of hair behind her ear with feigned casualness. "But that wasn't a precursor to jumping into bed. I was curious about what kissing you would feel like. My curiosity is satisfied and now we should continue our field research."

God, she sounded like a sanctimonious prig, as if she routinely kissed men for curiosity's sake and then walked away unaffected. So not true. Not only did she not recall her last kiss, she was pretty sure she'd been ruined for kissing other men ever again.

"No problem," Xavier said, his expression blank. "My mistake."

For once, Laurel was thrilled he'd maintained his cool. How crappy would that be, to finally rattle him with her backpedaling?

Her own hands were shaking from the influx of adrenaline that had nowhere to go and she'd have liked nothing more than to sweep him back into a passionate embrace. "I appreciate your graciousness."

He lifted an eyebrow. "Is that what it is? I heard a woman say she was done. There's no option B after that."

Laurel blinked. He wasn't going to remind her that he'd been the one to question whether taking this to the next level was a good idea? He'd even given her a chance to back out before he'd kissed her, which she should have taken and hadn't. But to refuse to call her on it? That was graciousness all day long and then some.

Underneath it all, Xavier was a gentleman, and dang it if that didn't just make her want him more.

Six

The next morning, Laurel swallowed her pride and tracked down Xavier in his office with the sole intent of finding out how badly she'd botched everything the night before.

It wasn't exactly bearding the lion in his den—Xavier was more of a lion statue. When he glanced up in response to her knock, his blank expression hadn't changed from last night.

Great. They were back to being at odds, then. She'd have to fix that or she'd never get the dirt she needed. Her problem was that she hadn't been prepared for how much kissing Xavier would affect her. Her plan to get him alone outside the office hadn't worked out quite like she'd hoped. If anything, they were *less* cozy than they'd been before.

"Did you need something?" he asked.

"I have to apologize for last night," she blurted out,

which had not been even number ten or twelve on the list of things she'd meant to say.

What did she have to apologize for? It was her right to back off if she wanted to. The problem was that she hadn't wanted to. She genuinely liked him, which might be her biggest stumbling block at the moment.

He lifted a brow with that maddening calm. "For what?"

"Because we never really talked strategy. We got… distracted."

"That we did." He leaned back in his chair and swept a hand at the empty chairs near his desk to indicate she should pick one. "Tell me what you thought of the exhibit."

Something pinged through Laurel's chest as she absorbed that he wasn't going to punish her for backing off last night. He'd even repeated "we" as if it was partially his fault, when in reality, Laurel had been the one to push him toward a cliff he hadn't seemed terribly eager to fling himself off of. At least, not until he'd jumped and then masterfully taken control of that kiss.

Bad thing to be thinking about. His lips pursed slightly as he waited for her response, and the memory of the way that man's mouth felt on hers sliced through her again with a muscle memory that centered in her core.

Her face flushed and she scrambled into one of the chairs, hopefully folding herself into it before he figured out how much that kiss was *still* affecting her.

"The exhibit was interesting," she began, praying her mojo would magically appear. "But I didn't like it as a fundraiser."

"Why not?"

She shrugged. "No one really wants edible art. To assume you'll sell pieces to wealthy patrons as the main means of generating donations is faulty logic."

"But the cost of admission was nothing to sneeze at." Xavier's dark blue eyes narrowed as calculations scrolled across his expression. "Surely ticket sales will bring up the total figure."

Yes, *this* was the conversation they should have had last night, but instead, she'd gotten all caught up in the vibe. "Doesn't work that way. The venue wasn't free unless the art gallery gave the autism group a block of time as a donation. Sometimes they do, but it's pretty rare, particularly if the event occurs during normal business hours. Because then the gallery is dealing with lost sales, as well, right?"

"Right. But they benefit from the publicity. So it can be a win-win situation to write off the loss."

God, the man was sexy when he was using his brain. She loved watching him think, loved how he woke up her blood with nothing more than a well-turned phrase. The best of both worlds—Xavier was smart *and* gorgeously built.

Why couldn't she have met him under different circumstances?

Shaking that off, she tapped the desk for emphasis. "There's still the cost of the buffet and bar. Again, possibly it was all donated, but that's even more unusual. Catering companies get requests for donations all the time, so they typically deny everyone in order to be fair. It's more common to pay event expenses out of donations."

"That seems counterintuitive," Xavier argued and leaned forward on the desk, folding his hands over the paperwork he'd been reviewing when she walked in. "The more money you spend, the less goes toward the cause. I don't like that at all."

She couldn't help but smile at his enthusiasm. Or what passed as such when it came to Xavier. Some people jumped around when excited. He leaned on his desk. But it was a victory nonetheless, since she had his absolute attention and she got to look at him as much as she wanted solely because they were talking.

The awkwardness from last night had completely vanished, thank God. Maybe she was finally getting it together.

"It's an age-old quandary, Xavier. That's why you hear so much about the percentage of a charity's funds that go to administrative costs versus how much is allocated to actual research or whatever. Do you want someone subpar running your charity who can't get a job anywhere else and is willing to work for a crappy salary? Or do you want someone of your caliber, with CEO experience, running it? You're not free, either."

His brows formed a line as he contemplated that. "Point taken. So our fundraiser needs to have low overhead and the probability of higher donation amounts."

"Pretty much."

She eyed him, trying to gauge how easily she could segue into the subject of fraud without tipping him off. The problem was, she didn't want to investigate that right now. The fundraiser discussion was much more fun and had fewer potential land mines.

Except that wasn't the sole reason she was here. Laurel squared her shoulders. Her career was at stake and so were the lives of the people being taken advantage of by a charity professing to be doing good.

That was the reason she was here.

"Sorry if this is stepping outside of bounds, but how do you not know all this?" she asked. "Isn't your last name the same as the woman who founded this place?"

"Yeah." It seemed as if he might clam up after that, but then he said, "It's not my world. It never was. I had to bury myself in diamonds to survive at LeBlanc. The jewelry business is not for the fainthearted."

"But these are basic principles," she said cautiously, feeling out how to proceed when she didn't want to be treading this ground in the first place. "Basic accounting. Surely you've glanced at LBC's books in the few months you've been here."

He shrugged. "Once or twice. Accounting is boring. I have people for that, here and at my real job."

The relief that poured through her shouldn't have been so swift and sharp. It didn't prove anything. He could be lying. But she didn't think he was. And if not, then he probably didn't have any idea about the fraud going on.

Alleged fraud—or, at least, it was until she found concrete evidence.

When she did, people would go to jail. People she'd likely spoken to and smiled at in the breakroom. The charity would probably be forced to close. If LBC somehow escaped that fate, donations would likely dry up and Val would be out of a job. He'd seemed like a good person in the interview, and whatever happened to LBC would affect Xavier, too, especially if whatever she found implicated his brother.

Xavier wouldn't have too many charitable thoughts toward the messenger, either.

That put a sickening swirl in her stomach she hadn't anticipated.

Why had she thought going undercover would be a good idea again? The sooner she found what she needed, the better.

She had to get out of here before she started caring about the people more than the story.

* * *

Laurel's discussion with Xavier ended up being cut short due to an emergency in the kitchen with a small fire that one of the volunteers had accidentally started. No one was hurt and the fire department arrived well after the flames had already been extinguished.

It was still a timely reminder that playing with fire wasn't a good plan.

In the name of her ethics, she should stay away from Xavier. Except that made it hard to do either of her jobs, which put her in a terrible quandary.

Once the fire department finished checking the immediate area to be sure the danger had passed, they left. Quite a few people, Xavier included, pitched in to clean up the mess from both the fire and the subsequent traffic in the area. It was the perfect time for Laurel to steal away so she could do a little sleuthing.

Adelaide kept her desk spotless, with a square box of tissues in the right-hand corner and a lone pen holder on the left, an unusual placement unless the owner of this configuration was left-handed like the new manager. Laurel had noted that the first day.

The odds of Laurel figuring out how to break into the woman's computer were about zero, and she didn't want to do that anyway, since any evidence she found would be inadmissible in court. Maybe the filing cabinet had something of value she could use in her story.

Laurel crossed to the squat, two-drawer beige stand-alone cabinet and pulled open the drawer. The loud screech of metal on metal crawled down her spine. Freezing, she waited to see if her presence in a place she wasn't supposed to be had just been announced. But no one materialized at the door. She gave her heart permission to start beating again and blew out a breath.

The covert part of the job she could do without. She liked the rush of knowing that she'd be the one to expose the truth. This sneaking around grated on her nerves, though. She'd compromise her position here if she got caught.

Laurel quickly flipped through the first few folders, pausing at one labeled Performance Reviews. That might be interesting. Someone could have received a bad review and decided to take it out on the charity by screwing around with the books.

She pulled the file and thumbed through it quickly, memorizing names and their scores. Since most of LBC's workforce came in the form of volunteers, there weren't that many and the file strictly held signed copies, not the full detail that was likely in digital form.

Nothing of value. Moving on. She pulled out a second file and that's when Adelaide strolled back into her office. Laurel's pulse skyrocketed.

The woman stopped short when she noticed Laurel and pushed her glasses back farther on her face. "Oh, I wondered where you were."

Casually, Laurel dropped the folder back into the drawer as if she had every right to be rifling through the woman's files. Sometimes faking that things were cool would fool other people even when they'd started out thinking something was amiss. "Is everything straightened up in the kitchen?"

"As well as can be. Jennifer is supervising the last of it and I was in the way. What are you looking for? I'll help you find it."

Busted. Laurel didn't have much room to act like she hadn't been looking for something, so she had to scramble. "That's generous. I was trying to find out what kind of fundraisers Val had done in the past. So I can find some ideas for Xavier to use. But you don't have to help. I'm fine on my own."

The lie sat awkwardly on Laurel's conscience, especially when Addy shook her head with a small *tsk* sound and gave her a smile. "Please. It's no trouble. I owe you big-time and I haven't repaid you."

"You don't owe me anything. What are you talking about?"

Instead of answering, Adelaide crossed the room and flung her arms around Laurel. Mystified, she hugged the shorter woman in return, and when Adelaide pulled away, she had genuine tears behind her glasses.

"I do! I'm not dumb. I know you were behind Mr. LeBlanc giving me this promotion. He never would have done that unless you'd prompted him and I'm just... I love this place so much and now I'm in charge. It's like a dream come true that never would have happened without you."

For some reason, that made Laurel feel worse, probably because she'd only pushed Xavier into the idea so she could get closer to him. But she wouldn't have done so if she hadn't thought Adelaide would shine in the role. "You're a natural. He just needed help seeing the forest for the trees. He's a man, isn't he?"

Adelaide nodded and rolled her eyes. "Very much so. He's not like his brother, that's for sure. Val cares about LBC and loves the people he serves. This isn't just a job, not for any of us. I don't think Mr. LeBlanc gets that."

"That's not true at all," Laurel corrected instantly. "Xavier and I went to a fundraiser last night to get ideas for LBC. He's more dedicated to this than you think."

What was she doing—*defending* him? And so quickly, too. But it didn't erase her absolute belief in what she'd claimed. Xavier did care.

When she'd last seen him, he'd been sweeping the floor alongside a few volunteers. She'd also spied him in the storeroom stacking boxes a few days ago. He didn't turn up his nose at any job, no matter how menial. That said a lot about his character.

Adelaide looked doubtful as she eased past Laurel to take her chair behind the desk as if they chatted like this every day and she always found Laurel with her hand in the filing cabinet.

"I'll have to take your word for it. Also, I don't think there's anything about fundraising in Marjorie's files. Maybe call Val? He's always got ideas."

The woman's devotion to her boss came through loud and clear, which boded well for her employment situation when Val returned to his normal position here at LBC and found that Laurel had passed her job to Adelaide. "I'm sure he does, but you're the manager. What would you do?"

Adelaide blinked so fast behind her glasses it was a wonder they didn't fly off. Had no one ever asked for her opinion before? The woman lived and breathed this place, which meant she had a vested interest in seeing it succeed. Her thoughts counted.

"I'd let the staff donate things they're good at making and auction them off," Adelaide said decisively, then glanced heavenward with a dramatic pause as if waiting for a burst of lightning from the ceiling that would fry her for being so forward. "I mean, everyone has a hobby. Like knitting or making patchwork quilts. There's a lot of downtime on some days, so we all bring our crafts to work and sit in the meal service area, so we get to see what other people can do. Some of the pieces are amazing."

The visual Adelaide had supplied unfurled in Laurel's

head and it was easy to envision the staff showing off crocheted afghans or beaded bracelets. The auction was a surprisingly good idea. She liked it instantly. The staff would be involved and thus help spread the word, plus they could advertise the wares as one of a kind.

Though the pieces would be made with love, they would not fetch high prices at an auction with donors who were used to the finer things in life. Regardless, the premise had potential, especially if Laurel goosed it a little. "It's a fantastic idea. I'll bring it up to Xavier. I'm so glad I ran into you."

Laurel edged toward the door, since that was a good segue to get her out before her guilty conscience made an appearance. The fundraiser had been on her mind but certainly wasn't the reason she'd sneaked into Adelaide's office.

"Oh, me, too," Adelaide said so enthusiastically that Laurel almost flinched. "You come by any time. I'm thrilled to have a confidante who listens to me. You're the best thing that's happened to LBC in a long time."

A *confidante*? Laurel's investigative journalist's ears perked up. "That's a huge compliment. Thank you. I am trying to help Xavier keep the wheels on. Speaking of which, would you mind if I stopped by, maybe tomorrow, to talk about some other areas for improvement?"

"Please do. My door is always open."

Laurel nodded at Adelaide, letting the other woman's infectious smile reflect in her own. The sweet lady would be a great partner in all things LBC. Much better than Xavier, whom she wouldn't have been able to stop undressing with her eyes even if someone offered her a million dollars.

Case in point: if she'd had half a brain, she could have found a friend in Adelaide much sooner, but no. She'd been too busy cozying up to the boss and letting herself get distracted.

"There you are."

Xavier's smooth, rich voice cut into her from behind and she whirled, only to get caught up in his deep gaze. He was so much closer than she'd anticipated and he reeked of masculinity, his biceps flaring out from beneath his T-shirt sleeves. She'd just seen him in his office a little while ago, but he'd been behind his desk. Now, there was nothing between them but raw need.

She breathed him in, losing herself in his potent presence as she unexpectedly relived that kiss from last night. She shouldn't be. She should…go somewhere. Or do something. What had she been about to do?

"Was I missing?" she asked and thankfully her voice didn't crack.

What was wrong with her? Why couldn't she remember that she wasn't supposed to be attracted to him?

Maybe because she'd worked so hard earlier to ease the tension, and here they were. No longer at odds.

She'd failed to consider the ramifications of being on the same side.

"I didn't see you after the fire," he said, his voice low, drawing her into his sphere where the rest of LBC didn't exist.

He'd noticed she'd ducked out? That was bad—how was she supposed to be covert if he had his eye on her?

And yet it pleased her enormously that her absence had been noted. "I was working on a fundraiser idea."

The lie flowed from her tongue far too easily. She didn't want to be good at lying to him.

"Tell me." Xavier crossed his arms and leaned against the wall, so casually sexy that her mouth went dry.

"It's Addy's idea actually. An auction."

His beautiful lips pursed. "Like where you put bachelors up on the block and little old ladies pay ten thousand dollars to have a hunky guy show up to bring them tea all afternoon?"

"Um, not exactly. But now that you mention it, that sounds intriguing." Her gaze slid down the length of his long, lean body almost automatically, and it was such a visual treat, she did it again, but this time more deliberately. "Would you volunteer?"

"Depends." One of his eyebrows quirked as he sized her up in kind, a decidedly wicked gleam climbing into his gaze. "Would you bid?"

Oh, man. This was not one of those times when honesty was in her best interests. The acrid scent of burned sheetrock and plastic still hung in the air, a pungent reminder of how easily a flame got out of control.

"Only on you."

Dang it.

That had slipped out. But it was the absolute truth, which seemed like her default around him, and it was dangerous times twelve. She couldn't keep letting herself get sucked into him, but what was she supposed to do about how he affected her—quit?

His long, slow smile spiked through her core. The vibe crackled between them, growing with intensity as the moment stretched out. It was so delicious that she forgot why she should cut it off.

She was *never* like this with men, so forward and flirty, mostly because she couldn't trust herself not to screw it up.

But with Xavier—she could be anyone she wanted. He didn't know she had the tendency to be awkward around men. With him, Laurel Dixon equaled sexy and fun.

"I thought I'd already satisfied your curiosity. Did

you come up with more questions that you have a burning desire for me to answer?" he asked, and the carnal thread running through his voice deepened.

Well, that was a leading question if she'd ever heard one.

"Maybe." God, she needed to reel it back, not vamp it up. This could not end well, but it felt as impossible to stop as it did to stuff a bullet back into the chamber once a gun fired. "The first one is—how good are you at making tea?"

He laughed, as she'd intended, and jerked his chin. "Sounds like you need to be the highest bidder in order to find out."

There were so many provocative things she could say in return and none of them were work appropriate. She *had* to back away from that cliff, the one she longed to fling herself from in order to soar right into his arms. This was just a conversation in the hallway about a fundraiser, nothing more. He wasn't serious; in reality, he'd done nothing but honor the fact that she'd been the one to cool things off last night. If she was smart, she'd keep things light, expectation free and, most important of all, impersonal.

"That's supposing that we're doing a bachelor auction when, in fact, we're not," she informed him, more disappointed than she had a right to be. "We would run out of bachelors too quickly."

"That's a shame." His blue eyes blazed with something she couldn't help but think might be disappointment. "I was really warming up to the idea."

She blinked. She had *no* business leading him on. None. It was unfair to him.

As much as she might want to pretend they were just having a conversation in the hall, there was entirely too much sizzling beneath the surface for that to be the case. Ignoring it wasn't helping and playing into it *really* wasn't helping.

She couldn't kiss him again or do anything else to act on the attraction swirling between them. If she'd been nothing more than a woman working at a charity, then all bets would have been off. Of course, if she had just been a woman working at a charity, she'd probably never have had the guts to speak to Xavier.

And she would have never willingly lied to a man she was interested in.

The entire thing made her sick to her stomach, but it was too late to backtrack now. And it was reprehensible to keep flirting with him when she hadn't told him the truth. She couldn't do that to someone she'd come to like more than she should.

"If you're on board with the idea of an auction, great," she said hoarsely, her throat tight with the realization that she couldn't have her cake and eat it, too. "You can help by talking to your friends and business associates about donating items. Instead of bachelors, the theme is One of a Kind. The more expensive, exclusive and special the items you talk them into donating, the better. Your crowd will love the idea of bidding on things they can't get anywhere else."

He nodded, seemingly unaware of the shift that had just occurred. Good. The less she had to talk about it, the better.

"I can do that. It's a good idea."

That small bit of praise meant more than just about anything else he'd said thus far. It might already be too late to avoid hurt feelings in this scenario—she just hadn't grasped that they'd be *hers*.

"Fantastic," she said as brightly as she could and

started edging away before she lost her mind. "I'll get started on it, then."

She fled in the direction of her small office and thankfully he didn't follow her.

Seven

Xavier gave Laurel breathing room, deliberately not seeking her out for several days. He'd come on too strong in the hallway after the fire. Obviously. She'd been flirty and fun for a few brief moments and then it was like he'd slammed headfirst into a brick wall.

Bam! She'd withdrawn, just like at the art gallery. It was maddening, but he'd finally figured out that the problem was his. Not hers.

He was screwing up the plan. Somehow. Thus far, he'd failed miserably at figuring out what she was hiding, and instead had discovered a woman he wanted to spend time with. A lot of time, and not just in bed. That was tripping him up.

So maybe the breathing room was for him, too.

He distracted himself by digging through business contacts and buddies from college to hit up for donations. The conversations came out stilted and too formal, so it wasn't surprising that the first few calls netted him exactly zero enthusiasm from the other end of the line. It was disastrous for more reasons than one, not the least of which was the looming deadline to earn his inheritance.

He could hear his father laughing from beyond the grave. It echoed in Xavier's mind, solidifying his grim determination to succeed. Edward LeBlanc could not be allowed to win at this chess game he'd posthumously organized, though it was easy to see that his father had set Xavier up to fail, for God knew what reason.

Xavier tried again with the next contact, but couldn't get his feet under him until all of sudden, in the middle of a sentence, Laurel's voice crowded into his head.

People don't give to fundraisers. They give to causes they believe in.

He wasn't selling anyone on the auction donations because he didn't believe in LBC's mission.

That was an unsettling realization. He didn't think of himself as a selfish person or one immune to the plight of those down on their luck. Hadn't he just helped restock the kitchen yesterday, carrying heavy bags of potatoes so Jennifer, the manager of that area, didn't have to?

Charity was in his blood. His mother had founded this place, pouring her time and effort into it. Honestly, he'd thought she'd done so out of boredom. Her husband had worked ninety hours a week; she'd needed something to do and had created a purpose for herself at the same time.

Then Val had followed her, taking up the cause when she'd retired. His brother had passion to spare, which Xavier had long dismissed as a personality flaw. Right at this moment, he might be close to admitting that his brother's inability to keep his heart off his sleeve was the reason Val ran LBC so well.

Xavier didn't have passion. He had interests. Things he enjoyed. Principles he lived by.

That obviously wasn't going to cut it here. If he wanted his five hundred million dollars, he had to be better than this, better than Val. He had to be like… Laurel.

She had passion. It had spilled over when she talked about her work at the women's shelter. Actually, she dripped conviction no matter the subject: Jolly Ranchers, the auction, Adelaide taking over management. Even her one-kiss-and-done speech had been firm, with no room for argument—the difference there being that he had a vested interest in changing her mind.

He pushed back from his desk and went in search of Ms. Dixon.

Her office was on the other side of the building, the only one that had been available once she'd given Marjorie's office to Adelaide. But she wasn't inside and her chair had been pushed up under the desk like she'd planned to be gone awhile, as opposed to having run to get coffee or something. Stymied, he scouted around for her and finally found her in one of the conference rooms.

She stood at the head of the long table talking to four extremely rapt audience members—volunteers from Northwestern University by the look of them. They were all young and wore expensive clothes that were deceptively casual. The university supplied a large number of LBC's volunteers, but this was the first time he'd realized that Laurel chipped in to help with their orientation.

Instead of interrupting her, he crossed his arms and leaned against the doorjamb to listen. And look. He wasn't blind; her sable hair hung down around her shoulders, so vibrant it was almost a living thing. He'd love nothing more than to be given an invitation to put his hands in her hair. Even brush it, something he'd never done in his life to a woman. But her hair begged to be explored.

Who could blame the newbie volunteers for hanging on her every word? The woman was gorgeous, articulate and so animated that his attention never wavered.

"So that's what we do here," she concluded. "Give people hope. The moment you start thinking that LBC is about food, that's when you lose sight of the person behind the mouth. Sure, food is important. Critical. But so is understanding what it represents. And for many of the guests, it's hope."

The four volunteers applauded and Xavier very nearly followed suit. But then she glanced up to see him standing there. A smile spread across her face that wiped all functional thought from his brain.

"A rare treat for you all today," she said and lifted a hand to indicate Xavier. "Mr. LeBlanc himself has come by to say hi."

The volunteers swiveled to take his measure, one immediately launching to his feet to cross the room and shake his hand enthusiastically. "I'm Liam Perry, sir. My father runs Metro Bank and has long been a customer of LeBlanc Jewelers. It's an honor to meet you."

"Simon Perry is your father?" Xavier asked needlessly, because of course he was. There was only one head of Metro Bank with the last name of Perry.

The kid nodded as if it was a perfectly reasonable question. "Yes, sir."

It was just that Xavier had always considered Simon Perry a peer and contemporary. Maybe not precisely the same age as Xavier, but close. And yet, the man had a college-aged son and probably other kids, too. A wife, most likely.

The concept of a family scared the mess out of him. Val's wife was pregnant and even that seemed like it had happened too soon, too fast. His brother seemed okay with it, but Xavier had never felt *ready* for something like that. And meeting Simon Perry's adult son brought it home in a different way. How did you get to a point where it didn't feel like you were signing up to get it wrong for the next two decades?

Parenting was a recipe for failure all day long. All at once, he wondered if Laurel worried about being a failure as a parent like he did. Even if she did, that did not make them alike, as she'd tried to insist was the case at the art gallery the other night.

Xavier shook off the weird revelations and made small talk with the Perry boy and the other volunteers for a minute. Then he hung out near the table while Laurel sent her charges off to Jennifer in the kitchen, where they'd be spending the afternoon prepping the evening meal.

Once they were finally alone, she contemplated him. "To what do I owe the pleasure?"

"I can't attend the orientation of new volunteers in my own charity if I want to?" Up close, she smelled like vanilla and citrus, which he would not have said went together. On her it became a magical blend that was downright erotic. "Speaking of which, when did you become the go-to for that?"

She lifted one shoulder. "I do whatever needs to be done. Marcy normally does orientations but she's taking her daughter to have her wisdom teeth extracted. So I volunteered."

These felt like things Xavier should know. It was Adelaide's job to manage the day-to-day operations, but he'd bet money Val knew who did orientations on a regular basis, plus the name of the woman's daughter. His brother would have already ordered flowers to be sent to the girl and no one would have ever introduced Val to volunteers as Mr. LeBlanc.

Yet that was the only part of this whole scenario that had felt natural to Xavier. Everyone called him Mr. LeBlanc. Xavier was too personal. Plus his name had a faintly exotic quality better suited to someone who frequented hookah lounges in Turkey and backpacked the Himalayas. Someone adventurous and irresponsible. Not the head of a near-billion-dollar corporation.

He wasn't dealing diamonds today, though. And he needed a shot of something to get him out of his fundraising slump—Laurel. How she'd become the answer, he didn't know, but he did trust his gut and it was screaming at him to embrace the idea of partnering with her.

Going it alone hadn't worked. Time for Plan B.

"Where did you get that speech?" He jerked his head toward the front of the room where she'd been standing when she told the volunteers not to forget the people behind the mouth. "Is that part of the orientation package and you were just reading it?"

"No. It's mine," she admitted freely with a sunny smile. "I just made it up. Because it makes sense. The volunteers don't necessarily want to be here in the first place, so I try to help them see what we do is more than slapping some food into a person's hand."

Slightly agape, he stared at her. "The volunteers don't want to be here? That's a new one on me. Isn't that the very definition of the term *volunteer*?"

"You would think. But a lot of times, they're fulfilling some type of requirement to get their degree or to earn a badge. Their place of employment encourages it, maybe. There are all sorts of reasons they end up here, and rarely is it because they have a burning desire to hang out with a bunch of homeless people."

All of this was so foreign, as if Laurel had started speaking in tongues. How had he never discovered this fact or thought to ask questions about the people who did the work at LBC? He'd been pretty focused on fundraising because that had been the stipulation in the will, but Laurel had just uncovered a whole new dimension to running this place that he'd left previously unexplored.

Probably his lack of engagement explained his lack of conviction about LBC's mission. If only he'd fully listened to Laurel's point about that from the beginning.

But he was here now. Listening. Absorbing.

"You're here hanging out with homeless people on purpose."

"I'm not a volunteer," she reminded him. "I choose to work here because it means something to me."

That was the line he needed to press. Deliberately, he shut the door to the conference room and leaned on it. Interruptions of any sort could wait. "What does it mean? Tell me why you believe in LBC."

"So you can write it down and repeat it?" She arched a brow that said she had his number and it was zero. "Tell me why *you* believe in LBC. What makes you walk through the doors every day?"

Money.

The word sprang to his lips but he couldn't spit it out. It was a cold, hard truth that money made the world go 'round. But he had money and Laurel asking the question forced him to reevaluate. What he wanted was his *due*. What he'd already thought he'd earned by running LeBlanc Jewelers the way he'd hoped would earn his father's approval.

Instead, upon his mentor's death, Xavier had been

handed a task that was nearly impossible because he lacked the fire needed to complete it. And the woman he'd hired to be his ace in the hole wasn't biting. She wanted *him* to figure it out.

So he would.

"I walk through the doors because I need to prove that I have what it takes," he told her with biting honesty. "I've been successful at everything I've tried, until now, and I cannot let this defeat me."

Her soft smile caught him sideways and he let it pour through him until he was filled to the brim.

"Exactly," she whispered. "Now imagine you're on the other side of the counter and think about what you just said from the perspective of someone who needs LBC's help."

Transfixed by her voice, he shut his eyes and did as she asked, letting the sheer helplessness of being unable to complete this fundraising task rush through him. He was no longer a CEO with all the privileges, headaches and responsibilities that came along with the role, or even a son whose father had forced him to confront his own weaknesses. He was a man who knew what it felt like to have odds stacked against him, to have no one to depend on but himself and no hope.

Laurel's soft touch nearly unglued him but he didn't open his eyes as she slid her hand into his and squeezed.

"It's okay that you're hungry and broken," she murmured, speaking to him as if he were one of the homeless masses. "I'm here. You don't have to figure this out all by yourself. Let me feed you. Then you'll have the strength to figure out where to go from here."

Yes. He held on to her hand like a lifeline, absorbing the truth she'd so eloquently revealed. He didn't have to do this alone. Neither did the hungry people of Chicago.

LBC cared enough to see the real need—and it wasn't food. It was the recovery of an individual's soul when all seemed lost. It was renewed belief in yourself.

He could sell that. Dear God, could he sell that.

His lids flew up and the look radiating from Laurel's silvery-gray eyes walloped him in places he didn't know existed. Did she fully get that she'd been talking him through his own demons as much as she'd been describing the plight of the people LBC served?

And did he really want to ask? The answer might open up dimensions to their relationship that he wasn't ready for. Neither did he care overly much for the idea of being knocked flat again if he tried to take things up a notch.

"Where did all of that come from?" he asked, his voice tight with emotion he couldn't control. "You've been here for five minutes. I've had a peripheral view of LBC for years and couldn't have articulated that so clearly."

"It came from here." She tapped her heart using her free hand without breaking their connection. "Because it's my story, too. I refuse to be defeated, but determination alone doesn't cut it."

Yesterday he would have argued with her, but today… "I'm starting to see that point."

Neither could he deny that she might have been spouting God's truth about how similar the two of them were. How else could she have verbalized the contents of his soul so easily?

"You know what hell is to me?" she asked him. "Having no one to count on. No one to support me when I've been kicked to the curb. Finding that helping hand is what gives me the strength to take the next step."

Okay, that part wasn't the same. But maybe it should be. That was the gist of this whole discussion. Determination was only the first step, and you could be determined all day long not to starve, but to prevent that, you had to take the hand of the person offering assistance.

Or in his case, he couldn't let go of the person already holding his hand.

Suddenly it all seemed so clear. Laurel had been stand-offish because she knew he had issues with trust. She could read him like a book, had proven that just now. How hard would it have been for her to pick up on the fact that he hadn't been totally up front about his interest?

God, he was a moron. Of course she sensed his reticence and it had fueled her own. That's probably what had tripped his suspicions in the first place. The woman had been nothing but an asset from day one and he'd bumbled around, ignoring the partnership she'd offered. The same one she'd *told him* he needed, and he'd blown it off like she couldn't possibly join him on his island of one.

His father had done a bigger number on him than he'd realized. He couldn't fully trust Laurel to work on his fundraiser, couldn't trust her enough to be all-in with his attraction to her, couldn't trust his gut.

But he could trust the sizzling chemistry between them. That had always felt exactly right.

So he reeled her in, slowly, giving her plenty of time to clue in to his intent in case she still wasn't on board with what he'd come to realize was inevitable between them. Her eyes flared as she got caught up in his gaze. Heat climbed between them, searing the air.

"Xavier," she murmured. "We can't."

"We can," he assured her but stopped just short of sweeping her deep into his embrace in deference to her protest, opting to brush the back of his hand down her cheekbone, instead. "Not here. But soon."

She shook her head, her cheek grazing his knuckles repeatedly, but she didn't pull away. "Then *I* can't. It's—"

"Shh. I get it. You're worried about the fact that we work together." Her skin felt like poetry and he wished he had the words to describe the way touching it made him feel. "Don't be. I'm only here for a blip and then Val will be back. Until then, we're going to do this fundraising task together. It only makes sense that we'll eventually give in to this *thing* we both feel. Why wait?"

"Because *I'm* not going to give in," she countered fiercely. "You're riding high on emotions, not logic. You've let yourself be swept up in the moment."

"Exactly!" Finally, everything had clicked into focus for him and this was the moment she picked to be obtuse? It actually made him laugh. "I've never been swept up by emotions. Never. This is a first for me. Don't kill it. Help me embrace it."

"Xavier—"

"No, Laurel, don't. I need you. Let me be passionate about this. Let me romance you while we're working on the fundraiser. I'm probably going to suck at all of the above, so you'll have to tell me when I'm screwing up." He smiled, pulling one from her, too. "What breathing woman would turn *that* down?"

Somehow, she managed to laugh and shoot him a dubious smirk at the same time. "If you'd let me get a word in edgewise, I—"

"Will say yes." He nodded once and tipped her head up to brush a thumb across her bottom lip. She didn't pull away, and in fact, leaned into his touch with a smile. It was enough.

Flying high on that small bit of acquiescence, he fused their mouths together, drawing her into an instantly deep kiss. Her squeak of protest died when she eagerly met his tongue in a hot clash of need. Her arms clamped around him, fingers sliding along the back of his neck as she held on, urging him forward.

He took the prompt and hefted her more solidly into his arms, reveling in the feel of her body snug against his. Yes, that was the theme of this kiss. *Feel.* He wanted to feel her skin, her hair, her hands racing down his body, but he settled for this fully clothed kiss in the conference room of LBC.

There was plenty to experience. Laurel tasted like the best combination of sweetness and heat as she kissed him. Apparently, he hadn't situated her properly enough for her liking because she burrowed deeper into his arms, her hips aligning with his so perfectly that it knocked all the air from his lungs. God, she was something. A live wire that electrified his whole body. If he didn't stop now, he feared his hair would end up singed.

He didn't stop. He tilted her head to find a new angle and it was so much better that he couldn't help letting his hands wander to her amazing backside. It was firm in his palms, promising that she would be spectacular naked. Not that he'd ever thought otherwise. But with that small preview, his need for her shot into the red.

"Laurel," he muttered huskily as he pulled back to rain nibbley kisses along her jaw. "Dinner. Me and you. Tomorrow night."

Her answering breathy sigh sounded like a yes to him. He nibbled on her earlobe, gratified to feel her sharp intake of breath as her chest expanded against his.

"Xavier, I—" She gasped as he sampled the skin below her ear, sucking on it probably a little too hard to leave it unmarked, but oh, well.

He liked the idea of Laurel wearing his lip marks. But it sounded even better to hide them beneath her clothing. It would be a secret that only the two of them knew. Carefully, he drew her blouse off one shoulder, following the line of her collarbone with open-mouthed kisses. Her body swayed toward him and he steadied her with one hand to the small of her back.

That creamy expanse of shoulder that he'd been dreaming about since the art gallery beckoned, and he abraded it with his mouth. Her hands came up to grip his T-shirt and then twisted, yanking him closer as more of those breathy sighs ruffled through his hair.

When he lifted his mouth, the red mark wasn't any bigger than a dime, but it gave him an enormous sense of satisfaction just the same. "After dinner, I want to put more of these marks on you. On your thighs. At the small of your back. The curve of your breast."

Her eyelids fluttered closed in an apparent quest for fortification. He hoped she didn't find it because he wanted her defenses down. He wanted her open and affected, wearing nothing but her enthusiasm for life.

"You can't say things like that," she whispered.

"Because it's inappropriate?"

"Because it makes me want that!" She blew out a frustrated breath. "This is all wrong. I'm not supposed to want you this much."

He couldn't help but grin. "I'm really not seeing the problem, then. Just let me take you to dinner. No pressure. I need a plus one. For a thing at Val's house. Very casual, other people there. No chance I'll drag you into a back bedroom and ravish you."

Or rather, there was a 100 percent chance he'd do exactly that if she gave him the slightest sign it was something she'd welcome, but she didn't have to know that. For some reason, she was holding back, probably because she still thought she sensed his hesitation. He couldn't let her think he continued to have suspicions about her when he was trying so hard to be different.

"Come on, Laurel," he pleaded, letting his expression convey what was going on in his head. "Just say yes. I promise I will keep my hands off you if that's what you want. We can just spend time together. I would enjoy that. If you would, too, I'll pick you up tomorrow night at seven."

"I should say no." But she shook her head with a laugh that didn't sound at all like a no. "You promise it's just dinner and nothing more?"

"Cross my heart." Xavier pressed his sudden advantage by dropping a quick kiss on her upturned cheek and then releasing her. "See? I can stop touching you if you tell me to."

She stepped back, her face flushed as she resituated her blouse. "I shouldn't go. But okay."

That was such a hard-won yes that he broke into a huge grin. There was no reason not to let her see how happy she'd just made him, so he didn't temper it.

He had thirty-six hours to figure out how to break down the remainder of her objections. Thirty-six hours to learn everything he could about how to romance a woman after he'd already been an idiot. Thirty-six hours to convince Val he'd love to host a dinner party for Xavier and his date because that was the only invitation she'd accept.

After the hurdles he'd just leaped over, all of that should be a piece of cake.

Eight

The next day, Xavier left LBC at noon to attend a seminar in uptown Chicago. The moment he walked out the door, Laurel sneaked into his office.

She had to find *something* she could use for her story. Anything. As long as it was concrete enough to submit her resignation before seven o'clock tonight. Then she could feasibly go on this date he'd tempted her into accepting. Otherwise, she *had* to cancel, as much as the thought of not spending the evening with Xavier made her eyes sting with unshed tears.

Yeah, she was a crappy, weak person who'd totally given into temptation. She should have stood her ground, refused to engage. Definitely she shouldn't have let him kiss her, but holy cow, how could she have stopped herself? The man had some kind of secret power that rendered her mute and stupid.

And she really wanted to go on the date. Like, a lot.

Men like Xavier didn't ask her out. They didn't notice her at all. But he had. And it was screwing with her head.

As she ducked through the door of his office, she noted he'd left his laptop, but it was shut and would require his credentials to unlock. That was fine. She'd find something in his filing cabinet. But as she flipped through the file folders, the worst sense of déjà vu slowed her fingers.

What if he caught her in here like Addy had done when Laurel had been snooping in her office? Telling him the truth under these circumstances would kill her, especially after everything that had happened yesterday when she'd forgotten that she was undercover. When he hadn't let her tell him the truth. She'd tried!

That scene in the conference room had been 100 percent Laurel, no holds barred, baring her true self and begging for Xavier to do so in kind. And he'd responded to that with something amazing. He'd been so deep and personal she'd hardly been able to keep her wits about her.

Kissing him had been a natural segue, just like his request to extend the vibe over dinner. Totally reasonable, assuming everyone in the room had been on the up-and-up. It had taken every ounce of will in her to say no and then he'd gone and done the one thing she could agree to—promising her it was just dinner and he'd keep his hands off. It was the only stipulation that would have passed her ethics test.

Well, that or calling off the investigation.

Her hands froze as she filtered the concept through her beleaguered senses.

What if she did that? What if she said forget it and gave up her investigative journalist hat in favor of Charity Worker Laurel? She had a legit job here at LBC. No one had to know she'd started her stint under false pretenses, only that she'd continued it for all the right reasons—to help people. She'd just be doing it in a slightly different way.

Then she could date Xavier without fear. What would that be like?

The thought of throwing away her entire professional career made her heart hurt, though. She couldn't stop digging. LBC had a bad apple somewhere. If she gave up, who would expose the fraud? It was even more unethical to abandon the fight strictly so she could sleep with Xavier and avoid a guilty conscience. Her investigation had merit and at the end of the day, he was just a man.

Except he wasn't.

Xavier was special—she could feel it when he held her hand, see it in his gaze when he looked at her. He made *her* feel special, like he'd been pulled into her orbit instead of the other way around. They could have something amazing and she'd never get to experience it because she'd boxed herself into a corner.

Blinking back the moisture that insisted on gathering at the edges of her eyes, she forced herself to flick through the file folder from front to back. Nothing jumped out. Thank God.

She shut the drawer as quietly as possible and went on to the next, then the next, pretending she was being as thorough as possible when deep down, she knew *haphazard* would be a better term for this investigation technique. What was wrong with her?

Really, the best strategy would be to find solid evidence, get out and never darken the door of LBC again. If she didn't see Xavier every day, she wouldn't want him so badly. The man even smelled like erotic suggestion. His aftershave had some kind of earthy note to it that made her think of sex. Or maybe that was just because *he* was that potent and pretty much any time she came in contact with him, images of the two of them twined together sprang to mind.

Oh, who was she kidding? She thought of that even when he wasn't in the room. She'd said yes to dinner because she'd secretly hoped some magical solution would present itself that would allow everything to work out.

Xavier's office had nothing she could use, no obvious hint of fraud lying around for her to find. Bummer. She had four hours to decide whether or not to stand him up for their date or go anyway while pretending that it was "just dinner." Instead of weighing that out, she ended up using those four hours to berate herself for letting her feelings for Xavier get to this point.

Bottom line—it was already too late. Her investigation had been irrevocably compromised.

Now what? Jump into Xavier with both feet and see how everything shook out? It was entirely possible that she'd never find evidence of fraud. Then she'd have given up this chance with Xavier for nothing.

While her conscience battled it out, Laurel got dressed for a casual dinner at Val's house because she'd already agreed to it. It would be bad form to cancel at this late hour, right? She could always invoke the hands-off rule; Xavier had said it was her call.

But when she opened the door at seven, the man on her doorstep took her breath. Xavier wore the hell out of a long-sleeved Henley the same color as his eyes and dark jeans that hugged the lines of his body so nicely she could almost feel the drool forming in her mouth.

"Just to be clear," she said, "if I say you have to keep your hands to yourself, do I have to follow the same rule?"

"Absolutely not," he replied instantaneously, a wicked gleam spreading through his gaze as if she made comments of that nature all the time and he liked it. "You don't have any rules. Not one. You feel free to touch me whenever and however you want."

"Noted. So, I guess we should stop all the make-believe and admit that this is not just dinner."

This was Xavier's inherent danger. She had no filter around him, because he made her brave. Every time he got within two feet of her, she forgot to be awkward and she could not possibly express how much she appreciated that.

"I don't know what you're talking about." Xavier spread both palms in the air in the classic hands-off gesture. "Val's having a get-together, and since he's going to be your boss at some point, it's a chance to socialize ahead of time. I was just invited because he's my brother. We'll eat and there will be some conversation. If you want to read into that solely because I'm imagining what you look like under that dress, I can't stop you."

Her smile shouldn't be so wide. In fact, she should take him to task for being so forward, but the time for that had long passed. "I've got on a matching pink panties and bra set that I bought to wear the next time I had a hot date. I figured it was time to pull it out since it's been sitting in the bag for something like six months."

The heated gleam in his gaze went thermonuclear. "I can envision it perfectly. Shame that's all I'm going to get to do, since this is just dinner."

Somehow, his insistence on maintaining their artificial distance despite her provocative comments put her in a daring mood. It was Friday night and she could separate her personal life from work. Plus, there was no guarantee she'd ever have to worry about the results of her investigation.

Especially if she kept up the half-hearted techniques

she'd used thus far. She'd really have to give herself a stern talking-to. Tomorrow.

Until there was something to worry about, there was no reason to keep refusing to explore what might be a really good thing with Xavier. Was it so bad to ignore the complications for a few hours?

She made an iron-clad deal with herself: if she did find anything, she'd bring it to him first and ask permission to report on it. If he was the kind of man she thought he was, he'd be glad she'd done so and agree to the story. She refused to believe he'd brush it under the carpet, but if he did, then she'd know he wasn't a man she could fall for, and she'd have every right to break the story without his consent. That was the best she could do under these circumstances.

As of right now, she wasn't an investigative reporter. She was Laurel Dixon, a woman with a great man on her doorstep who wanted to take her to a get-together at his brother's house.

Val lived in River Forest, which was so far from Laurel's tiny clapboard house it might as well be in Timbuktu. The gorgeous, sprawling home her future boss shared with his wife defied description. Laurel drank in the enormous trees and manicured lawns as Xavier wheeled his slick sports car up the drive.

So much for pretending this was a normal date with a nice guy she'd met at work. Of course, that had pretty much flown out the window the moment she slid into the buttery leather seat of the Aston Martin Xavier drove that probably cost double the amount of her college education.

"I'm guessing your house could give this one a run for its money," she commented wryly as the car slowed to a stop by the massive double front door.

Xavier glanced her. "I wasn't aware there was a contest. If it's age, then no, Val's house wins. It's historic. Not my thing, but he loves it."

Obtuse on purpose to steer the conversation away from the vast wealth of the LeBlanc family? Unnecessary. She knew they had a lot of money; after all, he'd picked her up for the art gallery gala in a limo—and she *could* read. Did he honestly think she'd never Googled him?

"No contest. It just occurs to me that I'm not in Kansas anymore."

"Does the money bother you?" he asked quietly as he switched off the car.

Silence fell inside the small, cockpit-like interior as she contemplated his face, made so much more intriguing by the landscape lighting that had thrown it into half shadows. "I just forget about it on occasion. At work, you wear casual clothes and it's hard to think of you as anything other than the guy I saw with a broom in his hand after a fire."

"That's the nicest thing anyone's ever said to me."

She rolled her eyes. "I'm being serious."

"So am I." He reached out and tipped her chin up to lay a brief kiss on her upturned lips, then immediately released her. "I'm not going to apologize for that. But I do promise to keep my hands off for the rest of the evening."

Her lips tingled as she stared at him, wishing he hadn't retreated so fast. "What if I don't want you to do either one?"

"Then you say the word," he murmured, his gaze catching hers in a tangle of heat and promise. "I'll give you a personal tour of my house. We'll start in the foyer, where I'll back you up against one of the marble columns as I strip you. I want to see your skin against it. Maybe next I'll introduce you to the couch in the library.

It's overstuffed, so plush you'd disappear into it, and it's a shame it never sees any action since it's wide enough for two. There's a skylight and I think it's perfectly positioned to spill moonlight all over you. I'd like to kiss every place it touches."

She shuddered as that image buried itself in her core and started simmering. "Stop. You had me at *then*."

He laughed, the low rich sound tumbling through her already-stimulated erogenous zones. "I've only just gotten started. I have a big house."

"I'll keep that in mind." That might take some effort when it was all she could think about. As he'd probably intended. The next few hours would be spent in extreme anticipation and she honestly couldn't remember a time when she'd been more enthralled by a man. "I didn't realize you were so poetic."

"I'm not." He contemplated her for a moment. "I'm only dictating what I see in my head when I think about you."

Geez. They hadn't even gotten to the really real date part of the evening and already he'd given her plenty of reasons to ditch the get-together. "How am I supposed to go hang out with actual people and make intelligent conversation when you say things like that to me?"

"The same way I've been functioning at LBC when I know you're across the building in an office where hardly anyone seeks you out," he told her flatly. "I have to stop myself at least once an hour from paying you a visit to see if your door would be strong enough to take what I've been thinking of doing to you up against it."

Well, then. Seemed like she'd given him the green light to share all his secret fantasies and she couldn't find a thing wrong with that. If this was how it was going to be between them now that she'd decided to treat this like a normal date, she was a fan.

"Maybe next time, don't stop yourself."

His gaze sharpened with hunger that thrilled through her. "I do believe you've officially blown my chances of concentrating at work on Monday."

She laughed, trying to decide if she should let herself be so charmed by him. "It's only fair. You blew my chances of concentrating at this shindig. I'm already thinking of a few excuses that can get us out of here early."

"I like the sound of that," he growled. "Maybe you can think of one that I can text to Val right now, and then we don't even have to go inside."

"That's…" She lost her train of thought as Xavier's hand settled into the hollow between her neck and shoulder, and his thumb brushed across her ear. "Um—we should at least make an appearance. They probably already know we're here."

He didn't release her. "Probably."

"We should go inside."

"We should."

And then he settled his mouth on hers in a long kiss that was clearly designed to untether her from her moorings, since that's what happened. She dropped into it, greedily sucking up every ounce of sensation. Their tongues clashed. The frissons of awareness and need that bloomed in her center sizzled along every nerve ending, and it was easily the most encompassing kiss she'd ever experienced in her life.

He palmed her jaw, one of his magic hands on each side, and angled her head to take her impossibly deeper still, as if he couldn't get enough. Good. She didn't want him to get enough. If he was never sated, he wouldn't stop. That *worked* for her.

He worked for her. He had something wholly unique that smoldered below the surface, something amazing and intense and profound. It called to her and she couldn't help but answer.

Far too soon, he backed off, his torso heaving with the effort. Or maybe that was hers. Hard to tell. There was a lot of touching and an inability to speak going on in Xavier's car.

"We should—" He nuzzled her ear and rained little butterfly kisses along her cheek. "Um…go—somewhere."

"Uh-huh." She tilted her head to give his questing mouth better access to her throat. "Like your house?"

He groaned, his lips vibrating against her skin. "I wish you hadn't said that. Because you really sold me on your point that we had to make an appearance. It would be crappy to just not go in. Right?"

"I guess. Maybe we can think of it as foreplay."

"Or we can have a prearranged signal. You caw like a bird and I'll meet you in the bathroom," he suggested hopefully.

"Gee, that's romantic for our first time." She elbowed him playfully and then laughed when he nipped at her shoulder. "Keep thinking."

"I'm thinking I have to get out of this car before I do something irreversible," he grumbled. "I never would have pegged you for a romantic."

Because she wasn't, and it pleased her enormously that he'd clued in to that, especially since she'd been totally kidding. But she didn't correct him. What would he come up with instead, now that she'd challenged him? She burned to find out.

Somehow they made it out of the car with all their clothing intact. Xavier held her hand as they stumbled up the front steps, whispering and giggling over secret jokes that had just become a thing between them. It thrilled her. Look what she would have missed out on if she'd stuck to her ethical guns. It would have been practically criminal to give up this breathless sense of anticipation and the grin she could not wipe off her face.

A uniformed woman with steel-gray hair ushered them inside the grand foyer and Laurel pulled her attention from the perfect curve of Xavier's earlobe so she could properly greet her soon-to-be boss if her investigation stretched out much further. Val introduced her to his wife, Sabrina, who had eyes for no one but her husband. It was sweet the way she shot him little loving looks when she thought no one was paying attention.

Laurel paid attention. Apparently, her investigative brain hadn't been completely saturated with Xavier. Somehow, there was enough heightened awareness flowing through her senses that she easily picked up on the vibes in the room. Val and Sabrina were clearly very much in love, and she had a glow about her that could create some extreme envy.

The uniformed woman passed out stemmed glasses of chardonnay but gave Val's wife a glass of deep red liquid—cranberry juice if Laurel didn't miss her guess. Laurel lifted her glass as Val made a lighthearted toast to crisp fall Friday nights. That was the kind of small moment she liked to celebrate, too. She and Val were going to get along famously.

If her investigation dragged out that long.

The thought set her back. She couldn't seem to stop wondering what it would be like if this was her real life. If she kept her job at LBC, where she could still make a difference, and kept dating Xavier until— Well, that was putting the cart before the horse.

Until what? They hadn't even slept together yet. Maybe he'd be a dud in bed.

That nearly sent her into a round of uncontrollable

laughter. Maybe the moon would turn into Swiss cheese, too. Her problem was that, so far, she liked being Laurel Dixon, charity worker, and she suspected that it was only going to get better.

"Sabrina's pregnant," Xavier said into her ear as Val's wife went to attend to a matter the caterer had brought to her attention while Val fiddled with the stereo system tucked into the entertainment center across the room.

"Oh?" It was such a personal thing to share. What was she supposed to do with that? "Should I congratulate her?"

"I'm not sure it's public knowledge."

She *really* didn't know what to do with the fact that Xavier didn't put her in the same category as *the public*. "Are you sure you should have told me, then?"

His brief smile tingled her toes. "I wanted to. It's kind of tripping me up."

"It is kind of a screwy thing," she said slowly, trying to parse out his intent. "Makes you think. I mean, not like, hey, I want one of those. But more about your own mortality."

His eyes flared with something she wished she could reach out and touch.

"Exactly," he murmured. "Though I don't know why I'm shocked that you read my mind. I guess we are a lot more alike than I had been willing to admit."

That's when it struck her that she'd finally gotten to the point where he was sharing his secrets with her—unsolicited. This kind of rapport couldn't be bought. It was gold for an investigative reporter. And it made her feel like crap that she was still lying to him about her identity.

There was a part of her that wanted nothing more than to stop the investigation cold. Right then and there. Make it vanish. It just didn't feel worth it in that moment.

Except, being undercover had been a convenient shield that allowed her to be much braver than she could credit herself with normally. Ever since her career had crashed and burned, her fear of failure was too ingrained to allow her to take chances with men. With that shield removed, would she shrivel up again, unable to have a conversation with a man who affected her as much as Xavier LeBlanc did?

Because that wasn't going to work at all.

She wanted to be this Laurel Dixon, the one Xavier shared things with because he trusted her, nuzzling her ear as he did it. She liked who she was with Xavier. She liked that he brought it out in her.

Was there a way to be both versions of herself without screwing it all up? Her track record didn't speak well for the possibility. But she couldn't stop walking down this path that had opened up to her in the span of a few glorious moments.

It was the worst dichotomy—she yearned to discover everything she could get her hands on, to turn over each rock and explore all the crannies, but she couldn't stop being afraid that very thing would cause her downfall.

She had no choice but to be *both* of those people.

Nine

Xavier had thought being around Sabrina again might be weird, since he'd dated her before Val had, but Laurel had taken up so much real estate beneath his skin, he forgot Val's wife was in the room the second she stopped talking.

Honestly, he'd never been all that into Sabrina in the first place and had moved on pretty easily after she'd dumped him. Sabrina was beautiful in the same way a frozen tundra dotted with snowy trees had appeal—the farther away you viewed it from, the better. That philosophy pretty well summed up how he'd always approached relationships. Maintaining distance came naturally as he worked ninety hours a week at LeBlanc Jewelers, and it also served to ensure women didn't get ideas about the longevity of their association with him.

He'd never thought twice about it, never missed a woman after she'd left, scarcely noticed if one never returned his calls.

Until Laurel.

She was so not his type. He'd have passed right by her as a potential lover if not for the fact that he'd been convinced she wasn't on the square. That suspicion had fueled their interaction from day one and he'd had a devil of a time letting it go, something he attributed to lingering bitterness over the way his father had forced him to jump through hoops.

But now he wasn't so sure. Seeing Sabrina again reminded him that he'd always kept women at arm's length, and not just because trust had become a scarce commodity in Xavier's world. He'd just never been that interested in diving deeper.

Until Laurel.

He had a feeling he'd be repeating that a lot over the course of the evening. Mostly because he wanted to do things differently, see how it felt to be fully engaged. To trust that things could only get better the more invested he became.

So…how did he do that?

After dinner was over, the couples moved to the casual living area off the kitchen. Laurel and Sabrina sat near each other on the long sofa near the fireplace, chatting up a storm. Val had set up camp near where Xavier stood by the double French doors leading to the covered patio that overlooked the pool. They'd been talking shop, mainly about the failing New England division under the LeBlanc Jewelers umbrella that Val had been struggling to correct. But that conversation had wound down and Xavier wasn't putting a whole lot of effort into starting a new one because watching Laurel was far more fun.

Somehow, he had to figure out how to stop automatically creating distance between himself and a woman. After the scene in the car, when it seemed he'd melted the last of her objections, he'd kind of thought everything would fall into place. Now he wasn't so sure.

"So," Val said, followed by such a long pause that Xavier glanced at him expectantly. "This is a thing, then. Between you and Laurel."

"Depends on your definition of a thing."

Xavier took a long, pointed pull from his beer. With his mouth busy, he couldn't say more and he didn't intend to. Mostly because he was still trying to work through his next steps. An audience wouldn't help.

Val didn't bother taking the hint to butt out. "A thing. As in you and Laurel are dating. Which I never saw coming, by the way. I wondered why you were so hot for me to invite you over tonight. Sabrina and I canceled our previous plans, you know."

"You shouldn't have," Xavier responded mildly. "And it's not a thing. It's…"

What was it? Complicated?

It shouldn't be. Tonight they'd turned a corner of sorts, and he couldn't wait to get Laurel alone. So why was he still here, still sorting through his strategy? This part should be a snap. He'd never had trouble getting a woman into his bed.

Except this one. It was still tripping him up. *She* tripped him up, had since day one.

Sometimes when he looked at her it felt like his brain had been sucked out of his head through his ear. What was he supposed to do about that? If he couldn't think, he couldn't maintain control, let alone ensure he could see what was coming. No surprises. No blindsides.

Of course, it didn't seem to matter how alert he tried to stay around her. She still managed to pull the carpet out from under him twice an hour.

Val's eyebrows quirked. "If it's caused you to be at

a loss for words, it's a thing. And that's why I canceled my plans. I had to see the lady firsthand who had prompted this round of finagling. Imagine my shock when you walked through the door with your new services manager."

"About that." Probably Xavier should have mentioned her role shift sooner, but it served multiple purposes to mention it now, not the least of which was a subject change. "Adelaide took over that position. Laurel is helping me with fundraising instead."

"It's like that, is it?" Val grinned, his dogged determination to stick with this subject apparent. "Keeping her close for some after-hours action?"

"No, it's not *like that*," Xavier countered fiercely and lowered his voice, one eye on Laurel in case she wasn't as involved in her conversation with Sabrina as he'd assumed. She didn't need any new excuses to throw up roadblocks. What would she think if she overheard their relationship being labeled something that she didn't agree with? "She's got a lot of great ideas and she's—I don't know. Inspiring. She makes me think about things a different way."

Wow. That had peeled off his tongue with literally no forethought, but it was pure truth. She was all of that and more. Five minutes ago, he'd have claimed that his sole focus with Laurel had to do with getting her into bed, but clearly there was more here than just sex. She did get him thinking in new directions when it came to his inheritance task. When it came to his approach to helming LBC as a whole. Was he supposed to feel so dazed to discover it, though?

"Yeah. That's what I meant. It's like that." In a totally unexpected move, Val socked him on the arm playfully, the way a brother who cared might. "She gets you fired up. When's the last time you raised your voice? Over anything? Laurel is obviously special. Just do me a favor and don't be yourself. I'd like to keep her at LBC."

"What the hell is that supposed to mean?" Xavier shot back and had to lower his voice again. Twice in one conversation? Laurel did have him twisted around—and they hadn't even slept together yet.

How much worse was all of this uncertainty going to get by dawn if he did get her into his bed tonight as he'd planned?

"Remember that she's a human being with feelings," Val said easily. "Women like it when you acknowledge their existence and take them out on dates occasionally."

"I'm here, aren't I?" he growled.

Which had pretty much been Val's point, as indicated by the look his brother gave him. "Yes, you are. Make the most of it. She's obviously good for you. Let her continue that trend."

Val broke off as Sabrina called to him to ask his opinion about moving to the patio. But Xavier held up a hand before his brother could answer.

"As much as we appreciate the invitation, Laurel and I will take a rain check on the rest of the evening, if you don't mind."

Hell if he couldn't take Val's hint. The reason he hadn't figured out his next steps yet had just crystalized—it was because he was supposed to do it *with Laurel*. This wasn't a solo journey. Besides, she'd been in the driver's seat since day one. Instead of wrestling back control, the key had to be letting go. It wasn't so hard to determine how this should work, after all. If he wanted to be different with a woman, he had to let the woman guide him.

Laurel met his gaze from across the room, and that otherworldly sensation rocketed through him again, like it had from the first. But this time, he recognized it as *connection*. She got him in ways he'd never wished for, never wanted.

It was too much. With nothing more than a look, she'd stripped him raw, exposing him, as if she could read the things written on his soul.

This was what he was supposed to embrace? It was madness.

Yet, he couldn't look away. She drew him into her chaos and he had zero desire to break free. Not when it felt like he was on the brink of something cataclysmic. The only thing he had to do was follow her.

Except he was the one who held the keys to their escape. It was on him to perform the extraction, so he said his goodbyes to his brother and Sabrina, then hustled Laurel into his car.

"That was the hastiest exit I've ever seen." Laurel's smile lit up the dark interior of the car as she let her fingers drift down his arm suggestively.

It was all he could do to grip the gearshift instead of sending his fingers on a quest of their own. "It was time to go. I have lots of evening left to fill and the things I have in mind can't be done at Val's house."

"I like the sound of that. Dare I hope that means you're taking me on a scenic drive along Lake Michigan?"

His mouth fell open a little wider than he'd have liked. "You're kidding, right?"

Her quick, sharp laugh loosened his lungs and had the odd effect of tightening everything else.

"I misspoke. What I meant to say was, where were we? I think your hand was under my dress, if I recall correctly," she said with a purr that vibrated through his erection, thickening it so hard and fast that he groaned.

His hand had been no such place, or they'd never have

gotten out of the car earlier. But who was he to argue? "Like this?"

He slid a palm along her bare thigh and skimmed under the hem of her dress, feathering her skin with his thumb as he went. When she didn't stop his progress, he kept going until his thumb brushed across the silk fabric between her legs. Pink, hopefully, as promised. He'd been anticipating getting a peek at the matching bra and panties set ever since she'd mentioned it earlier in the best sort of tease.

She sucked in a breath. The moment snapped with so much sexual tension that he was pretty sure his heart stopped.

"Something like that," she warbled so brokenly that he almost withdrew, but then she clamped her own palm down on his, grinding his hand deeper into her core. "But maybe more like this."

Yeah, that worked for him and then some. He circled the heel of his palm hard against her heat, yanking a gasp from Laurel that embedded itself in his nerve endings, enlivening them beyond anything he could stand. He wanted to touch her without the barrier of clothing in the way, without the center console of his car obstructing him from pulling her into his lap so he could do this properly.

"This is not the romance I promised you," he muttered. She deserved better, and he sure as hell could deliver something more fitting than a quick grope in the front seat like a randy teenager who didn't know a thing about a woman's body.

With a growl, he pulled his hand free and stabbed the starter button, then slung the car into Reverse. "I'm taking you to my house. If you'd prefer something else, speak now or forever hold your peace."

"I'd rather hold something else. Care to guess what it

is?" she asked saucily and slid her hand up his thigh in much the same fashion as he'd done to her, except she hadn't been driving at the time.

The side of Laurel's finger stroked his erection. It was the barest hint of a touch, but it felt like she'd encased his entire length in her warm palm and squeezed. The speedometer shot past ninety as the car careened up the entrance ramp to the freeway.

He forced himself to slow down before he killed someone and then he forcibly removed Laurel's hand from his lap. "Save that. We'll be there in less than five minutes."

Wisely, she chose not to press him and folded her hands into her lap. "I like your brother and his wife."

"Good," he said shortly. "I have zero interest in talking about them. If you're in a chatty mood, maybe you could list your favorite positions. Surfaces you favor. Water, yes or no? That kind of thing."

Her laugh washed over him. He glanced at her as he changed lanes to go around a minivan driving sixty-five in the fast lane, as if there weren't people behind them with a raging hard-on.

Laurel tapped her bottom lip as if contemplating. "I'm a fan of spooning. I don't like carpet but couldn't say if I did like something besides a mattress because I've never tried anything besides the two, and please clarify the water question. Would we be having sex in it or would you be pouring it over me?"

"Yes," he said instantly.

Water splashing down Laurel's body, droplets clinging to her pert breasts just begging to be licked off. Definitely that.

An image of her lounging on a stone ledge in his hot tub became superimposed over the previous fantasy. Yes to that, too. His mouth went desert dry as he imagined her spreading her legs for him in invitation, her head tipped back as she waited. The clear water would magnify her secrets, beckoning him to explore.

Why did Val have to live all the way over in River Forest? Civilized people lived in the Lincoln Park area. When he finally turned into his drive on Orchard Street and managed to get through the porte cochere opening to the garage without hitting anything, he considered it a minor miracle.

He left his car in the drive because it would take entirely too long to open the garage door. Would it be bad form to lift Laurel bodily out of her seat? Fortunately, she seemed to pick up on his urgency as her feet had already hit the pavement before he'd rounded the car to open her door. He chose to skip the admonishment. Next time, he'd get there in time to do the gentlemanly thing. Grabbing her hand, he led her to the door nearest the garage and ushered her inside.

She glanced around the darkened living area expectantly. "I seem to recall there was some talk about a marble column?"

"That's all the way in the front of the house," he said with a dismissive *tsk* and hustled her to the back staircase off the kitchen. "Way too far away. Forget I mentioned it. We'll tour the upstairs first."

They'd also skip the part where he was a moron because he hadn't had the foresight to give his staff the night off. No telling who might wander through the foyer while he was busy worshiping the goddess he'd brought home.

Once he got her into his bedroom, he shut the door and backed her against it. "This is oak. Close enough."

And then he sank into her lush mouth with a groan, molding it to his as he kissed her with every iota of pent-up longing. The awareness and anticipation that had begun simmering in the car in front of Val's house exploded into a firestorm that radiated outward to consume his entire body.

This was not the kiss he'd been envisioning. It was more. So much more. Never had he *wanted* so badly.

But he couldn't reel it back, couldn't think, couldn't do anything but feel. And she was doing plenty of that herself, her hands flat on his back, skimming downward to dip under his shirt to explore his bare skin.

The kiss deepened almost automatically as he devoured her, pressing into her delicious form until he scarcely knew where she began and he ended. Laurel's little moans of pleasure sang through him, heightening the experience even further. If he didn't hang on, he'd soar clear to the ceiling on an upward spiral of need.

Her mouth worked against his, sucking him deeper into this swirl of heat. She filled him with so many things: sensations, emotions, needs. None of which he recognized and neither could he stop the flood.

Still he didn't have *enough* of her inside him.

What was she doing to him? He never got this invested. Never got this *hot* for a woman. It was, indeed, madness in every sense of the word, as if his brain had been possessed.

He couldn't stop. He needed her skin bared, his hands on it. His mouth craved a taste of the curve of her breast, of the dew between her legs that would broadcast her desires.

As he slicked his hands down the sides of her thighs to grab the dress's hem, it occurred to him that he wasn't letting her guide him at all, and neither was he following. This was all 100 percent urgency and heat and uncontrollable desire. And yet…he struggled to find a problem with that. If they were both so overcome with eagerness, then there wouldn't be any room for weird otherworldly crap to distract him from what this was—sex. Only.

That worked for him. A beautiful woman in his bed he could handle. Why did it have to be anything else?

With a meaty growl, he picked her up in his arms and carried her to the bed. "We'll work on some other surfaces later."

She was too busy laving her tongue across his ear to do more than mumble, "That's a deal."

More gently than he'd have said his violent need would allow, he set her on the edge of the bed and leaned into her to kiss his way down her throat until he hit her dress. It was in his way. Not going to work. He yanked on the hem until it came free, then whisked the checkered print over her head.

"Holy hell." The moan that tore from his throat didn't even sound human, but who could blame him? "Pink is my new favorite color."

She smiled and fingered one of her bra straps, then drew it down her shoulder provocatively. "Maybe I'd look better out of it."

"That's not even possible." But then again… "I should probably check to make sure."

Her heated gaze latched onto his, holding it tight as he knelt between her legs to reach around her back. His fingers trembled with the effort not to rip the clasp apart. He didn't want to ruin it. But it wouldn't come apart. He cursed and gave up.

With a guttural growl, he ripped the hooks from their sewn-in prisons, the thread giving with little pops. "I'll buy you the contents of a Victoria's Secret tomorrow."

What use was money if he couldn't spend it when it really counted? He slid the bra free and forgot everything he'd ever learned—his name, how to breathe, whether he was supposed to direct the blood pumping through his heart. The perfection of Laurel's breasts called to him and he could do nothing else except answer.

Leaning forward on his knees, he lifted one beautiful globe into his palm and raised it to his mouth, sucking her nipple between his lips to taste. It was glorious. Her flesh hardened against his tongue as he licked the pointed peak.

She moaned and arched her back, pushing her breast against his mouth. He opened wider to take in more. Gasping, she clasped the back of his head, holding him in place with talon-like fingers, as if he might be interested in stopping sometime soon. Not happening. He could stay here for hours.

Except there was a whole other unexplored breast just begging for his attention. He switched sides and the second one was even more luscious than the first. Her nipple rolled between his teeth and he nipped at it, making her moan. *Again.* Harder this time. She cried out and squirmed closer, a stream of encouragement pouring from her mouth. *Yes, Xavier, like that, oh, yes...*over and over.

Emboldened, he pushed her back against the mattress, determined to build on that. Those pink panties taunted him. They covered the spot where he most wanted to be. Hooking his thumbs under the waistband, he yanked them down her thighs, then threw them somewhere. Didn't matter where. She wouldn't need them anytime soon.

"Beautiful," he murmured as he bent one of her knees so he could look his fill. There was nothing on earth more exciting than Laurel spread out on his bed, her thighs open wide in invitation. Her arousal grew more and more evident as glistening dew gathered under his watchful gaze.

Bending, he mouthed up one thigh and then settled between her legs to discover what she'd been hiding underneath that pink fabric. The first lick wound through his senses as he registered both her reaction and his all at once. Breathy sighs. Her erotic scent. Hips rolling. *Delicious*. Heat. His own gut tightening with long pulls of need.

The act of pleasuring a woman had never gotten him this worked up this fast. Sure, he liked the satisfaction of knowing he'd made a woman feel good, but this was different. Her cries inflamed him, shooting through his erection to the point where it was almost painful. He wanted *more*.

More Laurel, more feeling, more everything.

"I need you to come," he mumbled hoarsely against her sex, then increased the pressure and speed of his tongue to hurry things along. If she didn't slide over the edge in about four seconds, he'd… Well, he didn't know what he'd do, but he couldn't stand to be inside his own skin for much longer than that. He needed her more than anything he'd ever needed in his life, more than oxygen, blood, water.

And then she cried out as she clamped down on his neck with her fingers, her core pulsing against his tongue. He helped her draw it out, suckling at her pleasure bud until she sobbed his name.

The sound of her voice in the throes—it drove him wild. He'd be hearing that in his sleep for days. Weeks. It was better than music.

Now he could take care of himself.

He shed the clothes that he'd almost forgotten he was wearing and climbed up the length of Laurel's body, kissing everything he could reach. She'd apparently recovered enough to do some exploration of her own, her hot hands stroking down his back, over his buttocks, between his legs.

She loosely gripped his erection, brushing her thumb over the tip, and hell if that didn't almost end the party in one fell swoop. The sweet sting of his arousal sharpened so fast that he had to lock it all down so he didn't come in her hand.

"Laurel." He extracted himself with a stellar force of will he hoped he would never have to replicate. "Wait."

Blindly he fumbled in the bedside table's drawer for the box of condoms he kept there and somehow got one on without tearing a huge hole in it with his trembling fingers. This was easily the most turned-on he'd ever been, and doing anything while in the midst of this much passion didn't work so well.

He settled back between Laurel's thighs. She smiled up at him, her eyes huge and full of wonderful, mystical things. Okay, *this* worked extremely well. So well that he couldn't wait a second longer. Taking her lips in a torrid kiss, he rolled her into his arms, snugging their bodies together so perfectly that it was hard to remember a time when he and Laurel weren't in this exact position.

Everything about this felt right. Exquisite. No way it could get better. And then she took him to the next level, wrapping her legs around his, opening herself up so wide that he could easily push inside with hardly any effort. So he did.

Her tight, wet heat welcomed him and she was so ready for him that he buried himself to the hilt instantly. Light pinwheeled behind his eyelids as she closed around him, squeezing him with enough pressure to pull a groan from deep in his chest.

He needed to move. She took his thrusts and then some, undulating with him until the heat and friction drove him into the heavens. He needed an anchor, something real and weighty to keep him earthbound. *Laurel.* She was the realest thing he'd ever touched, the sole tether that held him to this world.

But as he met her gaze, something inside him snapped and he soared away on wave of sensation and heat. Laurel flew right along with him, climaxing again while he was inside her, and it was everything he'd never had in a relationship before.

Everything he'd never realized making love could be.

She'd shown him the way, after all.

The fragmented pieces of this experience swirled together into one bright moment of connection and then he shattered, coming so hard that he saw stars.

He emptied himself and let her fill him back up.

When he could see again, Laurel was lying in his loose embrace, her hair mussed around her face. He couldn't think, couldn't speak. All he could do was clutch her tighter and hope like hell that she wasn't planning on going anywhere for the next month or so. He'd only just begun to explore his recently discovered passion and Laurel Dixon was it.

Ten

Laurel had to get out of this bedroom. Now. Before the huge thing inside her cracked open and let a bunch of emotions out that she shouldn't be having.

Sleeping with Xavier had been a mistake. A giant, life-altering mistake. He didn't seem too keen to let her go, though, and frankly, she wasn't sure her bones still worked. After treating her to the orgasm of the century courtesy of his talented mouth, he'd then turned around and introduced her to the orgasm of the millennium less than fifteen minutes later. The man was *amazing*.

And if she wasn't careful, she'd ruin everything.

That's what she did. Something great happened; Laurel screwed it up. It was the world's worst cause and effect. Only this time, she was in danger of losing a lot more than solely a fraud story. Her job at LBC hung in the balance, too, and she'd only just come to realize how much she valued it.

Then there was Xavier.

She didn't want to think about how quickly and easily she could mess up, especially given the flood of things happening inside. Really, she had no business being here. But how could she have refused? Especially when she'd kind of thought it was supposed to be a hookup. No fuss, everyone got some satisfaction and no one had to think about anything other than sex.

In fact, she'd tried really hard to get some car boinking going, talking dirtier to Xavier than she ever had to a man in her life. At points, she hadn't even believed the stuff coming out of her mouth.

His response? Bring her home. Like they were a couple. And he expected her to spend the night. It felt too real, too big, too much like something she'd leap tall buildings to continue.

This was not her life. Not her real life, anyway. Undercover Laurel, sure. That girl could do anything, especially since Xavier was the one who goosed her actions. That was the world's best cause and effect. Somehow, she'd find a way to mess it up, though.

The longer she lay there, spoon-style in his strong arms, the deeper the panic winnowed.

"I can feel you winding up to flee," Xavier murmured and rubbed his lips against her temple in something halfway between a kiss and a caress. "I'm not going to let you, by the way."

His mouth made her shudder. Dear God, how could the man get her so worked up with nothing more than the brush of his lips on her skin? And her temple wasn't even an erogenous zone. Or, at least, she'd never considered it one before. Right this minute, her whole body apparently fell into the category of erogenous zone as his mouth ignited something inside her.

"You can feel me thinking about leaving?" she asked,

since it seemed as if her voice still worked. A minor miracle. Nothing else did, including her brain, because she couldn't remember why it was so critical that she get dressed. Only that she had to. "I didn't come prepared for a sleepover. It's better that I go."

That way she could keep pretending this was only sex.

Except he'd have to drive her or she'd have to find her phone and order a ride, which would probably take a million years on a Friday night in Lincoln Park. She was stuck for at least a little while.

"That's a complete lie," he countered and moved down to the hollow of her throat, sending her lashes fluttering as the spike of pleasure deepened. "You have all this bare skin I haven't explored yet. What more do you need for a sleepover?"

"Toothbrush," she managed to mutter. Somehow. Her skin had pebbled with goose bumps the moment he'd started talking about it.

"I have several extras. Next objection?"

"Are you just going to knock them down?"

"Pretty much. So you can save us both a lot of time by quitting while you're behind."

For some reason, his change-up of the saying made her smile. "Aren't you the one behind?"

"Why, yes, yes, I am." He punctuated that point by nestling his hips against her buttocks, announcing the fact that he'd regained a hard-on without saying a word. He pressed into the crevice with tiny, firm strokes that had her gasping instantly.

When his fingers started toying with her breasts, she nearly crawled out of her skin. How did he know all of the best ways to touch her?

"Xavier," she breathed, and it turned into a plea instead of a warning.

"Right here, sweetheart," he rumbled into her ear, and his hands slicked downward to hold her hips in place as he ground against her from behind. "This is your favorite position, right? I didn't get to it first because I'm a bad boy. Let me make it up to you."

She couldn't do anything but warble a moan in response. How was she supposed to refuse that? Answer: she couldn't. Not when his fingers crept toward her center, dipped inside and set up a slow rhythm that promised to pull her apart at the seams.

"I can't help but touch you," he continued in that slumberous voice that drifted through her very soul. "You're so sexy and warm, and I sort of lost my mind earlier."

"Ha," she said, or tried to. It came out more as a long sigh. "You've never lost anything, least of all your mind. I don't think I've even seen you get overly excited."

"You obviously have no idea what you do to me. I was nearly insane over how much I wanted you." His fingers played with her flesh as if he planned to do the same to her. Turnabout was fair play and all that. "Now that I've taken the edge off, I can do this for hours."

She didn't get a chance to revel in the victory of pushing him into something other than calm detachment. He underlined his promise with a particularly deep twist of his fingers that sang through her entire body. She bucked against his hand, instinctively seeking more. His other hand joined the party, rubbing in circles at her nub as he plunged into her core again. Pleasure knifed through her, arching her back, which allowed him to grind deeper against her buttocks.

The triple punch of sensations pushed her over the edge and she exploded in an exhilarating tsunami of passion, clenching around his fingers over and over. He did something magical, furled them in a way that elongated the orgasm, and the intensity ratcheted up exponentially.

He wrung so much pleasure out of her body that tears leaked from her eyes.

And then, after the brief crinkle of a condom wrapper, he plunged into her from behind, filling her so tightly, so fast, that it set off another round of ripples. He groaned into her ear as she kept closing around him, and that might have been the most erotic sound she'd ever heard.

Then he half rolled her to the mattress and began to move inside her, whipping her scarcely cooled center into a firestorm instantly. The heat raged as he pushed her further, demanding even more from her body, and he got it. She cried out as another intense climax seized her, and she came so hard that her legs went numb.

He followed her a few strokes later, his lips in her hair and his heavy body collapsing to cover hers as he pulsed inside her. They lay like that for an eternity until she became convinced that she'd passed into another dimension where this kind of pleasure happened to her on a regular basis.

"That was unbelievable," he croaked against her neck and rolled to settle her into his arms. "Even more so than the first time, and that's saying something."

Sweet air rushed into her lungs as his weight redistributed. She missed his body on hers instantly. Breathing was overrated. "That's one word for it."

"Give me another one," he said almost as a challenge.

"Looking for compliments?" she teased. "It was cataclysmic. Earth-shattering. Miraculous. Shall I go on?"

His lips grazed her cheek and she felt them curve upward. "You sound like a thesaurus."

Her insides froze and the silk sheet beneath her body turned cold in a flash. Of course she had a command of the English language. That's what an investigative reporter did—found the right words to describe the current situation.

The reminder was ill-timed. And yet perhaps apt. The longer she let herself stay here, the deeper she dug her own grave. After all, he still didn't know she was Undercover Laurel, and removing that barrier meant she lost all of this. Even if he didn't care, she couldn't be bold, saucy Laurel without a shield against failure.

"I feel you thinking about leaving again." His arms tightened around her, cutting off the flow of air to her lungs.

This time, it wasn't okay. She pushed at his arms until he realized what she wanted and released her, his gaze following her as she sat up.

"If you want to leave, I won't stop you," he said quietly. "I won't like it, but you do what pleases you."

That only made it worse. "Stop being so understanding."

"Okay."

"That's being understanding!"

Frustrated beyond measure, she pulled the sheet up to cover her bare breasts. Not that it mattered. He'd seen them plenty already. That was the problem, the thing she couldn't undo. They'd flung open Pandora's box, all right, and as advertised, she couldn't stuff everything back inside again.

She wanted to stay.

He didn't know the truth.

But this wasn't supposed to be serious. Any decision felt wrong, like a recipe for failure.

"You weren't 100 percent on board with coming here tonight, were you?" he asked, his voice betraying none of his thoughts. Even in this, she hadn't ruffled his feathers in the slightest.

"I was! Completely." She could own that all day long, and it was important for him to understand that she had never once felt coerced. But how did she explain the real reason she was flipping out? "I make my own choices. It's just... I don't know."

"I know," he announced, refreezing her heart.

"You do?" As in *everything*?

That wasn't possible. If he knew she'd taken the job at LBC under false pretenses, surely he wouldn't have brought her home and treated her like his own personal smorgasbord. Yet there was a part of her that craved to hear him say exactly that.

It's okay, Laurel. I love that you care enough to expose bad people in my organization. Have another orgasm or two.

"I think so. You just wanted to see how it felt to make love to me and now you're done. Just like when you kissed me at the gallery." His wry smile twisted her heart something fierce. "It's fine. My ego might be a little bruised but I'll live, as long as I did a good job satisfying your curiosity."

He was so patient, so instantly forgiving that she couldn't stand for him to think any of that. "That is so not it. I have a history of screwing up things and I refuse to do that in this situation."

Maybe that was too blunt. She'd just laid out her vulnerabilities, baring herself far more than he had when he'd stripped her clothing off. That's why she couldn't do this two-personality tango; it was too hard to juggle the woman who jumped into research with both feet and the woman who couldn't be trusted to get it right.

It wasn't her strongest play of the night, but he just nodded, taking it in stride. "You forget that we're alike. I hate failing, too, so I get that."

Oh, God, what was she supposed to do with that? Or with the little tugs at her heart that had started with his smile and had only gotten stronger with the possibility that he might actually understand her? Her vocal cords froze as she stared him, totally stricken into silence. Definitely not her finest hour.

But he didn't seem fazed at all. Gently, he took her hand, contemplating their twined fingers. "Given all of that, I've got to ask, Laurel. What do you think is going on here? If I want you to stay, am I moving too fast for you? Because that's not my intent. We're adults. I enjoy spending time with you. That's all. Don't make it into a bigger deal than it is."

She blew out a breath she hadn't realized she'd been holding. The crash and burn of her career had totally paralyzed her and it was far past time to get her head screwed on straight.

"I'm sorry. I'm being an idiot. Of course this thing between us isn't far enough along for me to be such a basket case."

Good. She could breathe. Everything was smoothing out, including her pulse.

"Basket case is going a little far," he said with a smile. "You reacted to me being an idiot, not the other way around. I don't do this kind of thing well, where I like a woman and figure out how to see more of her. Because tonight was great. Far more so than I was expecting, and selfishly, I want more of that."

"I tend to be a little cautious," she admitted. It seemed they were at a place where it was okay to confess a few things and no one had to run screaming from the room. "In the romance department. Strictly because of bad experiences."

He shook his head with a light snort. "Sweetheart,

you're the least cautious woman I've ever had the pleasure of getting naked in my bed. Whatever bad experience you had that caused you to believe such a lie, banish it from your mind."

She couldn't help but smile at that, even though the only reason she'd allowed herself to get naked in his bed had everything to do with trying not to be herself tonight. Look how that had turned out. She'd nearly botched the whole thing.

"Easier said than done," she said, well aware she was treading a fine line by trying to be this person Xavier saw—the person he helped her to be. She could easily lose her balance at any moment. "I'm probably going to need lots of reminding."

"Or I can just keep you naked and let you have your wicked way with me." His naughty smirk made her laugh. "No, no. I insist. We're partners. We'll do this together or not at all."

The promise of remaining Xavier's partner thrilled her. Especially when he'd extended it to the bedroom. He was basically saying he would continue to help her be that woman he saw, the one she could only be with his influence, and that it was okay. He got it. She didn't have to be afraid of screwing up because there was nothing to screw up since they weren't serious. They were just two people who enjoyed each other and wanted to continue doing so until one or both of them ended it.

She could do that.

"You're such a trouper," she teased. "Volunteering yourself like that. How did I get so lucky as to have a partner with such a selfless streak?"

"It's nothing, really. I do run a charity, obviously because I'm the kind of guy who likes to give back." Xavier shrugged good-naturedly and tugged on her hand until she lay back down, settling her head into the hollow of his shoulder. "Now that we've settled the subject of your untimely departure, there's something bothering me about this conversation."

Since they'd just decided she shouldn't be freaking out, she tried really hard to keep her voice level when she replied, "Oh?"

"At the gallery, you talked about jumping into voids and discovering what lay over the horizon. I was pretty moved by that speech."

"You were?" She didn't recall much of anything other than the feel of his mouth on hers. "You never said anything."

"I was trying to get a few things worked out in my head," he admitted. "I don't jump into stuff. It takes a certain kind of temperament to just blindly trust like that, and I've developed an inconvenient sense of caution lately. I'm trying to get past it. That's partially what tonight was about."

Oh, man. That spoke to her on so many levels. Emboldened, she smoothed a hand over his glorious pectoral muscle. "I'm glad I could be a part of your experimentation."

"You're not just a part of it. You inspire it."

Slowly, she absorbed that, trying to sort through what he was telling her. It sounded an awful lot like they'd just figured out yet another area they had in common. "I make you want to be bold?"

He shrugged, lifting her head a notch before letting it settle back into place. "To a degree, yeah. But I sense this hesitation in you and it's driving me nuts. I want to be all-in, Laurel, really experience what it's like to explore passion with someone. I hate this caution I've been feeling. I thought tonight would banish it, you know, if I jumped in, but then you started talking about your own caution, which doesn't jibe with the woman I've been getting to know. Maybe you're just saying that because you sense mine. I'm tripping you up."

Her eyelashes fluttered closed. Oh, God. No, that wasn't it at all. Her two-person tango was messing *him* up.

She'd never even considered that he'd pick up on all of her indecision and inability to just be herself. Of course he had. Xavier LeBlanc was not a stupid man. Yet, somehow, he'd decided that his limitations had caused hers.

"I'm sorry." What else could she say when confronted with the evidence that she'd managed to screw this up, after all?

"Don't be." He sat up, taking her with him. The covers puddled into their laps as he gripped her bare shoulders earnestly. "I'm saying I want that woman you let me glimpse at the gallery. Don't hesitate. Jump off a few cliffs in a row. I'll follow you. I want this crazy you make me feel inside. I'm sorry if the way I've held back thus far has contributed to your hesitation. Don't let it. That's all."

She stared at him, her insides a riot she could scarcely sort out. "Here's the thing. You're the one who makes me feel like I can jump. Like I can be courageous enough to put my fears behind me. Not the other way around."

A smile unfurled across his face, warming her instantly. "How about that? We're discovering how this works together. We really are a good team."

Something loosened in her chest. "I've been telling you that since day one."

Now she had to put her money where her mouth was. Xavier wanted her to be the bold, unapologetic woman she truly was inside, no fear. She had to trust that she wasn't going to mess up, trust that he was going to stick right by her side as she relearned how to be Laurel.

Because that was the best discovery of all—she wasn't two people. Just one who had forgotten how to be brave.

And brave Laurel took what she wanted.

Right now, that was Xavier.

Eleven

The weekend stretched into Monday morning and Laurel still hadn't left. That was fine by Xavier. He'd taken her shopping Saturday morning and spent an obscene amount of money ensuring she never had to leave if she didn't want to.

This was all new to him, but he liked where it was headed so far.

Especially when his alarm went off Monday morning at 5:00 a.m. and Laurel didn't stir. He'd tucked her into his embrace to fall asleep for the third night in a row, but at some point, she'd moved over to her own side, clutching her pillow like someone had tried to take it away from her. He watched her for a moment in the low light of the bedside lamp and opted not to disturb her as he went about his Monday morning routine.

Halfway through the middle of his workout, Laurel wandered into the gym. Her sable hair spilled down her back with mussed strands haloing her face, and she was easily the most beautiful woman he'd ever seen in his life. Even in sleep shorts and a tiny white tank top. Especially in that. In about four seconds, he was going to peel it off with his teeth.

"Good morning," she called with a sleepy smile. "This place is hard to find. I had to ask Greta where you were."

The immeasurable benefit of live-in staff. He rested the dumbbell in his hand on his thigh, which did nothing to free up his hands so he could pull her into his arms, but he *was* hot and sweaty. So he came up with a much better plan.

"I didn't want to wake you. But since you did that on your own, give me five minutes to finish my last set and we can take a shower together."

"Deal." She hesitated and just when he was about to remind her that he preferred it when she gave it to him no holds barred, she continued, "If you want to drop me off at home before work, that's fine."

"Why the hell would I want to do that?" He'd told her on multiple occasions that there was no expiration date to their affair and neither did he want to set one.

Sure, he was overly enthusiastic about continuing to sleep with Laurel on a regular basis. So? He had never been one to pull punches and he liked Laurel in his bed. When that changed, he'd let her know.

"Because, you know. The rest of LBC might not like it so much that I'm dating the boss."

"The rest of LBC can jump in Lake Michigan," he growled, but then had to concede that, while obviously Val knew he was seeing Laurel, the rest of the staff didn't necessarily hold the same views about dating in the workplace as Xavier did. Namely that it was none of their business.

Except he was supposed to be steering the ship until

Val's return. He couldn't do what he pleased without ram-ifications.

It was a tricky dynamic, one he'd never had to con-template before. What would happen when they stopped seeing each other? Would things grow uncomfortable be-tween them or would they remain friendly, working to-gether easily despite the fact that they no longer had the right to get each other naked behind a shut office door?

The idea of not having the right to sleep with Lau-rel put him in a foul mood. That was not on the horizon anytime soon, not if he had anything to say about it. Part of the problem was the fact that it wasn't all up to him. Laurel could decide at any point that she was done and there was nothing he could do to stop her.

Was it too soon to bring up the idea of something a little more permanent than whatever it was they were doing right now?

Xavier shook his head. Hard.

Yes. It was way, *way* too soon. What was he even thinking, that he'd blurt out an invitation for Laurel to move in? She'd laugh in his face and she should.

He needed to take a huge step back before he did something irreversible solely due to phenomenal sex.

"You have a point," he conceded. "The staff needs to get used to the idea that we're dating, but that doesn't mean we have to throw it in their faces. I'll drop you at your house on the way into LBC."

It was an easy solution to multiple problems. He didn't like it.

She nodded as if that had been the outcome she'd hoped for, but he couldn't muster the same enthusiasm. What if she didn't want to come back here tonight? Maybe she wanted her space. He didn't like space.

Laurel had cracked something open inside him, some-

thing that wished for more substance than a weekend affair, and now it was being threatened.

All the more reason to let her do as she pleased. He
blew out a breath. Space would be good for them both.
In fact, he should probably take a shower alone. This
house had five bathrooms. Surely he could find one that
would be Laurel free and then he didn't have to contemplate what had taken over his brain since Friday night.

"Once I have my car, I can drive myself back and forth
from your house to LBC," she said with a smile. "We'll do
it on the sly for a little bit until we figure out how big of a
deal this is going to be for people. Maybe, eventually, we
can drop the pretense and I'll just ride with you into the
office. Speaking of which, if we're taking a shower, we
should get started because I've been standing here aching for you to put your hands on me for a million years
and the things I want you to do to me will take a very
long time. We don't want to be late for work."

He got so hard so fast that he almost couldn't breathe.
But that didn't stop him from picking her up and carrying her into the closest shower off the gym. As the
hot water sluiced over them both, he lost himself in her
soapy, sexy body.

Space was overrated.

Of course she wasn't done with him. His trust issues
were rearing their ugly heads again, that was all. Until
he had something to worry about, he needed to relax and
enjoy the benefits of seeing a great woman who was allowing him to discover all the things he'd missed thus
far in a relationship.

Despite all of that, he still had a very difficult time letting her go later that morning. Finally, she sprang from
the front seat of his car, wrenching away from his kiss
with the promise that she'd come by his office later.

That at least made him smile as he drove to LBC in rush hour traffic with a raging hard-on. He'd have thought the shower sex would have sated him for the morning, but no. He wanted Laurel 24/7.

She let him cool his heels for an hour. His coffee had long grown cold, but every time he picked it up, he heard a noise outside his door that he hoped was Laurel, so he set it back down again, only to be disappointed.

Getting her naked behind closed doors had become his number one priority. The amount of work he'd accomplished since arriving—zero—attested to that more than he cared to contemplate.

He should be working on plans for the next fundraiser, not moping about like a lovesick teenager. When she finally blew through the door wearing a lime-green dress that ended just above her knees, everything but her drained from his head.

"About time," he growled. "That dress is the perfect color for what I have in mind to do to you."

She shut the door and leaned against it, her smile nothing short of naughty. "You want to make a margarita out of me?"

"More like suck the juice out," he said succinctly and pushed back from his desk, patting the space in front of him. "Up you go. Let's see if you taste as good as you look."

She didn't move but her gaze went heavy with arousal as she eyed the spot on his desk. "That sounds like a recipe for getting nothing accomplished today."

"Exactly. That was always going to happen."

"Then why did we bother to come in to the office?" she asked with maddening practicality. "We could have both taken a sick day and spent the entire morning in bed."

"Now you're talking." Why hadn't that occurred to him? "We'll do that tomorrow."

But she shook her head with an amused laugh. "We can't spend two days in a row doing nothing but boinking."

"Wanna bet?" *Boinking.* It was such a cute word for sex, especially the way they did it. Laurel had gotten him so hot a couple of times that he'd devolved into nothing but animalistic instinct. "We just spent the last two days in a row doing nothing but."

"That's not true—we went shopping. And I distinctly remember a movie. Maybe there was some eating."

Why was she still talking when he'd already told her he planned to pleasure her on his desk? Maybe he hadn't made it clear what he'd meant earlier. "Do you have some objection to me putting my mouth between your legs while we're at work?"

Her gaze went molten as she zeroed in on his lips. "Yeah, actually. I do."

Despite her protest, he'd watched her come enough times over the weekend that he could tell how turned on she was. It was doing a number on him imagining how wet she must be under that lime-green skirt. He crossed his arms over his chest and leaned back.

"Really? Because your face is telling me a different story."

"Wanting something is not the same as thinking it's a good idea." She crossed her own arms over her stomach, which tightened the fabric across her breasts, highlighting her hard nipples. "We have important work to do and I'm getting the distinct feeling you're using sex to avoid it."

That put enough of a hitch in his stride that his arousal fizzled a notch. As such, he couldn't let the comment go. "What's that supposed to mean?"

"The fundraiser. We've done nothing to plan it. We haven't even had one conversation outside of the initial one where I presented the idea of an auction. Why not?" The sensual vibe in the room vanished as they stared at each other. "Because it seems an awful lot like you want me in your bed but not your boardroom."

That stung. And put his back up at the same time. "You're being ridiculous. That's not true."

Even as he said it, he couldn't fully sell it to himself, though. With considerable effort, he took a figurative step back and examined her point.

She wasn't wrong.

He hadn't fully trusted her with details about his inheritance test. Actually, he hadn't trusted her at all. He'd maybe had a couple of discussions in the hallway once upon a time, but as a whole, he'd kept tight control over the fundraising aspect of his job. Because it was *his*. He needed to prove that he could do this task, despite having no idea why it had been thrust upon him.

And maybe that was the real reason he'd yet to share any of it with Laurel. If he didn't understand why his own father had turned on him, how would he recognize it when someone he didn't know as well did the same?

Someone like Laurel.

Keeping everyone at arm's length had become his coping mechanism. Passion hadn't even come all that easily, but he'd at least been able to quantify the benefits of that. His inheritance test? Whole other story.

Laurel was calling him on his crap and he'd never been more affected by a woman in his life.

She raised her brows. "If it's not true, then help me stop feeling like you're brushing me off when it comes to the partnership we've both agreed to."

Laurel deserved that explanation and probably a whole

lot more. He stood and pulled a chair around, setting it next to his, a pointed equal distance from his computer. "Let's talk."

Shooting him a smile that was far too forgiving, she skirted the desk and settled into her seat. "Did you talk to your friends about donating items?"

"A few. I got sidetracked."

A poor excuse, though he *had* been a little busy getting wound up with the woman in lime green. Before Laurel could call him on that, too, he held up a hand. "I had a hard time, okay? It didn't go very well. You helped me get my head on straight during our conversation in the conference room the other day after the orientation session, and then I never cycled back around to it. I absolutely should dive back in."

She glanced at his phone emphatically. "No time like the present."

That was fair. As a show of good faith, he picked up his phone and scrolled through the contacts. Under Laurel's watchful gaze, he dialed up Simon Perry, the head of Metro Bank and father to Liam from the orientation session. The man answered on the second ring. Odds were high Simon had Xavier in his contacts, and he took a moment to be grateful the LeBlanc name held enough weight to warrant such attention.

"Mr. Perry," Xavier began, struck all over again by how much further along in life his acquaintance was. "Xavier LeBlanc calling."

Unnecessary to identify himself, most likely, but this call justified formality.

"A welcome surprise," Simon said warmly. "My son mentioned that he'd met you the other day. Thank you for making him feel like he can make a difference in the world. It's an important concept I've tried to impart to him and I'm glad to hear he's finding similar influences in the business world."

"My pleasure," Xavier said and meant it. How about that? There was some actual emotional satisfaction in being the head of a place like LBC. Temporary head, though that qualification was coming a lot less quickly lately. Val had once mentioned that Xavier might be a better man for his time here. Perhaps this was what he'd meant.

"What can I do for you?" Simon asked.

Xavier launched into an unrehearsed spiel about the auction and within a few minutes, Simon had offered up a rare bottle of Macallan whiskey. While not a personal fan of the brand, Xavier knew the bottle would likely sell for upward of a hundred grand. It was a phenomenal donation and he told Simon so. They wrapped up the call after Simon tacked on a promise to send Xavier a few names of colleagues who might be willing to contribute.

"Well done," Laurel said softly when Xavier hung up.

"You don't even know how it went," he teased, even though he knew he wore a grin he couldn't quite control. Why should he, though? He'd taken her advice, done something he'd previously failed at and came out a winner this time. If that didn't warrant a smile, nothing did.

"Yes I do. I can see it in your face. It's breathtaking." Her quiet voice curled through him with warmth. Or maybe it was the content of her words that had such an unexpected effect.

"What is my face doing?" He couldn't help but ask.

"Everything. Your expression is typically very schooled. I like it better when you let me see what's going on inside you."

Since there was no point in trying to compose his features into something less revealing, he didn't bother trying. "Well, you're a limited audience of one who can actually read me with any degree of accuracy."

"I like that, too."

This whole conversation shouldn't be happening. It was far too intimate. But the real danger lay in how much more intimate he wanted to get, which should have been scaring the daylights out of him.

Instead of reeling it back, he leaned into her space and tipped up her chin to feather a kiss across her cheek that had nothing to do with getting her naked or even aroused; it was a small token of gratitude for the things he was feeling inside.

"You're good for me, apparently."

That pleased her immeasurably, judging by the light that dawned in her eyes. Maybe he was good for her, too. Wouldn't that be something?

For the first time in his adult life, he hadn't kicked a woman out of his bed and then promptly forgotten her. The uncharted waters he'd sailed into weren't as difficult to navigate as he would have guessed.

"Maybe you should make a few more phone calls while you're riding high," Laurel suggested wryly, intentionally moving out of his reach.

Yeah, yeah, it was getting too mushy in here for both of them. He got it. Plus she'd already called him out once for his avoidance tactics. Neither did he want to scare her away simply because he'd discovered something new and amazing.

He could wait to show her how much he appreciated her.

Twelve

Auction day started at five in the morning.

Xavier didn't typically get up this early on a Saturday, but he and Laurel had a to-do list a quadrillion items long. Even though they'd recruited as many volunteers from LBC as possible, the list never got shorter and Adelaide, who had turned out to be his second-greatest asset after Laurel, had to run the food pantry while they were off-site.

Xavier drove the truck they'd rented while Laurel rode shotgun, chattering a mile a minute about the changes she'd made to the catering menu. He listened with half an ear, not because her comments weren't important, but because he'd gotten more and more nerve-racked the closer they got to the venue.

This was it. The event they'd been planning for a solid two weeks. What if it didn't go as well as they'd projected?

Sure the appraised value of the donations had topped

three million dollars, but only for insurance purposes. Actual value might not even turn out to be half that. It all depended on whether the attendees opened their wallets. Scratch that—it all depended on how wide Xavier convinced them to open their wallets.

What if *he* was the reason it failed?

Worse, what if his father had set him up for exactly that? Instead of proving his father wrong, Xavier would be proving his father so very right.

The pressure mounted until his shoulders ached, as if the weight across them had real substance.

"I can feel you panicking," Laurel said into the silence, reading his mind.

"*Panic* is a strong word," he responded mildly.

"And when you start using your 'nothing's bothering me' tone, I have to believe *panic* is the right word." Her hand slid across his thigh and squeezed, imparting comfort and understanding. "Of course, if you don't want me to guess, you could always tell me what's going on."

The traffic light ahead of him turned red, but he waited until he'd come to a complete stop before answering her.

"I'm panicking, okay?" He scowled. Boy, he was really inspiring confidence here, in both of them. "I don't know why. I shouldn't be."

Her hand smoothed over his thigh again. "Because this is important to you. There's nothing wrong with that."

"But there is something wrong with letting it affect me. I can't fail today."

"You won't," she said fiercely enough to make him do a double take. "*We* won't. I'm here and we're going to do this thing together. Haven't you figured that out by now?"

Yeah. Maybe. Mostly, anyway.

After everything she'd said, all the conversations, the proof that she was aboveboard, there was still a part of him that automatically held back. He had to consciously loosen his grip on his worries, and sometimes that didn't go so well. It wasn't a crime. They were taking things slowly, or at least he was taking *that* part slowly. If she didn't like it, too bad.

"Why are you so invested in this, anyway? It's my deal," he grumbled, well aware that his nerves were causing him to be crabby.

He'd thrown that question in her direction strictly to change the subject, but now that it was out there, he realized it had been bothering him. They'd worked twelve hour days, even on the weekends. She had literally no skin in this game other than volunteering for the job.

"That's why, silly," she said with a smile, as if that should have been perfectly obvious. "You need me. Poof. Here I am."

He didn't deserve her loyalty, especially not when he was still deliberately holding back.

"But you don't even know why it's so critical," he blurted out and immediately wished he could recall the words. She was too sharp to let it pass.

His inheritance test was a can of worms he'd yet to open with her, and he'd just pulled into the lot of the hotel where they'd taken over one of the ballrooms. They had an enormous amount of work to do in order to get the venue decorated and ready for the auction, which would take place at eight o'clock sharp.

Not only did they have to transform the ballroom, they'd opted for black tie, which meant they both also had to change out of their T-shirts and jeans at some point. He didn't have time to get into the details of the inheritance test with her. And he really didn't want to have a conversation about why he hadn't told her about it already.

She cocked her head. "You mean, there's another objective besides the obvious?"

"Yeah." Now he had yet another reason not to go down this path—thus far, she'd apparently assumed he was fired up over fundraising strictly for altruistic reasons. And he didn't want to disappoint her. "Can we talk about it later?"

"Sure," she said immediately, and that made him feel even worse.

He had to tell her the truth. He owed it to her, if for no other reason than because she *did* have skin in the game: her time, her efforts, her faith in him. But also because this was where the rubber met the road. If he wanted to practice letting go of things and showing Laurel that he trusted her, this was what trust looked like. He had to lay out everything, even the ugly parts, and hope she didn't leap from the truck in disgust.

"Is this the part where I'm allowed to yell at you for being so understanding?" he asked. When her mouth quirked up, he returned the smile almost automatically. It was like a reflex; Laurel smiled and it made him happy. "My father's will…it's a little unconventional. Val and I had to switch places as a stipulation in order to get our inheritances."

"Oh." She drew the word out to about ten syllables. "*That's* why—"

"There's more." He hated interrupting, but he might not get this out if he had to wait. "I have to raise ten million dollars or I don't get a dime."

"That's ridiculous," Laurel returned immediately. "An inheritance shouldn't come with strings. What in the world did your father hope to accomplish by attaching fundraising to his will? It's not like he's around to see whether you succeed or not."

"Well…yeah. Exactly." Was he supposed to feel so relieved that she got it? That she'd latched onto the real culprit in all of this instead of lambasting Xavier for being so shallow? "I know diamonds. Not fundraising. It's been tripping me up to be so far out of my element."

"You listen to me, Xavier," she said sternly and slid her fingers through his hair to cup the back of his head, holding him in place so she could speak directly to him. "You're doing spectacular at fundraising. You're amazing and you've got this. We'll get your ten million dollars come hell or high water. If this auction doesn't do it, we'll keep going until we get there. I'm just mad enough on your behalf to dig my heels in."

"That's it?" he asked and couldn't even care that his incredulity was likely plastered across his face. Of all the possible reactions she could have had, that one was not even on his list. "You're all-in even knowing that I'm doing this for purely materialistic reasons?"

She flicked that question away with her hand as if it was a bothersome insect and shook her head. "You're not doing this for the money and there's not one single thing you can say to make me believe that you are. Your father insulted you, maybe even hurt you. You want to get back at him by succeeding. I get it."

"Uh, yeah, I guess you do." Dazed, he stared at her as something monumental shifted in his chest, making room for Laurel to settle inside as if she'd always been there. "Where did you *come* from?"

"Springfield," she said with a laugh. "Born and raised. I only came to Chicago to go to college and then I sort of stuck around."

He couldn't do anything else in that moment but grab her up in a fierce kiss, one she eagerly responded to. If they hadn't been in the cab of a panel truck, he'd have been stripping her at this very moment, determined to get to that place where she made him feel whole.

Hell, she was doing that right now, even dressed. For the first time, he fully believed he could complete this inheritance test. Laurel would stand by his side until he did. What more could he ask for?

The auction was a rousing success from the first moment to the last. Of course, it couldn't have been anything less given the involvement of LBC's staff, who had donated their own items handcrafted with love. As the master of ceremonies, Xavier had been magnificent. So much so, Laurel hadn't been able to peel her eyes from his gorgeous form all night.

Especially now, with his black tie unbound and hanging around his neck as he directed a couple of the volunteers who were removing the giant banner over the raised dais where the auctioneer had led the festivities.

Though dozens of people still milled through the ballroom, Xavier caught her watching him and slid her a secret grin that might mean any number of things, but she hoped it was an indicator of how thrilled he was with the outcome of the auction. As he should be.

Once the banner came down, he extracted himself from the volunteers and somehow managed to maneuver her into a private corner, where the foot traffic wasn't as heavy.

"The auction went far better than I had a right to expect," he said as he gathered her close in a celebratory hug that quickly grew into something more precious than air.

She let herself be swallowed by the enormous rush of emotions for about five seconds and then wormed out of his embrace. With regret. It was always hard to stop touching him, regardless of the location. But the longer she stayed in his arms, the more she wanted to whisper the things in her heart.

"There are way too many LBC staffers still here to be getting so cozy," she reminded him pointedly. They still hadn't announced to the world that they were dating.

Bold, brave Laurel had taken what she'd wanted and been richly rewarded over and over again for far longer than she would have expected. She kept waiting for everything to come to an immediate and abrupt halt when he told her he was through exploring.

"Then we should go home," he murmured, heat leaping into his gaze so fast that it made her dizzy.

Things *never* came to an abrupt halt because he kept saying stuff like that.

Home, as in his house. The place she'd started subconsciously calling home, as well. But it wasn't hers, no matter how hard he tried to make her comfortable there. Neither did she dare fall prey to the seductive idea that he might eventually ask her to stay permanently.

They weren't doing permanent. They were doing hot, uninhibited and adventurous. Nothing else, no matter how many times she found herself straying off in a fantasy that had a different end.

"Don't we still have work to do?" she countered breathlessly, as he treated her to a hungry once-over that affected her almost as strongly as it would have if he'd used his hands. Maybe more so because he wasn't touching her. They were in public and he couldn't. That somehow made it more delicious, more arousing.

"There's only one thing I want to do right now, and it has nothing to do with the auction," he told her. His low voice snaked through her, heating everything in its path. "We've been here almost all day. We have volunteers for a reason."

"I can't argue with that logic."

Before the entire sentence had left her mouth, he was steering her toward the door, murmuring wicked things in her ear until she shuddered. The valet had his Aston Martin waiting in the lane by the time they arrived at the curb, even though he'd driven the rental truck—a trick that she had no clue how he'd performed, but that she appreciated, especially when he threw the car into gear impatiently.

She'd learned to gauge exactly how turned on he was by the way he drove, and the screech of his tires around a corner said he was nearly thermonuclear.

Good. So was she.

They still hadn't explored the foyer, nor had he made good on his promise to back her up against a stone column, but she didn't mind. His bed worked for her. *He* worked for her.

Within seconds of hitting the threshold of his bedroom, he'd lifted the hem of her dress over her head and pulled her onto the mattress, twining their bodies together until she scarcely knew which way was up.

Then it didn't matter as he plunged her into a netherworld of sensation where only the two of them existed. Xavier drove her body to the heights of pleasure, wrung so much feeling from her very soul that she nearly sobbed with relief when she came. As he followed her, she clung tightly to his shoulders, anchoring herself lest she float away.

The longer she did this, the less certain she was about whether she'd walk away unscathed. But she'd agreed to help Xavier explore passion and she couldn't just stop cold turkey because she'd started assigning more importance to their relationship than she should.

This wasn't the precursor to something long term. It

couldn't be—she hadn't told him the truth about who she was and she didn't believe for a second that they were headed to a place where she needed to. They were sleeping together because they both enjoyed it and one day, that would stop being true. He'd even said they were helping each other be bold.

Plus, she'd pretty much decided that her story about the fraud was a no-go since she hadn't found any evidence. Besides, Xavier made her feel like she could focus on her flagging career and successfully find another story to break that would fix her mortifying gaff. She'd be better for her time with him and look back on it fondly.

But that's all there was to this.

It was just…when he snuggled her close and stroked his strong fingers through her hair, it didn't *feel* like they were winding down. She spent every night in his bed and they'd worked on the auction for hours upon hours outside of bed, yet she never got tired of being with him. Surely that meant something. But what, she couldn't wrap her head around.

"I still can't believe that Miro painting went for 1.4 million dollars," Xavier commented out of the blue as his lips toyed with her hair. "*One* piece fetched what I had braced myself to accept as the sum total of *all* the donations."

"You're the one who drove the price up," she reminded him, relieved to jump on something that would pull her away from the angst and drama in her own head. "It was like you'd been auctioneering your whole life when you got up on stage and announced to the audience that there were two collectors in the crowd, then got them bidding against each other."

He shrugged modestly, his muscles rippling against

her back and shoulders. "Helps that I knew so many people in attendance."

"Yes, it does. Whatever your father's posthumous game is with that will, it's not going to keep you from your inheritance."

Laurel could at least help give him that satisfaction before they ended this. At this point, she'd all but abandoned the idea of uncovering anything problematic at LBC. Not on purpose. She'd just been so busy with the auction that investigating had slipped in priority. Okay, maybe the slip had been a little more on purpose than she'd let herself admit. If she didn't investigate, she didn't have to worry about how to bring it up with Xavier, nor did she have to worry about making any mistakes.

"If all the money comes in from the auction as expected, I should be pretty close to the ten million," he said.

"If you want, I can meet with Addy and someone from accounting on Monday to get some solid numbers."

"Sure." Xavier mouthed down her neck to her shoulder, then lower, ratcheting up the intensity within seconds. Her body bowed beneath his talented lips as he worshipped one of her breasts, and she forgot all about the auction.

It wasn't until Monday morning, after she'd already taken a seat between Addy and Michelle from accounting, that it occurred to her that this was precisely the position she'd hoped to be in when she'd taken the job: trusted enough to be given access to LBC's books.

Her pulse drummed in her throat the entire time Addy and Michelle talked her through the numbers. Nothing calmed her ragged nerves, not even the news that Xavier was, indeed, very close to the ten-million-dollar mark. If he hosted another successful fundraiser, he'd hit his goal easily, as best she could tell from the preliminary figures.

That meant he might cut her loose soon and that hit her hard. She couldn't keep pretending that everything was going to work out fine, not when the thought of losing him hurt so deeply that she couldn't make it stop. It all seemed to be coming to a head but she couldn't see what the next steps were.

Laurel asked Michelle when she could check back to get final numbers and then scribbled out a few ideas Addy had for another fundraiser. The three women chatted and then Michelle and Addy segued into an entirely different conversation about a problem with the meal services area that apparently had been going on for some time.

Laurel listened with half an ear as she added her own notes to Addy's thoughts. The auction had been so successful because they'd heavily involved the staff and there was no reason to change that. In fact, Laurel wanted to take it a step further and involve the staff's families.

"Jennifer has been off with her estimates for so long, no one even thinks twice about it," Michelle said to Addy, flicking her fingers dismissively at the computer screen open in front her.

"Oh, I know." Addy rolled her eyes. "Marjorie used to complain about it twice a month, when Jennifer submitted her budget and then again when she submitted her expenses. I don't know why Jennifer bothers to come up with a budget at all."

"It's only because I make her," Michelle said with a laugh. "If I had to approve her expenditures, I'd go insane trying to match them to her budget. I'm more than happy to let Val handle that."

Laurel tried really, really hard to ignore the way her spine tingled. But it was no use. She'd heard every word and her vast experience with human nature told her there was more to this story than had been expressed thus far.

"Val approves all the invoices from the meal services area? Not someone in accounting?" Laurel asked.

"Yeah," Michelle offered readily. "Or he did. Xavier does now, because of the amount. LBC has a rule about who can approve over a certain dollar threshold."

Which wasn't uncommon. But it was somewhat irregular for no one to reconcile the budgeted amount to the actual spend, which didn't seem to be happening. Nor had anyone done anything about the discrepancy, if it extended as far back as when both Val and Marjorie had been involved.

Laurel tucked that information away, opting not to press Michelle on it since there was no evidence of any wrongdoing. Except, as the day wore on, Laurel couldn't quite dismiss the whole thing. Her original sources had mentioned discrepancies with accounting for items stocked in the supply closet, not with the meal services area, but who was to say there weren't issues in more than one area? Or it could be that there were no problems at all and all of this was unfounded suspicion that would be easily disproved.

That's what she'd come here to find out.

Either way, it was time to bring Xavier up to speed on what she'd heard. It was exactly what she'd promised herself she'd do if and when something like this came up. It would be a great test of his intentions toward her and definitely would reveal whether they were moving toward something better than what she'd braced for.

This whole matter would be decided, once and for all.

Thirteen

When Laurel appeared at the door of Xavier's office after a very long morning apart, the look on her face immediately eliminated the idea that she'd been thinking about him in a wholly non-work-related way. Which meant he couldn't boost her up on the desk and push her skirt to her waist like *he'd* been thinking about.

"Is this a business visit?" he asked, just in case he'd misread things.

She nodded and shut the door. Xavier closed his laptop and crossed his arms, though it was a sure bet neither would prevent him from angling for a way to get her onto the desk in a few minutes.

"I talked to Michelle in accounting a little while ago," she began and then hesitated.

His throat tightened as he recalled that Laurel had mentioned she'd ask for the fundraising numbers today. Surely he wasn't *that* far behind his ten-million-dollar goal. "Why doesn't your expression look like the news is good? I'm not that bad at math. I can't be more than a couple of million off."

"Oh, yeah, no, you're not." She waved that away, obviously startled that he'd mentioned it, as if fundraising hadn't even crossed her mind. "You're right on track. We just need one more good event like the auction and you're all set. Addy and I already hashed out some preliminary ideas that I'll run by you sometime."

"Okay, good. Why does that not make me feel better?"

She flashed a brief grin that warmed his insides, and that did make him feel better. As long as she kept smiling like that, nothing could go wrong.

"While I was talking to Michelle, some other stuff came up. About the accounting for the meal services area. I..." Laurel made a face. "Well, I hate to speculate, so I'm just going to tell you what she said and let you draw your own conclusions. Apparently there's a running joke that the manager of that area can't hit her budget. She's constantly over in her expenditures but no one has asked for an explanation."

A decade of monthly meetings where he'd scoured the balance sheet at LeBlanc rushed into his head in an instant and it was all he could do to remain calm. "You suspect fraud."

It wasn't a question, and the brief, bright flash in her gaze told him everything he needed to know. The calm he usually called up easily when dealing with the unexpected wouldn't surface.

"I don't know *anything*," she said simply, which didn't settle his stomach. "Only that Michelle mentioned that Val approves that area's expenses. And now you do."

"Okay." He had to start digging. Right now. "I hear you. This is my mess to clean up."

His stomach sloshed a bit more when she didn't immediately insist they were in this together or lean on the desk with fire in her eyes as she demanded that he let her be his clean-up partner. He couldn't focus on how much he wished she had, not when there was a potential issue festering beneath the surface of LeBlanc Charities.

If someone was stealing from LBC on Xavier's watch, there would be hell to pay. Then he could worry about why it felt like Laurel was slipping away.

Many long, grueling hours later, he and Michelle had run through enough of the numbers enough times to be convinced they'd only scratched the surface of the problem. The head of accounting had worn a sick expression on her face for the whole of the meeting. Xavier was pretty sure that same look had been etched on his.

"It's late," he told her and glanced at the clock, not at all shocked to see that it was past eight. "You should go home. I'll hire an independent audit firm in the morning to do a thorough excavation of the disarray our books are in."

And he meant "our" in every sense of the word. He'd signed off on some of the receipts and invoices, which appeared to have been inflated above their actual amounts. This was his to fix.

"Thank you for not firing me," she said quietly, her gratitude evident. "This should have been caught a long time ago."

"It's not all on you. Marjorie had a role in this, as does Val." Not to mention Jennifer Sanders, the manager of the meal services area who, it appeared, had been skimming off the top of LBC's operating capital for quite some time and rather blatantly, too. "I would ask that you keep this to yourself until we have enough evidence to bring up charges."

That was the real reason he hadn't fired anyone yet. He

needed facts before acting, and he couldn't trust the rage that seethed just under his skin. Until he had rock-solid proof from an unbiased third party about what had been happening, and for how long, he couldn't blame anyone 100 percent. Though Val topped his list at this moment.

His brother had some explaining to do.

Michelle slipped into a brown leather coat to brave Chicago's fall weather, then left without a backward glance. Xavier was too keyed up to go home, where Laurel was no doubt waiting for him, though he hadn't had a chance to really speak to her since she'd brought him the news that LBC wasn't being run as tightly as it could be.

He sent her a text message that was short and to the point: Don't wait on me for dinner.

Then he drove down by the lake, though the scenery wasn't all that pretty this time of year. Closer to New Year's, the trees would be bare of leaves and ice would form in large chunks on the shore. When the water froze, the lake looked like a giant sheet of glass, a testament to the power of an Illinois winter. That was his favorite. Tonight, the lake was choppy and dark and there was no moon to light the water.

He wanted to go home, despite how angry and heartsick he was over the suspected fraud. The problem was that he was even more heartsick over not understanding the reasons Laurel had basically dumped this in his lap and backed away. Was it because her role in his life was temporary and they were almost done? Maybe she wondered why she should get involved.

It wasn't that he wished for her to solve his problems. Only that he wished they were partners in this, too. That they could be partners in everything.

And he wished he could bring that up with her. It was too soon. He couldn't rush things.

Instead of heading for Val's house in River Forest, which was where he should be going, Xavier found himself on the North Shore. On a whim, he pulled up to the gate of his mother's neighborhood. The attendant nodded the moment he recognized Xavier and opened the gate to admit him, though he hadn't visited his mother since Thanksgiving last year. She wasn't expecting him.

If anyone would have some advice about how to handle this problem with LBC, it would be its founder. His mother answered the door of the palatial mansion herself, swinging one of the double doors wide as he came up the marble stairs. He hadn't even had a chance to knock.

"Xavier, what in the world are you doing here?" she asked, concern tightening her mouth. "Is everything okay?"

Patrice LeBlanc could pass for forty-five all day long and wore her ash-blond hair in a timeless style that women half her age envied. He studied his mother for a moment, struck all at once by the fact that that she'd run LBC by herself for a number of years until Val had joined her.

He hadn't fully appreciated the effort that had required until this moment. "Hi, Mom. I think we should talk."

She lifted her brows but didn't comment, ushering him into the salon she preferred. The sunny yellow always made her smile, as she'd gladly tell anyone who would listen. She didn't do so this evening, opting to take a seat on one of the brocade couches.

"You're scaring me, darling," his mom finally said as he settled into the leather chair at a right angle to the couch, though he knew she'd prefer it if he sat next to her.

They'd never been close. He'd been his father's son from an early age, while she'd favored Val, openly and unapologetically. Once upon a time, he'd been pretty jealous of the easy rapport she had with his brother, but he'd gotten over it, turning his slavish devotion to his father. Look where that had gotten him.

"Sorry, I didn't mean to drop in on you completely unannounced."

"Don't be silly. You're welcome here any time of day or night."

She meant it, too. How about that? He couldn't recall a time when he'd felt overly welcome at the house his parents shared before his father had died, but maybe that was on him. He hadn't tried to form any kind of bond with his mother, just retreated into his own misery over his father's will. Maybe it was time to change that.

"How are you doing, Mom?"

She laughed nervously. "Now you're really scaring me."

Because he didn't make a habit of asking after her health, emotional or physical, which shamed him more than he liked to admit. "It just occurred to me that I haven't given much regard to how lonely you must be with Dad gone."

The look on her face pretty well matched the confusion going on beneath his own skin. Where had that *come* from? But even as he asked that silent question, he answered it.

Laurel.

She'd opened up so many channels of emotion inside him, unlocking things he'd never considered before, things he didn't know existed or that he'd care about.

But he knew now.

"That's sweet of you to ask, darling. I'm doing okay, considering." She wagged her head back and forth. "Your father and I were married for nearly thirty-five years. It's hard to be alone. But I'm managing. Why did you really come by?"

He had to chuckle at her directness, which reminded him of his father for some odd reason. He'd have never said they were at all alike. But neither would he have claimed that about himself and Laurel. And he'd have been wrong.

"I uncovered some accounting issues at LBC. Looks like someone is stealing from us using fake invoices and receipts. I'm pretty upset."

"As you should be!"

Anger swept through his mother's expression, taking over her whole body, and she looked so much like Val in that moment that Xavier did a double take. That was the kind of passion he'd equate with his brother, all right, the same kind of all-in that Xavier had always avoided, with calculation. Hot heads didn't get results.

But he'd abandoned his emotion-free state in favor of a seductive lure in the form of Laurel Dixon. She'd enticed him to jump, holding her hand, as they soared into a free fall together. And as his reward? He would eventually be as alone as his mother, and he was suddenly very aware of how much he didn't want that.

"Tell me everything," his mother demanded, visibly bristling. "I might be retired, but my name is still LeBlanc."

Despite the somberness of the subject, that made him smile even as he laid out what he knew. Xavier concluded with the news that he'd already contacted an audit firm who specialized in nonprofit-sector accounting. His mother nodded and laid out a few of her own thoughts, namely that he needed to involve Val as soon as possible.

"I appreciate that you came to me first instead of Val," she told him. "It's a real testament to how far you've come since the reading of your father's will. I was against the idea of forcing you and your brother to switch places, at first, but Edward talked me into it."

"Why?" he blurted out, aching to understand once and for all why his father had hated him so much. "What possible good could have resulted from these ridiculous inheritance terms?"

"Darling." She shook her head, piercing him with a look that said he should have already figured this out. "If you hadn't been deep in the heart of LBC, would this theft have come to light? Would you have ever darkened my door? Your father worried that you were becoming too much like him and he didn't want you to get to the end of your life, only to have the same regrets he had."

Regrets? Over building an almost billion-dollar-a-year company? Something did not add up here. "Are you saying that Dad did this because *he* had regrets?"

But as she nodded, he couldn't summon a shred of anger. His mother was right; none of this would have happened if Xavier had stayed locked in his office at LeBlanc Jewelers.

Laurel wouldn't have happened.

And if he hadn't let her into his life, she might never have brought this theft to his attention. It had been the best combination of fate and design, but only by putting his trust in her had he gotten here.

"Sure. Regrets about not spending more time with Val, regrets about teaching you to be so hard, regrets about not traveling the world with me when he had the chance." His mother lifted a shoulder. "He had many."

Xavier would not have described himself as *hard*, at least, not prior to being propelled into LBC. LeBlanc Jewelers required a firm hand and, apparently, so did LBC, which he could provide. But he'd also learned that there were people at the cores of both enterprises that he'd over-looked—some of them, like Adelaide, to his detriment.

After standing at the helm of a charity for the last few months, he could at least take an objective step back and wonder if there was still more truth to uncover. Especially the one thing that still bothered him about all of this.

"If Dad did this to help me, where does Val fit into his master plan?"

His mother didn't miss a beat. "Val has his own chal-lenges, namely that he cares too much. He needs to learn how mix objectivity with his tendency to lead with his heart. Your father thought both he and LeBlanc Jewel-ers would benefit from the switch. I think he was right."

Xavier ran a hand through his hair and tried to make some sense out of his reeling thoughts. The will *hadn't* been a blunt instrument designed to wreck both Val's and Xavier's carefully constructed lives, if his mom could be believed.

He believed her.

And that meant he no longer defaulted to not trusting anyone, up to and including his family.

If he took anything from this conversation, it was that nothing was as it seemed. Which meant he had some more thinking to do about *all* of his next steps, not just the ones associated with the accounting issues at LBC.

He couldn't keep holding Laurel at arm's length and neither could he let her go.

It was far past time to admit he'd fallen in love with her.

When Xavier blew through the door of his bedroom and snatched Laurel up in a fierce embrace, she scarcely had time to yelp before he'd swallowed her whole with the most mind-altering kiss she'd experienced from him yet.

His hands were everywhere, in her hair, slicking down her back, holding her so tightly that she couldn't imagine being separated.

And they were still dressed. She didn't have enough working brain cells to question him about his meeting with Michelle, whether he'd eaten or what occasion had prompted such a display of raw need. She just let herself be taken by the storm until he finally pulled back and rested his forehead on hers.

"Hi," he murmured with a small smile.

Dragging in great big quantities of air, she scratched out her own *"Hi"* in response.

He followed that with, "I missed you."

Oh, God. She'd missed him, too, pacing up and down the length of the study downstairs that smelled like him, the best combination of man and sandalwood. Eventually she'd wandered back to his bedroom to bury her face in his pillow.

It shouldn't have been such a big deal to miss one night together, especially not when he'd been contending with the accounting issue. But they'd spent 24/7 in each other's company for weeks. Without him around, she'd fallen into withdrawal, seeking out anything she could find to give her even a small hit of Xavier.

And here he was, rocking her from the inside out with nothing more than a few simple words.

"I gathered something of the sort," she managed to get out. "I hope it was okay that I waited here at your house—"

"I wanted you to. In fact, I want you here all the time." He cupped her jaw, feathering his thumb across her lips. "Move in. Tomorrow. Let's make this official."

Yes. Yes, yes, yes.

Yes to discovering what it felt like to love him wholly

and completely. Yes to exploring what they could mean to each other. Yes to—

Oh, no. *No.*

Her throat closed so fast that she saw stars. A monumental weight dropped down on her chest as she struggled to extract herself from his grip. This *could not* be happening before she'd had a chance to tell him the truth. He finally let her go, ruefully rubbing the back of his neck as he stared down at her.

"Too fast?" he asked with a half laugh. "I practiced what I was going to say on the way home from my mom's house. It kind of all rushed out, so I'm sorry if I messed it up."

"You, um…" He'd gone to his mother's house? Strictly to work out how to upend her entire world or for another reason entirely? Her head spun. "You didn't mess up. At least, I don't think you did. What exactly are you saying?"

"I'm saying I'm falling for you, Laurel."

And with that one single devastating phrase, everything came apart. Her soul. Her plans. Her sanity.

"You can't drop that on me," she whispered, even as her heart greedily latched onto the idea that Xavier LeBlanc had just admitted he was *falling for her.* "Not now."

"When, then?" Confusion marred his beautiful face, which made the swirl in her stomach worse. "I don't hear you saying you don't feel the same. What's holding us back?"

The truth.

"The fact that you don't know who I really am," she burst out, wishing with all her might that she'd already told him so she could admit she'd fallen for him, too.

This wasn't supposed to be happening, not like this.

He took a step back, his expression veering between

such a wide range of emotions that she couldn't sort them all. "What are *you* saying?"

"That's what I'm trying to explain! Give me a minute to get my feet under me."

She took a deep breath. It didn't help. She still had no clue how to approach this conversation other than to jump and hope he took her hand on the way down.

Please, God, let that be what happens.

She wanted Xavier more than she wanted to breathe and it was all within her grasp. Or it never was and she'd ruined everything prior to even walking through the door of LBC by choosing not to reveal her true profession.

"I'm an investigative reporter," she said bluntly and prayed he'd take it with the spirit she'd intended. "I took the job at LBC to uncover the fraud I suspected was going on. I'm sorry. I should have told you sooner."

"But you didn't," he said slowly. "Why not?"

"I tried to! In the conference room. You interrupted me at least four times—"

"And I've kept a muzzle over your mouth every minute since then?"

"I didn't think we were serious, Xavier. I never expected to have a reason to mention it after that. But then I got into this with you so much deeper than I planned. I wanted to tell you, but I never found solid evidence until today. And then you blew in here and things got all jumbled up."

In that respect, he *had* moved too fast. But it was too late and she couldn't blame him, not when it was all her fault.

"Let me get this straight." He pinched the bridge of his nose, his eyes closed in apparent disbelief. "You aren't a fundraising wizard and you've been toying with me this whole time."

"No! Oh, my God, no." Horrified, she reached out without thinking and then flinched when he jerked out of her grasp. "Why would you think I was toying with you? I have done fundraising in the past. That part is true, just like the way I feel about you. Everything between us is real."

"Nothing between us is real," he corrected harshly. "I don't trust a single word coming out of your mouth right now."

"Xavier." She bit back at least four different trite phrases, all designed to prove her innocence, which wasn't fair. She wasn't innocent. "You're right, and I'm sorry. I shouldn't have hidden my reasons for being at LBC. But you're missing the most important part of this. I'm not going to do the story on the accounting discrepancies. That's why I told you about it. I changed my mind."

"Thank you for your generosity," he said flatly. "I plan to press charges against the likely suspect as soon as I get the proper evidence. If you'd broken the story in advance of that, she might have had time to cover her tracks. So we'll call it even. I won't fire you for taking the job under false pretenses and you'll turn in your resignation to Adelaide first thing in the morning."

Oh, God. He wasn't going to give her a second chance. Her heart tore in two and lay there in pieces, bleeding.

"That's it, then?" she asked in disbelief.

She didn't have to wait for his nod. She'd screwed up again, even though she'd been trying to do the right thing.

"What would you like me to say? Apparently we weren't that serious and I misunderstood our relationship."

His voice had taken on that quality she hated, the one that he adopted to make sure everyone understood he was above the petty emotions swirling through the room. Nothing fazed him.

Except she knew better. "I *wanted* it to be serious. I just didn't…"

There wasn't a good way to end that sentence.

"You didn't what? Think I deserved the truth? Think I'd find out? Think I'd care?" His gaze bored into hers. "I did. To all three."

Past tense. She got the message loud and clear. He didn't care anymore. And he was done with her at the exact moment that she figured out what she wanted— Xavier.

"Okay. I get that you're angry—"

"I'm not angry. I'm ambivalent, at best," he said with a shrug. "You can clear all of your things out of my house at your convenience. I won't be here."

With that, he calmly walked out the door, leaving her trembling in the middle of his bedroom wondering how she could have been so colossally stupid as to lose both the story and the guy in one shot.

Fourteen

Xavier ended up driving to Val's house, after all. There was nowhere else to go and he'd developed this eerie calm that had started to scare him.

After weeks of consciously letting go, of allowing himself to roll around in sensations and experiences, he couldn't seem to feel anything at all.

A blessing, really. Laurel *had* been hiding something from him. A pretty big something. She was a liar—and a really good one, at that. All this time, he'd taken the fall for his suspicions, blaming his father's will for instilling this inconvenient sense of caution that he'd had to work on overcoming. In reality, Laurel had been undercover, scheming to break open a scandal starring LeBlanc Charities. *On Xavier's watch*, no less.

He wanted to hate her. To bask in his righteous indignation. To wallow in his justifications for walking away from her. But he couldn't feel anything other than numb.

When he got to Val's, it was well past midnight. Probably because he'd taken the long way around via Naperville. He shouldn't go inside Val's house. If there was a prize for least-fit company, Xavier would win it. Given his mood, the last person he should be speaking to was Val when they hadn't hashed out the Jennifer Sanders problem yet.

Just as he hit the start button to gun the engine so he could jet out of there, Val materialized at the car's driver's-side door and tapped on the glass.

Xavier slid down the window. "What?"

"Laurel called me," Val explained without fanfare.

Val hadn't found it necessary to take Xavier to task for his snippy tone, so Laurel must have told him everything. Xavier sighed. He was the one in his brother's driveway disturbing an entire household when everyone had to work tomorrow. The least he could do was have the courtesy to let Val explain how someone could have been robbing LBC blind for months without the director's knowledge.

Xavier peeled out of the car and slammed the door, which didn't help his mood, and followed Val into the dimly lit house.

"Sabrina's asleep," Val whispered. "I'd like to keep it that way, since she's sleeping for two."

"Yeah, yeah." Rub it in his face that Val had it all figured out in the romance department while Xavier had literally been sleeping with the enemy.

Or the potential enemy. If she'd broken the story. Which she hadn't because… He didn't know why. Not enough evidence or something. Maybe Laurel had hoped Xavier would spill the beans to her after sex one night, once she'd gotten him good and pliant.

She wasn't like that. He knew she wasn't. Except she'd lied to him. Repeatedly. Was any of it real?

Wearily, he sank into a chair and let his head fall into his hands. He had to move on and stop thinking about her. Massaging his forehead, he glanced up at Val from under his fingers. "Start talking."

"I know Jennifer's skimming. I've known for months," Val said with a nonchalant shrug that belied the bomb he'd just dropped. "Her husband is dying of stage-four colon cancer and they're struggling to pay the bills. You know how insurance is these days. High deductibles and such. She won't take money from me. I tried to give it to her. Tell me what you'd do in that situation."

"None of that," Xavier countered immediately. "Letting employees steal from you is not how you run a profitable business. I'd fire her and let her lie in the bed she made."

And that was likely the very reason his father had conceived the inheritance switch. His mother's words flooded his mind and he flinched. Maybe *hard* was a better word to describe him than he'd been willing to admit.

"That's a crap answer, Z." Val raised his eyebrows, likely in deference to the fact that he hadn't called Xavier by his childhood nickname in many years. "That's Dad talking. What would *you* do?"

"I don't know," he mumbled as he thought about his mother being alone now and how horrible it must be to have to watch your husband die, knowing there was nothing you could do to stop it. That's why it was better never to trust in something as fleeting and unreliable as another human being.

It was too late to stop the subtle and powerful internal shifts, though. He'd already started thinking with his heart and knew he wouldn't fire the woman, though it would be within his power to do so as the acting director of LBC.

"Until you have an answer, don't press charges," Val suggested quietly. "Marjorie had a back door where she handled the accounting discrepancies, so we're okay on the audit front. I can get you details."

Of course Marjorie had been in on it. She would have to be, since the accounting manager, Michelle, had known nothing of this. And he had a feeling the independent audit firm would find exactly what Val had just told him. They were totally in the clear from a legal standpoint. Ethically, maybe not. But he could make an argument that Jennifer's judgment was impaired and thus she was not worthy of discipline.

"I'll sleep on it." *Alone*, apparently. And for some reason, the sudden image of his empty bed crawled through him, opening doors that had been shut so far this evening. The most profound sense of sadness weighed down everything, and that was the only excuse he could come up with for the reason he blurted out, "Laurel and I broke up."

Val just nodded, his expression troubled. "I know, she told me that part, too."

Was nothing sacred around here? "All of it? Like how she lied about everything?"

"All of it, like how much she loves working for LBC and how she wants to walk away from reporting. She asked if I could possibly forgive her deception and see a way to keep her on board after you go back to LeBlanc Jewelers."

Oh. She'd called to beg Val for her job. Probably she had done so strictly to curry Val's favor, since he'd be the one she'd be working for in the long term.

"You said yes," Xavier guessed grimly. "I suppose

you also told her it was okay if she worked there in the interim, too."

Why not? It would be fun and games to continue working with Laurel, at least as far as Val was concerned. It had been his idea to hire her in the first place, against Xavier's better judgment. He deserved a medal for not throwing that back in Val's face.

"That's your call."

"I see. So I get to make the decision about whether to keep the best fundraising partner I could have dreamed up? Is that what you're saying? I'm the one who gets to decide if I'd like to feel as if I've been eviscerated every time I see her, day in and day out? I suppose it's all supposed to be easy, then. I should just decide to stop being in love with her, too." Xavier smirked at Val and then everything inside caught up with what he'd just unwittingly blurted out.

Oh, God, there came the hurt.

That's what he'd been so successfully avoiding thus far. He didn't like feeling so out of control, so raw inside. The same way he'd felt after the reading of the will, with all of the questions and lack of answers and overwhelming sense of betrayal.

Only this was worse. Laurel had tripped his radar from day one and he'd consciously forced himself to let go of his caution. He'd *purposefully* walked into her executioner's ax.

And what had she done? Smiled at him as she let her ax fall.

He'd *told* her how messed up he was about his father's will and she'd *understood*. Claimed to, anyway. How *dare* she say she got it when she'd been keeping secrets from him?

The rage spread, burning the raw places inside. Everything hurt. He hated it.

"I'm sorry, man," Val murmured. "I know how rough you must feel."

"What do you know about it?" he snapped back and then sighed. "Sorry. I'm messed up."

Val nodded and put a comforting hand on Xavier's shoulder. The warmth bled through his T-shirt, reminding him that he hadn't put a coat on when he'd walked out of the house.

"That's the part I know," his brother said. "I was in the opposite boat, though. Sabrina is the one who got hurt because of me and I had to fix it. I'm lucky she didn't think too hard about my flaws before accepting the ring I put on her finger, or I'd still be messed up."

"That's totally different." Also, whatever Val had done to Sabrina couldn't be nearly as bad as what Laurel had done. His brother was a saint, running a charity with flair and figuring out how to let a woman whose husband was dying pay for expensive medical treatments without losing her job or her dignity. "What did you do?"

"I hurt her." Val closed his eyes for a beat, as if the memory alone caused him pain. "We weren't serious, and then she got pregnant. I didn't shift the way I treated our relationship in time. I should have. But it happened so fast. I'd never been serious with a woman before and it was all new. I made mistakes. Fortunately, she forgave me, which, by the way, is the secret to marriage. You never stop making mistakes because it's all new, every day, if you're doing it right. As long as you go into it with forgiveness, it all works out."

"Who said anything about marriage?" Dazed, Xavier tried to take in all the things his brother had just said. "I barely even got to the point where I asked her to move in."

Val raised his brows. "Maybe that's part of your problem. You treated the entire relationship casually until *you* were ready to move forward and then didn't give Laurel enough warning to shift the way *she* thought about your relationship."

"Did she say that to you?"

What was *wrong* with him, greedily begging for scraps of information about Laurel? He should be banishing her from his mind. Except when he tried, all he could picture was her face as she pulled him down for a kiss, or her laugh, the way her voice always curled up in his gut. She'd been all-in from the beginning, charging ahead, partnering with him on a million small things that, added together, formed a woman who had given him a reason to change the core of how he dealt with relationships.

That was the thing he couldn't get over. She'd come to mean a great deal to him but he couldn't see much evidence showing she felt the same about him.

"No," Val said. "She told me that she'd screwed up the best thing that had ever happened to her and she didn't want to do that with the second-best thing. That's why she called me in hopes of salvaging her job at LBC since she'd already lost you."

"Me?" He blinked. "I'm the best thing that ever happened to her?"

"I know, it was a shock to me, as well," Val said with a smirk. "This is the part where you get back in your car and go find her so she can apologize to you directly instead of through me."

It was a testament to how befuddling this entire conversation was that Xavier almost nodded and did exactly that. But then he beat back that impulse with some heavy reminders of Laurel's treachery.

"It doesn't matter how she apologizes. There are some things that are unforgivable."

"Like stealing?" Val gave Xavier a minute to absorb that. "If you take a specific action out of context, sure. But I hope your exposure to the less fortunate has given you a different frame of mind. Motivation is complex. People make mistakes. You can seek out ways to rise above the things people do to hurt you or be alone. Your choice."

"When did you get so smart?" Xavier grumbled without any heat because, yeah, he got it.

Val just laughed. "Hey, when I sit at the head of the boardroom table at LeBlanc Jewelers, I feel like the stupidest person in the room some days. You manage that environment day in and day out with so much success that you make it look easy. So I guess I'm saying we each have our strengths, and when we put them together, we do all right. That's what Dad wanted us to figure out, you know."

If so, Xavier had played into his father's hands all along because Laurel had been the one to truly teach him that. That much had been real; he could feel the difference beneath his skin. She'd made him into a better person. And if that was true, then there might be room to reevaluate her reasons for not telling him the truth.

Xavier made a face at his brother. "I already knew that. I have no idea what took you so long."

"Then take my advice." Val punctuated that by shoving Xavier's arm until he stood up. "Go. Talk to Laurel. Don't let anything stand in the way of your happiness."

Xavier wasn't sure he could actually take that advice. Having an academic understanding that Val was probably right didn't magically make the big black bruise inside go away. Neither did he feel like he should be the one to make the effort. Laurel had been in the wrong. Not Xavier. He shouldn't have to hunt her down.

Apparently, she was of the same mind, because when he got home, she was still there, quietly sitting on his bed as if she'd been willing to patiently wait for him, even if it took all night.

"What are you doing here?" He questioned her gruffly, even as he drank in her troubled face and his soul soaked up her presence.

"Not making another mistake," she informed him, her voice doing that thing where it felt like she'd climbed inside him. "I screwed up by not telling you the truth soon enough and I'm not screwing up again."

"Then you should leave—"

"No." Slipping from the bed, she stood and faced him, her hands by her sides, though it seemed as if it took some effort to keep them there. "I need you to hear what I have to say."

He crossed his arms before he went insane and pulled her into his embrace, which was feeling more and more likely the longer she stood there within touching distance. All of this could have been avoided if he'd ensured that she'd really left the first time. Or if he'd resisted trusting her.

If she hadn't been so wonderful, so easy to be with, so amazing. Or a million other things that hadn't happened that way.

What had happened was Laurel.

She hadn't left. Apparently she wasn't going to unless he gave her the floor. "Fine. I'm listening."

Her silvery-gray eyes latched onto his, bleeding into his soul. "Xavier, I fell for you, too."

And with that, the last piece of his heart broke open and sucked him under.

* * *

Laurel's nails bit into her palms as she waited for Xavier to say something. Anything. But he just kept staring at the floor as if he'd discovered a pattern there that fascinated him. Or he couldn't bear to look at her a second longer. Either way, it meant her gamble hadn't paid off.

It was over.

She'd apologized. She'd admitted that she'd fallen in love with him, opening herself up to that single point of vulnerability, and it wasn't enough.

But then he finally glanced up, his eyes damp. That punched her in the gut. She'd hurt him and he was allowing her to witness exactly how much. What was she supposed to do with that, mourn the loss of what she could have had with him? She had been mourning it, for several long hours.

"Say that again," he demanded.

"I fell for you," she repeated succinctly, happy to have an excuse to admit it all over again. "I've never been in love before. I had no idea it would scare me so much. It made me do stupid things that I can't take back."

He nodded. "I get that. We're more alike than you might think."

Dampness sprang into her own eyes and she had to smile at what had become a running theme with them. He couldn't be too mad if he was telling jokes. There might be a thread of hope here. "Do tell."

"I've never been in love before, either, and it's making me do stupid things, too. I don't trust easily, and then you broke the fragile bit I was able to scrape together."

Oh, God, that stabbed her through the chest.

He'd *trusted* her and she'd shattered him by not telling him the truth sooner. Not breaking the story, deciding to take the evidence to him, all the small moments—none of that mattered in the end because she'd done the one thing he couldn't tolerate.

"Darling, no." She rushed it out before he could complete the last word. "Don't you dare take any of this on you. I'm the one to blame here, and it is not stupid of you to have trusted me. You have every reason to be angry and I—"

"The stupid thing I'm doing is forgiving you," he interrupted and she was so shocked, she shut up. "I'm not sure what tipped the scales but I'd rather practice getting this right with you than be alone with my self-righteousness."

Stunned, she stared at him. He was forgiving her? And wanted to be with her? None of this made a lick of sense.

"I don't understand."

"Let me spell it out, then. Laurel, I love you. Stop talking and come over here so I can show you."

Just like that. So simple and yet so complex. *I love you*.

The words penetrated into every fiber of her body until it felt like her skin would burst from the fullness inside.

Obediently, she fell into his embrace, scarcely able to credit how she was being wrapped up in Xavier LeBlanc's warm arms without having to perform seven years' penance for her sins.

"How can you just forgive me like that and not even care that I misled you?"

"I care, sweetheart," he said into her hair, his breath sensitizing her. "It's because I do care that I'm giving you another chance. If I didn't care, I'd let you go and move on easily. I've done it many times. But I don't want to not care anymore. I want to love someone enough that when they screw up, it hurts. So here's the thing I'd ask of you in exchange. Try not to screw up any more. But if you do, I'm pretty sure I can forgive that, too. Just as long as you're here being my partner at all things in life."

She laughed even as the tears started falling. "You're very gracious. You should teach a class."

"Noted. I'd rather take you to bed, if it's all the same to you."

She nodded and squealed when he picked her up, then threw her on the bed, following her down to wind her body up with his until she couldn't move. That was perfect. If he wanted to get right to the makeup sex, that worked for her and then some.

Except…

"There's just one thing I don't understand," she said instead of kissing him senseless, which was what she should have been doing—not opening more cans of worms. "What changed between earlier tonight and now?"

Surely not her phone call to Val. Had his brother talked him into giving her another chance? If so, she owed Val about a million handwritten notes of gratitude.

"I remembered how much grace you gave me when I told you about my father's will," he muttered, color staining his cheeks. "I'd kept it from you for my own reasons and you didn't even seem to notice, just jumped right on the Xavier bandwagon, supporting me in my fundraising tasks with no questions asked. I decided I was being a little high-handed to throw away what we had solely because you hadn't yet figured out the right timing to share your guilty secret. I'm sorry."

"Did you just apologize to *me*?" Laurel choked on the phrase and not all of it came out audibly. "I'm the one who screwed up—"

"Shh. You did and you apologized." He stroked his fingertips down her face, enlivening everything under his gentle touch. "For me, this is what trust looks like, and I have to spend a lot of time getting it right. It's a concerted effort that I'm still working on. So, for now, just know that I'm over it."

"How can you say that? What if I'm lying about forty-seven other things?" She wasn't. But how could he blindly accept that?

"You forget how well we can read each other." He kissed the tip of her nose, his heart spilling all over his face. "Because we're so much alike. I'm not worried. Plus, I'm sure you'll have to forgive me on occasion when I screw up the trust thing. We'll figure it out together."

Greedily, she soaked it all up. She loved it when he let her see how much she affected him. Loved that he trusted her enough to do so. Loved him. What had she done to get so lucky as to find a man like him?

"If you can read me so well, what am I thinking about right now?" she asked, letting her heart bloom through her expression.

"A drive down the shore of Lake Michigan?" he guessed and levered one of his knees between her legs to bind them even closer together.

She snorted. "Try again."

But, instead, he just kissed her and that was exactly right. He really could read her mind.

Miraculously, Xavier was giving her the second chance she'd always craved but had never been granted. She didn't have to worry about making mistakes with him because he'd be right there with her, holding her hand as they both jumped into the unknown. Together.

Epilogue

The charity fashion show Xavier and Laurel had put together with Val and Sabrina's help started off with a bang. Literally. A glitter cannon rained sparkles onto the stage as the first model strutted down the runway dripping with LeBlanc diamonds.

This time, Xavier wasn't a nervous wreck. Not about the fundraiser, anyway.

Not only was the fashion show designed to raise money for LBC, it was also a showcase for LeBlanc's new jewelry line. The buzz for it had grown to a fever pitch, which, in turn, put the spotlight on the charity. Who would have thought that Xavier and Val could combine forces in such a seamless way?

Laurel and Sabrina, that's who. Laurel and Val's wife had become fast friends, burning the midnight oil to help pull this thing together. Xavier couldn't believe how hard the two women had worked, but he showed Laurel how much he appreciated her every night when they finally rolled into bed together.

They did everything together now, including showers and shopping. Xavier had never been happier to have given someone a second chance. He had reaped enormous rewards for it. She felt the same. How did he know? Because her actions always spoke louder than her words. Though she had plenty of those, and she told him often that she loved him, which he wouldn't mind hearing daily for the next fifty years.

Tonight, he hoped to permanently etch that into stone. A diamond, to be precise.

"You have the ring, right?" Val said in his ear as they stood at the back of the venue monitoring the show. "I cannot tell you how many favors I had to call in to get that thing done in time."

As Xavier surveyed the crowd, he noted that several celebrities they'd invited had shown. Val had been schmoozing them in order to get signatures on the dotted line for a new LeBlanc advertising campaign and their presence here meant he'd sealed the deal.

In response to Val's question, Xavier patted his pocket, where the one-of-a-kind diamond engagement ring nestled inside a velvet box. "I would have slept with it, but I didn't want to ruin the surprise. Laurel loves surprises, you know."

His brother made a face. "You don't say. That's only the nine thousandth time you've told me."

The thought of proposing choked him up a little, but he didn't temper it. Why should he care if Val knew the subject of marriage tripped him up?

"So I'm a little excited to ask the woman I love to marry me. Sue me."

Saying it out loud didn't alter the swirl inside his gut

one bit. *Excited* was the wrong word. Nervous, exhila-
rated, emotional, sick to his stomach that he'd get it so
wrong she'd say no. Any of the above might be more ac-
curate.

Rolling his eyes, Val clapped him on the shoulder. "I
would have thought you'd be more excited to hear that I
got the preliminary numbers from Roger. LeBlanc Jewelers is going to hit the billion-dollar mark in revenue for
the year by the end of this quarter."

Something bright bloomed in Xavier's chest and he
grinned at his brother. "You did it!"

"We did it," Val corrected instantly. "You stacked the
dominoes, I knocked them over. We're a team and that's
why this fundraiser is going to put you over the figure for your goal, as well. Our inheritances are almost
locked up."

Funny how the thought of having succeeded didn't
make him as happy as catching sight of Laurel Dixon
in the crowd did.

He watched her stop to speak to someone on her way
to the dais, where she'd announce to the crowd how they
could purchase the models' jewelry with all proceeds
benefiting LBC. Edward LeBlanc's will had stated Xavier
couldn't write a check to cover the ten-million-dollar
fundraising goal, but it had not stipulated whether LeB-
lanc Jewelers could make a sizable donation—which had
been Laurel's idea. Her passion for LBC had spilled over
as she'd sold both brothers on the idea.

It was a no-brainer to also let her win over the crowd.
It was also the perfect time to drop a surprise proposal
on her.

She took the stage, which was his cue to move. But
he was frozen, all at once. What if this was a mistake?
What if she had no interest in getting married? What if—

"Stop freaking out and go propose," Val muttered from behind him as Laurel's brilliant and beautiful voice rang out through the loudspeaker. "She's going to love that ring you designed. I approved the workmanship personally."

"Yeah, yeah." Somehow Xavier got his body moving and he hit the floorboards of the stage.

Laurel glanced over at him expectantly as she smoothly finished her sentence despite the unplanned interruption. Her silvery-gray eyes caught him sideways, warming him, loving him. His ingrained sense of caution vanished in an instant as he strode across the stage to take her hand.

This was right, no question in his mind.

"Laurel." He cleared his throat as she smiled, totally as caught up as he was, her attention on him instead of the hundreds of people watching them. "Before I met you, I spent a lot of time shutting people out and blaming it on the need to be clearheaded in order to run a company. You taught me that no one can do much of anything by themselves, then helped me figure out that I didn't want to, anyway."

Tears splashed down her face but she didn't interrupt, even when he pulled out the box and flipped the lid, letting her get a glimpse of the ultrarare, smoky gray diamond that matched her eyes.

"This is me, down on one knee, asking you to take my hand and jump." When she arched an eyebrow, he realized he'd forgotten to kneel and hastily corrected that mistake by dropping to the platform with a loud thud. "Both knees, then."

The crowd laughed along with Laurel, who promptly got down on her knees, too. Of course she had. That's what she'd always done—ensured he knew they were a team beyond a shadow of a doubt.

And he had none.

"Yes," she said into the microphone attached to the neckline of her dress. "I'll marry you, but only if you buy me that Jada Ness necklace on the third model as an engagement present. Did you guys see that thing? Gorgeous!"

With that, she turned off her microphone and dove into his arms for a scorching kiss that got the entire crowd cheering and hooting.

"Driving up the price of LeBlanc's donations?" he murmured when they finally came up for air.

She shot him a misty smile. "You see right through me."

How could an inheritance compare with this woman? It couldn't. And that was the real lesson he suspected his father had intended for his sons to learn.

Nothing could replace the people you let into your life.

* * * * *

ALL OR NOTHING

CATHERINE MANN

To Shelley, welcome to the family!
Love you much!

One

Monte Carlo, Casino de la Méditerranée

It wasn't every day that a woman bet her five-carat, yellow-diamond engagement ring at a roulette table. But it was the only way Jayne Hughes could think of to get her pigheaded husband to take the rock back.

She'd left Conrad messages, telling him to contact her attorney. Conrad ignored them. Her lawyer had called his, to no avail. Divorce papers had been couriered, hand delivered to Conrad's personal secretary, who'd been told not to sign for them under any circumstances.

As Jayne angled through the crush of gamblers toward the roulette table, her fist closed around the engagement ring Conrad had given her seven years ago. Since he owned the *Casino de la Méditerranée,* if she lost the long-shot bet, the ring would be back in his possession. All or nothing, she had to lose to win. She just wanted a clean break and no more heartache.

Jayne plunked down the ring on the velvet square for 12 red. The anniversary of their breakup fell on January 12, next week. They'd spent three years of their seven years married apart. By now Conrad should have been able to accept that so they could move on with their lives.

Familiar sounds echoed up the domed ceiling, chimes and laughter, squeals of excitement mixed with the "ahhhh" of defeat. She'd called these walls full of frescoes home for the four years they'd lived together as man and wife. Even though she moved with ease here now, she'd grown up in a more down-to-earth home in Miami. Her father's dental practice had kept them very comfortable. Of course, they would have been a lot more comfortable had her father not been hiding away a second family.

Regardless, her parents' finances were nowhere close to touching the affluence of this social realm.

Her ring had been a Van Cleef & Arpels, one-of-a-kind design that had dazzled her back when she believed in fairy tales.

Cinderella had left the building. Jayne's glass slipper had been shattered right along with her heart. Prince Charming didn't exist. She made her own destiny and would take charge of her own life.

Nodding to the croupier in charge of spinning the wheel, she nudged her ring forward, centering it on the number 12 red. The casino employee tugged his tie and frowned, looking just past her shoulders and giving her only a second's warning before…

Conrad.

She could feel his presence behind her without looking. And how damn unfair was that? Even after three years apart, never once laying eyes on him the entire time, her body still knew him. Wanted him. Her skin tingled under the silky beige gown and her mind filled with memories of spending an entire weekend making love with the Mediterranean breeze blowing in through the balcony doors.

Conrad's breath caressed her ear an instant ahead of his voice. "Gaming plaques can be obtained to your left, *mon amour.*"

My love.

Hardly. More like his possession. "And divorce papers can be picked up from my lawyer."

She was a hospice nurse. Not a freaking princess.

"Now why would I want to split up when you look hot enough to melt a man's soul?" A subtle shift of his feet brought him closer until his fire seared her back as tangibly as the desire—and anger—pumping through her veins.

She pivoted to face him, bracing for the impact of his good looks.

Simply seeing him sent her stomach into a predictable tumble. She resented the way her body reacted to him. Why, why, why couldn't her mind and her hormones synch up?

His jet-black hair gleamed under the massive crystal chandeliers and she remembered the thick texture well, surprisingly soft and totally luxurious. She'd spent many nights watching him sleep and stroking her fingers along his hair. With his eyes closed, the power of his espresso-brown gaze couldn't persuade her to go against her better judgment. He didn't sleep much, an insomniac, as if he couldn't surrender control to the world even for sleep. So she'd cherished those rare, unguarded moments to look at him.

Women stared and whispered whenever Conrad Hughes walked past. Even now they didn't try to hide open stares of appreciation. He was beyond handsome in his tuxedo—or just wearing jeans and a T-shirt—in a bold and brooding way. While one hundred percent an American from New York, he had the exotic look of some Italian or Russian aristocrat from another century.

He was also chock-full of arrogance.

Conrad scooped the five-carat diamond off the velvet, and she only had a second to celebrate her victory before he placed it in her palm, closing her fingers back over the ring. The cool stone warmed with his hand curling hers into a fist.

"Conrad," she snapped, tugging.

"Jayne," he rumbled right back, still clasping until the ring cut into her skin. Shifting, he tucked alongside her. "This is hardly the place for our reunion."

He started walking and since he still held her hand, she had no choice but to go along, past the murmuring patrons and thick carved pillars. Familiar faces broke up the mass of vacationers, but she couldn't pause to make idle chitchat, pretending to be happy around old friends and employees.

Her husband's casino provided a gathering place for the elite, even royalty. At last count, he owned a half dozen around the world, but the *Casino de la Méditerranée* had always been his favorite, as well as his primary residence. The old-world flair included antique machines and tables, even though their internal mechanisms were upgraded to state of the art.

People vacationed here to cling to tradition, dressed to the nines in Savile Row tuxedos and Christian Dior evening gowns. Diamonds and other jewels glittered, no doubt original settings from Cartier to Bvlgari. Her five-carat ring was impressive, no question, but nothing out of the ordinary at the *Casino de la Méditerranée*.

Her high heels clicked faster and faster against the marble tiles, her black metallic bag slipping down to her elbow in her haste. "Stop. It. Now."

"No. Thanks." He stopped in front of the gilded elevator, his private elevator, and thumbed the button.

"God, you're still such a sarcastic ass." She sighed under her breath.

"Well, damn." He hooked an arm around her shoulders. "I've never heard that before. Thanks for enlightening me. I'll take it under advisement."

Jayne shrugged off his arm and planted her heels. "I am not going up to your suite."

"Our penthouse apartment." He plucked the ring from her hand and dropped it into her black bag hanging from her shoulder. "Our home."

A home? Hardly. But she refused to argue with him here in the lobby where anyone could listen. "Fine, I need to talk to you. Alone."

The doors slid open. He waived the elevator attendant away and led her inside, sealing them in the mirrored cubicle. "Serving the papers won't make me sign them."

So she'd noticed, to her intense frustration. "You can't really intend to stay married and live apart forever."

"Maybe I just wanted you to have the guts to talk to me in person rather than through another emissary—" his deep brown eyes crinkled at the corners "—to tell me to my face that you're prepared to spend the rest of your life never again sharing the same bed."

Sharing a bed again?

Not a chance.

She couldn't trust him, and after what happened with her father? She refused to let any man fool her the way her mother had been duped—or to break her heart the way her mother had been heartbroken. "You mean sharing the same bed whenever you happen to be in town after disappearing for weeks on end. We've been over this a million times. I can't sleep with a man who keeps secrets."

He stopped the elevator with a quick jab and faced her, the first signs of frustration stealing the smile from him. "I've never lied to you."

"No. You just walk away when you don't want to answer the question."

He was a smart man. Too smart. He played with words as adeptly as he played with money. At only fifteen years old, he'd used his vast trust fund to manipulate the stock market. He'd put more than one crook out of business with short sales, and nearly landed himself in a juvenile detention center. His family's influence worked the system. He'd been sentenced by a judge to attend a military reform school instead, where he hadn't reformed in the least, only fine-tuned his ability to get his way.

God help her, she still wasn't immune to him, a large part of why she'd kept her distance and tried to instigate the divorce from overseas. The last straw in their relationship had come when she'd had a scare with a questionable mammogram. She'd desperately needed his support, but couldn't locate him for nearly a week, the longest seven days of her life.

Her health concerns turned out to be benign, but her fears for her marriage? One hundred percent malignant. Out of respect for what they'd shared, she'd waited for Conrad to come home. She'd given him one last chance to be honest with her. He'd fed her the same old tired line about conducting business and how she should trust him.

She'd walked out that night with only a carry-on piece of luggage. If only she'd thought to leave her rings behind then.

Standing here in the intimate confines of the elevator, with classical music piping through the sound system, she could only think of the time he'd pressed her to the mirrored wall and made love to her until she could barely think, much less remember to ask him where he'd been for the past two weeks.

And still he wasn't talking, damn him. "Well, Conrad? You don't have anything to say?"

"The real problem here is not me. It's that you don't know how to trust." He skimmed his finger along the chain strap of her black metallic shoulder bag and hitched it back in place. "I am not your father."

His words turned residual passion into anger—and pain. "That's a low blow."

"Am I wrong?"

He stood an inch away, so close they could lose themselves in a kiss instead of the ache of all this self-awareness. But she couldn't travel that path again. She stepped closer, drawn by the scent of him, the deep ache in her belly to have his lips on hers. The draw was so intense it took everything inside her to step back.

"If you're so committed to the truth, then how about proving *you're* not *your* father."

When Conrad had been arrested as a teen, the papers ran headlines, Like Father, Like Son. His embezzling dad had escaped conviction as well for his white-collar crimes thanks to that same high-priced lawyer.

In her heart she knew her husband wasn't like his

old man. Conrad had hacked into all those Wall Street companies to expose his father and others like him. She knew intellectually…but the evasiveness, the walls between them… She just couldn't live that way.

She reached into her large, dangling evening bag and pulled out the folded stack of papers. "Here. I'm saving you a trip to the lawyer's office."

She pushed them against Conrad's chest and hit the elevator button for her floor, a guest suite, because she couldn't stomach the notion of staying in their old quarters, which she'd once decorated with hope and love.

"Conrad, consider yourself officially served. Don't worry about the ring. I'll sell it and donate the money to charity. All I need from you is your signature."

The elevator doors slid open at her floor, not his, not their old penthouse, but a room she'd prearranged under a different name. Her head held high, she charged out and into the carpeted corridor.

She walked away from Conrad, almost managing to ignore the fact that he still had the power to break her heart all over again.

Conrad had made ten fortunes by thirty-two years old and had given away nine. But tonight, he'd finally hit the jackpot with his biggest win in three years. He had a chance for closure with Jayne so she wouldn't haunt his dreams every damn night for the rest of his life.

He stalked back into the lobby toward the casino to turn over control for the evening. Once he'd been alerted to Jayne's presence on the floor, he'd walked out on a Fortune 500 guest and a deposed royal heir, drawn by the gleam of his wife's light blond hair piled on top of her head, the familiar curve of her pale neck. Talking to Jayne had been his number-one priority.

Finding her thunking down her ring on 12 red hadn't been the highlight of his life, but the way she'd leaned into him, the flare of awareness in her sky-blue eyes? No, it wasn't over, in spite of the divorce papers she'd slapped against his chest.

She was back under his roof for tonight. He folded the papers again and slid them inside his tuxedo jacket. As he walked past the bar, the bartender nodded toward the last brass stool—and a familiar patron.

Damn it. He did not need this now. But there was no dodging Colonel John Salvatore, his former headmaster and current contact for his freelance work with Interpol, work that had pulled him away from Jayne, work that he preferred she not know about for her own safety. Conrad's wealthy lifestyle and influence gave him easy entrée into powerful circles. When Interpol needed an "in" they called on a select group of contract operatives, headed by John Salvatore, saving months creating an undercover persona for a regular agent. Salvatore usually only tapped into his services once or twice a year. If he used Conrad too often, he risked exposure of the whole setup.

The reason for the missing weeks that always had Jayne in such an uproar.

Part of him understood he should just tell her about his second "career." He'd been cleared to share the basics with his spouse, just not details. But another part of him wanted her to trust him, to believe in him rather than assume he was like his criminal father or a cheating bastard like her dad.

The colonel lifted his Scotch in toast. "Someone's in over his head."

Conrad sat on the bar stool next to the colonel in the private corner, not even bothering to deny Salvatore's implication. "Jayne could have seen you there."

And if the colonel was here, there had to be a work reason. The past three years in particular, Conrad had embraced the sporadic missions with Interpol to fill his empty life, but not now.

"Then she would think your old headmaster came to say hello since I'd already come to see another former student's concert at the Côte d'Azur." Salvatore wore his standard gray suit, red tie and total calm like a uniform.

"This is not a good time." Having Jayne show up unannounced had turned his world upside down.

"I'm just hand delivering some cleanup paperwork—" he passed over a disc, no doubt encrypted "—from our recent...endeavor."

Endeavor: aka the Zhutov counterfeit currency case, which had concluded a month ago.

If Conrad had been thinking with his brain instead of his Johnson, he would have realized the colonel would never risk bringing him into another operation this soon. Already, Jayne was messing with his head, and she hadn't even been back in his life for an hour.

"Everybody wants to give me documents today." He patted the tux jacket and the papers crackled a reminder that his marriage was a signature away from being over.

"You're a popular gentleman tonight."

"I'm sarcastic and arrogant." According to Jayne anyway, and Jayne was a smart woman.

"And incredibly self-aware." Colonel Salvatore finished off his drink, his intense eyes always scanning the room. "You always were, even at the academy. Most of the boys arrived in denial or with delusions about their own importance. You knew your strengths right from the start."

Thinking about those teenage years made Conrad uncomfortable, itchy, reminding him of the toxic time in his life when his father had toppled far and hard off the pedestal Conrad had placed him upon. "Are we reminiscing for the hell of it, sir, or is there a point here?"

"You knew your strengths, but you didn't know your weakness." He nudged aside the cut crystal glass and stood. "Jayne is your Achilles' heel, and you need to recognize that or you're going to self-destruct."

"I'll take that under advisement." The bitter truth of the whole Achilles' heel notion stung like hell since he'd told his buddy Troy much the same thing when the guy had fallen head over ass in love.

"You're definitely as stubborn as ever." Salvatore clapped Conrad on the shoulder. "I'll be in town for the weekend. So let's say we meet again for lunch, day after tomorrow, to wrap up Zhutov. Good night, Conrad."

The colonel tossed down a tip on the bar and tucked into the crowd, blending in, out of sight before Conrad could finish processing what the old guy had said. Although Salvatore was rarely wrong, and he'd been right about Jayne's effect.

But as far as having a *good* night?

A *good* night was highly unlikely. But he had hopes. Because the evening wasn't over by a long shot—as Jayne would soon discover when she went to her suite and found her luggage had been moved to their pent-

house. All the more reason for him to turn over control
of the casino to his second in command and hotfoot it
back to the penthouse. Jayne would be fired up.

A magnificent sight not to be missed.

Steamed as hell over Conrad's latest arrogant move,
Jayne rode the elevator to the penthouse level, her old
home. The front-desk personnel had given her a key
card without hesitation or questions. Conrad had no
doubt told them to expect her since he'd moved her
clothes from the room she'd chosen.

Damn him.

Coming here was tough enough, and she'd planned
to give herself a little distance by staying in a different suite. In addition to the penthouse, the casino had
limited quarters for the most elite guests. Conrad had
built a larger hotel situated farther up the hillside. It
wasn't like she'd snubbed him by staying at that other
hotel. Besides, their separation wasn't a secret.

She curled her toes to crack out the tension and focused on finding Conrad.

And her clothes.

The gilded doors slid open to a cavernous entryway.
She steeled herself for the familiar sight of the Louis
VXI reproduction chairs and hall table she'd selected
with such care only to find...

Conrad had changed *everything*. She hadn't expected the place to stay completely the same since she'd
left—okay, maybe she had—but she couldn't possibly
have anticipated such a radical overhaul.

She stepped into the ultimate man cave, full of
massive leather furniture and a monstrous television
screen halfway hidden behind an oil painting that slid

to the side. Even the drapes had been replaced on the wall-wide window showcasing a moonlit view of the Mediterranean. Thick curtains had been pulled open, revealing yacht lights dotting the water like stars. There was still a sense of high-end style, like the rest of the casino, but without the least hint of feminine frills.

Apparently Conrad had stripped those away when they separated.

She'd spent years putting together the French provincial decor, a blend of old-world elegance with a warmth that every home should have. Had he torn the place apart in anger? Or had he simply not cared? She wasn't sure she even wanted to know what had happened to their old furnishings.

Right now, she only cared about confronting her soon-to-be ex-husband. She didn't have to search far.

Conrad sprawled in an oversize chair with a crystal glass in hand. A bottle of his favored Chivas Regal Royal Salute sat open on the mahogany table beside him. A sleek upholstered sofa had once rested there, an elegant but sturdy piece they'd made love on more than once.

On second thought, getting rid of the furniture seemed like a very wise move after all.

She hooked her purse on the antique wine rack lining the wall. Her heels sunk into the plush Moroccan rug with each angry step. "Where is my bag? I need my clothes."

"Your luggage is here in our penthouse, of course." He didn't move, barely blinked…just brooded. "Where else would it be?"

"In *my* suite. I checked into separate quarters on a different floor as you must know."

"I was informed the second you picked up your key."
He knocked back the last bit of his drink.

"And you had my things moved anyway." What did
he expect to gain with these games?

"I'm arrogant. Remember? You had to already know
what would happen when you checked in. No matter
what name you use, the staff would recognize my wife."

Maybe she had, subconsciously hoping to make a
prideful statement. "Silly me for hoping my request
would be honored—as your wife."

"And 'silly' me for thinking you wouldn't embar-
rass me in front of my own staff."

Contrition nipped at her heels. Regardless of what
had happened between them near the end of their marriage, she'd loved him deeply. She was so tired of hurting him, of the pain inside her, as well.

She sank into the chair beside him, weary to her
toes, needing to finish this and move on with her life,
to settle down with someone wonderfully boring and
uncomplicated. "I'm sorry. You're right. That was
thoughtless of me."

"Why did you do it?" He set aside his glass and leaned
closer. "You know there's plenty of space in the penthouse."

Even if he wouldn't offer total honesty, she could.
"Because I'm scared to be alone with you."

"God, Jayne." He reached out to her, clasping her
wrist with callused fingers. "I'm fifty different kinds
of a bastard, but never—never, damn it—would I hurt
you."

His careful touch attested to that, as well as years together where he'd always stayed in control, even during
their worst arguments. She wished she had his steely
rein over wayward emotions. She would give anything

to hold back the flood of feelings washing over her now, threatening to drown her.

Words—honesty—came pouring out of her. "I didn't mean that. I'm afraid I won't be able to resist sleeping with you."

Two

With Jayne's agonized confession echoing in his ears and resonating deep in his gut, holding himself still was the toughest thing Conrad had ever done—other than letting Jayne go the day she'd walked out on their marriage. But he needed to think this through, and fast. One wrong move and this confrontation could blow up in his face.

Every cell in his body shouted for him to scoop her out of that leather chair, take her to his room and make love to her all night long. Hell, all weekend long. And he would have—if he believed she would actually follow through on that wish to have sex.

But he could read Jayne too clearly. While she desired him, she was still pissed off. She would change her mind about sleeping with him before he finished pulling the pins from her pale blond hair. He needed more time to wipe away her reservations and persuade her that sleeping together one last time was a good thing.

Pulling back his hand, he grabbed the bottle instead and poured another drink. "As I recall, I didn't ask you to have sex with me."

If she sat any straighter in that seat, her spine would snap. "You don't have to say the words. Your eyes seduce me with a look." Her chin quivered. "*My* eyes betray me, because when I look at you…I want you. So much."

Okay, maybe he could be persuaded not to wait after all. "Why is that a bad thing?"

A clear battle waged in her light blue eyes that he understood quite well. The past three years apart had been a unique kind of hell for him, but eventually he'd accepted that their marriage was over. He just refused to end it via a courier.

Call him stubborn, but he'd wanted Jayne to look him in the face when she called it quits. Well, he'd gotten his wish—only to have her throw him a serious curveball. She still wanted him every bit as much as he wanted her.

Granted, sex between them had always been more than good, even when they'd used it to distract them from their latest argument. One last weekend together would offer the ultimate distraction. They could cleanse away the gnawing hunger and move on. He just had to persuade her to his way of thinking

The battle continued in her eyes until, finally, she shook her head, a strand of blond hair sliding loose. "You're not going to win. Not this time." Standing, she demanded, "Give me my clothes back, and don't you dare tell me to go into our old bedroom to get them myself."

He'd been right to wait, to play it cool for now. "They're already in the guest room."

Her mouth dropped open in surprise. "Oh, I'm sorry for thinking the worst of you."

He shrugged. "Most of the time you would be right."

"Damn it, Conrad," she said softly, her shoulders lowering, her face softening, "I don't want to feel bad for you, not now. I just want your signature and peace."

"All *I* ever wanted was to make you happy." Tonight might not be the right time to indulge in tantric sex, but that didn't mean he couldn't start lobbying. He shoved to his feet, stepped closer and reached out to stroke that loose lock of hair. "Jayne, I didn't ask you to have sex, but make no mistake, I think about being with you and how damn great we were together."

Teasing the familiar texture of her hair between his fingers, he brushed back the strand, his knuckles grazing her shoulder as he tugged free the pin still hanging on. Her pupils went wide with awareness and a surge of victory pumped through him. He knew the unique swirl of her tousled updo so well he could pull the pins out of it blindfolded.

He stepped aside. "Sleep well, Jayne."

Her hands shook as she swept back the loose strand, but she didn't say a word. She spun away on her high heels and snagged her purse from the wine rack before making tracks toward the spare room. He had a feeling peace wasn't in the cards for either of them anytime soon.

Jayne closed the guest-room door behind her and sagged back, wrapping her arms around herself in a death grip to keep from throwing herself at Conrad. After three long years without him, she hadn't expected her need for him to be this strong. Her mind filled with fantasies of leaning over him as he sat in that monstrously big chair, of sliding her knees up on either side until she straddled his lap.

There was something intensely stirring about the times she'd taken charge of him, a scenario she'd half forgotten in their time apart. But she loved that feeling of sensual power. Sure, he could turn the tables in a heartbeat—a gleam in his eyes would make that clear—but then she would tug his tie free, unbutton his shirt, his pants...

She slid down the door to sit on the floor. A sigh burst free. This wasn't as easy as she'd expected.

At least she had a bed to herself without arguing, a minor victory. She looked around at the "tomato-red room" as Conrad had called it. He'd left this space unchanged and the relief she felt over such a minor point surprised her. Why did it mean so much to her that he hadn't tossed out everything from their old life?

Shoving back up to her feet, she tapped a vintage bench used as a luggage rack and skimmed her fingers along the carved footboard. He'd even kept the red toile spread and curtains. She'd wanted a comfortable space for their family to visit. Except Conrad and his older sister only exchanged birthday and Christmas cards. Since his parents and her mother had passed away, that didn't leave many relatives. Jayne definitely hadn't invited her father and his new wife...

Had she let some deep-seated "daddy issues" lead her to choose a man destined to break her heart? That was not the first time the thought had occurred to her—okay, how could she dodge the possibility when Conrad had tossed it in her face at least a dozen times? She'd forgotten how he had a knack for catching her unaware, like how he'd sent her clothes here rather than demanding she sleep in their old room.

Like the way he'd tugged the pin from her hair.

Her mind had been so full of images of them together, and she'd actually admitted how much she still wanted him. Yet, he'd turned her down even though it was clear from his eyes, from his touch—from his arousal—how much he wanted her, too. She knew his body as well as her own, but God, would she ever understand the man?

She tossed her purse on the bed and her cell phone slid out. She snatched it up only to find the screen showed three missed calls from the same number.

Guilt soured in her stomach, and how twisted was that? She wasn't actually dating Anthony Collins. She'd been careful to keep things in the "friend" realm since she'd begun Hospice care for his aged great-uncle who'd recently passed away from end stage lung cancer.

She'd seen a lot of death in her job, and it was never easy. But knowing she'd helped ease a person's final days, had helped their families as well, she could never go back to filling her time with buying furniture and planning meals. She didn't even want to return to working in an E.R.

She'd found her niche for her nursing degree.

While there were others who could cover her rounds at work, she wanted to resume the life she'd started building for herself in Miami. And to do that, she needed closure for her marriage.

She thumbed the voice mail feature and listened…

"Jayne, just checking in…" Anthony's familiar voice piped through with the sound of her French bulldog, Mimi, barking in the background since he'd agreed to dog sit for her. "How did your flight go? Call me when you get a chance."

Beep. Next message.

"I'm getting worried about you. Hope you're not stranded from a layover, at the mercy of overpriced airport food."

Beep. Next call from Anthony, he hung up without speaking.

She should phone him back. Should. But she couldn't listen to his voice, not with desire for Conrad still so hot and fresh in her veins. She took the coward's way out and opted for a text message instead.

Made it 2 Monte Carlo safely. Thanks 4 worrying. 2 tired to talk. Will call later. Give Mimi an extra treat from me.

More of that remorse still churning, she hit Send and turned off the power. Big-time coward. She pitched her phone back in her purse. The *clink* as her cell hit metal reminded her of the ring Conrad had slipped back inside. She'd won a battle by delivering the divorce papers, and she could think of plenty of charities that would benefit from a donation if—when—she sold the ring.

She may not have gotten to place her bet, but she'd won tonight. Right?

Wrong. She sagged onto the edge of the bed and stared at her monogrammed carry-on bag. Good thing she'd packed her ereader, because there wasn't a chance in hell she would be sleeping.

Parked on the glassed-in portion of his balcony, Conrad thumbed through the Zhutov document on his tablet computer.

Monte Carlo rarely slept at night anyhow, the perfect setting for a chronic insomniac like himself. Beyond the windows, yachts bobbed in the bay, lights glowing. No doubt the casino below him was still in full swing, but he'd soundproofed his quarters.

The divorce papers lay beside him on the twisted iron breakfast table. He'd already reviewed them and found them every bit as frustrating as when his lawyer had relayed the details. And yes, he knew the contents even though he'd led Jayne to believe otherwise.

She was insistent on walking away with next to nothing, just as she'd done the day she'd left. He'd already drawn up an addendum that created a trust for her, and she could do whatever the hell she wanted with the money. But he'd vowed in front of God and his peers to protect this woman for life, and he would follow through on that promise even beyond their divorce.

He hadn't made that commitment lightly.

Frustration simmered inside him, threatening his focus as he read the Zhutov report from Salvatore. He'd given up his marriage for cases like this, so he'd damn well better succeed or he would have lost Jayne for nothing.

The world was better off with that bastard behind bars. Zhutov had masterminded one of the largest counterfeiting organizations in Eurasia. He'd used that influence to shift the balance of power between countries by manipulating the strength of a country's currency. At a time when many regions were struggling for financial survival, the least dip in economics could be devastating.

And from all appearances, Zhutov had played his tricks out of an amoral need for power and a desire to advance his son's political aspirations by any means possible.

Helping Interpol stop crooks like that was more than a job. It was a road to redemption after what Conrad had done in high school. He'd committed a crime not all that different from Zhutov's and gotten off with a slap on the wrist. At the time he'd manipulated the stock market, he'd deluded himself into thinking he was some sort of dispenser of cosmic justice, stealing from the evil rich to give to the more deserving.

Utter crap.

At fifteen, he'd been old enough to know better. He'd understood the difference between right and wrong. But he'd been so caught up in his own selfish need to prove he was better than his crook of a father, he'd failed to take into account the workers and the families hurt in the process.

He might have avoided official prison time, but he still owed a debt. When Salvatore had retired as headmaster of North Carolina Military Prep and taken a job with Interpol, Conrad had been one of his first recruits. He'd worked a case cracking open an international insider trading scam.

The sound of the balcony door opening drew him back to the moment. He didn't have to turn around. Jayne's scent already drifted toward him. Her sea-breeze freshness, a natural air, brought the outdoors inside. She'd told him once she'd gotten out of the practice of wearing perfume as a nurse because scents disturbed some patients. And yes, he remembered most everything about her, such as how she usually slept like a log regardless of the time zone.

That she was restless now equaled progress. It was already past 2:00 a.m.

He shut down the file and switched to a computer game, still keeping his back to her.

"Conrad?" Her husky voice stoked his frustration higher, hotter. "What are you doing up so late?"

"Business." The screen flashed with a burst of gunfire as his avatar fought back an ambush in Alpha Realms IV.

She laughed softly, stepping farther onto the balcony silently other than the swoosh of her silky robe against her legs. "So I see. New toy from your pal Troy Donavan?"

Conrad had the inside track on video games since a fellow felonious high school bud of his now ran a lucrative computer software corporation. "It's my downtime, and I don't even have to leave town. Did you need something?"

"I was getting a glass of water, and I saw you're still awake. You always were a night owl."

More than once she'd walked up behind him, slid her arms around his neck and offered to help him relax with a massage that always led to more.

"Feel free to have a seat." He guided his avatar around a corner in dystopian city ruins. "But I can't promise to be much of a conversationalist."

"Keep playing your game."

"Hmm…" Alpha Realms provided a safe distraction from the peripheral view of Jayne sliding onto the lounger. The way the silky robe clung to her shower-damp skin, she could have been naked.

Her legs crossed at the ankles, her fuzzy slippers dangling from her toes. "Why do you keep working when you could clearly retire?"

Because his fast-paced, wealthy lifestyle provided the perfect cover for him to move in the circles necessary to bring down crooks like Zhutov. "You knew I lived at the office when you married me."

"I was like any woman crazy in love." She cupped a water glass between her hands. "I deluded myself into believing I could change you."

He hadn't expected her to concede anything, much less that. He set aside his tablet, on top of those damn divorce papers. "I remember the first time I saw you."

The patio sconce highlighted her smile. "You were one of the crankiest, most uncooperative emergency room patients I'd ever met."

He'd been in Miami following up on a lead for Salvatore. Nothing hairy, just chasing a paper trail. He would have been back in Monte Carlo by morning, except a baggage handler at the airport dropped an overweight case on Conrad's foot. Unable to bear weight on it even when he'd tried to grit through the pain, he'd ended up in the E.R. rather than on his charter jet. And he'd still protested the entire way.

Although his mood had taken a turn for the better once the head nurse on the night shift stepped into the waiting room to find out why he'd sent everyone else running. "I'm surprised you spoke to me after what an uncooperative bastard I was."

"I still can't believe you insisted you just wanted a walking boot, that you had an important meeting you couldn't miss because of what you called a stubbed toe."

"Yeah, not my shining moment."

"Smart move sending flowers to the staff members you pissed off." She scratched the corner of her mouth with her pinky. "I don't believe I ever told you, but I thought they were for me when they arrived."

"I wanted to win you over. Apologizing to your co-workers seemed the wisest course to take." He'd extended his stay in Miami under the guise of looking into investment property.

They'd eloped three months later, in a simple oceanside ceremony with a couple of his alumni buddies as witnesses.

Jayne sipped her water, her eyes unblinking as if she might be holding back tears. "So this is really it for us."

"Nice to know this isn't any easier for you than it is for me."

Her hand shook as she set aside her glass. "Of course this isn't easy for me. But I want it to be done. I want to move past this and be happy again."

Damn, it really got under his skin that he still hurt her even after all this time apart.

"I'm sorry you're unhappy." Back when, he would have moved heaven and earth to give her what she wanted. Now it appeared all he could give her was a divorce.

"Do you really mean that?" She swung her feet to the side, sitting on the edge of the lounger. "Or is that why you held off signing the papers for so long? So you could see me squirm?"

"Honest to God, Jayne, I just want both of us to be happy, and if that means moving on, then okay." Although she looked so damn right beside him, back in his life again. He would be haunted by the vision of her there for a long time to come. "But right now, neither of us seems to be having much luck with the concept of a clean break."

"What are you saying?"

Persuading her would take a lot more savvy than sending a few dozen roses to her friends. "I think we need to take a couple of days to find that middle ground, peace or closure or whatever the hell therapists are calling it lately."

"We've been married for seven years." She fished into the pocket of her robe and pulled out her engagement ring and wedding band set. "How do you expect to find closure in two days when we've been trying for the last three years?"

He did not want to see those damn rings again. Not unless they were sitting where he'd put them—on her finger.

"Has ignoring each other worked for you? Because even living an ocean apart hasn't gone so well for me."

"You'll get no argument from me." Her fingers closed around the rings. "What exactly do you have in mind?"

He sensed victory within his sights. She was coming around to his way of thinking. But he had to be sure because if he miscalculated and moved too soon he could risk sending her running.

"I suggest we spend a simple night out together, no pressure. My old high school buddy Malcolm Douglas is performing nearby—in the Côte d'Azur—tomorrow night. I have tickets. Go with me."

"What if I say no?"

Not an option. He played his trump card. "Do you want my signature on those divorce papers?"

She dropped her rings on top of the computer that just happened to be resting over the divorce papers. "Are you blackmailing me?"

"Call it a trade." He rested his hand over the five-carat diamond he'd chosen for her, only her. "You give me two days and I'll give you the divorce papers. Signed."

"Just two days?" She studied him through narrowed, suspicious eyes.

He gathered up the rings and pressed them to her palm, closing her fingers over them again. "Forty-eight hours."

Forty-eight hours to romance her back into his bed one last time.

Three

Gasping, Jayne sat upright in bed, jolted out of a deep sleep by...sunlight?

Bold morning rays streamed through the part in the curtains. Late morning, not a sunrise. She looked at the bedside clock: *10:32 a.m.?* Shoving her tangled hair aside, she blinked and the time stayed the same.

Then changed to 10:33.

She never overslept and she never had trouble with jet lag, thanks to her early years in nursing working odd shifts in the emergency room. Except last night she'd had trouble falling asleep even after a long bubble bath. Restless, she'd been foolish enough to dance with temptation by talking to Conrad on a moonlit Mediterranean night.

He'd talked her into staying.

God, was she even ready to face him today with the memory of everything she'd said right there between them? The thought of him out there, a simple door away, had her so damn confused. She'd all but propositioned him, and he'd turned her down. She'd been so sure she would have to keep him at arm's length she'd checked into the room on another floor. That seemed petty, and even egotistical, now.

He'd simply wanted the common courtesy of a face-to-face goodbye and he'd been willing to wait three years to get it. The least she could do was behave maturely now. She just had to get through the next forty-eight hours without making a fool of herself over this man again.

Throwing aside the covers, she stood and came face-to-face with her reflection in the mirror. A fright show stared back at her, showcased by the gold-leaf frame. With her tousled hair and dark circles under her eyes, she looked worse than after pulling back-to-back shifts in the E.R.

Pride demanded she shower and change before facing Conrad, who would undoubtedly look hot in whatever he wore. Even bed-head suited him quite well, damn him.

A bracing shower later, she tugged on her favorite black skinny jeans and a poet's shirt belted at the waist, the best she could do with what little she had in her suitcase. But she'd expected to be traveling back to the States today, divorce papers in hand. At least she'd thought to change her flight and arrange for more time off before going to bed last night.

Nerves went wild in her chest as she opened the door. The sound of clanking silverware echoed down the hallway, the scent of coffee teasing her nose. He'd said they would spend two days finding peace with each other, but as she thought about facing him over breakfast, she felt anything but peaceful.

Still, she'd made a deal with him and she refused to let him see her shake in her shoes—or all but beg him for sex again.

Trailing her fingers down the chair railing in the hall, she made her way through the "man cave" living room and into the dining area. And oh, God, he'd swapped her elegant dining room set for the equivalent of an Irish pub table with a throne at the head. *Really?*

And where was the barbarian of the hour?

The table had been set for two, but he was nowhere to be seen. A rattle from the kitchen gave her only a second's warning before a tea cart came rolling in, but not pushed by Conrad.

A strange woman she'd never met before pushed the cart containing a plate of pastries, a bowl of fruit and two steaming carafes. At the moment, food was the last thing on Jayne's mind. Instead, at the top of the list was discovering the identity of this stranger. This beautiful redheaded stranger who looked very at ease in Conrad's home, serving breakfast from a familiar tea cart that had somehow survived the "purge of Jayne" from the premises.

Jayne thrust out her hand. "Good morning. I'm Jayne Hughes, and you would be?"

Given the leggy redhead was wearing jeans and a silk blouse, she wasn't from housekeeping.

"I'm Hillary Donavan. I'm married to Conrad's friend."

"Troy Donavan, the computer mogul who went to high school with Conrad." The pieces fell into place and, good Lord, did she ever feel ridiculous. "I saw your engagement and wedding announcements in the tabloids. You're even lovelier in person."

Hillary crinkled her nose. "That's a very polite way of saying I'm not photogenic. I hate the cameras, and I'm afraid they reciprocate."

The photos hadn't done her justice, but by no means could Hillary Donavan ever look anything but lovely— and happy. The newlywed glow radiated from her, leaving Jayne feeling weary and more than a little sad over her own lost dreams.

She forced a smile on her face. "I assume that breakfast is for us?"

"Why yes, it is," Hillary answered, sweeping the glass cover from the pastries. "Cream cheese filled, which I understand is your favorite, along with chocolate mint tea for you and coffee for me."

And big fat strawberries. All of her favorites.

She couldn't help but dig to find out who'd thought to make that happen. "How lovely of the kitchen staff to remember my preferences."

"Um, actually..." Hillary parked the cart between two chairs and waved for Jayne to sit. "I'm a former event planner so nosy habits die hard. I asked Conrad, and he was wonderfully specific."

He remembered, all the way down to the flavor of hot tea, when he'd always preferred coffee, black, alongside mounds of food. As she stared at the radically different decor, she wondered how many other times he'd deferred to her wishes and she just hadn't known.

Jayne touched the gold band around a plate from her wedding china. "I didn't realize you and your husband live in Monte Carlo now."

"Actually we flew over for a little unofficial high school reunion to see Malcolm's charity concert tonight. Word is he's sold out, set to take the Côte d'Azur by storm."

They were all going in a group outing? She felt like a girl who thought she'd been asked to the movie only to find out the whole class was going along. How ironic when she'd so often wished they had more married friends.

"I have to confess to having a fan girl moment the first time I met Malcolm Douglas in person." Hillary poured coffee from the silver carafe, the java scent steaming up all the stronger with reminders of breakfasts with Conrad. "I mean, wow, to have drinks and shoot the breeze with the latest incarnation of Harry Connick, Jr. or Michael Bublé? Pretty cool. Oh, and I'm supposed to tell you that evening gowns are being sent up this afternoon for you to choose from, since you probably packed light and it's a black-tie charity event. But I'm rambling. Hope you don't mind that I'm barging in on you."

"I'm glad for the company. Not many of Conrad's friends are married." When Troy had come to visit, she'd wished for a gal pal to hang out with and now she finally had one…too late for it to matter. "And when we were together, none of his classmates had walked down the aisle yet."

"They're getting to that age now. Even Elliot Starc got engaged recently." She shook her head laughing. "Another bad boy with a heart of gold. Did you ever get to meet him?"

"The one who was sent to the military high school after too many arrests for joy riding." Although according to Conrad, the joy riding had been more like car theft, but Elliot had influential friends. "Now he races cars on the international circuit."

"That's the one. Nobody thought he would ever settle down." Hillary's farm fresh quality, her uncomplicated friendliness, was infectious. "But then who would have thought my husband, the Robin Hood Hacker, would become Mr. Domesticity?"

The Robin Hood Hacker had infiltrated the Department of Defense's system, exposing corruption. After which, he'd ended up at North Carolina Military Prep reform school with Conrad. Malcolm Douglas had joined them later, having landed a plea bargain in response to drug charges.

Taking their histories into account, maybe she'd been wrong to think she could tame the bad boy. Was Hillary Donavan in for the same heartbreak down the road?

Shaking her head, Jayne cut into the pastry, cream cheese filling oozing out. "You're not at all what I expected when I read Troy got married."

"What *did* you expect?"

"Someone less…normal." She'd always felt so alone in Conrad's billionaire world. She hadn't imagined finding a friend like the neighbors she'd grown up with. "I seem to be saying all the wrong things. I hope you didn't take that the wrong way."

"No offense taken, honestly. Troy is a bit eccentric, and I'm, well, not." She twisted her diamond and emerald wedding ring, smiling contentedly. "We balance each other."

Jayne had once thought the same thing about herself and Conrad. She was a romantic, and he was so brooding. Looking back now, she'd assumed because of his high school years he was some sort of tortured soul and her nurse's spirit yearned to heal him.

Silverware clinked on the china as they ate and the

silence stretched. She felt the weight of Hillary's curious stare and unspoken question.

Jayne lifted her cup of tea. "You can go ahead and ask."

"Sorry to be rude." Hillary set aside her fork, a strawberry still speared on the end. "I'm just surprised to see you and Conrad together. I hope this means you've patched things up."

"I'm afraid not. The divorce will be final soon." How much, if anything, had he shared with his friends about the breakup? "We had some final paperwork to attend to. And while I'm here, I guess we're both trying to prove we can be civil to each other. Which is crazy since our paths will never cross again."

"You never know."

"I do know. Once I leave here, my life and Conrad's will go in two very different directions." Jayne folded her napkin and placed it on the table, her appetite gone.

She couldn't even bring herself to be mad at Hillary for being nice and happy. And Jayne hoped deep in her heart that Troy would be the bad boy who'd changed for the woman he'd married.

She'd been certain Conrad had changed, too, but he'd been so evasive about his travels, refusing to be honest with her when she'd confronted him again and again about his mysterious absences. He didn't disappear often, but when he did, he didn't leave a note or contact her. His excuses when he returned were thin at best. She'd wanted to believe he wasn't like his father… or her father. She still wanted to believe that.

But she couldn't be a fool. He kept insisting she should trust him. Well, damn it, he should have trusted her. The fact that he didn't left her with only two conclusions.

He wasn't the man she'd hoped, and he'd very likely never really loved her at all.

This little fantasy two-day make-nice-a-thon was just that. A fantasy. Thank God, he'd turned her away last night, because had she fallen into bed with him, she would have regretted it fiercely come morning time. Her body and her brain had never been *simpatico* around her husband.

But she had a great big broken heart as a reminder to listen only to her common sense.

Common sense told him that keeping his distance today would give him an edge tonight. But staying away from Jayne now that she'd returned to Monte Carlo was driving him crazy.

Seeing her on the security camera feed from the solarium didn't help his restraint, either.

But the secure room offered the safest place for him to hang out with a couple of his high school buds—Donavan and Douglas—who'd also been recruited for Interpol by Colonel Salvatore. The colonel had his own little army of freelancers drafted from the ranks of his former students. Although God knows why he'd chosen them, the least conformist boys in the whole school. But they were tight with each other, bonded by their experiences trying to patch their lives back together.

They'd even dubbed themselves "The Alpha Brotherhood." They could damn well conquer anything.

Now, they shared a deeper bond in their work for Salvatore. For obvious reasons, they still couldn't talk freely out in public. But a vaulted security room in his casino offered a place of protected privacy so they could let their guards down.

The remains of their lunch lay scattered on the table.

Normally he would have enjoyed the hell out of this. Not today. His thoughts stayed too firmly on Jayne, and his hand gravitated toward her image on the screen.

Donavan tipped back his chair, spinning his signature fedora on one finger. "Hey, Conrad, I picked up some great Cuban smokes last week, but I wouldn't want to start Malcolm whining that his allergies are acting up."

Douglas scratched at the hole in the knees of his jeans. "I do not whine."

"Okay—" Donavan held up his hands "—if that's the story you want to go with, fine, I'm game."

"I am seriously going to kick the crap out of you—" Douglas had picked fights from day one "—just for fun."

"Bring it."

"I would, but I don't want to risk straining my vocal cords and disappoint the groupies." Douglas grinned just like he was posing for the cover of one of his CDs. "But then, you've been benched by marriage so you wouldn't understand."

Some things never changed. They could have all been in their barracks, seventeen years ago. Except today Conrad didn't feel much like joining in. His eyes stayed locked on the screen showing security feed from his place.

Or more precisely, his eyes stayed locked on Jayne at the indoor pool with Donavan's wife. He couldn't take his eyes off the image of her relaxed and happy. Jayne wore clothes instead of a swimsuit, not that it mattered when he could only think of her wearing nothing at all. She was basking in the sun through the solarium windows.

Donavan sailed his hat across the room, Frisbee

style, nailing Conrad in the shoulder. "Are you doing okay, brother?"

Conrad plucked the hat from the floor and tossed it on the table alongside his half-eaten bowl of ratatouille. "Why wouldn't I be?"

"Oh, I don't know…" Malcolm lowered his chair legs to the ground again. "Maybe because your ex-wife is in town and you haven't stopped looking at her on that video monitor since we got in here."

"She's not my ex-wife yet." He resisted the urge to snap and further put a damper on their lunch. "Anybody up for a quick game of cards?"

Donavan winced. "So you can clean me out again?"

Malcolm hauled his chair back to the table. "Now who's whining?"

Pulling his eyes if not his attention off Jayne, Conrad swept aside the dishes and reached for a deck of cards.

Between their freelance work for Interpol and their regular day jobs, there was little time left to hang out like they'd done during the old days. Damn unlucky for him one of those few occasions happened to be now, when they were all around to witness the final implosion of his marriage.

And what if he didn't get one last night with Jayne? What if he had to spend the rest of his life with this hunger gnawing at his gut every time a blonde woman walked by? Except no woman, regardless of her hair color, affected him the way Jayne did.

No matter what he told his brothers, he was not okay. But damn it, he would be tonight after the concert when he lay Jayne back on that sofa and made her his again.

Jayne hadn't been on a date in three years, not even to McDonald's with a friend. How ironic that her first post-separation outing with a man would be with her own estranged husband. And he'd taken her to a black-tie charity concert on the Côte d'Azur—the French Riviera.

Although she had to admit, his idea of finding a peaceful middle ground had merit—even if he'd all but blackmailed her to gain her cooperation.

At least seated in the historic opera house she could lose herself in the crowd, simply sit beside Conrad and enjoy the music, without worrying about temptation or messy conversations. Malcolm Douglas sang a revamp of some 1940s tune, accompanying his vocals on the grand piano. His smooth baritone voice washed over her as effortlessly as the glide of Conrad's fingers on her shoulder. So what if her husband had draped his arm along the back of her seat? No big deal.

In fact, she'd been surprised at how little pressure he'd put on her throughout the day, especially after their intense discussions, their potent attraction, the night before. Waking up alone was one thing. But then to have him spend the entire day away from her...

His amenability was good. Wasn't it?

That niggling question had grown during the rest of the afternoon without him. Lunchtime passed and she started to question if she'd heard his offer of a date correctly. Except Hillary had mentioned it, as well. Then the staff brought a selection of evening wear in her size. She'd chosen a silver gown with bared shoulders, the mild winter only requiring a black satin wrap.

By the time Conrad arrived at their suite to pick her up, her nerves had been strung so tightly, she was ready to jump out of her skin. The sight of him in a tuxedo, broad shoulders filling out the coat to mouthwatering perfection, had just been downright unfair. All the way to the limo, she'd thought he would make his move, only to find Troy and Hillary Donavan waiting in the limousine, ready to go out to dinner with them before the concert. But then hadn't Hillary said Troy and Conrad were having some kind of reunion?

The evening had been perfect.

And perfectly frustrating.

Conrad's thumb grazed the sensitive crook of her neck, along the throb of her pulse. Did he know her heart beat faster for him? Her breath hitched in her throat.

Hillary leaned toward her and whispered, "Are you all right?"

Wincing, Jayne resisted the urge to shove Conrad's arm away. "I'm fine, just savoring."

Savoring the feel of Conrad's hand on her bare skin. Damn it.

He shifted in his seat, his fingers stroking along the top of her arm and sending shivers along her spine. She struggled not to squirm in her seat and draw Hillary's attention again. But that was getting tougher and tougher to manage by the second. He had to know what he was doing.

Still, if he'd been trying to seduce her, he could have been a lot more overt, starting with ditching the other couple. Her mind filled with vivid memories of the time he'd reserved a private opera box for a performance of *La Bohème* and made love to her with his hand under her dress.

Only one of the many times he'd diverted an argument with sex.

Yet now, he turned her down. Why?

The lights came up for intermission, and Conrad's

arm slid away as he applauded. She bit her lip to keep from groaning.

He stood then angled back down to her. "Do you and Hillary mind keeping each other company while Troy and I talk shop? He's developing some new software to prevent against hackers at the casino."

"Of course I don't mind." She'd given up the right to object when she'd walked out on him three years ago. Soon, their breakup would be official and legal.

"Thanks," he said, cupping her face in a warm palm for an instant before straightening. At the last second, he glanced back over his shoulder. "I didn't think it was possible, but you look even more beautiful than the night we saw *La Bohème*."

Her mouth fell open.

The reference to that incredible night had been no accident. Conrad had known exactly what he was doing. No doubt, her savvy husband had planned his every move all day with the express purpose of turning her inside out. The only question that remained?

Had he done so just for the satisfaction of turning her down again? Or did he want to ensure she wouldn't back away at the last second?

Either way, two could play that game.

Four

Conrad downshifted his Jaguar as he took the curve on the coastal road, Jayne in the passenger seat.

After the concert ended, he'd sent Troy and Hillary off in the limo, his Jaguar already parked and waiting for the next part of his plan to entice Jayne. She'd always loved midnight rides along the shore and since neither of them seemed able to sleep much, this longer route home seemed the right idea for his campaign to win her over.

When he took her back to the penthouse, he wanted to make damn sure they were headed straight for bed. Or to the rug in front of the fireplace.

Hell, against the wine rack was fine by him as long as he had Jayne naked and in his arms. The day apart after the fireworks last night seemed to have worked the way he'd hoped, giving the passion time to simmer. Even after three years away from each other, he understood the sensual side of her at least.

He glanced over at her, moonlight casting a glow around her as she toyed with her loose blond hair brushing her shoulders. His fingers itched to comb through the silky strands. Soon, he promised himself, looking back at the winding cliff road. Very soon.

She touched his arm lightly. "Are you sure you wouldn't rather visit with Malcolm tonight?"

Instead of being with her?

Not a chance.

"And steal Malcolm away from his groupies?" He kept his hand on the gearshift, enjoying the feel of her touch on him. Too bad the dash lights shone on her empty ring finger. "Even I wouldn't be that selfish."

"If you're certain." Her hand trailed away, searing him with a ghostly caress.

His hand twitched as he shifted into fourth. He winced at the slight grind to the finely tuned machine. "We had a chance to shoot the breeze this afternoon with Troy."

"Malcolm seems so different when he's away from the spotlight." She stretched her legs out in front of her, kicking off her silvery heels and wriggling her painted toes under the light blast of the heater. "It's difficult to reconcile the guy in holey blue jeans jamming on the guitar in your living room to the slick performer in suits and ties, crooning from the piano."

"Whatever gets the job done." He forced his eyes back on the road before he drove them over a cliff. "You and Hillary seem to have hit it off."

"I enjoyed the day with her, and it was nice to have another woman's opinion when I picked out which dress to wear tonight." She trailed her thumb along her bared collarbone, her black wrap having long ago slipped down around her waist.

The silver gown glistened in the glow of the dash, all but begging him to pull over and devote his undivided attention to peeling off the fitted bodice....

Eyes on the road.

He guided the Jag around another curve, yacht lights glinting on the water far below.

She angled her head to the side. "What are you thinking about?"

Nuh-uh. Not answering that one. "What are *you* thinking about?"

"Um, hello?" She laughed dryly. "Exactly what you intended for me to think about. The night we went to see *La Bohème.*"

How neatly she'd turned the tables on him.

He liked that about her, the way she took control, too, which reminded him of how she'd seduced him in his favorite chair once they'd gotten home from *La Bohème.* "That was a, uh, memorable evening."

"Not everything about our marriage was bad," she conceded.

"Italian opera will always hold a special place in my heart."

Except he'd thrown out that damn chair when she left, then found he had to pitch most of the rest of his furniture as well, including the dining-room table, which also held too many sensual memories of her making her way panther-style toward him with a strawberry in her mouth. The only place they'd never made love was in that tomato-red room since she'd said it was meant for guests, which somehow made it off-limits for sex.

She inched her wrap back up and around her shoulders, the night having dipped to fifty degrees. "I thought *Don Giovanni* was your favorite opera."

"The story of a hero landing in hell for his sins?" Appropriate. "A longtime favorite. Although I'm surprised you remember that I liked it."

"You remembered that I prefer cream cheese pastries and chocolate mint tea for breakfast."

He'd made a mental note of many things she liked back then, working his ass off to keep her happy as he felt their marriage giving way like a sandy cliff. "We were together for four years. I intended to be with you for the rest of my life."

"And you think I didn't?" Pain coated her words, as dark as the clouds shifting over the stars. "I wanted to build a family with you."

Another of her dreams he'd crushed. The ways he'd failed this woman just kept piling on, compacting his frustration until he was ready to explode.

Not trusting himself to drive, he pulled off the road and into a deserted rest area. He set the emergency brake and wished the anger inside him was as easy to halt. Anger at himself. "I gave you a puppy, damn it."

"I wanted a baby."

"Okay…" He angled toward her, half hoping she would slap his face, anything but stare at him with tears in her eyes. "Let's make a baby."

She flattened her hands to his chest, hard, stopping just shy of that slap he'd hoped for. Although a telltale flex of her jaw relayed her rising temper. "Don't you dare mock me or my dreams. That's not fair."

"I'm very serious about being with you."

"So you stay away from me all day?" she shouted, her fingers twisting in the lapels of his tuxedo. "You stay away for three whole years?"

Her question stopped him cold. "That bothered you?"

"For three years you ignored my attempts to contact you." She shoved free and leaned against the door, arms crossed under her breasts, which offered too beautiful a view. "Did you or did you not manipulate me on purpose today?"

He chose his words carefully, determined to get through the tough stuff so they could make love without the past hovering over them. "I figured we both needed space after last night if there was any chance of us enjoying our evening together."

"That makes sense," she conceded.

"I'm a logical man." He rested a hand on the back of her seat, his fingers dangling a whisper away from her hair. He was so damn close to having her, he could already taste her.

"You may think you're logical, but I don't understand half of what you do, Conrad. I do know that if you'd really loved me, truly wanted to stay married, you would have been honest. Whatever game you're playing now, it has nothing to do with love." Words tumbled from her faster and faster as if overflowing from a bottle. "You just don't want to lose. I'm another prize, a contest, a challenge. The way you've played me today and for three years? It's a game to you."

"I can assure you," he said softly, his fingers finally—thank God—finally skimming along her silky hair. "I consider the stakes to be very high. I am not in the mood to play."

"Then what are you doing? Because this back and forth, this torment, has nothing to do with peace."

"I have to agree." He traced her ear, down to the curve of her neck.

Her eyes slid closed and the air all but crackled. "Are you doing this to make me stay?"

"I told you what I want. A chance for us to say good-bye." He thumbed the throbbing pulse along her neck, his body going hard at the thought of her heart beating faster for him. "Leaving was your choice, not mine, but after three years I get that you mean business."

Her lashes fluttered open, her blue eyes pinning him. "And you really accept my decision."

"You *were* yelling at me about thirty seconds ago." He outlined her lips, her breath hot against his palm.

"Are you accusing me of being a shrew?" She nipped his finger.

He forgot to breathe. "I would never say that."

"Why not? I've called you a bastard and worse."

"I am a bastard, and I am far worse." He took her face in both hands, willing her to hear him, damn it, to finally understand how much she'd meant to him. "But I'm also a man who would have been there for you every day of your life."

She searched his eyes, her mouth so close to his their breaths tangled together. Something in her expression stopped him.

"Every day, Conrad? Unless it's one of the times you can't be reached or when you call but your number is blocked."

Damn it. He pulled away, slumping back in his seat. "I have work and holdings around the world."

"You're a broken record," she said, her voice weary and mad all at once. "But who am I to judge? You're not the only one who can keep secrets."

A chill iced the heat right out of the air. "What the hell does that mean?"

"Do you know what finally pushed me over the edge?" Her eyes filled with tears that should have been impossible to hold back. "What made me walk out?"

"It took me a couple of days to return your calls, and you'd had enough." He'd fired the secretary that hadn't put her calls through. He'd honestly been working at being more accessible to Jayne.

"Seven days, Conrad. Seven." She jabbed a finger at him, her voice going tight and the first tear sliding down her cheek. "I called you because I needed you. I'd gotten a suspicious report back on a mammogram, and the doctor wanted to do a biopsy right away."

Her words sucker punched *everything* out of him, leaving him numb. Then scared as hell.

He shot upright and started to grab her shoulders, only to hold back at the last second, afraid to touch her and upset her even more. "God, Jayne, are you all right? If I had known…"

"But you didn't." She pushed his hands away slowly, deliberately. "And don't worry, I'm fine. The lump was benign, but it sure would have been nice to have you hold my hand that week. So don't tell me you would have been there for me every day of my life. It's simply not true."

The sense of how badly he'd let Jayne down slammed over him. He closed his eyes, head back on his seat as he fought down the urge to leap out of the car and shout, punch a wall, anything to ease the crushing weight of how he'd let her down.

One deep breath at a time, he regained his composure enough to turn his head and look at her again. "What happened to the puppy?"

"Huh?" She scrubbed the backs of her hands across her wet cheeks.

"What did you do with Mimi after you left?" Mimi, named for the heroine in *La Bohème*.

"Oh, I kept Mimi, of course. She's with…a dog sitter."

Of course she'd kept the dog. Jayne wasn't the kind of person to throw away the good things in her life. He was.

He pinched the bridge of his nose, stared out the window at the churning night sea below and wished those murky waters held some answers. Jayne's ocean-fresh scent gave him only a second's warning before she took his face in her hands and kissed him.

Desperate to forget the past, Jayne sealed her lips to Conrad's. Right or wrong, she just needed to lose herself in the feel of his body against hers. The roar of the waves crashing against the shore echoed the elemental restlessness inside her.

With a low growl, he wrapped his strong, muscled arms around her. He took her mouth as thoroughly as she took his. The taste of coffee from dinner mingled with the flavor of him. And what a mix of the familiar and a first kiss wrapped up in one delicious moment. Goose bumps sprinkled along her arms, shimmering through her, as well.

Her hands slid from the warm bristle of his face to his shoulders and she held on. Because, God, this was what she'd wanted since the second she'd sensed him walk up behind her in the casino, drawn by the intoxicating warmth and bay rum scent of him. The way his hands smoothed back her hair, stroked along her arms, stoked a familiar heat inside her. She'd been right to instigate this. Here, in his arms, she didn't have to think about the pain of the past. To hell with peace and resolving their problems. Rehashing old issues just brought more pain. She wanted this bliss.

And then goodbye.

His mouth trekked to her jaw as he dipped lower, his late-day beard a sweet abrasion against her neck. Her head lolled to the side, a moan rolling up her throat. She stroked along the fine texture of his tux over bold muscles, up and into his hair. Combing through his impossibly soft strands, she urged him to give more, take more. She tugged gently, bringing his mouth back to hers.

Bittersweet pleasure rippled through her, reminding her how good they'd been together. Her breasts ached for his touch and she wriggled to get nearer, pressing against the hard wall of his chest. She struggled to get closer, swinging a knee over and bumping the gearshift.

"Damn it," Conrad's muffled curse whispered against her mouth but the thought that he might stop was more than she could bear.

She shoved her hands under his tuxedo coat, sinking her fingernails into the fine fibers of his shirt. Three years of being without sex—without *him*—crested inside her, demanding she follow through. His hand skimmed up her leg, tunneling under her dress as he'd done years ago. The rasp of his calluses along her skin ignited a special kind of pleasure and the promise of more.

Except that private theater box had been a lot roomier than his Jaguar. And she wanted more than just his *hands* on her.

"Take me…" she gasped.

"I intend to do just that." His voice rumbled in his chest, vibrating against her.

"Not here. Home. Take me home."

He angled back to look at her as if gauging the risk

of pausing. He grazed his knuckles along her cheek. "Are you sure?"

"Absolutely." As sure as anyone could be about making love with the person who'd broken her heart. She scored her nails down his back. "I know what I want. I won't change my mind about being with you tonight."

It wasn't a matter of winning or losing anymore. It was just a matter of stopping the ache and praying for some of that peace. Because wanting him was tearing her apart.

Angling into him, she nipped his bottom lip. "Conrad, I think it's time we break in your new furniture."

Conrad hauled Jayne into the private elevator and willed the doors to close faster. He may have hoped to clear the air of past issues during their drive before jumping right to sex, but now that Jayne had taken that decision out of his hands, he was all in.

He'd made record time driving back to the casino, determined to get to the penthouse before she changed her mind. God help him—both of them—if she backed out now. After tasting her again, touching her again, he was on fire from wanting to be with her. Wanting to bury himself heart deep inside her until they both forgot about everything but how damn good they were together.

Until in some way he made up for how deeply he'd let Jayne down.

He jammed his key card into the slot and the elevator doors slid closed. The mirrored walls reflected multiple images of his wife, tousled and so damn beautiful she took his breath away.

"Come here, now," she demanded, taking control in that way that turned him inside out. She grabbed his jacket and tugged him to her. "You've been tormenting me all night with the way you look at me."

He pressed her against the cool wall as the elevator lifted. "You've been tormenting me since the day I met you."

"What are we going to do about that?" She arched against him, her hips a perfect fit against his.

"I suggest we keep right on doing this until we can figure out how we're ever going to quit." He angled his mouth over hers, teasing her with light brushes and gentle tugs on her bottom lip.

"That makes absolutely no sense," she whispered between kisses.

Nothing about the way he felt for her made a damn bit of sense. But then he'd wanted her since the first time he saw her. That had never changed, never lightened up. He gathered her hair in his hand and—

"Conrad," she gasped, "stop the elevator."

"You want me to *stop?*" Denial spiked through him.

"No, I want you to stop the elevator—" she kissed him "—between floors—" stroked him "—so we don't have to wait a second longer."

He slapped the elevator button.

Jayne opened her arms, and he didn't even have to think. He thrust his hands into her hair, the familiar glide of those silky strands against his skin as arousing as always. Images scrolled through his mind of her slithering the blond mass over his chest as she nibbled her way down, down, down farther still until her mouth closed around him… Desire pounded in his ears in time with the bass beat of the elevator music.

As if she heard his thoughts, understood his need to have her touch him again, her fingers grazed down the front of his pants, rubbing along the length of him until he thought he would come right then and there. He gripped her wrist and eased her hand away. Soon, he promised himself, soon they could have it all.

Her hips rocked against him, and he pressed his thigh between her legs, rewarded by her breathy moan of pleasure. The gauzy length of her gown offered little barrier between him and the hot core of her.

Memories of that night at *La Bohème* seared his brain and fueled his imagination. He bunched up her dress in his fist, easing the fabric up her creamy-white legs until he reached the top of her thighs. Only a thin scrap of satin stayed between him and his goal. Between him and her.

They were completely alone in the privacy of his domain. And even if someone dared step into his realm, he shielded her with his body. Never would he leave her vulnerable to anyone or anything. She was his to protect, to cherish.

To please.

He tucked a finger into the thin string along the side and twisted until…the fabric gave way. She purred into his mouth and angled toward his touch. He wadded the panties in his fist and stuffed the torn scrap into his pocket before returning to her.

Stroking from her knee to her thigh again, he nudged her dress up until his fingers found her sweet, moist cleft. He stroked along her lips, swollen with the passion he'd given her. Without rushing, he stroked and explored, giving her time to grow accustomed to his touch, to let her desire build while he kissed her, murmuring against her mouth how damn much she drove him crazy. His other hand cupped the perfect curve of her bottom and lifted her toward the glide of his caress.

Her gasps grew faster, heavier, the rise and fall of

her breasts against his chest making him throb to be inside her. He slipped two fingers into the hot dampness of her, the velvety walls already pulsing around him with the first beginnings of her orgasm. He knew her body, every telltale sign. His fingers still buried deep within her, he pressed his palm against the tight nub of nerves and circled. She writhed against him in response, gasping for him not to stop, she was so close…

He burned to drop to his knees to finish her with his mouth, to fill his senses with the essence of her, but he didn't dare risk leaving her that exposed unless they were behind locked doors. But soon, before the night was over he would make love to her with more than his hand. He would bring her to shattering completion again and again, watching the bliss play across her face.

Her head fell back against the glassed wall, her hands clamped to his shoulders, her nails digging deep. He grazed his mouth along the throbbing pulse in her neck just as she arched in his arms. Her cries of completion echoed in the confines of the elevator, blending with the music drifting from the speakers. And he watched—God, how he watched—every nuance on her beautiful face, her eyes closed, her mouth parted with panting gasps. The tip of her tongue peeked out to run along her top lip and he throbbed impossibly harder. For her. Always for her.

Her body began to slide as she relaxed in the aftermath, her arms slipping around his neck. He palmed her back, bringing her against him, although his feet weren't as steady as he would like right now. The music grew louder, sweeping into a crescendo until…

An alarm pierced his ears, jolting through him. No wait, that was the floor lifting again, the elevator rising.

"Conrad?" Her eyes blinked open, passion-fogged.

He understood the feeling well.

His head fell to rest against the mirrored wall. "That's the backup system in case the elevator breaks."

"Oh…" She froze against him then wriggled, smoothing her gown back in place. "That would have been really embarrassing if we hadn't noticed and the doors had just opened."

"This is only a temporary delay." He cupped her head and kissed her soundly before stepping into the penthouse.

She kicked her shoes off, her eyes still steamy blue, her pupils wide with desire. He flung her wrap over the wine rack and backed her down the hall. Except he didn't intend to stop at the chair or in front of the fireplace. He wanted his wife in his bed again. Where they both belonged.

Later, he would figure out why the notion of one weekend suddenly didn't seem like near enough time with her.

He reached for the light switch only to realize…

Crap. The chandelier was already glowing overhead and he always turned the lights off when he left. Cleaning staff never came at night.

How had he let his instincts become so dulled that he'd missed the warning signs?

Someone was in his penthouse, and he should have noticed right away. His lapse could put Jayne in danger, and all because he'd let himself get carried away making out with her in an elevator. His guilt fired so hot her panties damn near burned a hole in his pocket. He moved fast, tucking her behind him as he scoped the living area and found his intruder.

Wearing his signature gray suit and red tie, Colonel

Salvatore lounged in a chair in front of the fireplace, a cell phone in hand.

Conrad's old headmaster and current Interpol handler set aside his phone and stood, his scowl deeper than usual. "Conrad, we have a problem."

Five

Her head still fogged from her explosive reaction to Conrad in the elevator, Jayne stared in confusion at their unexpected guest sitting in the living room like family. She recognized Conrad's old headmaster and knew they'd kept in touch over the years, but not to the extent that the man could just waltz into their home while they were out.

Conrad's home, she reminded herself. Not hers. Not anymore.

Had her almost-ex-husband grown closer to Colonel Salvatore over the past three years? So much time had passed, even though their attraction hadn't changed one bit, it wasn't surprising there might be things she didn't know about his life anymore.

Although that wouldn't stop her from asking.

Praying she didn't look as mussed as she felt, she walked deeper into the living room, all too aware of her bare feet and hastily tossed aside heels. Not to mention the fact that she wasn't wearing panties. "Colonel Salvatore? There's something wrong?"

Conrad stepped between them, his broad back between her and their "guest." He stuffed his hands into his tuxedo pockets only to pull them back out hastily. "Jayne, I'm sorry to leave, but Colonel Salvatore and I need to talk privately. Colonel? If you'll join me downstairs in my office…"

Except Salvatore didn't move toward the door. "This concerns your wife and her safety."

Safety? Unease skittered up her spine, icing away the remnants of passion from the elevator. If this problem involved her, she wasn't going anywhere. "Whoa, hold on. I am completely confused. What does your being here for some kind of problem have to do with me?"

The colonel looked at Conrad pointedly. "You need to tell her. Everything."

Conrad's shoulders braced. His jaw went hard with a familiar stubborn set. The tender lover of moments prior was nowhere to be seen now. "Sir, with all due respect, you and I should speak alone first."

"I wouldn't advise leaving her here by herself, even for us to talk." Salvatore's serious tone couldn't be missed or ignored. "The time for discretion has passed. She needs to know. Now."

Jayne looked from man to man like watching a tennis match. Something big was going on here, something she was fast beginning to realize would fundamentally change her life. The chill of apprehension spread as her legs folded. She didn't know what scared her more—the fact that this man thought she was in serious danger, or that she could be on the verge of finally learning something significant about her ultrasecretive husband. She sat on the edge of Conrad's massive leather chair, her bare toes curling into the Moroccan carpet.

Muscles twitching and flexing with restraint under his tux jacket, Conrad parked himself by the fireplace. He didn't sit, but he didn't protest or leave, either. Whatever John Salvatore wanted of Conrad, apparently he intended to follow through. The way the colonel issued orders spoke of something more official, almost like a boss and employee relationship, which made no sense at all.

"Jayne," Conrad started, scratching along the same bristled jaw she'd stroked only minutes earlier, "my lifestyle with the casinos gives me accessibility to high-profile people. It provides me with the ability to travel around the world, without raising any questions. Sometimes, authorities use that ability to get information."

"Accessibility to what? Which authorities? What kind of information?" Her mind swirled, trying to grasp where he was going with this and what it had to do with some kind of threat. "What are you talking about?"

Salvatore clasped his hands behind his back and rocked on his heels. "I work for Interpol headquarters in Lyon, France, recruiting and managing agents around the world."

"You work for Interpol," she said slowly, realization detonating inside her as she looked at her husband, all those unexplained absences making sense for the first time. "*You* work for Interpol."

All those years, he hadn't been cheating on her. And he hadn't been following in his criminal father's footsteps. But she didn't feel relieved. Even now, he was ready to make love to her with such a huge secret between them.

Anger and betrayal scoured through her as she thought of all the times he'd looked her in the face while hiding such intense secrets. For that matter, he wouldn't have confided in her even now if his boss hadn't demanded it. She'd had a right to know at least something about a part of Conrad's life that affected her profoundly. But he'd rather ditch their marriage than give her the least inkling about his secret agent double life.

To think, she'd been a kiss away from tearing her clothes the rest of the way off and jumping back in bed with him, even though he hadn't changed one bit. Even now the moist pleasure lingered between her legs, reminding her of how easily she'd opened for him all over again. Part of her hoped he would deny what she'd said, come up with some very, very believable explanation.

Except, damn him, he simply nodded before he turned back to John Salvatore. "Colonel, can we get back to Jayne's safety?"

"We have reason to believe the subject of your most recent investigation may have stumbled on your identity, perhaps through a mole in our organization. He's angry, and he wants revenge."

Salvatore's veiled explanation floated around her brain as she tried to piece together everything and figure out what it had to do with her husband. "Who exactly is after Conrad?"

They exchanged glances and before they could toss out some "need to know" phrase, she pressed on. "If I'm uninformed that puts us both in more danger. How can I be careful if I don't even know what to be careful about?"

Salvatore cleared his throat. "Have you heard of a man named Vladik Zhutov?"

Her heart stopped for three very stunned seconds. "Of course I've heard about him. He was all over the news. He's responsible for a major counterfeiting ring. He single-handedly tried to manipulate some small country's currency to affect the outcome of an election. But he's in jail now. Isn't he?"

The colonel dabbed his forehead with a handkerchief. "Even in prison, he has influence and connections, and we have reason to fear he might be trying to use those against Conrad."

She flattened her hand to the nearest chair to keep her legs from giving way underneath her. Her husband had always been so intent on separating himself from anything to do with his father's world. Even though his parents were both dead, Conrad wouldn't even visit their graves.

Was he on a vendetta of his own? Had he placed his life at risk to see that through?

Anger at Conrad took a backseat to fear for his safety. Her stomach knotted in horror, terror and a total denial of the possibility of a world without Conrad's indomitable presence. "Are you saying this individual has taken out some kind of hit on Conrad?"

She looked back and forth from the two men, both so stoic, giving away little in their stony expressions. How could someone stay this cool when her whole world was crumbling around her? Then she saw the pulse throbbing in Conrad's temple, a flash of something in his eyes that looked remarkably like…raw rage.

Salvatore sat on the chair beside her, angling toward her in his first sign of any kind of human softening. "Mrs. Hughes—Jayne—I'm afraid it's more complicated than that. Intelligence indicates Zhutov has been in contact with assassins, ones who are very good at

what they do. They understand the best way to get revenge is to go after what means the most to that person.
You, my dear, are Conrad's Achilles' heel."

Conrad was certain his head would explode before
the night was through. What more could life catapult
at him in one weekend?

The thought that someone—*anyone*—would dare
use Jayne to get back at him damn near sent him into
a blind rage. Only the need to protect her kept him in
check.

Later, he would deal with the inevitable fallout from
Salvatore ignoring Conrad's request to shield Jayne
from the messiness of his Interpol work. He could think
of a half-dozen different ways this could have been
handled, all of which involved *not* telling Jayne secrets
that could only put her in more danger.

Since Salvatore had dropped his "Achilles' heel"
bombshell, the colonel had taken charge as he did so
well. He'd shown Jayne his Interpol identification and
offered to fly her to headquarters in Lyon, France. He
would do whatever she needed to feel reassured, but it
needed to happen quickly for her personal protection.

One thing was clear. They had to leave Monte Carlo.
Tonight.

Salvatore continued to explain to Jayne in even, reasonable tones designed to calm. "When you make arrangements for work and for your dog, you need to give
a plausible story that also will lead Zhutov's people in
the wrong direction."

She twitched, but kept an admirable cool given everything she'd been told. "My phone is tapped?"

"Probably not." Salvatore shook his head. "And even
if it is, the penthouse is equipped with devices that

scramble your signal. However, that doesn't stop listening devices on the other end. We can use that to our advantage, though, by scripting what you say."

"This is insane." She pressed a trembling hand to her forehead.

"I agree." Salvatore played the conciliatory role well, one he sure as hell hadn't shown a bunch of screwed-up teenagers seventeen years ago. "I sincerely hope we're wrong and all of this will be resolved quickly. But we can't afford to count on that. You need to tell them that you're ironing out details of the divorce with Conrad and it's taking longer than you expected."

Nodding, she stood, hitching her evening bag over her shoulder. "I'll step into the kitchen, if that's not a problem."

"Take your time, catch your breath, but keep in mind we need to leave by sunup."

Jayne shot a quick glance at her husband, full of confusion, anger—betrayal—and then disappeared into the kitchen.

Conrad reined in his temper, lining up his thoughts and plans while his wife's soft voice drifted out.

Salvatore cleared his throat. "Do you have something to say, Hughes?"

Oh, he had plenty to say, but he needed to narrow his attention to the task at hand. "With all due respect, Colonel, it's best that I keep my opinions to myself and focus on how the hell we're going to keep Jayne off of that megalomaniac's radar."

"I have faith you'll handle that just fine."

The colonel's blasé answer lit the fuse to Conrad's anger. He closed the gap between them and hissed low between his teeth so Jayne wouldn't overhear. "If you have such faith in me, why the big show in front of my wife?"

"Big show?" He lifted an eyebrow.

What the hell? Conrad was not sixteen and a high school screwup. This was not the time for games. "Scaring the hell out of her. Springing the whole Interpol connection on her."

"I still can't believe you never told her. I thought you were smarter than that, my boy."

"It doesn't matter what you think. That was my call to make. I told you when I married her I didn't want her involved in that side of my life, for her own safety."

"Seems to me you've put her in more danger by not clueing her in. Even she picked up on that."

There was no way to know for sure now. But the possibility chapped at the worst time possible. "Thanks for the insights. Now, moving on to how we take care of Zhutov? If my cover's been compromised…"

The ramifications of that rolled over him, the realization that even once he had Jayne tucked away safe, this line of work and the redemption it brought could be closed to him forever. Later, he would sift through that and the possibility that without Interpol in his life, he could have his wife back.

Right now, he could only concentrate on making sure nobody touched so much as one hair on her head.

Sagging back against the polished pewter countertop, Jayne hugged her cell phone to her chest. The lies she'd just told left a bad taste in her mouth. Not to mention the fact she'd just been put on an unpaid leave of absence from her job.

This was supposed to have been such a simple trip to tie up the loose ends in her marriage…

Hell. Who was she kidding? Nothing with Conrad had ever been simple.

As if conjured from her thoughts, he filled the archway leading into the kitchen. He'd ditched his tuxedo jacket and tie, the top button of his shirt open. A light scratch marked his neck and she realized she must have put it there sometime during their grope fest in the elevator, along with spiking his hair in her desperate hunger to touch him again. Thank God she hadn't followed through. How much worse this moment would have been had that elevator stayed shut down and she'd made love with him standing up in that cubicle of mirrors.

She set her phone down. "Can I have my panties back?"

He quirked an arrogant eyebrow before dipping into his pocket and passing over the torn scrap of satin. It was ridiculous really, asking for the useless piece of underwear back, but it felt like a statement of independence to her, reclaiming ground and putting space between them.

She snatched the dangling white scrap from his hand. "Thank you."

She jammed the underwear into the trash, a minor victory, before turning back to confront him. "You work for Interpol."

Hands in his pockets, he lounged one shoulder against the door frame. "Apparently I do."

Apparently?

His dodgy answer echoed too many in their past. The time he'd missed their first anniversary weekend retreat that they'd planned for weeks. Or when he'd bailed on going with her to her half brother's incredibly awkward wedding. And no explanations. Ever.

She couldn't keep quiet. Not now with her emotions

still so raw from their explosive discussion in the car and their passionate encounter in the elevator. Even now, a need throbbed between her legs to finish what they'd started, to take him deeply inside her.

"You still won't admit it? Even when your boss confirmed it to me? What kind of twisted bastard are you? Do you get some sick pleasure out of yanking me around this way?"

His eyebrows shot up. "I kept you in the dark for your protection."

"I'm not buying it. I know you too well." Anger, hurt—and yes, more than a little sexual frustration—seethed inside her. "You didn't tell me because then you would have to commit, one hundred percent, to our marriage. You never wanted it to last, or you would have found a way to put my mind at ease all these years."

He could have told her something. Anything. But he hadn't even tried to come up with a rationale for his disappearances. He'd just *left*.

"I thought you would worry more," he said simply.

Although she wondered if there was a flash of guilt in his mocha-brown eyes. That would go a long way toward keeping her from pummeling him with fruit from the bowl on the counter.

"And you think I didn't worry when I had no clue where you were or what you were doing?" Those sleep-less nights came back to haunt her. "In the beginning, I was scared to death something had happened to you those times I couldn't locate you. It took me a long time to reach the conclusion you must be cheating on me, like my father fooled around on my mom."

He straightened, his eyes flinty hard. "I never slept with another woman."

"I get that." She raised a hand. "Hell, I figured that out even then. But you still lied to me. You cheated on me with that damn job."

He scrubbed a hand over his scowl. "Do you think operatives have the luxury of printing out an itinerary for their spouses?"

"Of course not. I'm not that naive." More like she'd let herself stay oblivious, clinging to the hope she might be wrong about him hiding things from her. "But Colonel Salvatore made it clear tonight you could have told me something and you chose not to."

"I chose what I thought was best for you." His mouth went tight.

Well, too damn bad. She had every right to be upset.

"You thought it was best to sacrifice our marriage? Because that's the decision you made for both of us, without even giving me the option of deciding for myself."

"I won't apologize for keeping you safe."

His intractable words made her realize how far apart they were from seeing eye to eye on this.

"Fine. But consider how you'd feel if the tables were turned and it was me disappearing for days on end without a word of explanation. Or what you would have thought if I'd left you to celebrate your anniversary by yourself." He'd flown her to a couples retreat in the Seychelles. The island country off the coast of Africa had been so romantic and exotic. Except he'd left her sitting in a dining room full of hormones all alone.

He'd said nothing, as per usual.

Knowing she'd let herself be turned into some kind of doll adorning his arm and decorating his world perhaps stung most of all. "And to think I was that close to falling in your arms again. Well, no worries about that now. I am so over you, Conrad Hughes."

She angled sideways past him, through the door.

He gripped her arm. "You can't leave now. No matter how angry you are with me, it's not safe for you out there."

"I got that from your boss, thanks. I'm just going to pack. In my room. *Alone.*"

His hand slid down her arm, sending a traitorous jolt of awareness straight to her belly until she pressed her legs together against the moist ache still simmering.

"You were able to arrange things with work and for Mimi?"

Standing this close to Conrad with her emotions on overload was not a smart idea. She needed to wrap this up and retreat to her room to regroup. "She's settled, but Anthony can't watch her indefinitely. He travels with his job. But I'll figure that out later."

She brushed past.

"Anthony."

Conrad's flat, emotionless voice sent prickles up her spine. She turned slowly, her evening gown brushing the tops of her bare feet. "He's the nephew of a former patient."

Not that she owed him any explanation after the way he'd walled her out for years.

"And he watches our dog while you're out of town." Conrad still leaned in the doorway, completely motionless other than the slow blink of his too-sharp eyes.

"It's not like he and I are dating…"

"Yet. But that's why you came to Monte Carlo, isn't it? So you would be free to move on with Anthony or some other guy." Conrad scratched his eyebrow. "I think I pretty much have the picture in place."

And clearly he wasn't one bit happy with that image. Well, too damn bad after all the tears she'd shed seeing his casino pictured in tabloids, him with a different woman on his arm each time. "You don't get to be mad at me. I'm the one who's been lied to."

"Then I guess that makes it easier for us to spend time alone together." He shoved away from the door frame, his shoulder brushing hers as he passed. "Pack your bag, sweetheart. We're taking a family vacation."

Six

The bulletproof, tinted windows on his balcony offered Conrad the protection he needed while escaping the claustrophobic air of the penthouse.

Jayne had already picked out his replacement. He realized now that she'd come to Monte Carlo to end their marriage so she could move on with another man. If she hadn't already.

Scratch that.

He didn't think she was sleeping with the guy, not yet. Jayne was an innately honorable woman. And while he didn't assume she would stay celibate for three years, she wouldn't have almost had sex with him if she'd already committed to another man.

Her integrity was one of the things about her that had drawn him right from the start. She had a goodness inside her that was rare and should be protected. For the first time, it hit him how much she must have missed her career when she lived with him, and even though Monte Carlo was his primary residence, he'd traveled from holding to holding too often for her to secure a new job. He'd never thought about how long and lonely her days must have been.

Looking back, he probably should have left her the hell alone. He deserved Jayne's anger and more. He'd been wrong to marry her in the first place knowing he would never choose to tell her about his contract work with Interpol. He'd deluded himself that he held back out of a need to protect her, but deep down he knew he'd always feared he needed the job more than he needed her. That he needed that outlet to rebel, a way to channel the part of his father that lived inside him, the part that had almost landed him in jail as a teenager.

He'd been so damn crazy for Jayne he'd convinced himself he could make it work.

He'd only delayed the inevitable.

Now she was paying the price for his mistake. He resisted the urge to put his fist through a wall. Her life could be at risk because of him. He wouldn't be able to live with himself if anything happened to her.

He scoured the cove below, every yacht and cruise ship lighting up the shoreline suddenly became suspect.

A sound from the doorway sent him pivoting fast, his hand on the 9mm he'd strapped into a shoulder harness.

Troy Donavan lounged in the entrance, his fedora in hand. "Whoa, hold up. Don't shoot your body double."

"My what?"

Donavan stepped out onto the balcony. "Your double. I'll travel as you and you travel as me. If anyone manages to track either of our movements, they'll still be led in the wrong direction." He dropped his hat on the lounger. "Salvatore said we're not heading out for another couple of hours. I can keep watch over Jayne while you catch a nap."

"I'm cool. But thanks. Insomnia has its perks." He glanced sideways at his best friend of over seventeen years. "Did Salvatore send you here to check on me after the showdown with Jayne?"

"He alerted me to the crap with Zhutov and the concerns for your wife. I know how I would feel in your shoes, and it's not pretty."

Damn straight. He didn't know how Donavan handled having Hillary keyed into the Interpol world. She'd even started training to actively participate in future freelance missions.

"I have to get Jayne as far away and under the radar as possible." How long would this nightmare last? Would she end up spending the rest of her life on the run? He wouldn't leave her side until he knew she was safe. He'd wanted to grow old with her, but sure as hell not that way.

"I promise you, brother, if Zhutov has so much as breathed Jayne's name, he will be stopped. You have to believe that."

"After this is over, I have to let her go." Those words were tough to say, especially now with the image of her building a life with another man. "I was wrong to think I could have her and the job."

"People do dangerous jobs and still have lives. You can't expect every cop, firefighter, military person and agent not to have families. Even if we don't get married, there are still people in our lives who are important to us. The best thing you can do for Jayne is stick to her, tight."

"You're right."

"Then why aren't you smiling?" Donavan clapped him on the shoulder. "Want to talk about what else is chewing you up?"

"Not really."

"Fair enough."

And still he couldn't stop from talking. "She just… gets to me."

He remembered the way she'd called him on the carpet for teasing her on the ride home tonight, giving him hell for talking about that evening they saw *La Bohème* together. As if he knew that would turn her inside out the same way it did him. Damn, he'd missed that spark she possessed.

"That's what women do. They burrow under your skin." Donavan grinned. "Didn't you get the memo?"

Conrad didn't feel one damn bit like smiling. He stared down at his clenched fist, at his own bare ring finger. "She's seeing someone else."

"Damn," Donavan growled. "That's got to really bite. But it's been three years since the two of you split. Did you really expect you would both stay celibate?"

Conrad looked out over the harbor, the sea stretching as far and dark as each day he'd spent apart from Jayne.

Troy straightened quickly. "Whoa, wait. Are you telling me you haven't seen anyone else while you've been separated?"

Still, Conrad held his silence.

"But the tabloids…"

"They lie." Conrad smiled wryly at his friend. "Didn't you get the memo?"

Donavan stared back, not even bothering to disguise his total shock. "You haven't been with anybody in *three years?*"

"I'm married." He thumbed his empty ring finger. "A married man does not cheat. It's dishonorable."

Donavan scrubbed both hands over his face then shook his head as if to clear the shock away. "So let me get this straight… You haven't seen your wife since she left you. Which means you haven't had sex with anyone in *three years?*"

"You're a damn genius."

Donavan whistled softly. "You must be having some serious quality 'alone time' in the shower."

Understatement of the year. Or rather, that would be *three* years. "Your sympathy for my pain is overwhelming."

"Doesn't sound like you need sympathy. Sounds like you need to get—"

"Thanks," he interrupted, not even wanting to risk Donavan's words putting images in his head. "I can handle my own life."

"Because you're doing such a bang-up job at it lately. But wait." He thumped himself on the forehead. "Poor choice of words."

Against his will, a smile tugged at Conrad's face. "Really, Donovan. Don't you have some geeky computer tech support work that needs your attention before we all leave?"

"You can call me a geek all night long, brother, but I'll be sleeping next to a woman." Donavan punched him in the arm.

Conrad lifted an eyebrow, but preferred the joking to sympathy any day of the week. Something his best friend undoubtedly understood. "Hit me again, and I'm going to beat the crap out of you."

Donavan snagged his fedora from the lounger. "Everybody wants to beat the crap out of me today. What's up with that?"

"Get out of here before I break you in half."

"Because I feel very sorry for you, I'm just going to walk away." He spun his hat on one finger. "But I'm taking a bottle of your Chivas with me so you won't feel bad for scaring me off."

"Jackass."

"I feel the love, brother. I feel the love." He opened the French doors and paused, half in, half out. "See you inside later?"

"Absolutely." He nodded once. "And thank you."

Donavan nodded back. No more words were needed.

His friend had helped him decompress enough to see clearly again. He needed to keep his eye on the goal now, to keep Jayne safe at all cost.

He might not be the man she deserved, but he was damn well the man she needed.

Jayne rolled her small bag out into the living room, having used the past couple of hours to change out of her evening gown and generally get her head together. If that was even possible after her world had been so deeply shaken in such a short time.

The sun hadn't even risen yet.

If they hadn't been interrupted, she would have been in Conrad's bed now, completely unsuspecting of *this*.

She realized his secret had noble roots, a profession that brought justice, so different than her father's secret life, his hidden second family with a mistress and two children. But the fact that she'd been duped so totally still hurt on a deep level. Trusting her heart and her life to Conrad had been very difficult.

How could she reconcile the fact that she hadn't

even begun to know the man she'd married? Walking away with any kind of peace when she'd thought she understood him was tough enough. But now with so much mystery surrounding Conrad and their life together, she felt like every bit of progress she'd made since leaving had been upended.

And with this possible threat lurking, she didn't even have the luxury of distance to regain her footing.

The Donavans sat in the leather chairs, talking over glasses of seltzer water. She felt uncomfortable having Troy and Hillary pose as decoys for them. The thought of anybody in harm's way because of her made her ill. But she hadn't been given any say on the matter.

She also couldn't help but note how seamlessly Hillary had been brought into the plan. Apparently not all Interpol operatives kept secrets from their spouses.

The stab of envy for that kind of compatibility wasn't something she was proud of. But, damn it, why couldn't she have found her way to that sort of comfort with her husband? What was wrong with her that Conrad had never even considered confiding in her?

Just as she rolled her bag the rest of the way in, Conrad stepped out of his suite. His normal dark and brooding style of clothes had been swapped out for something more in keeping with Troy's metro style. She couldn't take her eyes from the relaxed look of her husband in jeans and a jacket, collar open, face unshaved, his thick black hair spiked.

Troy looked back over the chair, water glass in hand. "Good timing. Salvatore should be done any minute now. He's arranging the travel plans, complete with diversionary stories going out to the press." He glanced over at his wife. "Did I forget anything?"

"Just this." Carrying one of her husband's hats, Hillary walked to Conrad. "You should wear this. And maybe slick back your hair a bit. Here…" She reached for her water glass. "Use some of this since you didn't have time to shower."

Troy choked on his drink.

Conrad glared at him.

Jayne wondered what in the world was wrong with both of them.

Her husband took the fedora from Hillary. "I'm good. Thanks. I'll take good care of his hat."

"Take good care of yourself while you're at it," Hillary said just as her husband looped an arm around her waist and hauled her to his side. "Yes?"

Troy held up his phone. "Text from Salvatore. Time to roll."

With a hurried goodbye, Troy and Hillary stepped into the elevator, his head bent toward hers to listen to something. The two of them looked so right together, so in sync even in the middle of chaos.

Jealousy gripped Jayne in an unrelenting fist.

The doors slid closed and she wished her feelings could be as easily sealed away. She turned back to her husband. "Where are we going?"

Conrad thumbed through his text message, Troy's fedora under his arm. "To the jet."

"And the jet would be going to…"

He looked up, his eyes piercing and closed off all at once. "Somewhere far away from here."

His evasive answer set her teeth on edge. "Now that I know about your double life, you can drop the tall, dark and mysterious act."

She yanked the fedora from under his arm, his jacket parting.

A shoulder holster held a silver handgun.

"Oh," she gasped, knowing she shouldn't be surprised, but still just... "Oh."

He pulled his jacket back over the weapon. "The people I help nail don't play nice. They are seriously dangerous. You can be as angry at me as you want, but you'll have to trust me, just this once, and save your questions for the airplane. I promise I'll tell you anything you want to know once we're airborne. Agreed?"

Anything she wanted to know? That was one promise she couldn't resist. Probably the very reason he'd said it, tossing irresistible temptation her way. But it was an offer she intended to press to the fullest.

She pulled out a silk scarf to wrap over her blond hair. "Lead the way."

Once the chartered jet reached cruising altitude, Conrad took his first easy breath since he'd found Salvatore waiting for him in the penthouse. He was that much closer to having Jayne tucked away in the last place anyone would think to find either of them.

Jayne hadn't moved her eyes off him since they'd left the penthouse. Even now she sat on the other side of the small table, tugging her silk scarf from hand to hand. He watched the glide of the deep purple fabric as it slid from side to side. Until now, he hadn't realized she dressed in bolder colors these days. A simple thing and inconsequential, but yet another sign that she'd moved on since leaving him. She'd changed and he couldn't go back to the way things were.

But back to the moment. Without a doubt, the boom was going to fall soon and he would have to answer her questions. He owed her that much and more. He reached for his coffee on the small table between them, a light breakfast set in front of them.

He wasn't interested in food. Only Jayne. He could read her well and the second she set aside the scarf in her hands he knew. She was ready to talk.

"We're airborne, and you owe me answers." She drizzled honey into her tea. "Tell me where we're going."

"Africa."

Freezing midsip, she stared at him over the top of her cup. "Just when I think you can't surprise me. Are we staying somewhere like the island resort where we planned to spend our first anniversary?"

"No." He couldn't miss the subtle reminder of when he'd bailed on their first anniversary retreat in Seychelles. Without a doubt, he owed her for all the times he'd shortchanged her in the past. He raised the window shade, the first morning rays streaking through the clouds. "We're going to West Africa. I have a house there."

"Another thing I didn't know about you." Her voice dripped with frustration as thick as the extra honey she spooned into her tea. "Do you mean something like a safari resort?"

"Something like that, nothing to do with business, though." She would see for herself soon enough, and he had to admit, he wanted to see her reaction without prior warning. "I purchased the property just before we split. A case led me to… It doesn't matter. You're right. I should have told you about an acquisition that large."

"If it's your home, can't we be found there?"

"The property was purchased under a corporate name, nothing anyone would connect with me. There's not much point in a retreat if the paparazzi can find you."

"Well, if the press hasn't found out about it, then the

place must be secure." She half smiled. "So do we plan to hide in Africa indefinitely?"

"What did you tell Anthony?" He set down his coffee cup carefully.

"It's my turn to ask the questions, remember?" she reminded him gently. Her eyes fell away, and she stared into her cup as if searching for answers of her own. "But in the interest of peace…I told him what we planned for me to say, that divorcing my husband wasn't as simple as I'd expected. That you and I needed time to sort things out. He was understanding."

"Then he isn't as big a threat as I thought." He couldn't wrap his brain around the notion of ever being okay with the prospect of Jayne and some other guy hooking up. His hand twitched around the cup.

"Conrad, not everyone is all alpha, all the time."

He looked up fast, surprised at her word choice then chuckled.

"What did I say? And remember, you promised to answer my questions."

At least he could tell her this and wondered now why he never had before. "Back in high school, my friends, we called ourselves the Alpha Brotherhood."

"You're all still so close." She frowned. "Do they *all* work for…"

"Please don't ask."

"You said I could ask anything," she pressed stubbornly.

He searched for what he could say and still stay honest. "If something were to happen to me and you needed anything at all, you could call them. They can get in touch with Salvatore. Is that answer enough for you?"

She stared at him for so long he thought she might push for more, and truly there was more he could say but old instincts died hard after playing his life close to the vest.

Nodding, she leaned back in her leather seat, crossing her arms. "Thank you. Get back to the Alpha Brotherhood story."

"There were two kinds of guys at the academy, the military sort who wanted to be there to jump-start a career in uniform and a bunch of screwed-up rule breakers who needed to learn discipline."

Did she know that when she'd leaned back her legs stretched out in a sexy length that made him ache? He wanted to reach down and stroke her calf, so close to touching him. The sight of her in those jeans and leather boots sent another shot of adrenaline to his already overrevved body.

He knocked back another swallow of hot coffee to moisten his suddenly dry mouth. "Some of us in that second half realized the wisdom of channeling those rebellious tendencies if we wanted to stay out of jail. After we graduated from college, Salvatore offered us a legal outlet, a way to make amends and still color outside the lines—legally. Honorably."

"That's important to you, honor." She crossed her legs at the ankles, bringing her booted foot even closer to brushing him. "You've been so emphatic about never lying even when you hold back the truth."

He looked up sharply, realizing how much he'd revealed while ogling her legs like some horny teenager. And he realized she was playing him. Just like he'd played her in the past, using sexual attraction to steer their conversations.

It didn't feel good being maneuvered that way.

Remorse took his temperature down a notch. He sat up straighter, elbows on the table as he cradled his coffee. "My father was a crooked bastard, Jayne. It makes me sick the way the rest of the world all thought he was this great philanthropist. He made a crap-ton of money and gave it away to charities. But he made it cheating the same kinds of people he was pretending to help."

Her hand fell to rest on his. "I understand what it's like to lose faith in your father. It hurts, so much."

How strange that he was holding hands with his wife and he couldn't remember the last time he'd done that. He'd touched her, stroked her, made love to her countless times, but he couldn't recall holding her hand.

"I guess we do have that in common. For a long time, I bought into my old man's hype. I thought he was some kind of god."

"You've never told me how your mother felt about your father's crimes?"

"She's his accountant." He shrugged, thinking of all the times he got an attaboy from his parents for making the grade. It never mattered how, as long as he won. "Colonel Salvatore was the first person to ever hold my feet to the fire about anything. Yes, I have my own code of honor now, Jayne. I have to be able to look myself in the mirror, and this job is the only way I know how to make that happen."

"How weird is it that we've been married for seven years and there are still so many things about you I don't know." Her blue eyes held him as tangibly as her hand held his beside the plate of croissants and éclairs.

"That's my fault." He squeezed.

"Damn straight it is." She squeezed back.

The jet engine droned in the silence between them, recycled air whooshing down.

He flipped her hand in his and stroked her lifeline with his thumb. "What happens now?"

"What do you mean?" Her voice came out breathy, her chest rising and falling faster.

Although he could see that even in her anger she still wanted him, he was now beginning to understand that desire alone wouldn't cut it any longer.

"In the elevator we were a zipper away from making love again."

Her hand went still in his, her eyes filled with a mix of desire and frustration. "And you want to pick up where we left off?"

"How will your dog sitter feel about that?"

She sighed. "Are you still jealous even after I told you I'm not dating him?"

"Are you planning on seeing him after you leave?" He had to know, even if the answer skewered him.

What had the other guy given her that he couldn't? He'd lavished her with every single thing a woman could want, and it hadn't been enough for Jayne.

"Honestly," she said, "I thought I might when I flew to Monte Carlo, but now, I'm not sure anymore."

He started to reach for her but she stopped him cold with a tight shake of her head.

"Damn it, Jayne—"

"I'm not done." She squeezed his hand hard. "Don't take what I said as some sign to start tearing our clothes off. I *am* certain that I want a normal life with a husband who will be there for me. I want the happily ever after with kids and a real family sitting down to dinner together, even if it's hamburgers on a rickety picnic table at a simple hometown park. Maybe that sounds boring to you, but I just can't pretend to fit into this jet-set lifestyle of yours where we share a bed and nothing else. Does that make sense?"

He closed his eyes, only to be blindsided by the image of her sitting on a porch swing with some other lucky bastard while their kids played in the yard. "The thought of you with someone else is chewing me up inside."

"You don't have the right to ask anymore," she said gently. "You know that, don't you? We've been separated for three years."

"Tell that to my chewed-up gut."

She tugged her hand free. "You've already moved on. Why shouldn't I?"

He looked up sharply. "Says who?"

"Every tabloid in the stands."

"Tabloids. Really?" He laughed. Hard. Not that it made him feel any better. "That's where you're getting your news from? I thought you graduated from college magna cum laude."

Finally he'd shocked her quiet, silencing those damn probing questions.

But not for long.

Jayne's hand clenched around her discarded scarf. "You're saying it's not true? That you haven't been with other women since we split up?"

He leaned across the table until his mouth was barely an inch away from hers. He could feel her breath on his skin and he knew she felt his. Her pupils widened in awareness, sensual anticipation. And still, he held back. He wouldn't kiss her now, not this way, when he was still so angry his vision clouded.

Not to mention his judgment.

He looked her in the eyes and simply said, "I am a married man. I take that commitment very seriously."

She was his wife. The only woman he'd ever loved.

He should have the answers locked and loaded on how to keep her happy. He was a damn Wall Street genius, entrepreneur billionaire and Interpol agent, for God's sake.

Yet right now, he didn't have a clue how to make things right with Jayne, and he didn't know if he ever would.

Seven

The gates swung wide to Conrad's home in Africa, and Jayne had to admit, he'd shocked the hell out of her twice in less than twenty-four hours.

She'd expected a grand mansion, behind massive walls with sleek security systems that made Batman's cave look like something from last generation's game system. This place was…

Understated.

And the quiet beauty of it took her breath away.

She leaned forward in the seat, as the Land Cruiser took the uphill dirt road. A ranch-style house perched on a natural plateau overlooking a river. She'd spent four years poring over renovations and perfect pieces of furniture for their different residences, perhaps hoping she could somehow create an ideal marriage if she could only put together an ideal home. She would guess the place was built from authentic African walnut. Everything about the house looked real, nothing prefab or touristy about it.

Porches—and more porches—wrapped around the lengthy wooden home, with rockers, tables and roll down screens to overlook the nearby river. Palm trees had a more tropical than landscaped feel. Mangrove trees reached for the sky with their gnarled roots twisting up from the ground like wads of fat cables.

She glanced at her husband, wondering what led him to purchase this place just before they'd split. But his stoic face wasn't giving away any clues. Although, Lord, have mercy, he was as magnificent as the stark and unforgiving landscape.

With the day heating up fast, he'd ditched the sports coat and just wore jeans with his shirtsleeves rolled up. Like his home, he didn't need extravagant trappings to take her breath away. As if she wasn't already tempted enough around him.

Although the gun still tucked in the shoulder harness gave her more than a little pause.

Their game of twenty questions during the plane ride hadn't helped her understand him one bit better. If anything, she had more questions, more reservations. Being here alone together was complicated now. They'd moved past the idea of sex for the hell of it as some farewell tribute to their marriage. That didn't mean the attraction wasn't still there, fierce as ever, just beneath the surface of their tentative relationship.

Tearing her gaze away, she pressed her hands to the dash. "This isn't at all what I expected."

"How so?" He slowed the SUV then stopped at the half-dozen wooden steps leading to the front door.

"No bells and whistles chiming. No gambling rich and famous everywhere you look."

"The quiet appeals to me." He opened the door and circled the hood to her side.

She stepped out just as he reached her and avoided his outstretched hand, not ready to touch him again, not yet. "If you'd wanted somewhere to be quiet, there were places a lot closer to home than Africa."

The dusty wind tore at her hair. She tugged her scarf from around her neck and tied back the tangled mess.

"True. But this is the one I wanted and since I'm sinfully rich," he said, pulling out her roll bag and a duffel for himself, "I can have the things I want, if not the people."

Was this quieter persona one he donned for his missions or was this a part of her husband she'd never seen? She shivered in spite of the temps already sending a trickle of sweat down her spine. "What about security? I don't see any fences or cameras."

"Of course you didn't see them as we drove up. They're the best, thanks to our good friend Troy. If anyone crosses the perimeter, we'll know." He jogged up the stairs and flipped back a shutter to reveal an electronics panel. "You'll be briefed on how everything works so you're not dependent on me if an emergency arises."

Now wasn't that an eye opener?

She trailed her fingers along a rocker, setting it in motion and thought of his casino with the glassed-in balcony overlooking the sea. And she realized he loved the outdoors. Even now, his ear tipped toward the monkey chattering from some hidden tree branch.

"Jayne?" he called from the open door. "Are you ready?"

"Of course," she lied and followed him inside anyway.

This was definitely not a safari lodge after all.

There weren't any animal heads mounted on the walls, just paintings, an amalgamation of watercolors, oils and charcoals, without a defining theme other than the fact each one portrayed a unique view of Africa.

And in such a surprisingly open space.

Conrad had a style of his own—and a damn good one. But she'd fallen into a stereotypical assumption that he would put a foosball table in her living room if she turned over the reins to him. She thought back to his penthouse remodeling. She'd been so focused on the shock of all her things swept away she'd failed to notice the sense of style even in his man cave.

How much of his "hiding" of himself had she let happen?

She stepped deeper into the room with a massive stone fireplace in the middle. A wood frame sectional sofa dominated the space, piled with natural fiber cushions and pillows. There were no distractions here, just the echo of her footsteps and the sound of the breeze rustling branches outdoors.

The place was larger on the inside than it looked from outdoors, likely another means of security. Her entire condo back in Miami could have fit in the living area with room to spare. A glance down the hall showed at least five other doors, but she was drawn to the window overlooking the river. A small herd of antelope waded in for a drink, while a hippo lazed on the far side of the shore.

Conrad's hand fell on her shoulder. "Jayne?"

She jolted and spun to face him, finding him so close her heart leaped into her throat. Her hands started to press to his chest, but she stopped shy of the silver gun.

"Uh, I was just enjoying the view." She gestured over her shoulder at the window.

"You've been standing there awhile. I thought you'd dozed off." He tugged the end of her scarf, her hair sliding loose again. "You must be almost dead on your feet since we didn't sleep last night, so I'll save the grand tour for later. There's just one place you need to see now."

The kitchen for a snack? His bed to make love before they both fell into an exhausted slumber?

He stopped in front of a Picasso-style watercolor of people in bright colors dancing. He slid the painting to the side to reveal another panel like the one she'd seen on the front door. After a quick tap along the keypad, he stepped back. Boards along the wall slid automatically and stacked, revealing a passage.

"This is the panic room." Conrad pressed a card into her hand with a series of numbers. "This is the code. Do not hesitate to use it in case of an emergency. Don't wait for me. I can take care of myself a helluva lot better if I'm not worrying about you."

Salvatore's words from earlier came back to haunt her, about how she was Conrad's Achilles' heel. Her presence placed him in greater danger. Somehow in the rush to leave Monte Carlo, she'd lost sight of that revelation.

Tears burned her eyes, and she ached to reach for him.

"Jayne, it's going to be okay." He brushed her hair over her shoulder. "You need to sleep, and I need to check the place over. We'll talk more later."

She tried not to feel rebuffed. He was doing his job. *She* had pushed *him* away after Salvatore's revelation.

Her hands fell to her sides. Of course he was right. She couldn't possibly make rational decisions with her head cottony from lack of sleep. And if she couldn't think clearly she became even more of a liability to Conrad.

Yet as he showed her to the guest room, she still couldn't help wishing she could sleep in his arms.

Conrad punched in the code to the safe room where he stored all his communication gear and security equipment. The entire place ran off solar power and a satellite feed, so he couldn't be cut off from the outside world. He kept enough water and nonperishable food in storage to outlast a siege.

Call him paranoid, but even in his infrequent freelance role with Interpol, he'd seen some intense crap go down in the world.

The windowless vault room in the middle of the house had everything he needed—a bed, an efficiency kitchen, a bathroom and a sitting area, small, but useful down to the last detail. A flat screen was mounted on the wall for watching the exterior. And an entire office's worth of computers were stored away, ready to fold out onto the dinette table like an ironing board lowered out of a wall.

He parked himself in front of the secured laptop and reached for the satellite phone. He needed to check in with Salvatore. Halfway through the first ring, his boss answered.

"Yes," the colonel barked.

"We've arrived, and we're settled. No red flags here that I can see. What do you have on your end?"

"The money in Zhutov's wife's account has been withdrawn and we have images—which I'm forwarding to you now—of his known associates in discussion with a hit man. We've got trackers on both individuals."

"I'll review his wife's bank accounts again. Why her assets haven't been frozen is beyond me."

"We do what we can, and you know that."

"Well, let's damn well do more." Scrolling through computer logs of account transfers, Conrad tucked the phone between his shoulder and ear, not wanting to risk speakerphone where Jayne might wake up and overhear.

"Hughes, my people are on it. You should sleep. You'll be more alert."

"Like you sleep?"

The colonel was a well-known workaholic. When they'd all been in school they'd theorized that their headmaster was a robot who didn't need mere mortal things like sleep. Seemed as if he was always walking the halls, day and night.

Salvatore sighed. "Go spend some time with your wife. Repair you marriage. Put your life back together again."

"Sir, with all due respect, you saw her back in Monte Carlo. She was pissed."

"I saw a woman who looked like she'd just been kissed senseless in an elevator."

"You're not helping the problem at hand by playing matchmaker." He'd need more of a miracle worker to untangle the mess he'd made of his life.

"I sincerely hope you and she had a long talk on the airplane about your work with me."

Just what he needed right now, a damn lecture on all the ways he'd screwed up his marriage. "Thank you for your input, sir. I'll take that under advisement."

The colonel laughed darkly. "Still as stubborn as ever, Hughes. Leave the sleuthing to my end this time.

Your job is to fly under the radar, keep you and your wife safe. Let me know if you need anything."

The call disconnected, and Conrad set the phone aside.

Three fruitless hours of database searching later, he slammed the computer shut in frustration. He couldn't figure out if the clues just weren't there. Salvatore's words echoed through his head, about his job being to protect Jayne. The old colonel was right. Conrad wouldn't be any good to her dead on his feet.

Resigned to surrendering, at least for now, he left the panic room and sealed it up tight again. The sectional sofa looked about as inviting as a bed of nails, but it was the best place to keep an ear out for Jayne— other than sleeping next to her, which didn't appear to be an option tonight.

And speaking of Jayne, he needed to check on her, to leave her door open a crack so he could hear her even in his sleep. He padded barefoot down the hall to her room and eased her door open.

Bad idea.

Looking at Jayne sleeping was torture. And apparently he was a masochist tonight because he stepped deeper into her room. Her legs were tangled in the sheets, long legs bared since her nightgown had hitched up. Her silky hair splashed over the pillow in a feathery blond curtain.

She slept curled on her side, with a pillow hugged to her chest just the way he remembered. If they'd still been together, he would have curled up behind her, their bodies a perfect fit. He still didn't understand how something so incredibly good could fall apart like their marriage had.

Tired of torturing himself tonight, he pivoted away and walked back out to the living room. He yanked a blanket off the ladder rack against the wall and grabbed two throw pillows. Even if his mind resisted shutting down, his body demanded that he stretch out and rest. But still his brain churned with thoughts of Jayne and how damn close they'd been to making love again.

If Salvatore hadn't been waiting for them in the penthouse, they would have ended up in bed. He could still hear her cries of pleasure from the elevator. He could feel the silken texture of her clamping around his fingers.

They may have had their problems communicating, but when it came to sex, they'd always been beyond compatible. And they'd had other things in common, too, damn it. They shared similar taste in books and politics. She enjoyed travel and appreciated the beauty of a sunset anywhere in the world.

And they both enjoyed the opera.

In fact, he'd planned to take her to the opera during their forty-eight hours of romance, back when he'd been enough of an idiot to think he could let her go again. He'd chartered a jet to fly them to Venice for a performance. He'd reserved a plush, private opera box where he could replay their *La Bohème* date.

He could still remember what she wore that night, a pale blue gown, feathery light. He'd been riding the rush of a recent mission, adrenaline making him ache all the more for his wife. The moment he'd seen her walk out of their bedroom wearing the dress, he'd known he wouldn't rest until he found out what she had on underneath.

Before Act One was complete, he'd known....

Dreams of Conrad during that hazy realm of twilight sleep always tormented her the most. Fantasy and reality blended until she didn't know whether to force herself awake or cling to sleep longer.

La Bohème echoed through her mind, the opening act, except that didn't make sense because she was in Africa with Conrad. So why was the opera playing out on a barge on the river? Confusion threatened to pull her awake. Until the glide of Conrad's hands over her breasts made her cling to the dream realm where she could sit with her husband on the porch and listen.

Savor.

His hands slid down her stomach to her leg. With skillful fingers he bunched her gauzy blue evening gown up, up, up her leg until his hand tunneled underneath. She felt his frown and realized she had jeans on underneath her formal dress?

Confusion churned in her brain as she stared down at her bare feet and well-worn denim. She kicked at the hem of her gown, frustrated, needing to free herself of the voluminous folds so she could wear her jeans.

And so she could feel Conrad's touch.

The roar of frustration grew louder, and louder still until the porch disintegrated from the vibrations. She stood in the rubble, a herd of elephants kicking up dust on the horizon.

Her bare feet pedaled against the covers. She fought harder, frantic to wake herself up and outrun the beasts chasing through her head. Elephants thundered behind her, rumbling the ground along with an orchestra segueing into the closing act. Her chest hurt, and she gasped for air.

She tripped over the gnarled roots of a mango tree. Her hands slapped the ground, but it gave way, plunging her into the Mediterranean Sea outside Conrad's casino. The farther she sank, the darker the waters became until she hit bottom.

Sealed in a panic room.

A window cleared along the top and she looked up, searching for a way out. Desperation squeezed the air from her lungs. Conrad stood on the balcony far, far above, watching her, drinking his Chivas. She couldn't reach him, and he couldn't hear her choked cries of warning to watch out for the thundering herd.

Wasn't a guy always supposed to hear his mermaid call him?

Except she wasn't the one in danger.

His balcony filled with thick, noxious smoke until Conrad disappeared…

Jayne sat up sharply.

Wide-awake, she blinked in the dark, unfamiliar room. Gauzy mosquito netting trailed from all four corners of the canopy. Just a dream, she reminded herself. Not real.

Well, the charging elephants weren't real, but the panic room was very real, along with a looming threat.

Fear for Conrad still covered her like a thick blanket on a muggy day. She'd put him in danger just by being with him. A crummy way to pay him back for all the years he'd tried to keep her safe from a dangerous job. Now that she was past some of the worst feelings of betrayal, she could feel the inevitable admiration beneath it. He was a good man, and she—unknowingly—had been his Achilles' heel.

That hurt her to think about. She had so many regrets about her marriage, and their future had never been more complicated. Her body burned for his touch.

With the pain of losing him still so fresh in her mind, she knew without question, she *had* to be with him tonight.

Conrad stared at the ceiling fan swirling around and around, the click so quiet he knew that couldn't have woken him.

So what had?

The alarms were set. He'd cracked the door to Jayne's room. No one would get in without him knowing, and Jayne wouldn't so much as sneeze without him hearing.

Muffled cries? He'd absolutely heard those.

Hand on his 9mm, he raced down the hall, careful to keep his steps quiet so as not to alert an intruder. He pushed through the guest bedroom door.

And found Jayne standing a hand's reach away in an otherwise empty room. She jumped back to avoid the swinging door. The sight of her hit him clean in the libido.

His hand fell away from his gun.

An icy-blue nightgown stopped just shy of her knees, lace trim teasing creamy flesh. The pale blue was so close to the color of the gown she'd worn to *La Bohème* that memorable night it almost knocked his feet out from under him. The silk clung to her curves the way his hands ached to do, the way he'd dreamed of doing every night since she'd walked out on him.

"Is something wrong? I heard you cry out in your sleep and I just needed to be sure you're all right." Good enough cover story for why he'd burst into the room.

"Just a nightmare. How cliché, huh?" She thrust her hands in her hair, pushing it back—and stretching the fabric of her nightgown across her breasts. "I cry out.

You run to me in my bedroom, afraid something happened to me. I'm still rattled by my bad dream."

He tore his eyes off the pebbly tightness of her nipples against silk. "God forbid we should ever be cliché."

She stepped closer, padding slowly on bare feet, her eyes narrowed with a sensual intent he'd seen—and enjoyed—many times in the past.

"Although, Conrad, clichés become clichés because they worked well for a lot of other people. And if we follow the dream cliché to its conclusion, the next step would be for me to throw myself in your arms so we can make love."

Jayne stopped toe-to-toe with him, still not touching him, and if she did, his control would be shot all to hell. For whatever reason, she was taking charge and seducing him. Except she would be doing so for all the wrong reasons, vulnerable from whatever had frightened her in the dream.

He couldn't take advantage of her while she was riding the memories of a nightmare. But he also couldn't leave her in here upset and alone.

Grabbing the door to keep from reaching for her, he stepped back into the hall. "I think we need to get out of this bedroom."

"Why?" She nibbled her bottom lip.

He swallowed hard. "We need to go. Trust me."

She laughed softly. "Trust you? That's rich, coming from you."

"Fair enough, I deserve that." He always had liked the way she never pulled punches and found it every bit as arousing now as he had when they lived together. "Or you could just trust me because you're a nicer person than I am."

"All right, then." She placed her hand in his, her soft fingers curling around his.

And holy crap, she leaned in closer to him as they walked down the hall. The light scent of her shampoo teased his nose. The need to haul her into his arms throbbed harder, hotter. Damn it, he was supposed to be protecting her, comforting her. He reined in thoughts fueled by three years of abstinence.

Three. Damn. Years.

Out in the main living area, he guided her to the sectional sofa, wide palm ceiling fans clicking overhead. "Have a seat, and I'll get us a snack from the kitchen."

She settled onto the sofa, nestling in a pile of pillows. "Just some water, please."

That would give him all of sixty seconds to will back the raging erection. Hell, he could spend an hour creating a five course meal and it wouldn't be enough time to ease the painful arousal.

He snagged two bottles of water from the stainless-steel refrigerator in a kitchen he'd actually learned to use and returned to the living room. He twisted off a cap and passed her the Evian. "Let's watch a movie."

"A movie?"

"I can pipe anything you want in through the satellite." He opened his bottle. "I'm even open to a chick flick."

"You want to watch a *movie?*" She shifted in the mass of throw pillows, looking so much like a harem girl he almost dropped to his knees.

"Or we can talk." And he realized now that Salvatore was right. He should talk to Jayne and tell her more about the man she'd married, the man she thought she wanted to crawl back in bed with. He needed to be sure her eyes were wide-open about him before he could even consider taking her up on what she offered.

She was stuck here because of him. They were both forced to watch over their shoulders—also because of him and the choices he'd made. While he couldn't see much he would do differently, at least he owed her a better perspective on why he'd broken the law.

Why he'd ruined so many lives, including theirs.

He sat by her, on the side that didn't have his gun in the way. On second thought, he unstrapped the shoulder harness and set the whole damn thing on the teak coffee table.

Too bad his past couldn't be tucked away as easily.

He wrestled with where to start and figured what the hell. Might as well go back to the beginning.

Elbows on his knees, he rolled the water bottle between his palms. "You know what I did as a teenager, but I don't think I've ever really explained why."

She sat up straighter, her forehead furrowing, but she didn't speak.

"A teenage boy is probably the dumbest creation on the planet. Pair that with a big ego and no moral compass, and you've got a recipe for trouble."

Seventeen years later and he still couldn't get past the guilt of what he'd done.

"You were so young," she said softly.

"That's no excuse. I was out of control and hating life. This girl I liked had dumped me because her parents didn't want her around my family." He glanced at her. "Her dad was a cop. My ego stung. And I decided to show him and the justice system what screwups they were, because I—a teenager—was going to do what they couldn't. I would make the corrupt pay." Starting with two leches he'd caught hitting on his sister, damn near assaulting her, and his dad hadn't done more than shrug off his friends' behavior by insisting no harm, no foul.

"You had good intentions. All of the news reports I read said as much. And yes, I searched every one of them since you're usually closemouthed about your past." She set aside her drink and clutched his forearm, squeezing. "While it's admirable you feel bad, you can also cut yourself some slack. You were exposing corrupt corporations."

"Not so much. See, I could have infiltrated my dad's records and those of his crooked friends, then turned them over to the authorities. And I could have had a better motivation than getting back at some girl or showing up my old man. But I wanted to make a statement. I wanted to make him see that even if I didn't do things his way, damn it, I was still every bit as smart. Because I would get away with it."

She didn't rush to reassure him this time, but she hadn't pulled away in disgust. Yet.

"Twisted, isn't it?" He set aside his water bottle to keep from shattering it in his fist. "I wanted to bring him—as well as a couple of his friends—down *and* make him proud of me."

"That had to make getting caught all the worse." She gathered a pillow to her, her voice steadier than her hands.

"That's the real kick in the ass irony." His hand fell to the lacy edge on the short sleeve of her nightgown and he rubbed it between two fingers. "I didn't get caught. I would have gotten away with it."

"Then how did you end up in reform school?"

"I found out that one of the CEOs of a business I'd helped tank with my short sales… He took his life."

Acid fired at the lining of his stomach, burning up to his throat with a guilt that would never leave, no matter how many missions he completed or how much money he donated to charity. "I turned myself in to the police, with all the information on what I had done, everything I could dig up on my father."

"And the police gave you a more lenient sentence because you came forward." Her hand settled on his back, soothing. "What happened was horrible, but you did come forward with all that evidence, even when it incriminated you. That counts for something."

Laughter rumbled around in his chest, stirring the acid and mixing in some shards of glass for good measure to flay his insides. "Turning myself in didn't count for jack. I only got sent to that school instead of juvie because my dad hired the best lawyers. He got off of every major charge, and I could not beg my way into prison."

His dad's lawyers had made sure the press learned—through an "anonymous" leak—that every targeted company had been guilty of using child laborers in sweatshops overseas.

Once the media got wind of that part of his case, he'd been lauded the white knight of orphans. The pressure had nudged the judge the rest of the way in cutting him a deal. Through the colonel's mentorship, he and his friends had learned to channel their codes of right and wrong. Now they had the chance to right wrongs within the parameters of the law.

"I'm just damn lucky I landed in Salvatore's program. I owe him more than my life, Jayne." His voice strangled off with the emotion clogging his throat and squeezing his chest. "I owe him my self-respect."

Wordlessly she slipped her arms around him and

pulled him to her. He pressed his forehead into her shoulder and drew in the pure, clean scent of her. She was too good for him, always had been. There just hadn't been anyone in her life to warn her away from him the way his teenage girlfriend's dad had.

"Conrad, Colonel Salvatore couldn't have built something within you if the foundation and all the essential parts weren't already there. You're a good man."

He didn't know how long they sat there, and a part of him knew he should let her go back to bed before he took anything more from her. But having her this close again felt better than he'd remembered, different, too. The glide of her fingers along the back of his neck soothed as much as they aroused. She was such a mix of contradictions, everything he wanted and all he didn't deserve.

She turned her face to graze a kiss across his temple before taking his face between her hands and looking him in the eyes. "I think we've both been hurting long enough."

Oh, God, this was it. The moment she would send him packing for good. She wouldn't wait around for him to sign the papers. She would pursue the divorce without his consent, an option that had always been open to her due to their lengthy separation. He hadn't realized until now how much hope he'd been holding on to. Like a sap, with every day that passed and no divorce, he'd allowed himself to believe there was a chance they would reconcile.

Now he had to face up to the fact that it was over between them, and she would move on to live the life she deserved. The one he'd never come close to offering her. She would find the man she deserved who would give her a real home and cute babies.

Forcing out words to set her free damn near split him in half. "Jayne, I never wanted to hurt you." He clasped her wrists, holding on to her for what would be the last time. "I only want you to be happy."

She angled back to stare deep in his eyes. "Then make love to me."

Eight

Leaning forward, her hip digging into the sofa cushions, Jayne skimmed her mouth over Conrad's, praying he wouldn't push her away again.

Desperate to see this through.

His admissions, his outpouring from deep in his soul only confirmed her conviction that he was a much better man than he realized. And regardless of whatever else had happened between them, she wasn't turning back from right now, right here with Conrad.

She sensed his restraint, his lingering concerns about protecting her from her dream or from herself. Whatever. To hell with holding back. She poured all her frustration and bottled emotions into the way her body ignited around him. Arching upward, she swung her leg around and over until she straddled him, bringing her flush against the hard length of his erection. She rocked once, twice, her hips to his until she felt the growl rumble in his chest. His arms shot up and around her, locking her to him.

A purr of relief spiraled up her throat.

"Jayne, are you sure this is what you want?" he asked between possessive kisses.

"Absolutely. We've both waited long enough. Stop talking and take me, damn it."

And thank heaven he listened and agreed. Angling her back onto the sofa, his solid body pressed her into the welcoming pile of pillows. He hooked a finger along the lacy edge of one sleeve, sliding along her shoulder and around until he skimmed her breast, launching delicious shivers of anticipation.

Desire surged liquid heat through her veins in a near-painful, all-over rush. She'd laid awake so many nights, aching for him, tempted to reach for the phone and just hear the sound of his voice. The rumbling timbre of him speaking her name then and now sent her spine bowing up toward him, as she wriggled to get closer.

She thumbed the buttons on his shirt free and yanked the fabric off his shoulders, sending it sailing to rest on a water bottle. Sighing, she splayed her fingers over his chest, up along his shoulders to pull him to her again. The heat of his bare flesh seared through her nightgown, her breasts tingling with awareness. How had she made it through the past three years without him, without this?

Her hand slid between them, down the front of his jeans, stroking his erection straining against his fly until he throbbed impossibly harder against her touch. She fumbled with the top button then eased the zipper down. Her fingers tucked inside his boxers, and he groaned low in his throat.

The steely length of him fit to her hand, familiar even after years apart. Although in some ways it seemed like no time at all, given all the hungry dreams she'd had of him coming to her bed again. Or in some of her more uninhibited fantasies he'd come to her in other places. Whisking her away from work to make love in the car. Joining her on a beach walk where they slipped behind a sand dune together. Or appearing next to her in a dark theater...

But she always woke up alone, unfulfilled and knowing he would never come for her. She had to move on with her life.

God, her thoughts were running away from her, threatening to steal this moment from them again.

Conrad shifted on top of her, and she gripped his shoulders to hold him in place. "Where are you going?"

"Jayne, I'm not leaving." His hands never stopped moving and arousing her even while he talked. "I packed a box of condoms in my suitcase, because even though I didn't just assume we would sleep together, I sure as hell wasn't going to lose the chance due to poor planning."

"Guess what?" She slid her hands around, digging her nails into his buttocks. "I'm a good planner, too."

"Then lucky for us, we have plenty to get through the night." He slid off her and stood, wearing nothing but his jeans, open and low slung on his hips in a tempting V. "So do I go get mine and come back, or do we move to the bedroom?"

Her brain was so fogged just staring at him that she struggled to form an answer. She didn't want to think. She just wanted to feel him over her, moving into her. But if they stayed here, there would be the awkward moment afterward when they pulled themselves together afterward and walked to separate bedrooms—which was insane, since she was his wife. For now at least.

And she realized exactly what she wanted. To be in his bed, to make love there and sleep in his arms.

"Let's go to your room."

Before she could say another word, he swept her against his chest in such a macho show of strength she smiled just before she flicked his earlobe with her tongue then drew it between her teeth, enjoying the slightly salty taste of him.

The lingering scent of his aftershave mixed with the musk of perspiration on his skin. She drew in the smell of him, the feel of him, until even the silk of her nightgown felt itchy against her oversensitized skin. The hard wall of his muscled chest wasn't the one of a paper pusher or a man who'd become soft from years of high living. He could take charge in every realm, intellectually and physically, and that duality turned her on all the more.

He shouldered open his door, revealing a massive teak bed sprawling in front of a window overlooking the river. Then she didn't see anything other than the linen drapes on the ceiling over the bed as he settled her in the middle of a simple cotton comforter. He angled to his suitcase on the stand, pulled out a box of condoms and tossed it on the bed before leaning over her again.

With competent and quick hands he bunched her gown in his fists and swept it away. The breeze over her skin made her want the press of his body but he sprinkled kisses along her stomach, took the edge of her bikini panties between his teeth and tugged. She thought of the panties he'd torn from her body in the elevator, of how he'd given her such an intense release.

At the first nuzzle between her legs, her knees fell

apart and her bones turned to liquid. The flick of his tongue and gentle suckling brought her to the edge too fast, too soon. She clawed at his shoulders, drawing him up, but he stopped, teasing the tight nipple the way he'd licked and laved the tight bud of nerves.

He had her writhing on the comforter, aching to take this further, faster. His hand slid down to replace his tongue with a knowing touch. He inched his way back up her body until his mouth settled on her breast and his fingers between her legs teased in synchronicity, playing her perfectly. He knew her, just like the night at *La Bohème*. Except now she was naked and they were alone so he had free rein for more. He stroked the tight bundle of nerves with his thumb while sliding two fingers deep, crooking at just the right spot.

She gasped and pressed harder against his hand even as she wanted all of him. "No more playing. I just want you inside me."

"And you can be damn sure that's exactly where I want to be." He rolled her nipple lightly between his teeth. "But I want that—want you—so much and it's been so long, I'm not going to last. I need to take care of you first."

She circled him, stroking…her thumb rolling over the damp tip. And yes, she was every bit as close to coming apart.

"That works both ways you know, the part about having gone without sex for too damn long." She reached for the condom box and tugged free a packet. "No more waiting. If we come fast, then we get to linger later, but I can't wait anymore."

Determined to delay not a second longer, she sheathed him with a familiarity and newness that she still didn't quite comprehend. The fan rustled the curtains around their haven.

He held her face, looked into her eyes and said, "There hasn't been anyone since you. No one comes close to turning me inside out the way you do. And even when I resent it like hell, there's no denying it. I only want you."

His words stilled her hands. *No one* since her? For three years?

She wanted to believe him, ached to believe him. Because she felt the same. She even understood the part about resenting the way this feeling for each other took over her body and her life.

And then he kissed her. He thrust his tongue as he pushed inside her. Filling her, stretching her with more of that newness after so damn long away from each other. The sweet abrasion of his chest rasped along her nipples. The hard roped muscles of his legs flexed with each pump of his body. She dug her heels into the mattress and angled up against him until the gathering tension in her pulled even tighter, bringing her closer.

Her hand flung out to grab the headboard, the intense sweetness was almost too much. She wanted to hang on to the sensations as tightly as she held the headboard, but he'd taken her too close to the edge with his mouth and his skillful touch.

One more deep stroke finished her. Pleasure rippled from her core, pulling through her, outward until the roots of her hair tingled. She bowed upward into him, even as her head thrashed on the pillow.

He chanted encouragement as her release pulsed and clamped around him, his voice growing hoarse until he hissed between gritted teeth. And while she'd doubted so much about their relationship, she knew he'd told her the truth about the past three years. He belonged to her.

She hugged him in the aftermath as he collapsed on top of her. The ceiling fan overhead click, click, clicked, gusts shifting the drapes around the towering teak bed. She trailed her fingers along his broad back, her foot up his thigh, and didn't take for granted the feel of him.

Not anymore.

It was one thing to be angry at him for the past thirty-six months. And another altogether to accept he'd been every bit as torn apart by their breakup as she had. With what he'd shared about his father tonight, she started to realize she'd never fully grasped what made him tick. Maybe if she dug for more clues about his relationship with his father in particular, she might understand how he'd arrived at his place of such emotional isolation.

Because she realized more than ever that she couldn't just walk away again.

Conrad held his wife spooned against him while she slept. She was back in his bed. He'd won.

And he didn't feel one bit peaceful about letting Jayne go.

Moonbeams reflected on the river water, the dock light glowing. If she was awake, he would have liked to sit out there with her and just listen to the night sounds, then walk with her up to the house, shower with her in the outdoor stall with the stars above them.

He'd made love to her twice more and still it wasn't enough. He rested his chin on her head, the sweat of their lovemaking lightly sealing their bodies, her spine against his chest. Each breath pressed her closer again, stirring his hard-on to a painful intensity. His hand slid around to cup her breast, filling his palm with her creamy roundness. She moaned in her sleep, her nipple drawing up into a tight bead.

She was in his blood. Rather than clearing away the past, making love with her had churned up all the frustration of the past three years. The thought of letting her go—unbearable. But he couldn't envision taking her back to Monte Carlo.

Although, how to blend her into his old life could be a moot point. If his cover had been blown, his Interpol work would be over. He angled to kiss her shoulder over the light red mark of his beard bristle from last night. He could have Jayne back and no more unexplained absences.

But the thought of ending his Interpol work… hell. He wouldn't have considered it before. Although since Zhutov might have taken that choice from him, he might as well make the best of the situation. And he couldn't just let Jayne wander off with God knows what kind of threat looming. These sorts of crooks did not forget.

His path became clear.

Protect Jayne.

His life came into focus. He realized his past mistake. He'd tried too hard to blend her into his world in Monte Carlo. He'd let her too close to the darker side of himself. Somehow, he must have known that, since he'd chosen to bring her here, to a place that represented the man he'd once wanted to be.

Jayne shifted in her sleep, arching her breast into his hand, her bottom wriggling against him. He throbbed against the sweet dip in her spine and the beginning of his need for her pearled along the tip of his erection. He clamped a hand on her stomach to hold her still.

Sighing, she looked back over her shoulder at him with sleepy half-awake eyes.

"Is it morning?" she asked in a groggy voice.

"Not yet. Keep sleeping." He had a packed day planned, showing her the full extent of the compound he'd built here. "We have plenty of time."

"Hmm... Except I'm not sleepy." She reached behind her to stroke his hair. "What's on the agenda for today?"

He nuzzled her hair. "I have some ideas. But what do you want?"

"At some point, breakfast. A very big breakfast, actually. After last night, I'll need more than pastries and tea."

"I'm certain I can figure something out."

"You cook?"

He was a little insulted by the assumption that he didn't, until he remembered all the times he'd burned toast when they were still together. His cooking was a more recently acquired skill. "I make some pretty fierce eggs Benedict these days."

"Sounds heavenly." Her head rested back against his chest. "I also noticed you've taken up redecorating."

Did he detect a note of pique in her voice? He opted for honesty. "Having your things around brought back too many memories. It was easier to move forward if I got rid of them."

Her feet tucked between his. "But you didn't replace everything. The red room stayed the same."

"That was the only room in the penthouse where we never had sex."

"So let me get this straight. You tossed out every piece of furniture that reminded you of the two of us having sex there."

"Pretty much."

She stayed silent, and he wished he could see her face to gauge her mood. So much of her was familiar and then other times not so much. She'd changed. So had he. They were both warier.

Finally she smiled back at him over her shoulder. "Good thing we never made love in the Bentley. It would have been a damn shame for you to have to get rid of such a cool collector's item."

"You have a point." He kissed her, wondering if he would have to burn this bed if she walked out on him again. "I guess we've both made some changes. What prompted you to swap from being an E.R. nurse to Hospice care?"

"You've obviously kept tabs on me. Why do you think?"

Was that a dig? "You know you don't have to work, right? No matter what happens between us, I will take care of you."

She flipped back the covers and started to sit up. "I don't need to be 'taken care of.'"

"Whoa… Hold on now." He looped an arm around her waist. "I didn't mean to offend you. I was just commenting on the fact that we're married. What's mine is yours. Fifty-fifty."

"Don't let your lawyer hear you give up your portfolio that easily."

"Not. Funny."

Still, she sat on the edge of the bed, the vulnerable curve of her back stirring his protective urges. She could shout her independence all day long. That wouldn't stop him from wanting to give her nice things. And more importantly, it wouldn't stop him from standing between her and anything that threatened her.

Shifting up onto an elbow, he rubbed her back and tried to backtrack, to fix what he'd screwed up. "Tell me about your new job."

Was it his imagination or did the defensive tensing of her shoulders ease?

"When I came back to Miami, my old job had obviously been filled. I took the Hospice opening as a temporary stopgap until a position more in my line of expertise became available. Except I found I didn't want to leave the job. It's not that I was unhappy with my work before, but something changed inside me."

"Like what?" He smoothed his hand down to the small of her back, the lolling of her head cluing him in to keep right on with the massage.

"I think I was drawn to E.R. work initially because there wasn't as much of a chance of my heart being engaged." She glanced back. "I don't mean to say that I didn't care for the patients. But there wasn't time to form a relationship with someone who's out of your care in under an hour. I had a set amount of time to help that person, and then we moved on."

He massaged along the tendons in her neck. "Your dad's stunt hiding a second family really must have done a number on you."

"I had trouble connecting with others." She sagged back onto the bed and into his arms. "Now I find there's a deep satisfaction in bringing comfort to people when life is at its most difficult. It may sound strange…"

"Not at all," he said as he tucked her tight against him, this amazing woman he damn well didn't deserve but couldn't bring himself to give up.

"Enough depressing talk about the past. I don't know about you, but I can think of a far more enjoyable way to spend our time now that I am completely awake."

She stretched out an arm to slide a condom from the bedside table and pressed it into his palm.

Smiling seductively over her shoulder, she skimmed her foot along his calf, her legs parting ever so slightly for him, inviting him. And call him a selfish bastard, but he wasn't one to turn down an invitation from Jayne. He'd been without her for so long he couldn't get enough of her. Time and time again he'd been tempted to fly to Miami and demand she come home.

Like that would have gone over well.

Instead he'd sent back those damn divorce papers repeatedly, knowing eventually she would have to come to him. She'd been well worth the wait. He skimmed his fingers around her again, slipped them down between the damp cleft, stroking as she opened farther.

With two fingers, he circled, faster, pressing and plucking with the amount of pressure he knew she enjoyed, bringing a fresh sigh from her. And just when he'd brought her to the edge, he hooked his arm under her knee and angled his sheathed erection just right, so close to everything he'd dreamed of and fantasized about when he'd taken those long and unsatisfying showers without her.

As he slid inside Jayne, *his wife,* he vowed he would not lose her. And he would never, never let anything from his past touch her again.

Jayne stood at the river's edge and watched the gazelle glide through the tall grasses on the other side of the mangrove swamp. The midmorning sun climbed up the horizon in a shimmering orange haze, echoing the warm glow inside her after a night of making love with Conrad.

Again and again. He'd given her explosive orgasms

and foreplay to die for. He'd brought her a late-night snack in bed of flatbreads and meats, fed to each other. He'd fed her perfectly prepared eggs Benedict this morning. They'd talked and laughed, everything she'd dreamed could happen for them again.

How different might things have been if they'd come here for their first anniversary? If they'd talked through all the things they were only beginning to touch on now?

And she couldn't completely blame him anymore. As she looked back, she accepted the times she'd let things slide rather than push him, because deep in her heart she was scared she wouldn't be able to walk away.

Her mother hadn't deserved what happened to her. God knows Jayne hadn't deserved it, either.

But she refused to be passive any longer. If—and that was a *big* if—she and Conrad stood a chance at patching things up, he needed to be completely open with her. They needed a true partnership of equals.

Glancing over her shoulder up to his home on the plateau, she saw her husband pacing, talking on his cell phone. He'd said he needed to check in with Salvatore before he took her on a tour of the property. Apparently there were other buildings and even a small town beyond the rolling hills and she had to admit to curiosity about what drew him here. The home—the whole locale—was so different from the glitz of his other holdings.

It gave her hope.

So much hope that she'd called Anthony. She'd arranged for a friend from work to pick up Mimi. If she was going to even consider making things work with Conrad, she had to cut off any ties to Anthony, a man she'd considered dating.

Watching Conrad walk down the incline toward her now, she wasn't ready to pack her things and bring Mimi across the ocean yet, but for the first time in three years, she was open to the possibility. She just needed the sign from Conrad that he would compromise this go-round.

He closed the distance between them, stopping at the shoreline with tall grasses swaying around his calves. He draped an arm around her shoulder. "Salvatore's staff is still wading through backlogs of visitors, letters, emails, any contact with the outside world. A suspicious amount of money was moved from Zhutov's wife's account. Salvatore hopes to have concrete answers by the end of the day."

The threat sounded so surreal, but then Conrad's whole hidden career still felt strange to her. "What about Troy and Hillary?"

"They're safely in the Bahamas at a casino and no signs of anyone tracking them, either. By all accounts, they're enjoying the vacation of a lifetime."

"So this could all be a scare for nothing?"

He kissed her forehead. "Not nothing. We're here, together."

For how long? Long enough to find a path back together? She wished they could stand here by the river watching the hippo bathe himself in mud.

She tucked closer to Conrad's side, the sun beaming down on them. "Did you get any sleep last night?"

"Three or four hours. I'm good."

"Yes, you are." Turning in his arms, she kissed him good-morning and wondered just how private this spot might be. She looked at the dock, then up the incline at the deck and the outdoor shower stall. Her mind swirled with possibilities.…

With a final kiss to her forehead, he angled back. "Ready to go for the tour?"

"Absolutely." Walking alongside him to the Land Cruiser, she tucked away her fantasy for another time, intensely curious about this tour and the opportunity to dig deeper into what made her husband tick.

The wilds of Africa were definitely a world away from Monte Carlo. Instead of flashy royalty in diamonds and furs, a spotted cheetah parted the grasslands not far from a mama giraffe with her baby. They walked with a long-legged grace much more elegant than any princess.

She rolled down her window, letting the muggy air clear away the images of the glitzier lifestyle, immersing herself in the present. "We know each other well in some ways and in others not at all—no dig meant by that. I feel like it's my fault, too."

"None of this is your fault. I'm the one responsible for my own choices and actions, no excuses from the past." Wind tunneled in his white polo shirt, his faded jeans fitting to his muscled thighs.

It wasn't about the clothes with him. She couldn't help but think—not for the first time—how he had a powerful presence just by existing, whether he was in a tuxedo in Monte Carlo or dressed for the desert realms of Africa.

She studied the hard line of his jaw, peppered with stubble. "Why can't you let me feel sorry for what you went through as a teenager?"

"I don't want sympathy. I want you naked." He shot a seductive grin her way. "We can pull over and…"

"You're trying to distract me." And she was determined to talk. "You promised to answer my questions."

Only the wind answered, whispering through the

window as they drove toward a small cluster of build-ings in the distance, with cars and lines of people, adults and kids. Perhaps this was a school?

Regardless, her time to talk would be cut short soon.

"Conrad? You promised," she pressed as birds ducked and dove toward their windshield only to break away at the last instant.

He winced, looking back at the narrow rural road. "You're right. I promised."

"Where did you stay on school breaks? Or did you stay at the school, like juvenile hall or something?"

The smile left his eyes. "I went home for holidays with an ankle monitor."

Thoughts of him as a teenager walking around with that monitoring device chilled her. "That had to have been awkward after you tried to turn in your father."

"My dad told me I could make it all up to him by connecting him with the families of my new friends." He steered around a pack of dwarf goats in the road. "Why don't we talk about your dad instead, Jayne?"

He guided the car back on the road again, leading them closer to the long stucco building, surrounded by smaller outbuildings. The slight detour off the road jounced her in the seat, hard, almost as if he'd deliber-ately bounced her around.

She held up her hands in surrender. "Okay, mes-sage received."

Her husband wasn't as open to talking this morn-ing, but she wouldn't give up. She would simply wait for a better opening while they spent their day at... Not a school at all.

He'd driven her to a medical clinic.

Nine

Conrad watched his wife, curious as to what she would think of the clinic he'd built. Because yes, he'd built it as a tribute to her and the light she'd brought to his world. Regardless of how their marriage had broken up in the end, his four years with her were the best in his life.

She asked him all those questions about his father and the arrest, looking for ways to exonerate him because she had such a generous and forgiving heart. But she didn't seem to grasp he'd done the crime. He was guilty of a serious wrong, no justification.

His life now had to be devoted to a very narrow path of making things right. The small hospital was a part of that thanks to a mission to the region nearly four years ago that had left a mark on him. He'd been aiding in an investigation tracing heroin traffic through a casino in South Africa, the trail leading him up the coast. He wasn't an agent so much as a facilitator to lend effective covers and information about people in his wealthy world. They'd taken down the kingpin in that case, but Conrad hadn't felt the rush of victory.

Not that time.

His nights had been haunted by visions of the *Agberos,* street children and teens also known as "area boys." They were loosely organized gangs forced into crime. And no matter how many kingpins Conrad took out, another would slide into place. There was no Salvatore to look after those boys, to change their lives with a do-over.

Conrad opened Jayne's car door, her reaction so damn important to him right now that his chest went tight with each drag of air. Lines of patients filed into the door, locals wearing anything from jeans and T-shirts to colorful local cloths wrapped in a timeless way. They were here for anything from vaccinations to prenatal care to HIV/AIDS treatment.

The most gut-wrenching of all? The ones here for both prenatal care and HIV treatment. There was a desperate need here and he couldn't help everyone, but one at a time, he was doing his damnedest.

He wasn't a Salvatore sort, but he could at least give these kids some relief in their lives. He could make sure they grew up healthy, and those that couldn't would have a fighting chance against the HIV devastating so many lives in Africa.

Jayne placed her hand in his and stepped out of the SUV. "Interesting choice for an outing."

"I thought since you're a nurse, you would like to see the facility."

"It's so much more than I would have expected in such a rural community."

"It feeds into the population of three villages, and there are patients who drive in from even farther."

She shaded her eyes against the sun, turning for the full three-hundred-and-sixty-degree view of everything from the one-story building to storage buildings. The place even had a playground, currently packed with young kids playing a loosely organized game of soccer, kicking up a cloud of dust around them. A brindle dog bounded along with them, jumping and racing for the ball, reminding him of little Mimi.

Patients arrived in cars and on foot, some wearing westernized clothes and others in brightly colored native wear. A delivery truck and ambulance were parked off to the side. Not brand-spanking-new, but well maintained.

They'd accomplished a lot here in a few short years.

He pointed to the doctor pushing through the front double doors. Conrad had given the doc a call to be on the lookout for them. "And here's our guide. Dr. Rowan Boothe."

Another former Salvatore protégé.

Jayne halted Conrad with a hand on his arm. "Is it okay if we just wander around? I don't want to get in anyone's way or disrupt anyone's routine."

The doctor stopped at the end of the walkway, stethoscope around his neck, hands in the pockets of his lab coat.

"Ma'am, don't worry about the tour. He owns the place." Boothe said it in a way that didn't sound like a compliment.

Not a surprise.

He and Boothe hadn't been friends—far from it. From day one, the sanctimonious do-gooder had kept to himself. Getting a read off him had been tough. On the one hand, he'd picked fights and then on the other, Boothe damn near martyred himself working community service hours.

The doc didn't much like Conrad, and Conrad didn't blame him. Conrad had given Boothe hell over his do-gooder attitude. But Conrad couldn't deny the guy's skill and his dedication. Boothe was the perfect fit for this place, and probably even a better fit for Jayne.

Damn.

Where the hell had that come from?

Suddenly it mattered too much to him that Jayne approve of the clinic. He was starting to want her to see him as the good guy and that was dangerous ground.

Damn it all to hell. He needed distance, or before he knew it, she would start asking more questions, probing around in his past for an honorability that just wasn't there.

"Jayne, you're in good hands here. I'm going to tend to some business."

Jayne's head was spinning as fast as the test tubes in the centrifuge. Her slip-on loafers squeaked along the pristine tile floors as she turned to follow Dr. Boothe into the corridor, her tour almost complete.

One wing held a thirty-bed hospital and the other wing housed a clinic. Not overly large, but all top-of-the-line and designed for efficiency. The antibacterial scent saturated each breath she took, the familiarity of the environment wrapping her in comfort.

She'd expected Conrad to romance her today. That's what Conrad did, big gifts and trips. He remembered her preferences from cream-filled pastries to Italian opera.

But this? He'd always seemed to think her nursing

was just a job and she'd followed his lead, figuring someone else needed the job she would have taken up. She'd had plenty of money as his wife... But God, after six months, she'd become restless and by the end of the first year, she'd missed her job so much her teeth ached.

Walking down the center hall of the clinic, she couldn't stop thinking maybe he had seen her need there at the end, that he'd been planning this for her. Had she given up on them too soon?

Dr. Rowan Boothe continued his running monologue about the facilities and their focus on childhood immunizations as well as HIV/AIDS treatment and education.

She was impressed and curious. "You and Conrad seem to know each other well. How did you meet?"

The doctor looked more like a retired model than a physician. But from what she'd heard so far, his expertise was undeniable. "We went to high school together."

North Carolina Military Prep? Was he the kind who'd gone in hopes of joining the military or because of a near brush with the law? Asking felt...rude. And then there was the whole Salvatore issue...an off-limits question altogether. "Hmm, it's nice when alumni can network."

He quirked a thick blond eyebrow as they passed the pharmacy. "Yes, I was one of the 'in trouble' crowd who now use their powers for good instead of evil."

"You have a sense of humor about it."

"That surprises you?" he asked as he held open the door for her, a burst of sunshine sending sparks in front of her eyes.

"What you face here, the tragic cases, the poverty, the limited resources and crime..." She stepped onto the front walkway, shading her eyes. Where was Conrad? "How can you keep that upbeat attitude under such crushing odds?"

"People are living longer here because of this clinic. Those children playing over there would have been dead by now without it." He gestured to a dozen or so boys kicking a soccer ball on a playground beside the clinic. "You said you're a Hospice nurse now, an E.R. nurse before that. You of all people should understand."

He had a point.

"You're right, of course." Her eyes adjusted to the stark sunshine and out there in the middle of the pack of boys, her husband joined in, kicking the soccer ball.

Laughing?

When was the last time she'd heard him laugh with something other than sarcasm? She couldn't remember. The sound of him, the *sight* of him, so relaxed took her breath away. He looked...young. Or rather he looked his age, a man in his early thirties, in the prime of life. Not that he'd looked old before but he'd been so distant and unapproachable.

She glanced at Dr. Boothe. "What was he like back in high school?"

"Moody. Arrogant. He was gangly and wore glasses back then, but he was a brilliant guy and he knew it. Folks called him Mr. Wall Street, because of his dad and what he did with the stock market." He glanced at her. "But you probably could have guessed all of that."

She just smiled, hoping he would keep talking if she didn't interrupt.

"I didn't come from money like most of the guys there, and I wasn't inordinately talented like Douglas. I had a monster chip on my shoulder. I thought I was better than those overprivileged brats. I caught a lucky break when I was sent there. I didn't fit in so I kept my distance." He half smiled. "The sense of humor's a skill I acquired later."

"Yet, Conrad brought you here. He must respect you."

"Yeah, I guess. I have the grades, but so do a lot of doctors who want to save the world. If we're going to be honest, I'm here because of a cookie."

"Pardon me? I'm not sure I understand."

"My mom used to send me these care packages full of peanut butter cookies with M&M's baked into them. Damn, they were good." The fond light in his eyes said more about the mother who sent the baked goods. "One day, I was in my bunk, knocking back a couple of those cookies while doing my macro-biology homework. And I looked up to find Conrad staring at those cookies like they were caviar. I knew better than to offer him one. He'd have just thrown it back in my face."

He leaned against a porch pillar. "We were all pretty angry at life in those days. But I had my cookies and letters from Mom to get me through the days when I didn't think I could live with the guilt of what I'd done."

He shook his head. "But back to Conrad. About a week later, I was on my way to the cafeteria when I saw him in the visitation area with his dad. I was jealous as hell since my folks couldn't afford to fly out to visit me—and then I realized he and his dad were fighting."

"About what?" She couldn't help but ask, desperate for this unfiltered look into the teenager Conrad had been during a time in his life that had so tremendously shaped the man he'd become.

"From what Conrad shouted, it was clear his father wanted him to run a scam on Troy's parents and convince them to invest in some bogus company or another. Conrad decked his dad. It took two security guards to pull him off."

The image of that betrayal, of the pain and humiliation he must have felt, brought tears to her eyes she knew her overly stoic husband would never have shed for himself. "And the cookie?"

"I'm getting there. Conrad spent a couple of days in the infirmary—his dad hit him back and dislocated Conrad's shoulder. The cops didn't press charges on the old man because the son threw the first punch. Anyhow, Conrad's first day out of the infirmary, I felt bad for him so I wrapped a cookie in a napkin and put it on his bunk. He didn't say anything, but he didn't toss it back in my face, either." He threw his hands wide. "And here I am today."

Her heart hurt so badly she could barely push words out. "You're killing me, you know that don't you?"

"Hey, don't get me wrong. He's still an arrogant ass, but he's a good guy if you dig deep." He grinned. "Really deep."

She looked back out at her husband playing ball with the kids. His voice rode the breeze as he shouted encouragement and tips, and she couldn't help but think of the father that had never been there for him. No wonder he was wary of being a parent himself.

But if he could only see himself now. He was such a natural.

She'd dreamed of them having children one day, and she'd hoped he could be a good father. But she'd never dared imagine him like this. She should be happy, hopeful.

Instead she was scared to death. It was one thing to fail at her second chance with Conrad if she would have had to walk away from the same failed marriage she'd left before. But everything was different this time. What if she lost the chance to make Conrad genuinely happy? This chance to touch lives together in Africa?

That would level her.

An older boy booted the soccer ball across the field, a couple of smaller boys chasing it down. The ball rolled farther away, toward a moving truck stacked with water jugs. The vehicle barreled along the dirt road without the least sign of slowing even as the child sprinted closer on skinny little legs.

Her heart leaped into her throat. Dr. Boothe sprang into motion but there was no way he would make it to the child in time.

"Conrad!" Jayne screamed, again and again.

But he was already sprinting toward the kid, who was maybe six or seven years old. Conrad moved like a sleek panther across the ball field, faster than should have been possible. And in a flash, he'd scooped the child up with one arm and stopped a full ten yards away from the truck. He spun the kid around, sunshine streaming down from the sky around them. The little boy's giggles carried on the breeze as if all was right in the world. And it was. Conrad had the situation firmly in hand.

Her heart hammered in her ears.

A low laugh pulled her attention away from her husband and back to Dr. Boothe. A blush burned up her face over being caught staring at her husband like a lovesick teenager.

God, her feelings for Conrad were so transparent a total stranger could read her.

What did her husband think when he looked at her? Did he think he'd won her over today? If so, she needed to be damn clear on that point. Yes, she was hopeful,

but that didn't mean she was willing to compromise
on her dreams.

But what about his dreams?

This close brush with danger revealed her husband's
competence in a snapshot. She'd spent so many nights
worried about why he hadn't called home, but seeing
him in action gave her a new appreciation for how well
equipped he was for quick action in risky work. He was
smart, strong and he had resources. Furthermore, he
had lightning reflexes and a will to help others.

Was she being as selfish as she'd once accused him
of being by denying him a job that obviously meant a
lot to him? A job that was, she now understood, a con-
duit to forgiving himself for his past? Clearly Conrad
needed his work as badly as she needed hers.

That realization hurt, making her feel small and
petty for all the accusations she'd hurled at him. He'd
deserved better from her then, more understanding.
She couldn't change the past and she didn't know if
they had a future together or not.

But she could control what she did today.

Conrad started the Land Cruiser, sweat sticking his
shirt to his back from the impromptu ball game and
the surprise sprint to keep the little Kofi from dash-
ing in front of a moving truck. His head still buzzed
with the kick of fear when he'd seen the kid sprint toward the vehicle, unaware of anything but reaching
that soccer ball.

Thank God the worst hadn't happened.

Playing with the kids was the high point of these
visits for him, something he always did when he had
time here. But today, he'd also needed the outlet after

watching Jayne with Boothe, their heads tucked together as they discussed the ins and outs of the clinic.

The day had been a success in every way that mattered, and he was a petty bastard for his foul mood. He wanted to blame the stress on Zhutov, and God knows that added to his tension. There wasn't a damn thing he could do but wait until the enemy made a move. And once that wait was over?

Hell. The need to take his wife home and imprint himself in her memory, deep in her body, took hold of him. And he couldn't think of a reason why he shouldn't follow through on the urge to make love to her until they both fell into an exhausted sleep.

He put the car in Drive and accelerated out of the parking lot. His wife sat beside him with that expression on her face again, like she'd put him under a microscope. He prepped for what he knew would come next.

"That was amazing how fast you reacted when the child ran toward that truck."

"I just did what anyone would have." And he'd also had a word with the truck driver about the dangers of speeding past a playground. "Kofi—the kid—spends a lot of time here with his older brother, Ade. Their mother comes regularly for her HIV treatments."

"Do you know all the kids' names?"

"Some," he answered noncommittally.

She sighed in exasperation. "You said before we got on the plane you would tell me anything. Did you mean that?"

"I should have put a limit on how many questions you could ask." A flock of geese scattered in front of him.

"I'll go easy on you then. What's your favorite kind of cookie? I realize I should already know that, and I feel awful for having to ask when you have my favorite pastry memorized, but I realized I really don't know."

Cookie? What the hell? "Um, anything with M&M's. I'm, uh, partial to M&M's in my cookies."

She smiled and touched his knee. Apparently he'd answered that one correctly.

"Next question?"

"Why don't you wear glasses anymore? And why didn't you ever mention that you used to? You'd think there would be pictures."

"Boothe," he said simply. Now he understood why they'd been standing under the awning so long. Boothe had been spouting out crap about the past. "I had Lasik surgery on my eyes so I don't need glasses anymore. As for photos of me wearing them? They perished in a horrible accident, a trash can fire in Salvatore's office. A fire extinguisher was sacrificed in the line of duty."

Her hand stayed on his knee. "You have a sense of humor when you want to—sarcastic, sure but funny."

She stroked higher up his thigh and he damn near drove into a ditch. He clasped her wrist and moved her back to her side of the car.

"You'll need to put that thought on hold."

Laughing softly, she hooked an elbow out the window, her blond hair streaking across her face. "I want to know more about your job with Interpol."

Apparently the easy questions had just been to soften him up.

"What do you want to know?"

"I keep trying to wrap my brain around the whole notion of you and your friends living a James Bond life, and it's blowing my mind. How did I miss guessing for four years?"

Because he was a damn good liar?

That didn't seem like a wise answer. He measured out a smarter answer, balancing it with what was safe to tell her.

"We're more freelancers, and we don't take jobs often. It actually keeps the risk of exposure down." But the longer he went between assignments, the more restless he grew. If this Zhutov case blew up in his face, would Salvatore cut him out or relegate him to some paper-pushing research? "I only worked six 'projects' in the entire time we were together. An assignment could take anywhere from a week to a month."

She nodded, going silent while she stared out the window at an ostrich running on pace with them at forty-two miles per hour. Her deep breath gave him only a flash of a notice that she wasn't giving up.

"Sounds to me like your Alpha Brotherhood has morphed into a Bond Brotherhood." She tipped her face into the wind, her eyes closed, her neck arched and vulnerable. "Troy is definitely the Pierce Brosnan Bond type, with his charm and his metro-sexual style. Malcolm is the Roger Moore type, old school Bond with his jazz flair. I only recall meeting Elliot Starc once, but he fits well enough for the Timothy Dalton slot, rarely seen but very international. The doctor, Boothe, he's the Daniel Craig Bond, the tortured soul."

"Who said Boothe was part of the Alpha Brotherhood?" And yes, he noticed she'd aptly insinuated they were all working for Salvatore as well, something he didn't intend to confirm.

"Just a guess." She glanced at him, her perceptive blue eyes making it clear she hadn't missed the nuance. "By the way, *you* are absolutely the Sean Connery Bond."

"I think you're paying me a compliment." He

glanced over and found her staring at him with a familiar sensual glint.

He went hard at just a look from her—and the promise in her eyes.

"You're sexy, brooding, arrogant and too damn mesmerizing for your own good. It's not fair, you know."

"I'm not sure where you're going with this."

"Just that I can't resist you. Even now, I'm sitting here fighting the urge to jump you right here in the middle of nowhere. I'm trying to play it cool and logical because I don't want either of us to get hurt again."

"Can we go back to the Sean Connery discussion?" He hooked an arm around her and tugged her to his side.

She adjusted her seat belt and leaned against him. "I wonder sometimes if we were drawn to each other because of feeling like orphans."

He forced himself not to tense as she neatly shifted the conversation again. "We had parents."

"Don't be so literal."

"Don't be such a girl."

"Um, hello? I have breasts."

"Believe me." His hand slid along the generous curve. "I noticed."

"You're not paying attention." She linked fingers with him, stopping his caress.

He squeezed her hand, driving with the other hand down the deserted private road leading back to his house. "You have my complete and undivided attention."

"Good, because there will be a quiz afterward," she said smartly.

He nuzzled her hair, and wondered when just sitting beside her, holding her hand had become such an incredible turn on. "I've missed you."

"I've missed you, too." Her head fell to rest on his shoulder. "That's what I was getting at. You have your brotherhood, but you lead these separate lives with just periodic high octane reunions. Day by day, neither of us has a family."

He laughed darkly. "Dysfunctional is drawn to dysfunctional, I guess."

"Not exactly how I would have phrased it, but that works well enough." Her hand fell to rest on his knee, stroking lightly.

To arouse or soothe?

"Jayne, your dad's a loser just like mine was." Anger simmered in his gut over how her father had hurt her. "End of story. We overcame it."

"Did we?" She drew circles on his jeans, her touch heating him through the denim. "Or are we still letting them control our lives?"

His hand clenched around the steering wheel. He wanted to be with her, but damn it, she needed to leave discussions of his father in the past. He'd said all he cared to say about the old man who didn't warrant his time. This whole twenty questions game was officially over.

"If I wanted therapy I would pay a shrink." He turned off the road, hitting the remote for the gate, which also triggered a timed release for the other layers of security along with a facial recognition program.

"Wow, Conrad," she said, sliding back to her side of the vehicle, "that was rude."

He reined his temper in even as sweat beaded his brow. "You're right." He stopped the car beside the house. "Of course."

"If you don't agree," she snapped, throwing her door open wide, "then just say so."

"I disagree, and I'm rude." He threw his arms wide as he circled to the front of the car. "I agree, and you tell me not to?"

"I just meant disagree politely." She crossed her arms over her chest, plumping her breasts in the simple white T-shirt.

His hard-on throbbed in his jeans, aching as much as the pain behind his eyes.

"I just want to get a shower and some lunch." He yanked his sticky polo shirt off and pitched it on the porch. To hell with this. He stalked toward the outside shower stall along the side of the house. "Not pick a fight."

"Who's picking a fight?" Her voice rose and she all but stomped a foot. "Not me. I'm just trying to have an honest discussion with you."

"Honest?" He barely kept his voice under control. That shower was sounding better and better by the second. Maybe it would cool down his temper. "You want to talk honest then let's talk about why you want to rewrite history so I'm some pathetic sap who blames the world for all his problems."

She stalked closer to him one step at a time until she stopped an inch shy of her breasts skimming his bare chest. "Conrad? Shut up and take me to the shower."

Ten

As much as Jayne ached to find answers that would give them a path to reconciliation, clearly Conrad didn't want to talk anymore. And to be honest with herself, the trip to the clinic had left her more than a little vulnerable. She'd seen a side to her husband she hadn't known existed. Beyond just funding a building, he was obviously hands-on at the place, well-known and liked. The way he'd played with the kids still tugged at her heart until she could barely breathe.

She definitely needed to give them both time and space. She was a patient woman, and right now she could think of the perfect way to pass that time.

Making love to her husband.

And if she was using sex to delay the inevitable? Then so be it. She couldn't leave the protection of this place so she might as well make the most of this time.

She linked fingers with Conrad and tugged him toward the side of the house.

"Jayne, the front door's that way."

"And the exterior shower is this way." She walked backward, pulling him with her. "Unless there's some reason we should stay inside? I figured since we walked around the grounds earlier, the security system outside is as good as inside."

"You are correct. I wouldn't have built an outdoor shower if it wasn't safe to use it. No one can get within a mile of this place without my knowing about it." He reassured her with a fierce protectiveness in his voice and eyes.

The magnitude of that comforted her and unsettled her at the same time. She was a dentist's kid from Miami. Prior to meeting Conrad, the extent of her security knowledge included memorizing the pin code for the security box on the garage leading into her condo.

She shoved aside distracting thoughts and focused on the now. Seducing Conrad. She pulled a condom from her purse and tucked it into his hand. "And that takes care of our last concern."

He flipped the packet between his fingers. "You were planning this all day?"

"Actually—" she tossed aside her purse "—I intended to get you to pull over on a deserted side road—since this whole place is essentially deserted that wouldn't have been tough—and I would seduce you in the car. Since the Land Cruiser is conveniently roomy, we would finish off the fantasy we started in the Jaguar in Monte Carlo."

He jerked a thumb over his shoulder. "Do you want to go back to the car?"

"I want you. In the shower. Now."

He hooked his thumbs in her jeans. "Happy to accommodate."

She grabbed the hem of her T-shirt and peeled it over her head, baring her white lacy bra. Late afternoon rays heated her skin almost as much as his eyes as she toed off her canvas loafers. The gritty earth was warm beneath her feet, pebbles digging into her toes.

Her hands fell to her belt buckle, and she unfastened her jeans, never taking her eyes from his sunburnished face. She wriggled denim down her hips, enjoying the way his gaze stroked along each patch of revealed flesh. One last shimmy and she kicked aside her jeans, grateful she'd invested in new satin and lace lingerie before this trip.

That panty set forced her to admit she'd been hoping for just this when she'd come to Monte Carlo to deliver her five-carat ring and divorce papers. Deep in her heart, she'd hoped he would tear up the papers and slide the ring back on her hand.

Life was never that clear-cut. Today's answers had shown her more than ever how far more complex the situation—and her husband were.

But one thing was crystal clear. She had amazing lingerie and her husband's interest. And she intended to enjoy the hell out of their afternoon together.

She teased the front clasp open and tossed her bra aside. The extravagant scrap of satin and lace landed on top of her jeans. After they'd met in Miami, he'd rented a yacht to live on while he concocted business reasons to stay in town. Even though she'd been tempted to sleep with him from the first date, she'd held back, overwhelmed by his wealth, concerned about his past. But two months into the relationship, she couldn't ignore her heart any longer. She'd fallen irrevocably in love with him.

They'd made love on his yacht that night. They'd eloped four weeks later.

Memories of the optimism of that day and the heart-break that followed threatened to chill her passion. She refused to let that happen, damn it.

Turning toward the shower, she called over her shoulder, "Someone's way overdressed for this party."

His eyes took on a predatory gleam, and he walked toward her, taking off his jeans and boxers with a speed and efficiency that sent a thrill of anticipation through her.

He stalked toward her, his erection straining hard and thick up his stomach. She reached behind her, her fingers grazing along the teak cubicle until she found the latch. She pulled the door open.

The slate tile floor cooled her feet after the scorched earth outside. She turned on the shower just as Conrad filled the entrance with his big, bold presence. The spray hit her in a cold blast, and she squealed, jumping back.

Laughing, Conrad stepped deeper inside, hooking an arm around her waist and hauling her against the delicious heat of his body until the spray warmed. She arched up on her toes to meet his kiss, water slicking over her skin in thousands of liquid caresses. She knew they couldn't continue like this forever. They were merely delaying the inevitable decision on where to take their relationship next.

That only made her all the more determined to indulge in every moment now. She scored her nails lightly down his back, down to his hips, her fingers digging into his flanks to urge him closer. The rigid press of his arousal against her stomach brought an ache and moisture between her thighs that had nothing to do with the sheeting water.

He caressed her back, her breasts, even her arms, the rasp of his callused fingertips turning every patch of her skin into an erogenous zone. One of his hands fell away, and she moaned against his mouth.

"Patience," he answered, his hand coming back into sight cupping a bottle of shampoo.

He raised his arm and poured a stream onto her head before setting aside the bottle. Suds bubbled, dripping, and she squeezed her eyes shut a second before he gathered her hair and worked up a lather. Pure bliss.

The firm pressure of his fingers along her scalp was bone melting. She slumped against the sleekly varnished walls. With her eyes closed, her world narrowed to the sound of the shower, the wind, the distant cackle of monkeys, a natural symphony as magnificent as any opera.

Certainly Conrad played her body well, with nuances from his massage along her temples to the outlining of her ears. Bubbles rolled down her body, slithering over her breasts and between her legs. She rubbed her foot along the back of his calf, opening her legs wider for the press of his erection against the tight bud of nerves already flaming to life. Each roll of her hips, each thrust of his fingers into her hair took her higher, faster.

The pleasures of the whole incredible day gathered, fueling the tingling inside her. He'd always been a generous lover and their chemistry had been explosive from their first time together. She opened her eyes and found him watching her every reaction.

Time for *her* to take *him*.

She scooped the bar of soap from the dish and

worked up a lather. He lifted an eyebrow a second before she used her hands as the washcloth over his chest, down his sculpted arms and down to stroke his erection, cupping the weight of him in her hands. He twitched in her clasp, bracing a hand against the shower wall.

He clamped her hand to stop her.

"Jayne—" his voice came out choked and hoarse "—you're killing me."

"As I recall…" She sipped water from his chest, her tongue flicking around the flat circle of his nipple. "You never complained in the past when I took the initiative."

"True enough." He skimmed his hand over her hair, palming the back of her head.

"Then why won't you let me…"

He stepped back, the shower spraying between them. "Because you've called the shots for the past three years."

That was debatable, given how many times he'd sent her papers back unsigned. "Then this is a punishment? I'm not sure I like the context of that mixed with what's happening between us."

"Do you want to stop?" His question was simple enough, but the somber tone of his voice added weight and layers.

They were talking about the future. She wasn't ready to have this discussion with him.

"You know I don't want to stop. I never have. How about my turn now, yours later?" Clamping hands on his shoulders, she nudged him down to the shower seat. "Any objections to that?"

"None that come to mind." He spread his arms wide. "I'm all yours."

"Glad to hear it."

Anticipation curled through her. Kneeling in front of him, she took him in her mouth, the shower sheeting along her back. She gripped his thighs. The flex of muscles thrilled her as she took in every sign of his arousal increasing. His head thudded back against the cubicle wall, and yes, she delighted in tormenting him as much as he'd teased her last night, drawing out the pleasure.

She knew his body as well as he knew hers, thanks to years of great sex and exploring what drove the other crazy. And she drew on every bit of that stored knowledge now until his fist clenched in her hair, gently guiding her off him. She smiled, reveling in the powerful attraction, the connection that couldn't be denied even after three years apart.

His hands slid under her arms, and he lifted her onto his lap. She straddled him, the tip of him nudging between her legs, and she almost said to hell with birth control. Never had she been more tempted, her womb aching to be filled with his child. Aching to have a whole damn soccer team with this man. But after what her parents had put her through, she wouldn't risk bringing a child into an unstable relationship.

And, damn it, even thinking about those lost dreams threatened to wreck the mood. She grabbed the condom from the soap dish and passed it to him. Her hands were shaking too much to be of any help.

Her hands braced on his shoulders, and she raised up on her knees, taking him deep, deeper still inside her, lifting again. She slid her breasts up and down his chest. Every brush of flesh against flesh launched a fresh wash of goose bumps over her. Faster and faster they moved, his hands on her hips, guiding her as he thrust in synch with her.

Moans rolled up her throat, wrung from her, each breathy groan answered by him. And yes, she took added pleasure in controlling this much of her life, bringing him to the edge, knowing that his feelings for her were as all-consuming as her own were for him.

His hands slid under her bottom and he stood, never losing contact, their bodies still linked. He pressed her back to the wall, driving into her, sending her the rest of the way into a shattering orgasm. Her arms locked around him, her head on his shoulder as her cries of completion rippled through her.

Thank goodness he held her because she couldn't have stood. Even now, her legs melted down him, her toes touching the slate floor. His hot breath drifted through her hair as he held her in the aftermath of their release.

They'd made love in a shower numerous times and the tub, too, but never in an outdoor shower. His adventurous nature had always appealed to her. She'd always been such a cautious, practical soul—her mother had always been so stressed, Jayne had worked overtime to be the perfect daughter and that regimen eventually became habit. Rigid attention to detail was a great trait for a nurse, but not in her personal life. Then Conrad had burst into her world.

Or rather he'd hobbled into the E.R. on that broken foot, stubbornly refusing to acknowledge just how badly he'd been hurt. Even in a cast, he'd been more active than any human she'd met. He'd swept her off her feet, and for the first time in longer than she could remember, she'd done something impulsive.

She'd married Conrad after only knowing him for three months.

If they'd dated longer might they have worked through more of these issues ahead of time? Had a stronger start to their marriage, a better foundation?

Or would she have talked herself out of marrying him?

The thought of having never been his wife cut through her. She wanted a future with him. She couldn't deny that, but she also couldn't ignore what a tenuous peace they'd found here.

And the least bump in the road could shatter everything.

Conrad lounged on the shower bench with the door open, watching his wife tug her clothes back onto her damp body. Damn shame they couldn't just stay naked, making love until the world righted itself again. "I read once that 'The finest clothing made is a person's skin, but, of course, society demands something more than this.'"

She tugged her T-shirt over her head, white cotton sticking to her wet skin and turning translucent in spotty places. "Where did you read that?"

"Believe it or not, Mark Twain."

"I always think of you as a numbers man." She pulled her hair free of the neckline, stirring memories of washing her, feeling her, breathing in the scent of her.

Her legs glowed with a golden haze, backlit by the sunset. There was still time left in this day.

He gave her a lazy smile. "You've been thinking of me, have you?"

"I do. Often." Her smile was tinged with so much sadness it socked him right in the conscience.

He stood and left the shower stall, sealing the door after him. He reached for his jeans. "And where do you think of me? Somewhere like in bed? Or in the shower? Because I thought of you often in the shower and now…"

She rolled her eyes. "Where doesn't matter."

"It's been a long three years without you. I'm making up for lost time here." He tried to lighten the mood again, to bring them back around to level ground. "That's a lot of fantasies to work through."

"If only we could just have sex for the rest of our lives. That would probably cure your insomnia." She gave her jeans an extra tug up her damp legs, her breasts moving enticingly under the T-shirt.

She'd been his wife for seven years and still his mouth watered when he looked at her. Her blond hair was slicked back wet, her face free of makeup, and she was the most beautiful woman he'd ever seen.

"The last thing I think about when I'm with you is sleep." What a hell of a time to remember how their marriage had cured his insomnia in the beginning.

"Eventually we would wear out." She sauntered up to him and buttoned his jeans with slow deliberation, her knuckles grazing his stomach.

"Is that a challenge?" His abs contracted in response to the simple brush of her fingers against him.

And he could see she knew that.

She patted his chest before stepping back. "You enjoy a challenge. Admit it."

He grabbed her hips, hauled her against him and took her mouth. He would eat supper off her naked body tonight, he vowed to himself. He would win her over and bring her into his life again, come hell or high water. The past three years without her had been hell. The thought of even three days away from her was more than he could wrap his brain around.

The possibility that he might not be able to persuade her started a ringing in his ears that damn near deafened him. A ringing that persisted until he realized...

Jayne pulled back, her mouth kissed plump and damp. "That's my cell phone. I should at least check who it is."

Disappointment bit him in his conscience as well as his overrevved libido. "Of course you should."

She snatched her purse from the ground and fished out her cell phone. She checked the screen and frowned before pushing the button. "Yes, Anthony? What can I do for you?"

Anthony Collins? Conrad froze halfway down to pick up his polo shirt off the ground. What the hell was the man doing still calling Jayne? She said she'd ended any possible thoughts of romance between the two of them.

The way her eyes shifted away, looking anywhere but at Conrad wasn't reassuring, either. He didn't want to be a jealous bastard. He'd always considered himself more logical than that. But the thought of Jayne with some other guy was chewing him up inside.

She turned her back and walked away, her voice only a soft mumble.

Crap. He snatched his shirt off the ground and shook out the sand. He stood alone, barefoot, in the dirt and thought of all the times he'd isolated Jayne, cut her off from his world without a word of reassurance. He was a bastard. Plain and simple. She'd deserved better from him then and now.

Jayne turned around, and he willed back questions he'd given up the right to ask. He braced himself for whatever she had to say.

"Conrad." Her voice trembled. "Anthony said he's been getting calls from strangers claiming to be conducting a background check on me for a job I applied for. It could be nothing, but he said something about the questions set off alarms. He wondered if it might be someone trying to steal my identity. But you and I know, it could be so much worse than that…."

Her voice trailed off. She didn't need to state the obvious. His mind was already shutting down emotion and revving into high gear, churning through options for their next move.

And most of all how to make sure Jayne's safety hadn't been compromised.

Up to now his gut had told him Zhutov didn't have a thing on him. He didn't make mistakes on the job. But he couldn't ignore the possibility of Zhutov's reach when it came to Jayne so he'd been aggressively cautious.

Had he been cautious enough? Or had something slipped through the cracks while he was lusting after his wife? He shut down his emotions and started toward the house.

"We need to get inside now. I have to call Colonel Salvatore."

Jayne hated feeling useless, but what could she do? She wasn't some secret agent. Hell, she didn't even have her car or access to anything. She felt like she'd been turned into an ornamental houseplant—again.

Conrad had locked the house down tight before going to the panic room to talk to Salvatore and access his computers. She padded around the kitchen putting together something for supper while listening to one side of the phone conversation, which told her absolutely nothing.

Only a couple of hours ago, he'd shown her the clinic and it was clear he'd been trying to reach out to her by sharing that side of his life. Although the spontaneous soccer game had touched her just as much.

She tugged open the refrigerator and pulled out a container of Waldorf salad to go with the flaky crois-sants on the counter. And she vowed, if she found one more of her favorite anything already waiting here for her she would scream.

How could the man have ignored her for three years and still remember every detail about her food prefer-ences? For three long years her heart had broken over him. She would have given anything for a phone call, an email, or God, a surprise appearance on her door-step. Did he really think they could just pick up where they left off now?

She spooned the salad onto plates, her hands shak-ing and the chicken plopping on the china with more than a little extra force. Would he have continued this standoff indefinitely if she hadn't come to him? She couldn't deny she loved him and wanted to be with him, but she didn't know if she could live the rest of her life being shut out this way.

Slumping back against the counter, she squeezed her eyes shut and forced herself to breathe evenly. She thought about that teenage Conrad whose trust had been so horribly abused by his father. Conrad, who'd grown into a man who built a health clinic and de-voted his life to a job he could never claim recogni-tion for doing.

Boothe was right. Conrad was a good man.

She just needed to be patient. And instead of peppering him with questions nonstop, she could start offering him parts of her past, things that were important but that she'd been hesitant to dredge up. But, good God, if she couldn't tell her husband, who could she talk to?

Yes, she still loved Conrad, but she wasn't the same woman she'd been three years ago. She was self-reliant with a clear vision for her future and a sense of her own self-worth.

She also knew that her husband needed her, whether he realized it or not. Pushing her own fears aside, she opened a bakery box full of cookies.

No matter how hard he worked to shut down emotions, still he couldn't ignore the weight of Jayne's eyes on him, counting on him. At least they had one less thing to worry about.

He leaned against the kitchen doorway. "Salvatore's looking into the calls, but so far he said everything looks on the up-and-up. He's confident it was just a hiring company for a hospital running a background check."

"Thank God. What a relief." Her eyes closed for an instant, before she scooped up two plates off the counter. "I made us something to eat. We missed lunch. Could you pour us something to drink?"

She walked past him, both plates of food in her hands. He opened a bottle of springwater, poured it into two glasses with ice then followed her into the dining room. Already, she sat at her place, fidgeting with her napkin.

No wonder she was on edge. All the pleasure of their day out, even making love in the shower, had been wrecked with a cold splash of reality. He sat across from her and shoveled in the food more out of habit than any appetite.

Jayne jabbed at the bits of apple in her salad. "Did I ever tell you why I'm such an opera buff?"

He glanced up from his food, wondering where in the world that question had come from. But then he had given up trying to understand this woman. "I don't believe you did."

"I always knew my parents didn't have a great marriage. That doesn't excuse what my father did to us— or to the family he kept on the side. But my parents' divorce wasn't a huge surprise. They argued. A lot."

He set his fork aside, his full attention on her. "That had to have been tough for you to hear."

"It was. So I started turning on the radio to drown them out." She shrugged, pulling her hair back in her fist. "Opera worked the best. By the time they officially split, I knew all the lyrics to everything from *Madame Butterfly* to *Carmen*."

The image of her as a little girl sitting in the middle of her bed singing *Madame Butterfly* made him want to time travel to take her bike riding the hell away from there. But was he doing any better at protecting her in the present?

She leaned forward on her elbows. "Just so we're clear, you have absolutely no reason to be jealous of Anthony. Nothing happened with him, and I made sure he understood that when I spoke to him yesterday. I even had a friend from work pick up Mimi. I would never, never betray your trust that way."

"I believe you." And he did. He knew how she felt about what her family had been through with her father's longtime affair.

"What's wrong then?" She clasped his arms, holding on tight, her eyes confused, hurt and even a little angry. "Why are you so…distant? You know those walls destroyed us last time."

He shoved away from the table, holding himself in check. Barely. But he wouldn't be like her father, shouting and scaring the hell out of her. "This whole mess with Zhutov and you having to second-guess every call that comes into your life. Do you expect me to be happy that there are people asking around about you? That I had to take you to a remote corner of the world to make sure no one is after you—because of me?"

"Of course you have a right to be worried, but if Colonel Salvatore says there's nothing to worry about, I believe him."

"Nothing to worry about—this time."

"We don't always have to assume the worst here."

A siren split the air like a knife, cutting her off midsentence.

He recognized the sound all too well. Someone had tripped the alarm on the outer edges of his property.

Holy crap. His body went into action, his first and only priority? Securing Jayne.

"Conrad?" Her face paled with panic. "What's that?"

"The security system has been tripped. Someone's trying to break into the compound." He grabbed her by the shoulders and hustled her toward the front steps. "You need to lock yourself in the panic room. Now."

Eleven

Jayne hugged her knees, sitting on a sofa in the panic room. Her teeth chattered with fear for her husband. She'd barely had time to process Anthony's confusing call before the alarm had blared. Conrad had hooked an arm around her waist, rushed her indoors and opened the panic room. He ushered her in and passed over a card with instructions for how to leave…

If he didn't return…

Horror squeezed her heart in an icy fist with each minute that ticked by. She'd already been in here for what felt like hours, but the clock on her cell phone indicated it had only been sixteen minutes.

Someone was trying to break in and there was nothing she could do except sit in this windowless prison while the man she loved faced heaven only knew what kind of danger. Desperately, she wanted to be out there with him, beside him. But Colonel Salvatore had been right. She was Conrad's Achilles' heel. If he had to worry about her, he would be distracted.

She understood that problem well.

There wasn't anything she could do now other than get her bearings and be on guard. Surveying the inside of her "cell," she took it in, for all the good that did her.

As far as prisons went it wasn't that bad, much like an efficiency apartment, minus windows and with only two doors—one leading out and the other open to a small bathroom. A bed filled a corner, a kitchenette with a table in another. A table and television rounded out the decor.

A television? She couldn't envision anyone in a panic room hanging out watching their DVD collection. Angling sideways, she grabbed the remote control off the end table. She turned on the TV. A view of the front yard filled the flat screen.

Oh, my God, she was holding the remote to a surveillance system. She wasn't isolated after all. Relief melted through her. She could help by monitoring the outside. She yanked her cell phone from her pocket and saw…she still had a signal so the safe room hadn't blocked her out.

She thumbed through the remote until she figured out how to adjust the views—front yard, sides, the river—all empty. Her eyes glued to this thin connection to Conrad, she clicked again to a view of the outward perimeter including the clinic.

Not empty.

In fact, a small crowd gathered outside, even this late in the day with the sun setting fast. In the middle of the crowd, four lanky figures sat with their hands cuffed behind their backs.

Teenagers.

Probably not more than fifteen.

And if she guessed correctly, they were some of the same kids who'd played soccer with Conrad just that afternoon.

She clicked the remote, the camera scanning the view until she found Conrad standing with Dr. Boothe. Her husband had his phone out, talking to the doctor while thumbing the keypad. She sagged back on the sofa. If there was any danger to her here, Conrad wouldn't be so far away.

Still, she stayed immobile, waiting for his call. She wouldn't be the fool in the horror films who walked right into a killer's path in spite of all the warnings. But how many times in her life had she sat waiting and worrying, unable to connect or help? She couldn't be a helpless damsel in distress or a passive bystander in her own life.

Her cell phone buzzed beside her, and she saw an incoming text from Conrad.

All clear. Just a break-in at the clinic for drugs. I'll be home soon.

A moment of sheer fright was over in an instant. Was this how Conrad lived on the job? Not fun by any stretch of the meaning. But then, not any more stressful than the time she'd been working in the E.R. when a patient pulled a knife and demanded she empty the medicine cabinet. He'd been too coked up to hold the knife steady, and the security guard had disarmed him.

There weren't any guarantees in life, regardless of where she lived.

She picked up the clearance code and punched in

the numbers to open the door back into the house. She texted Conrad an update.

Made it out of the panic room. No problems with the code.

She hesitated at the urge to type "love you" and instead opted for...

Be safe.

Seconds later the phone buzzed in her hand with an incoming text.

This will take a while. Don't wait up.

Not so much as a hint of affection coated that stark message, but then what did she expect? He was in the middle of a crisis. She shook off the creeping sense of premonition.

For a second, she considered returning to the panic room and just watching him on the screen, but that seemed like an invasion of his privacy. If she wanted this relationship to work between them, she needed to learn to trust him while he was gone. And he needed to learn to trust that she could handle the lifestyle.

So what did a woman do while her man was out saving the world? Maybe she didn't need all the answers yet. She just needed to know that she was committed to figuring them out.

She knew one fact for certain. Living without Conrad was out of the question.

The moon rose over the clinic, lights blazing in a day that had run far too long. Bile burned his throat as he watched the last of the *Agberos* loaded into a police car. Ade, a teen from the soccer game, stared over the door at him with defiant eyes that Conrad recognized well. He'd seen the same look staring back at him in the mirror as teenager.

Jayne and the house were safe, but four teens he'd played with just this afternoon had tried to steal drugs from the clinic. While one of them tried to escape, he'd strayed too close to the house. Boothe had said the attempts were commonplace. *Agberos* weren't rehabilitated in a day—and many of the Area Boys could never be trusted.

Now wasn't that a kick in the ass?

Intellectually he understood what Boothe had told him a million times. In a country riddled with poverty and lawlessness, saving even a handful of these boys was a major victory.

Still, defeat piled on his shoulders like sandbags.

The ringleader of this raid really got to him. Conrad had played soccer with Ade and his younger brother Kofi earlier. He thought he'd connected with them both. And yeah, he'd identified with Ade, seen the seething frustration inside the teen, and wanted to help him build a stable life for himself. Would the little Kofi follow in his big brother's footsteps?

There wasn't a damn thing more Conrad could do about it tonight. He jerked open the door to the Land Cruiser, hoping Jayne had turned in for the night, because he wasn't in the mood for any soul searching.

The drive home passed in a blur with none of his regular pleasure in the starkly majestic landscape that had drawn him to this country in the first place.

Ahead, his house glowed with lights.

The house where Jayne waited for him, obviously

wide-awake if the bright windows were anything to judge by.

Conrad steered the Land Cruiser along the dirt road leading up the plateau, his teeth on edge and his temper rotten as hell. He floored the Land Cruiser, the shock absorbers working overtime. He couldn't put enough space between him and the mess at the clinic, now that the cops had everything locked down tight again.

He parked the Land Cruiser in front of the house, but left the car in idle. He couldn't just sit here thoughtlessly losing himself in his wife's softness in order to avoid the obvious. He needed to take action, to do something to resolve the questions surrounding Zhutov. And he needed to tuck Jayne somewhere safe—most likely somewhere far the hell away from anything in his world since his judgment was crap these days.

Bringing her here had been a selfish choice. He'd wanted to be alone with her. Like some kid showing off an A-plus art project, he'd wanted her to see his clinic, to prove to her there was something good inside him. There were plenty of other places she could stay that were safer. He would talk to Salvatore once Jayne was settled for the night.

He turned off the car, leaped out and slammed the door. Already, he could see her inside on the sofa, lamps shining. He should have tinted these windows rather than depending on the security system.

Just as he hit the bottom step, Jayne opened the front door. Her smile cut right through him with a fresh swipe of guilt.

"Welcome back." She leaned in the open door, a mug of tea cradled in her hands. "What a crazy evening. But at least you know your security system works as advertised."

"You figured out how to work the surveillance television?" If so, that should cut down on the questions for tonight, a good thing given his raw-as-hell gut.

"I did, although I'm still a bit fuzzy on the details." She followed him inside, the weight of her gaze heavy on his shoulders.

"Some of the local *Agberos* tried to steal some drugs from the clinic. When the alarms went off at the clinic, one of the kids—Ade—ran away and tripped the security system here."

"Thank goodness they didn't get away with it. And I'm glad everything was resolved without anyone getting hurt."

"A guard was injured during the break-in." He pinched the bridge of his nose, pacing restlessly past a ladder against the wall covered with locally woven blankets. He needed to get to his computer, to plug into the network and start running leads.

"Oh, no, Conrad. I'm so sorry." Her hand fell to rest on his shoulder. "Will he be all right? Do they need my help at the clinic? I'm sorry now that I didn't go with you."

Her touch made him restless, vulnerable.

He walked to the window, looking out over the river. "You were here, safe. That's the best thing you could do for me."

"What's wrong?" She stopped beside him. "Why are you avoiding me?"

Because if he lost himself in her arms right now, he would shatter, damn it. His hands clenched. "This isn't the right time to talk."

She sighed, a tic tugging at the corner of her eye. "It's never the right time for my questions. That's a big part of what broke us up before." She squeezed his forearm. "I need for you to communicate with me."

Her cool fingers on his skin were a temptation, no question. She'd always been his weakness from the day he'd met her.

"I would rather wait for any discussion until we get the report in from Salvatore."

"What changes if we hear from him?" She frowned, staring into his eyes as if reaching down into his soul. "You think if that man Zhutov has blown your cover, then you don't have to make tough choices. You won't have to do the work figuring out how to let me into your life if you keep the job."

"Or maybe I'm not sure if I'll be a man worthy of you without the job." The admission hissed out between clenched teeth, something he'd known deep in his belly even if he hadn't been willing to admit it until now.

Her eyes went wide. "How in the world could you think that?"

"I'm looking reality in the face, and it sucks. You saw it all on the surveillance camera. You saw those kids in the handcuffs." The memory of it roared around inside him, echoing with flashes from his arrest, the weight of an ankle monitor, the sense of confinement that never went away no matter how freely he traveled the world. "They were stealing drugs to sell. And we could dig into why they needed the money, but bottom line is that they stole medication that's hard as hell to replace out here and they injured a guard in the process."

She gripped his arm harder, with both hands. "It had to be painful seeing the boys you'd played with betray you that way."

The sympathy in her eyes flowed over him like acid

on open wounds. "Damn it, Jayne, I was one of those kids. Why can't you get that?"

"I do get it. But you changed, and there's a chance they'll change, too. Is that such a horrible thing? To believe in second chances?"

The roar inside him grew until it was all he could do to keep from shouting. She didn't deserve his rage. She didn't deserve any of this.

"I'm not the good guy you make me out to be. Yes, I took the job with Interpol to make amends, but I do the work because it gives me a high. Just like when I was in high school, like when I broke the law. I've only figured out how to channel it into something that keeps me out of jail." He looked her dead in the eyes and willed her to hear him. "I'm not the family guy you want, and I never will be."

"What if I say I'm willing to work with that? I think we can find a balance."

He would have given anything to hear those words three years ago, to have that second chance with her. But he knew better now. "And I don't. We tried, and we failed."

"Are you saying this because you're afraid I'll get hurt from something related to your job?"

Holding back a sigh, he dodged her question. He'd had plenty of practice after all. "If that was the case, I would just say it."

"Like hell. You would stage a fight to get me to walk. It's cliché, just like when I woke up with night-mares, and we're not cliché kinds of people. We lead our lives doing difficult jobs that rational people would shy away from. I love that about you, Conrad. I love you."

Damn it, why was she pushing this tonight? Did she want to end things?

And ultimately, wouldn't that be the best thing for her?

"Jayne, don't make this harder on both of us. We've been separated for three years. It's time to finalize the divorce."

Too stunned to cry, Jayne closed the bedroom door and sagged back on the thick wood panel. At least she'd made it out of that room with her head high and her eyes dry.

How in the hell was she supposed to sleep in here tonight with the memories of a few hours ago still so fresh in her mind, the scent of their lovemaking still clinging to the sheets?

Damn him for doing this to her again. And damn her for being such an idiot.

She ran to her suitcase and dug through it, tossing things onto the floor until she found the little black shoulder bag she'd worn to the casino that first night. She dug inside and pulled out her wedding ring set, the five-carat yellow diamond and matching diamond-studded band.

Her fist clenched around the pair until the stones cut into her palm. She grounded herself in the pain. It was all she could do not to run outside and throw the damn things into the river.

She squeezed her eyes closed and thought back over their fight.

Conrad meant every word he'd said. She'd seen the resolution in his eyes, heard it in his voice. And while she still believed he'd made the choice out of misconceptions about himself, she also accepted she couldn't change his mind. She couldn't force him to let go of his past.

She'd waited for him for three years. She'd come here to try one last time to get through to him, only to have him tear her heart to shreds all over again. She didn't regret trying. But she knew it would be a long time before she got over loving Conrad Hughes, if she ever did.

Now there was nothing left for her but to leave with her head high.

Putting the pieces of her life back together would be beyond difficult and, God, she needed a shoulder to cry on, someone to share a bucket of ice cream and put life into perspective. Her mother was gone. She didn't have any sisters. Seeing Anthony again was out of the question, and her friends from work would never understand this.

The answer came to her, a place to go where Conrad couldn't argue about her safety, a person who could offer the advice, support and the sympathetic shoulder she needed. She placed her wedding rings on the bedside table, letting go of them and of Conrad for the final time. She wasn't chasing after him anymore.

She picked up her cell phone and called Hillary Donavan.

She was gone. He'd lost her for good this time.

Watching the lazy hippo roll around in the mud, Conrad sat on the dock with a bottle of Chivas, hoping to get rip-roaring drunk before the sun set. The night had been long, sitting on the couch and thinking about her in the next room. He'd prepared himself for the torment of watching over her until Salvatore cleared him to leave.

But she'd walked out first thing in the morning with her own plan in place, already cleared by Salvatore. A solid plan. As good as any he could come up with himself. Boothe would take her to the airport where Hillary would meet her.

Jayne was a smart and competent woman.

He tipped back his glass, not even tasting the fine whiskey, just welcoming the burn in his gut.

The rumble of an approaching car launched him to his feet. Then he recognized Boothe's vehicle and dropped back down to sit on the dock. He must be returning from taking Jayne to the airport.

Just what he needed. His old "friend" gloating. He topped off his drink.

Boothe's footsteps thudded down the embankment, rustling the tall grass. "You're still sitting around here feeling sorry for yourself. Damn, and I thought you were a smart guy."

Conrad glanced over his shoulder. "I don't need this crap today. Want a drink?"

"No, thanks." Boothe sat beside him, a handful of pebbles in his fist.

"Always the saint."

He pitched a pebble in the water, ripples circling outward. "People see what they want to see."

"Is there a reason you came by?"

"I've been thinking about offering your wife a job. Since you live here and own the clinic, I thought I should run the idea past you first."

Boothe surprised him again, although hadn't he had the same thought about moving Jayne to Africa and settling down? Would she actually take the position even though their paths would cross? "And you're asking my permission?"

"She's a Hospice nurse. She's already on unpaid leave from her other job because of what we do. Only seems fair to help her out." He flicked a couple more pebbles into the water. "Or did you just plan to assuage your conscience by writing her a big fat check?"

Damn, Boothe went for the jugular. "You're offering her a job to get back at me, aren't you?"

"Contrary to what you think, I don't dislike you... anymore."

"So you concede you hated my guts back then, even if you had the occasional weak moment and shared your cookies with a soulless bastard like me."

Boothe's laugh echoed out over the river, startling a couple of parrots and a flock of herons. "Hell, yes, I resented you. You were an arrogant bastard back then and you haven't learned much since."

"Remember that I write your paycheck." Conrad knocked back another swallow. "I fund your clinic."

"That's the only reason I'm here, because I'm grateful." He flung the rest of the pebbles into the water and faced him. "That woman is the best thing that's ever going to happen to you. So, because I owe you a debt, I'm going to give you a piece of advice."

"Thanks. Can I have another drink first?"

Boothe ignored him and pressed on. "In the work world, you're aggressive. You go after what you want. Why the hell haven't you gone after your wife?"

The question stunned him silent through two more rolls of his pet hippo out there.

Disgusted with himself, Conrad set aside his glass.

"She wants a divorce. She's waited three years. I think that's a good sign she's serious."

"Maybe." Boothe nodded slowly. "But is that what you want? You made her come to you again and again. And if you do get back together again, she's stuck waiting for you, repeating the old pattern that wrecked her the first time."

"You're more depressing than the alcohol."

Boothe clapped him on the back, Salvatore style. "It's time for you to quit being a stupid ass. I'll even spell it out for you. Go after your wife."

"That's it?" Just show up? And he hadn't realized until now how much he'd been hoping Boothe might actually have a concrete solution, a magic fix that would bring Jayne home for good this time. Even though he'd told her to leave, the quiet afterward had been a damn hefty reminder of how empty his life was without her. He'd made a monumental mistake this time and Boothe thought that could fixed with a *hey, honey, I'm home?* "After how badly I've screwed up, that doesn't seem like nearly enough."

"For her, that's everything. Think about it." He gave him a final clap on the back before he started walking up the plateau again.

Conrad shoved to his feet, his head reeling from a hell of a lot more than booze.

"Boothe," he called out.

Rowan stopped halfway up the hill. "Yeah, brother?"

Conrad scratched along his collarbone, right over the spot that had once been broken. "Thanks for the cookie."

"No problem." The doctor waved over his shoulder.

As Boothe's car rumbled away, Conrad let his old

classmate's advice roll around in his brain, lining up with memories of the past. Damn it, he'd fought for his wife. Hadn't he?

But as he looked back, he had to accept that he'd expected the marriage to fail from the start. He'd expected her to walk every bit as much as she'd expected him to follow the pattern of her old man. And when she didn't walk this time, he'd pushed her away.

Except Jayne wasn't like his parents. She couldn't be any further from his criminal of a dad or his passively crooked mother and he should have realized that. Countless times he'd accused Jayne of letting the past rule her, and he'd done the same thing. Convinced she would let him down, because, hey, he didn't deserve her anyway. So he'd pushed her away. He might not have been the one to walk out the door, but he hadn't left her any choice by rejecting her so callously. He hadn't left physically, but no question, he'd emotionally checked out on her.

She deserved better than that from him. She'd laid her heart out, something that must have been tough as hell for her after all they'd been through. He should have reassured her that she was his whole world. He worshipped the ground she walked on and his life was crap without her.

And his life would continue to be crap if he didn't get himself together and figure out how to make her believe he loved her. He'd panicked in telling her to leave. He realized now that even though he wasn't good enough for her, he would work his ass off every single day for the rest of his life to be a man worthy of her. No matter what Salvatore uncovered, regardless of whether Conrad had a career or not, he wanted to spend his life with Jayne. He trusted her with anything. Everything.

He would even answer her million questions, whatever it took to make her trust him again.

To make her believe he loved her.

Twelve

The Bahamas shoreline was wasted on Jayne.

She lounged in a swimsuit and sarong on the well-protected balcony with Hillary. Most people would give anything for a vacation like this at a Nassau casino with a friend to look out for her. Her new gal pal sure knew how to nurse a broken heart in style. But for all Jayne's resolve to stand her ground, this split with Conrad hurt so much worse than the one before and she was only one day into the new breakup.

The familiar sounds drifted from the casino below and wrapped around her, echoing bells and whistles, cheers of victory and ahhhs of disappointment. Glasses clinked as the drinks flowed in the resort, while boaters and swimmers splashed in the ocean. This place had its differences from Monte Carlo, a more casual air to the high-end vacationers in sarongs and flowing sundresses, but there were still plenty of jewels around necks, in ears…and in navels.

She wasn't in much of a gambling mood. Besides, she'd left her rings behind.

What had Conrad thought as he looked at them? Did he have any regrets about pushing to finalize the divorce? How could she have been so wrong to hope he would come around this time and fight for their marriage the way he tackled every other challenge in his life?

God, she wanted to scream out her pain and frustration and she would have had she been alone. She turned to Hillary, who was stretched out on a lounger with a big floppy hat and an umbrella to protect her freckled complexion.

"Thanks for taking me in until Salvatore can clear everything up. Once he gives the go-ahead, I'll be out of your hair and back to work."

Hillary looked over the top of her sunglasses, zinc oxide on her freckled nose. "You know you never have to work again if you don't want. I don't mean to sound crass, but your divorce settlement will be quite generous."

Jayne hadn't wanted Conrad's money. She wanted the man. "I don't see myself as the dilettante type."

"Understandable, of course." Hillary twirled her straw in the fruity beverage, not looking the least like an undercover agent herself. "During my years planning events, I met many different types of people—everything from conspicuous consumers to truly devoted philanthropists. It's amazing to have the financial freedom to make a difference in such a sweeping fashion. Just something to think about."

Like opening a clinic in Africa? Conrad had definitely used his money and influence to change the world for the better. Why the hell couldn't he accept the happiness he'd earned?

The sound of the French doors opening pulled her attention back to the present.

Hillary sat up quickly, her fingers landing on the folded towel that covered a handgun. "Troy?"

A tiny canine ball of energy burst through in a frenzy of barking. Jayne gaped, stunned. Surely it couldn't be her little...

"Mimi?"

Her French bulldog raced on short legs in a black and white blur straight into her arms. Oh, my God, it *was* her dog. Mimi covered her chin in lapping kisses.

Jayne's heart tumbled over itself in her chest because there was just one way Mimi could have gotten here. Only one person who would have known how important it was to have her dog with her right now.

The final question that remained? Had Conrad delivered the dog in person as a peace offering or just arranged the travel in a final heartbreaking gesture of thoughtfulness? She squeezed her eyes shut and buried her face in Mimi's neck to hold off looking for a moment longer, to hold on to the possibility that her husband might be standing behind her even now.

Bracing herself, she looked back and found, thank God, Conrad stood in the open doorway. Her heart leaped into her throat and her eyes feasted on the sight of him after a nightmarish day of thinking she would never see him again. He wore jeans, a button-down shirt with rolled-up sleeves—and dark circles under his haunted eyes.

She didn't rejoice in the fact that he'd been miserable, too—okay, maybe she did a little—but above all she wanted him to be happy. He deserved to be happy. They both did.

A rustling sounded from the lounger beside her as Hillary stood. "Is there word on Zhutov?"

Jayne sat upright, swinging her legs to the side of her own lounger. Why hadn't she considered he might be here for that reason? If Zhutov had broken Conrad's cover, ending his career with Interpol, then she would never know if he would have returned to her on his own. Trust would be all the tougher when they already had so much between them.

Bottom line, she wanted what was best for him, his cover safe, even if that meant he walked away from her.

Conrad shook his head. "No word on Zhutov yet. I'm here for Jayne. Just Jayne."

He stared straight into her eyes as he spoke, his voice deep and sure. She almost forgot to breathe. And while she was disappointed not to have Salvatore give them the all clear, she couldn't help but be grateful that whatever Conrad had to say wasn't motivated by losing his work with Interpol.

Hillary grabbed her bag and her hat. "I'll, uh, just step into the kitchen and make, um… Hell. I'll just leave." Her hand fell on Jayne's shoulder lightly. "Call if you need me."

Angling sideways past Conrad, Hillary slipped away into the suite, closing the door behind her.

Jayne hugged her dog closer as Mimi settled into her lap. "This was thoughtful of you. How did you get her here?"

He stuffed his hands in his pockets and eyed her warily. "I phoned your friend Anthony and asked for help retrieving the dog."

"You spoke to him?"

Conrad nodded, pushing away from the door and stepping closer. "I did. He's a nice guy actually, and he was glad to pick up Mimi and take her to the airport because he knew seeing her would make you smile." He crouched beside her, one knee on the ground. "Which I have to tell you, makes me feel like a mighty small bastard, because I should have thought to do this sooner. I should have thought to do and say a lot of things. But I'm here to make that right."

The hope she'd restrained in her heart swelled as she heard him out, her thoughtful husband who knew she would appreciate her precious dog far more than a lifeless diamond bracelet. "I'm listening."

"I'm sorry for telling you we should make the divorce final. I was certain I would let you down again, so I acted like an idiot." He drew in a shaky breath as if…nervous. The great Conrad Hughes, Wall Street Wizard and casino magnate was actually anxious. "I'm a numbers man, always have been, ever since I was a kid counting out my French fries into equal piles. I'm not good at seeing the middle ground in a situation. But I'm getting there."

"What do you propose?" she asked and saw no hesitation in his eyes as he opened up and answered her.

"Compromise." He met her gaze full-on, such sincerity in his espresso dark eyes they steamed with conviction. "On *my* part this time. When we were together before I asked you to do all the changing and insulted you by giving nothing in return."

And clearly that was tearing him apart now.

"Not nothing. You're being too tough on yourself. You always are." She sketched her fingers along his unshaven jaw. Apparently he hadn't wasted a second getting to her, between arranging to pick up Mimi and flying to the Bahamas. He hadn't even stolen a second to shave.

"Then you'll help me work through that." He pressed a kiss into her palm. "Jayne, I've faced down criminals. Made and given away fortunes. But the thought of losing you nearly drives me to my knees. I see you with all that unconditional love in your eyes, a total openness I never gave back. You knew the truth about me and my crooked family, and you loved me anyway. I'd put us in an all-or-nothing life. Well, the past three years of 'nothing' has been hell."

"I completely agree with you there." Her eyes burned, but with happy tears and hope.

"But back to my compromise. And if it's not good enough, tell me and I promise you, I will listen to you this time. After you left, I realized I can't go through this again. I let you go once, and it almost killed me."

"Conrad? I don't know what to say." How funny that *she* was the one speechless now. She'd hoped for a moment like this, prayed that Conrad could find the peace to embrace a life together, but the reality of it sent joy sparkling through her.

"If you want me to quit the Interpol work, I will."

"Shh!" She touched her fingertips to his mouth, moved that he would offer, hopeful that he truly was willing this time to make the compromises needed to build a life together. "You don't have to do that. I just need reassurances that you're all right."

He nipped her fingers lightly, smiling his appreciation. "I can do that. I will tell you everything I'm cleared to share about my work with Salvatore. I can promise you I'll check in every twenty-four hours so you won't worry."

"And that's safe for you?"

"We have the best of the best technology. And I intend to make use of it to keep you reassured—and to keep you well protected. I kept pushing you away to keep you safe, but all it did was tear us both apart. I will do better. And if you change your mind about the job with Interpol, say the word, I'm out. I would give up anything to keep you. I honest to God love you that much, Jayne."

Unable to hold back any longer, she leaned forward into his arms and kissed him, pouring all the love, hope and dreams out and feeling them flow right back to her, from him. There was something different in him now; the restlessness was gone. And while it had shredded her heart to walk away from him again, maybe that's what it had taken to make him see what she'd already realized—they needed each other. Two pieces of the same whole. Conrad seemed to understand that now. He'd found a new peace and maybe even some forgiveness for himself.

Mimi squirmed to get free, squished between them. Laughing, they eased apart and her dog—their dog—jumped from Jayne's lap to sniff the balcony furniture and potted plants.

Jayne looked back at Conrad, still kneeling in front of her. "Is it all right to have a dog here?"

"I bought the place two years ago. I can have a whole damn pack of dogs inside if I want."

"And is that what you want? A pack?" She toyed with the open V of his collar, the fire rekindling inside her.

"Actually I was thinking more like a soccer team of kids. Our kids, babies first, of course."

Shock froze her. She stared into his eyes and found one hundred percent sincerity.

"I'd like that, too," she whispered.

She'd learned to leave the past behind and step outside her safety zone without losing the essence of herself. Life wasn't an all-or-nothing game. It was a blending of the best of both sides. A marriage.

Her marriage.

Just as she started to reach for her husband, the French doors opened and Hillary stuck her head out, cell phone in hand. "Folks, you're going to want to hear this update from Salvatore."

Jayne's stomach knotted. Was it bad news? Could their newfound peace be so short-lived? She felt Conrad take her hand and squeeze reassuringly. She looked into his eyes and realized she wasn't alone—and neither was he. They truly were a team now and whatever happened, they would face it together.

She turned back to Hillary, and realized the woman was smiling so brightly the news couldn't be that bad.

Conrad said, "We're ready. What's the update?"

Hillary tapped speakerphone and Salvatore's voice rumbled over the airwaves, "Authorities apprehended Zhutov's hired assassin and given his confession and the photos he had on his cell phone, we're certain you two were not the targets. You're in the clear. Your cover is secure."

Grinning, Conrad grabbed Jayne around the waist, lifted her from the chair and spun her around. Mimi barked, dancing around their feet. Laughing, Hillary put the phone to her ear and stepped back into the hotel suite.

Jayne grasped Conrad's shoulders as he lowered her back to the ground again. "Oh, my God, that is amazing news."

"Damn straight it is." He hauled her to his chest, a

sigh of relief rattling through him. "And Lord willing, the day's about to get even better."

Stepping back again, he pulled his hand out of his pocket, their wedding rings rested in his palm. "Jayne, I've loved you from the first time I saw you and will love you until I draw my last breath. Will you please do me the honor of wearing this ring?"

She placed her hand over his, their rings together in their clasped hands. "I'm all in. I want to be a part of your big, bold plans for the future, to help others in the clinic in Africa and build more clinics in other parts of the world. I accept you, as you are... I *love* you as you are."

His hand slid into her hair, and he guided her mouth to his with a fierce tenderness that reached all the way to her soul.

The stakes had been high, but she knew a winning hand when she saw one.

Smoothly, Conrad slid on his wedding band and then he slipped hers back on her finger. Where it would stay put this time.

Because one pair, the two of them, had won it all.

Epilogue

Two months later

Coming home to his wife was one of life's greatest pleasures.

Conrad parked the Land Cruiser beside the clinic where his wife worked. Their clinic, in Africa. He'd offered Jayne diamonds and a splashy jet-set lifestyle, but his wife had chosen a starkly majestic home in Africa, caring for the ill and orphaned in the area villages.

God, he loved her and her big, caring heart.

His eyes were drawn to her like a magnet to the purest, strongest steel. He found her on the playground with the kids, kicking the soccer ball, her hair flying around her.

She'd stepped in to help run the foundation that oversaw the clinic. In the two months since she'd relocated here, she'd already come up with plans and funding to add an official childcare center so when adults came for treatment they didn't have to bring their kids inside where they could catch anything from pneumonia to a simple cold.

He'd tried to tell her she didn't have to work this hard, but she'd only rolled her eyes and told him they could sneak away for an opera once a month—if he promised to be incredibly naughty before intermission. In spite of his efforts to pamper her, he'd discovered his wife had grown fiercely independent. The way she took charge, her visionary perspective, reminded him of Colonel Salvatore.

Zhutov was no longer even a remote threat. One morning a month ago, guards had found him dead in his bunk, smothered. Most likely by someone as payback for any one of his criminal acts over the years.

Life was balancing out.

Conrad started toward the soccer field. Now that the loose ends had been tied up this past week he'd spent at Interpol Headquarters in Lyon, France, he was free until the next assignment rolled around.

He liked coming home to her, here. He could manage his holdings from a distance with good managers in place, and he could jet over with his wife whenever she was ready to take in an opera.

Right now, though, he just wanted to have dinner with his wife. The soccer ball came flying in his direction, and he booted it back into play. Jayne waved, smiling as she jogged toward him.

"Welcome home," she called, throwing her arms around his neck.

He caught her, spinning her around under the warm African sun. Already, she whispered about her plans for making love in the shower before supper and how good it would be to sleep next to him again.

And he had to agree, his insomnia was now a thing of the past. Everything was better with her in his life. He knew, in his wife's arms, he'd finally come home.

* * * * *

LET'S TALK
Romance

For exclusive extracts, competitions
and special offers, find us online:

- facebook.com/millsandboon
- @MillsandBoon
- @MillsandBoonUK

Get in touch on 01413 063232

For all the latest titles coming soon, visit
millsandboon.co.uk/nextmonth

JOIN US ON SOCIAL MEDIA!

Stay up to date with our latest releases, author news and gossip, special offers and discounts, and all the behind-the-scenes action from Mills & Boon...

 millsandboon

 millsandboonuk

 millsandboon

It might just be true love...

MILLS & BOON

MODERN

Power and Passion

Prepare to be swept off your feet by sophisticated, sexy and seductive heroes, in some of the world's most glamourous and romantic locations, where power and passion collide.